**Praise for Cleo Coyle's
Coffeehouse Mysteries**

MURDER BY MOCHA

"[A] tasty espresso-dark tale of multigenerational crime and punishment lightened by the Blend's frothy cast of lovable eccentrics."
—*Publishers Weekly*

"A delicious mystery!"
—*Woman's World*

"This rich and entertaining mystery blends atmosphere, unforgettable characters, and a killer plot that will keep readers hooked until the very end."
—*RT Book Reviews*

"Like a great cup of coffee, I can't get enough of Cleo Coyle's Coffeehouse Mysteries . . . This terrifically written, can't-put-it-down series . . . is a must-read for cozy fans who enjoy a great story with well-developed characters and a new twist in every chapter."
—*Cozy Corner*

"A specially blended mystery . . . inside of an action-packed series . . . Filled with twists, used coffee beans, and false leads, readers will wonder who the killer is (over mocha)."
—*Midwest Book Review*

ROAST MORTEM

*A BookReporter.com Reviewer's Pick
Favorite Book of the Year!*

"Coyle incorporates a taste of the real-life bravery of the New York City Fire Department into her brilliantly fast-paced mystery, giving readers a glimpse into the lives of some of the hardest-working men and women in America."
—*Fresh Fiction*

D0059401

"Coyle's strong ninth coffeehouse mystery (after 2009's *Holiday Grind*) pays tribute to New York City firefighters . . . Coyle (the wife-husband writing team of Alice Alfonsi and Marc Cerasini) provides an appendix of useful tips and tempting recipes."
—*Publishers Weekly*

HOLIDAY GRIND

"Other honorable mentions for new holiday booking . . . *Holiday Grind* by Cleo Coyle, a new addition to the Coffeehouse Mystery series that . . . adds in jolts of souped-up coffee, sweet cooking . . . and super sleuthing to deliver a fun and gripping fa-la-la-la-latte surprise."
—*The Huffington Post*

"Coyle's greatest strength is writing characters that feel real. Clare and company are some of the most vibrant characters I've ever read . . . Coyle also is a master of misdirection and red herrings. I challenge any reader to figure out whodunit before Coyle reveals all."
—*Mystery Scene*

ESPRESSO SHOT

"Coyle's Coffeehouse books are superb examples of the cozy genre because of their intelligent cast of characters, their subtle wit, and their knowledge of the coffee industry used to add depth and flavor to the stories . . . Highly recommended for all mystery collections."
—*Library Journal* (starred review)

"Clare visits underground restaurants, temples to high fashion, and the hotel room of a seductive Italian sculptor in her attempts to keep the bride alive . . . A realistic depiction of New York City high and low life. The smattering of recipes, romance, and caffeine-fueled detection add up to a lively tale."
—*Kirkus Reviews*

continued

FRENCH PRESSED

#1 Paperback Bestseller
Independent Mystery Booksellers Association

"Engaging . . . Keeps the reader in suspense to the very end, *French Pressed* is well worth reading."
—*New Mystery Reader Magazine*

"Once again, Cleo Coyle has written an enjoyable, fast-paced mystery that features a perky heroine who has gone from single mother to savvy business owner . . . Readers may be stumped until the very end." —*The Mystery Reader*

DECAFFEINATED CORPSE

#1 Paperback Bestseller
Independent Mystery Booksellers Association

"Great characters, smooth plotting, and top-notch writing, it's no wonder these books are bestsellers." —*Cozy Library*

"Coyle displays a deep understanding, not only of coffee . . . but also of coffee shop culture. She treats espresso shop work as an honorable profession . . . Coyle knows her coffee so well that even I have learned new coffee bits by reading her books . . . If you have not yet discovered the Coffeehouse Mystery series by Cleo Coyle, you should . . . I heartily recommend them." —Eric S. Chen, *BARISTO*

MURDER MOST FROTHY

"Exciting, delicious fun, with coffee trivia, recipes, a vicarious adventure for those of us at home reading of things we'd rather not face ourselves but understanding Clare Cosi's motives and morals." —*Gumshoe Review*

LATTE TROUBLE

"Anyone who loves coffee and a good mystery will love this story. Rating: Outstanding."
—*Mysterious Corner*

THROUGH THE GRINDER

"Coffee lovers and mystery buffs will savor the latest addition to this mystery series . . . Fast-paced action, coffee lore, and incredible culinary recipes . . . All hail the goddess Caffina!"
—*The Best Reviews*

ON WHAT GROUNDS

#1 Paperback Bestseller
Independent Mystery Booksellers Association

"A great beginning to a new series . . . *On What Grounds* will convert even the most fervent tea drinker into a coffee lover in the time it takes to draw an espresso."
—*The Mystery Reader*

"A hilarious blend of amateur detecting with some romance thrown in the mix . . . I personally adored this book and can't wait to read the rest of the series!"
—*Cozy Library*

Visit Cleo Coyle's virtual Village Blend at
www.CoffeehouseMystery.com,
where coffee and crime are always brewing . . .

HOLIDAY BUZZ

CLEO COYLE

BERKLEY PRIME CRIME, NEW YORK

THE BERKLEY PUBLISHING GROUP
Published by the Penguin Group
Penguin Group (USA) Inc.
375 Hudson Street, New York, New York 10014, USA
Penguin Group (Canada), 90 Eglinton Avenue East, Suite 700, Toronto, Ontario M4P 2Y3, Canada
(a division of Pearson Penguin Canada Inc.) • Penguin Books Ltd., 80 Strand, London WC2R 0RL,
England • Penguin Ireland, 25 St. Stephen's Green, Dublin 2, Ireland (a division of Penguin
Books Ltd.) • Penguin Group (Australia), 707 Collins Street, Melbourne, Victoria 3008, Australia
(a division of Pearson Australia Group Pty. Ltd.) • Penguin Books India Pvt. Ltd., 11 Community
Centre, Panchsheel Park, New Delhi—110 017, India • Penguin Group (NZ), 67 Apollo Drive,
Rosedale, Auckland 0632, New Zealand (a division of Pearson New Zealand Ltd.) • Penguin Books
Rosebank Office Park, 181 Jan Smuts Avenue, Parktown North 2193, South Africa • Penguin China,
B7 Jaiming Center, 27 East Third Ring Road North, Chaoyang District, Beijing 100020, China

Penguin Books Ltd., Registered Offices: 80 Strand, London WC2R 0RL, England

This is a work of fiction. Names, characters, places, and incidents either are the product of the author's
imagination or are used fictitiously, and any resemblance to actual persons, living or dead, business
establishments, events, or locales is entirely coincidental. The publisher does not have any control over
and does not assume any responsibility for author or third-party websites or their content.

PUBLISHER'S NOTE: The recipes contained in this book are to be followed exactly
as written. The publisher is not responsible for your specific health or allergy needs that
may require medical supervision. The publisher is not responsible for any adverse
reactions to the recipes contained in this book.

HOLIDAY BUZZ

A Berkley Prime Crime Book / published by arrangement with the author

PUBLISHING HISTORY
Berkley Prime Crime mass-market edition / December 2012

Copyright © 2012 by Penguin Group (USA) Inc.
Cover illustration by Cathy Gendron.
Cover design and logo by Rita Frangie.
Interior text design by Kristin del Rosario.

ISBN: 978-0-425-25535-3

BERKLEY® PRIME CRIME
Berkley Prime Crime Books are published by The Berkley Publishing Group,
a division of Penguin Group (USA) Inc.,
375 Hudson Street, New York, New York 10014.
BERKLEY® PRIME CRIME and the PRIME CRIME logo are trademarks of
Penguin Group (USA) Inc.
A COFFEEHOUSE MYSTERY is a registered trademark of Penguin Group (USA) Inc.

PRINTED IN THE UNITED STATES OF AMERICA

10 9 8 7 6 5 4 3 2 1

ALWAYS LEARNING   **PEARSON**

A good conscience is a continual Christmas.

—Benjamin Franklin

Prologue

∽∾∽∾∽∾∽∾∽∾∽∾∽∾∽∾∽

> *It couldn't have happened anywhere but in little old New York.*
>
> —O. HENRY

SHE'S coming. I see her . . .

Short and slight with blunt-cut bangs and a cheap black coat, the little assistant baker wended her way through the well-heeled crowd like a crow strutting through peacocks. The night was near freezing, yet the girl's coat hung open. As she walked along, she took drags from a cigarette.

"Here I am," the little baker announced, waving the burning butt.

"Obviously," the figure said.

The two stood in the chilly shadows of a broken carousel, just beyond the brilliance of the city park's skating rink, where children lapped the ice, laughter rose on the frosty air, and bouncy tunes spilled out of speakers.

"Well?" the figure asked. "Did you bring it?"

"I did," the girl said.

"Then let me see it!"

"All right! Keep your knickers on!"

The figure stiffened, holding back a retort. The girl was nobody, hardly memorable, excepting that low-rent Irish accent and gallingly direct tone. Correcting her would be a waste of breath—and, anyway, in another minute, her attitude wouldn't matter.

Sixty yards away stood the park's exclusive restaurant. Inside that glass box, wealthy monsters and A-list idiots nibbled gourmet goodies. Out here, nannies shivered around a block of ice, laser focused on paychecks with legs skating around the brightly lit rink. No attention had been given to the single young woman who'd marched into this circle of darkness.

While the girl fumbled at her apron, the figure asked, "Who have you told about this?"

"No one! I kept it to myself. You can feel certain of that . . ."

The figure dipped a gloved hand into a deep coat pocket, feeling the hard, heavy object hidden inside. This was a better kind of certainty.

At last, the girl produced the reason for this meeting. "Have a look," she said, holding out the paper. The figure reached for it, intentionally missing. The paper fluttered down.

"I'll get it," the girl offered.

The figure nodded, and the girl bowed, like the servant she was, toward the floor of the lifeless merry-go-round.

One last time, the figure glanced around, then pulled the solid object from its hiding place, raised up a hand, and—

Down came the blow. Thin and weak, the girl fell hard, like a baby bird from its mother's nest, her short, sharp chirp barely audible above the blare of holiday noise. The second blow stopped all movement. Merciless strikes followed, just to be sure.

Finally, the basher rose, cleaned up quickly, and disposed of the murder weapon. Amid the shadowy tableau of painted horses, a chilly breeze ruffled the girl's hair, now matted holiday red. Her cigarette rolled away, sending up dying smoke signals.

Close by, skaters glided and swirled to "Jingle bells, jingle bells, jingle all the way . . ."

Inside the park's restaurant, children licked candy

canes; mommies laughed with daddies; couples held hands, toasting their romance; while outside a forsaken smoke stick went cold, sending a final plume to heaven.

"Oh, what fun . . ." the basher sang.

So many eyes. And none of them saw.

One

～～～～～～～～～～～～～～～～～

When a star falls, a soul goes up to God.
　　　　　—HANS CHRISTIAN ANDERSEN,
　　　　　　"THE LITTLE MATCH GIRL"

$\mathcal{E}$ARLIER *that day* . . .

"So how's the weather outside?" I asked. "Frightful?"

"Far from it," said Tucker Burton, pulling a woolen stocking cap off his floppy brown mop. "There's not even a *hint* of snow . . ."

There was no hint of murder, either. Not then.

I was still hours away from finding that poor girl's bludgeoned body; and soon after, I, Clare Cosi, would be the one to find her cold-blooded killer. At this hour, however, standing behind my coffeehouse counter, I wasn't thinking about murder weapons or contextual evidence. I didn't plan on interrogating a reality show diva; hoodwinking a New York hockey player; or butting heads with a conniving Cajun cook. And I certainly wasn't expecting to trump one of the biggest forensic freaks in the NYPD—or withstand one of the worst shocks of my early midlife.

On this particular December afternoon, my chief concern wasn't murder. It was weather.

My lanky assistant manager had entered the Village Blend with a blast of frosty air, but I found his tidings warmer than our crackling fireplace. *No snow* was good news! (Not that Currier or Ives would agree.)

Personally, I loved the stuff.

Growing up in a run-down factory town, I couldn't wait for the season's first snowfall. That sparkly blanket instantly beautified rickety buildings and cracked concrete. It even made the local mill's sooty smokestacks look more like the chimneys of Santa's workshop.

Moving to New York, I learned to love snow for a different reason. Back then, I was barely twenty, an art school dropout, adjusting to a new husband, new baby, and new way of life. My rhythms had been set by small-town living. Manhattan, on the other hand, was an island of beings on a continual series of seemingly dire quests. Rushing uptown and down, men and women glanced off one another with barely a grunt.

Heaven's magic crystals calmed all that, quieting the traffic and culling the crowds. Snowfall forced a period of contemplation on a perpetually racing population.

For going on two decades now, that peaceful oasis was what I tried to provide for my coffeehouse customers—no matter the weather. We were a cocoon of comfort on an island of chaos, and the hectic holiday season was the time of year people needed us most.

At three weeks to Christmas, festive shopping bags and gift-wrapped boxes joined smartphones and laptops at our marble tables. Our tree was duly decorated, its piney branches scenting the air. Jazzy renditions of holiday classics drifted from our sound system, and flickering red orange flames sent a glow of warmth from our exposed brick fireplace.

Shoppers took a load off to sip an eggnog latte or nibble a candy cane–frosted brownie. At last, their crazy-busy worlds had calmed down.

Ironically, my own work schedule was ramping up to full throttle.

Tonight my baristas and I were in charge of the beverage

service for the first of three exclusive parties in the Great New York Cookie Swap, an annual tradition that gave city bakers a showcase while raking in a Santa's sleigh of cash for charity.

Unfortunately, many of tonight's well-heeled guests would be driving in from tony suburbs; and the approaching snowstorm could kill the event. On the other hand, the blizzard might bypass us completely. The meteorologists, who sounded more like bookies than weather reporters, were currently giving us a "fifty percent chance" of dodging the snow bullet.

My pop, who was an actual bookie, didn't like fifty-fifty odds, but the way I saw it, when latte mugs were half empty, they were also half full.

"I haven't seen a flurry since last February," Tucker complained. "And the almanac predicts a dry winter. At this rate, New York's chance for a white Christmas is about on par with my chances of dating Channing Tatum." He swung a bright red sack off his narrow shoulders. "Not in this lifetime."

"You already have a boyfriend," I pointed out. "And I'll take a white Christmas on December twenty-fifth. Not tonight . . ." Beyond our French doors, the December sky remained free of clouds, its cobalt hue as clear as my favorite cop's steady gaze. Now all it had to do was stay that way.

"Yes, fret not, oh worshipper of the Hallmark moment . . ." Hands on her zaftig hips, Esther Best emerged from behind our espresso machine. "Santa's sleigh doesn't blast off for three weeks, and that's plenty of time for your cherished whiteout."

Esther Best (shortened from Bestovasky by her grandfather) was my senior barista. An NYU grad student and the most popular slam poetess on Hudson Street, Esther had Rubenesque cleavage, wild dark hair, currently tamed into a half beehive, and an array of cheerful Internet handles, which included *MorbidDreams* and *SnarkCandy*.

Pushing up her black-framed glasses, she eyed Tuck's

bright red bag on our blue marble counter. "So what does Santa's little helper have in his crimson pack? Theatrical hand-me-downs no sane person would be caught dead wearing?"

"Don't be so terminally hip," Tuck scolded. "When it comes to Christmas, you must have kitsch, especially when kids are involved."

"Kids? Who said anything about kids?" Esther asked.

"The Cookie Swap parties are family events," I explained. "We'll be serving in the Bryant Park Grill, but the park skating rink is reserved for the party—so there'll be plenty of children."

"In other words, be ready to serve a lot of Belgian Chocolate Cocoa and Sugar Cookie Steamers?"

"Precisely," I said. "And while our aprons are professional, they're not exactly festive, which is why I asked Tucker for help. You know what I always say—"

"Yeah, yeah," Esther droned, "serving is theater."

"And I'm a firm believer in recycling costumes!" Tuck noted. "So choose anything you like from my bag of thespian tricks."

Esther folded her arms. "I don't know. Red and green clashes with my zombie eye makeup . . . And I'm not hiding these luscious curves under some hand-me-down Santa suit."

"If anyone's playing Santa, it's *moi*," Tuck said, pulling out a jingle bell–trimmed candy cane scarf that looked longer than my holiday to-do list. "And these aren't mere 'hand-me-downs' my Dark Queen of Urban Angst. These are high-quality goodies left over from last year's Ticket to the North Pole party at the New York Public Library. You remember that blowout, don't you, Clare?"

"A North Pole party? Deadly!" another voice chimed in. "Sounds like great *craic*!"

Moirin Fagan, the newest addition to our shop, swept among us with her latest tray of fresh-baked cookies— gingery brown morsels glistening under a crystalline sheen of shimmering sugar.

"Great crack?" Tucked blinked. "Excuse me, but as far

as I know, Santa's white powder does *not* require a cocaine pipe."

"Not that kind o' crack!" Moirin laughed. "*Craic* is Irish slang for . . . well, it means a few things. What I meant was it sounded like a *fun time*."

Esther made a show of sniffing the air then gestured to Moirin's tray. "Those Gingerbread Crackle Cookies smell like crack to me."

Tuck shot me a meaningful look. "It *does* smell like Mrs. Claus's kitchen in here."

I smiled. "That's the idea."

In New York, the battle for holiday buzz was fierce, and every year I searched for a way to see that the Village Blend came up a winner. This year my weapon was the evocative smell of Christmas cookies.

The scents of cinnamon, ginger, caramel, molasses, and chocolate not only filled our shop, but also drifted outside (via my strategically placed vent and fan), where they lured passersby to come in from the cold, indulge, *and* bring a friend. (Buy two coffee drinks, get two cookies free!) The cookies were so good that customers almost always purchased more to eat, along with a box to take home.

It was a new idea for us, worked out through an arrangement with Janelle Babcock, a friend and pastry chef who rented us the small convection oven and sold us the refrigerated cookie dough.

Every hour between 2 and 8 PM, a different batch of cookies went into the Blend's oven, thanks to Janelle's (borrowed) baker's assistant Moirin Fagan, aka "M."

(I found Moirin's name easy enough to pronounce—really, who couldn't remember *Mur-in*?—but from her first day she insisted we call her by her first initial, and so we did.)

Confident and opinionated, M was the kind of girl my grandmother would call "mouthy," Madame (the Blend's owner) would call "sassy," but I simply called "perfectly equipped for Manhattan retail."

She handled good customers with friendly efficiency; bad ones with firm control. And a shift didn't go by without her teaching us some new word of Irish slang from her native Emerald Isle. To wit—

Craic meant a fun time, but also the news, as in "What's the craic?" *Deadly* was good. *Tiz me berrys* meant *you're kidding me.* The bathroom was *jax*; police officers were *guards*; *daycent* meant decent, and something terrible was *nawful.* If you were drunk, you were *demented*; and a jerk of a customer was an *eejit.*

My staff liked her immediately. In fact, we all liked her so much that we invited her to participate in our annual Secret Santa tradition. The presents were already piling up in a special area of our back pantry—beside the eight-inch-high, battery-operated Christmas tree and plastic, motion-activated Bing Crosby. Tucker provided the latter. "Whenever we hear Bing croon 'White Christmas,' we'll all know someone is back there, adding a Secret Santa gift to the pile!"

The next sound I heard that afternoon wasn't Bing, but our front doorbell. The fresh-baked cookies brought in a few new customers along with my shift-change baristas.

With a wave to Vicki and Gardner, I turned to Tucker.

"Okay," I said. "Time for a preparty costume meeting— *with* cookies."

I grabbed a corner café table, and Esther poured us coffees. Then Tuck dug into his bag and dangled a scrap of red velvet, trimmed in fake fur.

"What do you think, Esther? Want to be Santa's Little Helper?"

Esther's eyes went wide as she crunched her crinkle. "I've seen wider belts than that skirt. Maybe I will take a Santa suit after all."

Shuddering, I snatched the flimsy material out of Tuck's hand and stuffed it back into his bag.

"But it's Santa's Little Helper," Tuck wailed. "Don't you remember, Clare? You wore it last Christmas to—"

"Never again. And there'll be no skimpy outfits in this coffeehouse."

"Glad to hear you say that, yeah!" Moirin's head bobbed in appreciation. "I once worked a pub job with a whacker of a manager. It was pure dose! He made all the girls wear skirts up to their navels. We didn't bend over—unless we *wanted* to moon the bartender, and I reckon some of the girls did."

"Well, for catering, I don't require my staff to wear anything but black pants, black shoes, white shirts, and our Village Blend aprons—with the exception of this evening." I speared Tucker. "*Tell me* you have *hats* in that bag of tricks."

"Of course!" Tuck fumbled through it. "Here we go . . ."

One by one, the chapeaus appeared: two snowman top hats; a penguin hat (complete with orange bill); and a Jack Frost dangling icicles cap.

"These are great," I said. "You know what? I think all the baristas should wear them—in the shop, too."

Esther groaned.

"Oh, come on," Tucker said, in agreement with me. "It'll be fun! I've got the perfect one for you, Esther . . ."

He pulled out a "kiss-me!" mistletoe hat—a green bowler with a red edge featuring a wire that dangled a sprig of plastic mistletoe, presumably for the wearer to approach unsuspecting targets and demand a holiday kiss.

Esther raised her hands in mock horror. "Not me. Not in this lifetime. Give it to Moirin."

We waited for her reaction. She blinked and stared. The pause struck me as odd.

"M?" Esther prompted.

She tilted her head. "Yes? What?"

"Do you want this hat?"

"*That* hat? Tiz me berrys!" she cried. "I'd sooner wear the flimsy skirt!"

Tuck shrugged and tossed the cap aside.

"How about this one?" he asked, pulling out a green joker's cap, complete with fake ears. Tiny bells were affixed to its many points, and when he shook it, the hat jingled.

"I couldn't hear myself think with all those tinkling bells," Moirin said with a toss of her black bangs.

"Give it to Nancy," Esther said. "She's got that terrible crush on Mr. Boss."

Tuck raised an eyebrow. "So you want to bell the cat to warn the canary?"

"The canary being Matt?" I asked.

Esther nodded.

"That's rich," I said. "Sorry, but I just can't see Matt as a canary . . ."

As anthropomorphic analogies went, my ex-husband (who also happened to be the son of the Blend's owner and my business partner) was more like the tomcat who ate one.

"The bell hat goes on Nancy," I agreed. "And any hat for Matteo Allegro should have big, obvious horns."

"Got it!" Tuck sang, pulling out a reindeer hat with long brown antlers.

"Perfect."

The throbbing beat of club music interrupted us. Moirin silenced her ringtone and checked the caller ID. A quiet look of smugness came over her face; not triumph, exactly, but more like a cat who was *about* to eat a canary.

"Excuse me. I've been expecting this call!"

"Now that looks like a girl with a plan," Esther said as Moirin headed for the back pantry. "Probably her precious Dave."

That's when my own pocket started playing "Edelweiss," my favorite tune from *The Sound of Music*, and I knew who was trying to reach me—my precious Mike.

In his midforties, Detective Lieutenant Mike Quinn was a few years my senior and a full foot taller. His caramel brown hair was nearly always in Spartan trim. His voice was low and patient; his bearing stoic; and his gaze a midnight blue. On the job, his eyes were chillier than an arctic lake; and in the bedroom, they melted into shimmering pools.

"Please tell me you're at Penn Station."

"Sorry. Still in DC."

Tiz me berrys! "What happened?"

"Frosty the Snowman left my boss grounded in Chicago, which put me on the hook to run a major briefing . . ."

Until five months ago, Mike had spent his entire career in the NYPD. A confluence of events (the primary one involving me) had landed him on a U.S. Attorney's anti-drug task force for the year, which meant ours was currently a commuter relationship.

"Not to worry," he assured me. "I'll find a seat on an afternoon flight and come right from LaGuardia."

"That's not what concerns me . . ."

Over the last twelve hours, towns in Michigan, Ohio, and Pennsylvania had been crippled by the snowfall; which meant traveling anywhere in the Boston–Washington corridor today could be treacherous.

Sure, I hadn't kissed Mike in nearly a week (a month in dog years, and my heart agreed). I didn't relish spending another night alone, but the man should have been on that early train. Not trying to travel now!

"Have you checked the Doppler?" I demanded. "Frosty the Whiteout is rolling our way. It's stupid to risk—"

"Don't worry, sweetheart. It'll all work out . . ."

Those were Mike's last words before I lost his signal. I tried to get him back, but all I could reach was voice mail. So I left a firm message, telling him to stay put—at least for tonight. I assured him I would deal with his ex-wife and take care of his two kids at the skating party.

"Wait till the storm blows over and hop a flight tomorrow. *Please*, Mike? I don't want you to risk—"

That's when I heard it, a quiet singing in our Secret Santa pantry, a tinny, mechanical crooning that gave me a forbidding chill. Just like Tucker, our battery-powered Bing was dreaming of a white Christmas.

Two

~~~~~~

THE rest of that afternoon and evening, I stayed focused on the Cookie Swap, and for a few hours, I was actually free of worry. But now it was close to eleven o'clock, the party was over, the cleanup work done; and in all this time, Mike Quinn hadn't shown *or* called.

I didn't know what to think.

My baristas were gone, rushing off with late-night plans. And Moirin had disappeared halfway through the party (much to Janelle's chagrin). At eight thirty, the girl had taken a cigarette break and had never come back.

I was flummoxed by this.

Moirin Fagan had never ducked out on a shift in my coffeehouse, and leaving her boss alone was completely irresponsible. Feeling badly for Janelle, I sent a member of my staff to her display table, where she helped out for the rest of the night.

Now I was calling it a night.

Grabbing my white parka off a hanger in the coat check, I wished the restaurant's janitorial staff a happy holiday.

Then the glass doors closed behind me, the lock clicked into place, and I stood alone in the shadows of Bryant Park.

Phone in hand, I tried to reach Mike again—with no luck.

Giving up, I began to cross the park just as a blast of arctic air swept through the city's steel and glass canyons. The gust muted the roar of the nighttime streets and carried the sting of ice crystals, the first chilly breath of the approaching monster.

Shivering, I flipped up my hood, barely acknowledging the dazzling holiday wonderland around me. Thousands of tiny bulbs twinkled on the London plane trees. Beside the brightly lit ice rink, a lavish Christmas tree blazed with primary colors. Then, with no warning, the private park went suddenly dark.

I froze, midstride. Skyscrapers towered above me. Their windows shone like near-earth stars, but they were too far away to help me see. Good thing 40th Street paralleled the park. The trees diffused its streetlamps, but the ambient glow was strong enough to light my way.

I began moving again and heard approaching footsteps. The sound might have alarmed me, but it came with girlish giggles and male laughter. A well-dressed young couple emerged out of the gloom ahead.

The young man held a bottle of champagne. The young woman tottered on high-heeled boots. She tripped on a paving stone and nearly fell. Her companion caught her, and they both found this hysterical.

The two loudly moved toward the darkened carousel and walked through the unlocked gate. That's when their laughter stopped. In appalled tones, they whispered back and forth then walked quickly away, passing me.

"What's wrong?" I asked.

The boy pointed. "Some drunken woman is sleeping it off on that merry-go-round."

"Yeah, nasty!" added the girl.

"A woman?" I asked. "Are you sure?"

"Of course, we're sure! She's right there on the floor."
The girl rolled her eyes and tugged on her boyfriend's thick
overcoat. "Come on . . ."

The temperature was falling. The wind was getting
stronger, the frigid flakes of snow biting my face. But Jack
and Jill's discovery troubled me.

The sleeping woman might be drunk, or she might be
homeless and need help. Either way, death from exposure
was a real possibility on a night like this, so I strode to the
carousel to speak with this stranger. If the woman could not
walk away on her own, I would call 311 for help.

Right outside the carousel gate, I tripped. Just like Tipsy
Girl, my heel caught on a loose paving stone—unusual for
a private park like this one. It was a lawsuit waiting to happen. I nearly fell, but there was no boy to catch me, so I
caught myself.

Regaining my balance, I moved forward.

"Hello?" I called, my voice competing with the wind.

The carousel was shrouded in darkness, and the circular
platform rocked slightly as I stepped aboard. I maneuvered
around the masterfully carved horses, each one frozen mid-
prance, eyes wide and staring.

Finally I spied the woman. She lay faceup, her limbs
sprawled, as if she were making a snow angel on the
wooden floor. Under blunt-cut bangs, her eyes appeared
glassy, just like the frozen horses, but her gaze was fixed on
the painted ceiling.

A black shadow masked her features, so I stooped down
for a closer look just as headlights from a bus on 40th flash-
lit the scene. I finally saw her entire face—and the halo of
blood around her head.

Stifling a scream, I dropped to my knees beside her.

This woman wasn't homeless or some nameless party
guest. She was my part-time employee, poor, missing Moirin Fagan. And she wasn't sleeping or passed out drunk.

She was dead.

THREE

~~~~~~~~~~~~~~~~~~~~~~~~~~~~~~~~

THIRTY minutes later, Moirin and I were no longer alone, and the park was lit up again, but not with Christmas lights.

My frantic 911 call brought wailing sirens. Four police officers responded in two cars. Two of the cops led me away from Moirin's body and asked me to wait near the skating rink rail, outside their police perimeter.

Paramedics arrived next. Then came plainclothes detectives, the Crime Scene Unit, private park security, and a Con Edison crew. Now flashes of red, orange, and yellow glinted from official vehicles along 42nd Street.

The snow wasn't yet sticking to the ground, but it was aggressively swirling. A figure approached me through the pelting flakes. This cop I recognized—Detective Lori Soles.

Her ivory cheeks were rosy, her yellow cherub curls squashed under a brown fedora. I looked around for her usual partner, Sue Ellen Bass, but I didn't see her.

For years, Soles and Bass had been regular customers of my Village Blend. The two had started their detective careers as partners in the Village's Sixth Precinct. Dubbed "the Fish Squad," they had been transferred recently to a midtown station.

"How are you, Clare?" Lori began.

"I'm fine." But hot tears stung my eyes as I said it. I swiped at them with a gloved hand, and Lori handed me a personal pack of tissues.

"Your nose is running," she said.

And my mind is spinning.

Half an hour earlier I'd approached the park's carousel in an attempt to save a human being from a hazardous situation. But there was no saving Moirin Fagan. Not now. Not ever.

She'd been more than lively at the party; she'd been *alive*, and I couldn't help but feel that I'd failed her. When she disappeared, I assumed she was shirking work. I never even tried to look for her. That hard truth was tearing me up inside.

What in the name of heaven happened?! Who did this to her and why?!

"You knew the victim, is that correct?" Lori asked.

Too choked up to speak, I nodded. Then I blew into the tissue and cleared my throat. "Her name is Moirin Fagan, but she preferred we call her 'M.' She's an Irish immigrant."

"Could you clarify your relationship with Ms. Fagan?"

"Moirin worked for me part-time. She's a holiday season hire."

"What were you doing inside the park so late, Clare?"

"Earlier this evening, there was a private party at the Bryant Park Grill. I managed the specialty coffee service. I stayed late to help with cleanup, and . . ."

"And?"

And wait for Mike Quinn, who never showed.

"Clare?"

The state I was in, I wanted to spill every thought in my head—about Mike's travel plans, my frustration with his changing decisions, my fight at the party with his ex-wife. But Lori knew Mike as a fellow detective, and it was all so embarrassing. It also felt incredibly trivial in the face of Moirin's murder.

"And," I finally replied, "that's all."

"Ms. Fagan was at this event? Is that right? Working for you?"

"She was there, but she was working her primary job, as an assistant to a pastry chef."

The wind kicked up, low thunder rumbled in the distance, and chunks of hail began to mix with the flakes. On the carousel, the detectives in sterile white CSU suits began to look like blurry abominable snowmen.

"Do you have any idea who might have wanted to hurt Moirin?" Lori asked, blinking against the bitter onslaught.

I thought back over the day. "There were a few odd incidents, at my shop and then at the party. I think they're worth noting—"

Before I could continue, an impatient voice interrupted us.

"Detective Soles? Could you finish up quickly with that witness, please? The *real* work is over here."

Lori's answer was flat. "I'll be right there, sir."

She frowned at me. "Sorry, Clare. Please wait for me here. I'll be back soon to finish taking your statement."

I grabbed her arm. "Let me go with you. Your colleague may have questions for me."

"Detective Endicott doesn't like to question witnesses. He prefers to review written statements."

"What?"

"You heard me."

"But I knew the victim. And I was around Moirin for much of the day. I can help piece together a timeline for you—and tell you about some odd encounters I witnessed at the party that involved Moirin. They may be important to note."

I could see the tug-of-war behind Lori's gaze. She didn't want to piss off her sergeant. But she clearly agreed with me. "Okay, come with me," she said. "But be warned, Cosi. Fletcher will want a DNA sample from you."

"Fletcher? That's his first name?"

"Detective Sergeant Fletcher Stanton Endicott."

"*Stanton* as in?"

"Our current mayor, Warren J. Stanton. They're first cousins on his mother's side. And, yes, he uses that connection—without shame—whenever and wherever it will advance his person."

"And *he's* your boss?"

"My new senior partner—*temporary* partner." She didn't have to add *thank goodness*, I could see it in her eyes.

"What happened to Sue Ellen?"

"Medical leave."

"Is she okay?"

"Line of duty injury. Broken arm and some serious bruises."

"Oh my goodness. I hope it was worth it."

"She thinks it was. Some gangbanger made the mistake of roughing up an elderly woman in a purse-snatch within sight of her. The guy had a running start, but my girl brought him down like a cheetah on the veldt. They both plowed into a pile of garbage cans and a fight ensued."

Yeah, that sounds like Sue. "Is the perp in the hospital, too?"

"He's lucky he is."

"What do you mean?"

"I'm a crack shot. If I'd been at the scene, he'd be in the grave."

O-kay. "So what's the story with Endicott? Is the man as insufferable as his tone?"

"You're a smart one, Cosi. You'll figure it out—"

"Detective Soles? Are you *hearing impaired*?" the man called again. "You're needed!"

"You heard him," she said as she led the way to the crime scene.

THE carousel was illuminated, but not with its own cheerful lights. Standing halogen spots were positioned around the ride, their harsh beams focused on the corpse. In the cruel radiance, Moirin's waxy face contrasted with a crown of ink black hair and the scarlet blood splatter that haloed her battered head.

Two technicians in matching white CSU overalls and paper booties cautiously moved around the body, snapping photographs, gathering samples of hair, of litter, of anything that might prove to be a clue. They worked fast, attempting to capture what evidence they could before snow began covering the scene.

When Lori and I tried to pass through the carousel gate, a barked command stopped us.

"I *do not* want this crime scene contaminated! Remain outside the perimeter."

A man stepped away from the CSU white-suits, and I was suddenly in the presence of Detective Fletcher Stanton Endicott. A head shorter than the men around him, the detective was nattily dressed in a tweed jacket and maroon sweater vest, visible beneath transparent plastic coveralls that swathed him from head to ankle. Endicott also wore paper booties, thick protective glasses over small, round spectacles, and a cellophane hat that revealed a receding blond hairline.

With one gloved hand he held up a digital recorder. "Soles, my notes on chapters one through five of my new novel have taken up nearly all of my memory. Do you carry a digital recorder?"

"Sorry—" She waved her narrow, leather-bound notebook. "I still do it the old-fashioned way."

"Fine. I'll dictate my preliminary report, and you will take notes and transcribe them back at the precinct."

Lori stiffly nodded, teeth noticeably clenching.

"Step closer to the fence, please, so I do not have to shout, and *remember* to stay *outside* the perimeter."

As we carefully approached, I caught Lori's eye. "New novel?"

"He writes crime novels," she whispered.

Endicott frowned at me, his eyebrow arching. "Excuse me. *Who* is this?"

"This is Clare Cosi," Lori replied, "the victim's employer. She discovered the body—"

Before she could continue, Endicott scowled and stated: "Ms. Cosi has contaminated the crime scene. I'll need hair samples and clothing fibers from everything she's wearing."

Before I could say a word, he gave us his back. Then his head suddenly swiveled, and he locked eyes with me. "You weren't chewing *gum*, were you?"

"Of course not."

"Then I think we can forgo the DNA swab—for now."

Lori grunted. "You got off lucky," she whispered.

"And what's going on with the electricity?" Endicott bellowed. "Why can't we get this carousel's lighting system to work? Between the floodlights and horses, I'll have nothing but glare and shadows in my photos!"

"Con Ed's working on it," a technician replied. "But it may be half an hour or more before it's powered up."

Endicott massaged the bridge of his nose between his thumb and index finger and glanced up at the miasma of snow-filled sky. "We're battling weather, so the floodlights will have to do, but subpar documentation of transient contextual evidence will *not* help our pretrial presentations."

I cleared my throat. "Excuse me, Detective Endicott. Isn't it a little premature to talk about a trial? You haven't caught Moirin's murderer—unless you already have a suspect in mind."

"I have *science* in mind, Ms. Cosi." He flashed a smirk. "Modern forensics will reveal the killer's identity."

"So you don't have a suspect?"

"I don't have a *name*. But if our CSU detectives do their jobs right, we'll find the key to the killer's identity inside this perimeter."

"Moirin has been working closely with me for six weeks. Perhaps I can help."

"Ms. Cosi could be an asset for us, Detective," Lori jumped in. "We're lucky she knows the victim. She has good instincts, and members of the PD have reached out to her before."

"Why? Is she a private investigator?"

"I manage a landmark coffeehouse in Greenwich Village," I explained. "I've been part of the community for a long time. People in the neighborhood trust me and I try to—"

"You're an informant, is that what you're trying to say?" Endicott finished with disdain. He shook his head at Lori. "You know how I feel about informants. They're akin to glorified gossips. Such methods are not reliable—which means they're not *my* methods. You know that, Detective Soles."

Lori shot me an apologetic look. After clearing her throat, she tried again.

"But Ms. Cosi has informed me that she witnessed *pertinent* encounters at a party involving the victim."

"That's true," I chimed in. "The incidents seemed unimportant, but looking back, I think you should hear the details. One of the encounters involves her boyfriend, another a high-profile sports figure, and I also witnessed—"

"High-profile sports figure, you say?" Endicott's eyes lit up. "Yes, perhaps I should hear this background personally. Take notes, Soles."

"Yes, sir. Go ahead, Clare . . ."

"Well, it all started with the wooden stirrers."

"Wooden what?"

"Coffee stirrers. About two hours into the Cookie Swap, we ran short. So I ducked back to the restaurant's supply closets and found Janelle Babcock already there."

"And who is Janelle Babcock?"

"She's the pastry chef who employed Moirin on a full-time basis. M worked in my shop only part-time. Tonight Janelle needed her behind her cookie display table."

"Go on."

"Like I said, when I got back to the supply area, I found Janelle there in a desperate search for doilies."

"Excuse me? Did you say doilies?"

"Yes, Detective . . ."

Four

〜〜〜〜〜〜〜〜〜〜〜〜〜〜〜〜〜〜〜〜〜

"**Paper** doilies!" Janelle exclaimed with a good-humored frown. "I'm almost out of them!"

"Let's team up," I suggested. Flipping back the cotton tail of my Mrs. Claus hat, I told her about my stirrer crisis.

Apparently *everyone* wanted to try our new Caramel Swirl Latte, a drink you were supposed to stir between sips to boost the caramel flavor. Tuck called it *interactive*. I called it a *bona fide hit*.

The buttery-sweet caramel sauce looked delectably decadent oozing down the glass mugs, and the buzz for the drink had swept the party. I hadn't anticipated this, however, and my wooden stirrer supply was nearly depleted.

"You check the closets on the right," I said, "and I'll check the ones on the left."

"Oh, girl, I'm tellin' you. My doily issue is worse," Janelle pattered as she ripped open one door after another.

She looked adorable tonight in her special chef's jacket and toque. This wasn't her usual baker's whites. The Mardi Gras party jacket was a tie-dyed tribute to her New Orleans roots. The green, purple, and gold tones complimented her café mocha skin, and the custom cut of the jacket flattered her ample hips.

"I was all ready to serve two cookies per doily, but the models and actresses in *this* crowd—they're all demanding, 'Just *one* cookie, no more,' which completely threw off my doily-to-cookie ratio!"

"I can't find any doilies," I called. "How about plain paper napkins?"

"Sorry, but my little babies look their best on lace!" She slammed another door. "I mean, c'mon, y'all, can't you enjoy a few extra calories? It's the holiday season. No, they say. 'Just one please' and I'm going through doilies faster than you-know-what goes through a goose!"

"Found some!" I waved a box of small paper lace doilies, one hundred count.

"You're a lifesaver, Clare!" She clutched her disposable treasures. "And before I forget, please tell Tucker he's a lifesaver, too. His 'Storybook Cookie' idea was genius . . ."

Janelle was referring to the first Cookie Swap baker's challenge. Tonight's donations benefited a major literacy program, so the theme for this challenge was "Storybook Cookies: Treats Inspired by the Tales of Christmas."

The New York Public Library provided books and prints as props, and the pricey tickets entitled guests to free cookies from all of the participating bakers' tables—including a take-home Swap box—and beverages from my Village Blend station.

"I've handed out almost as many business cards as I have these dang doilies!" Janelle happily informed me.

"I'm not surprised. Your table is beautiful . . ."

At Tuck's suggestion, Janelle based her cookie creations on O. Henry's "The Gift of the Magi." The impoverished husband of the story longs to give his wife the jewel-rimmed tortoiseshell combs for her lustrous hair. The wife wants only to give her husband a shining platinum fob chain for his prize possession—a gold pocket watch. The climax of the tale is timeless.

"Did you see Lisa Logan, the actress from that bizarre new Christmas movie?" Janelle asked.

"*Santa Claus, Zombie Hunter?* No, haven't had that pleasure."

"Well, Ms. Logan made a big show of taking one of my jewel-candy-rimmed comb cookies and sticking it into her hair while a bunch of paparazzi took her picture! Last time I saw her, she was *still* wearing my cookie! You can't *buy* that kind of publicity, Clare. And the little kids love—I mean *love*—my gold pocket watch cookies! Most of them just learned to tell time, and I set each watch at a different hour. So Moirin and I quiz the kids who come to our table. If they're right about the time on their pocket watch cookies, we give them Sugarplum Fairy cake ball treats as a prize!"

"That's wonderful. But I have to warn you: Tuck saw your display and he has a nit to pick. The wife's gift in the story is a fob *chain*, not a watch."

Janelle raised a hand. "Listen here, I *tried* making a cookie out of a watch *chain*. They came out of the oven looking like a tray of swamp snakes!"

"Point taken."

Janelle glanced at the wall. "Speaking of clocks, is that the right time?"

I checked my watch. "It's a little fast. I have ten minutes to eight."

"I've got to hustle. Roger Clark from New York One is supposed to interview me with two other pastry chefs at eight o'clock!"

"Then get moving. I'll deliver the doilies to Moirin."

"You saved my bacon again—but what about your stirrers?"

"Don't worry, I'll find some. Go and wow 'em!"

We parted at the kitchen door. Janelle headed to the Grill's patio, where the local media had set up cameras by a Christmas display, and I moved to the dining room, where the crowd was thickest.

For the first ninety minutes of the party, the big excitement had been around the ice rink, where the captain of the New York Raiders hockey team was hanging with the kids, taking photos and giving impromptu lessons. From what I saw through the Grill's big windows, the children were having the time of their lives.

At this hour, the hockey star was off the ice, but the kids were still skating their hearts out, while inside the restaurant, costumed carolers now serenaded the adults, who continued mingling, nibbling, and sipping.

My spirits had been flagging, but they were lifted by Janelle's positive energy—and then I reached her display table, where a wall of hard muscle, swathed in Armani and a whiff of alcohol, brought me to a puzzled halt.

"Come on, you must have *something* with booze in it," the ice blond giant insisted. "A whiskey scone or a rum raisin something or other?"

"Sorry, big guy," Moirin replied, hands linked behind her back in a professional posture. "This party's dry."

"No, it's not," the giant replied, "I just sucked down some spiked whipped cream from inside those 'Little Match Girl' Brandy Snaps. No buzz, though. You *must* have something with booze in it over here!"

"I'm not tweekin' you," Moirin assured him. "We've got nothing with spirits at this table."

Muscle man flashed a grin full of cornpone charm, but the good humor didn't quite reach his chilly blue eyes. "I don't know about that. You sound like you got a *lot* of spirit."

Almost certainly a professional athlete, it was clear this man was also a *player* of another sort.

"Hey, I've seen your cute tail," he said, tone flirtatious, "downtown—at Cheshire and Daddy-O. You're a club girl, aren't you?"

"I follow a few bands, that's all."

"Are you a hockey fan?"

That's when it hit me, who this guy was—

"I'm Ross Puckett, captain of the New York Raiders . . ."

Puckett was the reason Mike Quinn's son was so excited

about this party. Earlier, I'd glimpsed the hockey star, handing out free jerseys and tousling hair. But on the ice he'd worn his helmet and bulky uniform. I hadn't recognized him without all the hockey gear. Obviously, he'd done a quick change in the men's room before joining the adult section of this party.

Grinning at Moirin, he thrust out a meaty hand, but he wasn't looking for a polite shake. "How about you put your personal flask in my palm, and I'll cross yours with a dead president."

Moirin blinked under her black bangs. "Which one?"

"Ben Franklin."

Her lips twitched. "Franklin's on the U.S. hundred, that's true. And he is dead. But he was never your president."

"Oh, you are a cute one." His grin grew. "Give it over."

Moirin sighed. "Now why would you be thinkin' I carry a flask?"

"You're Irish, aren't you?"

Oh man. What a jerk. To M's credit, she kept her temper. "I reckon I am Irish. But believe me, Mr. Puckett. I don't have one. I don't even own one."

Puckett's response was to step around the cookie display.

M stepped back, surprised and a little intimidated by the giant man's nerve. "Shoo, now, mister," she said, clearly trying to keep things light. "On the other side of the table with you!"

"Not until I search you, lassie."

Was this Puckett's ham-handed way of flirting? Or was he just a pushy alkie, getting off on intimidation?

I could see Moirin struggling with this one. If she were on the street or in a club, I had no doubt she'd put him in his place. But this wasn't *any* guy. Causing a scene with a celebrity like Puckett could embarrass Janelle.

Well, I could handle myself, too. As he reached out to paw her, I stepped up. "So, how is your evening going, M?!"

Ross Puckett blinked, a little surprised when I moved

behind the display and elbowed my way between them, *hard*.

"Janelle told me you had a supply problem. She sent me over with this box of doilies!"

I waved the box, "accidentally" bouncing it off Ross Puckett's rock-hard chest.

"Oops! Sorry about that, sir! Listen, Janelle had specific instructions about the display. You'd better let me arrange these for you . . ."

"Oh yeah, Clare. That's *daycent* of you," M said, biting back her laughter.

I tore open the box and laid out the doilies in four neat piles of twenty-five each. As I worked, I made sure to "accidentally" bump and elbow Giant Man. Finally, I tromped on the shiny leather toes of his *very* expensive shoes.

That did it. He'd had enough.

By the time I was finished "arranging things" not much was different, except that the display's doily supply had been replenished, and Ross Puckett was in front of the display again.

"There. All set," I declared.

"*Thanks*, Clare," Moirin said. "For everything."

"So," I said, addressing Ross Puckett this time. "I see by those half dozen Brandy Snaps in your pocket that you visited Rita Limon's table. I haven't met the woman, but I hear her display is fantastic."

"Yeah," he said, still a bit dazed by my passive-aggressive intervention.

"Did you know those Brandy Snaps were inspired by the Hans Christian Andersen story 'The Little Match Girl'? See how the tubular brown cookies look like matchsticks? And the cherries on the ends—I see your cherries are gone—resemble the red match head?"

"I ate the cherries," Puckett said. "Sucked out the spiked cream inside, too, but, uh . . . not much *fire* for a match, if you get my drift."

"I do understand . . ." I turned on my "difficult customer" smile. "How about I fix you up with a nice Irish coffee—heavier on the Irish than the coffee? That's what you need, right?"

"Sounds good," Puckett said, then his eyes narrowed. "So long as I don't have to stand too close to *you* while you pour it."

"It's a deal. Follow me to the coffee bar." I set off with the giant in tow.

"Catch you later, club girl," Puckett called over his shoulder.

M didn't reply.

I grabbed Esther's arm a moment later and explained the drink order.

"Make it a double," Ross Puckett called.

"Coming right up," Esther promised beneath her green Grinch Peruvian Beanie (believe it or not, this was her holiday hat of choice). "By the way, boss, where are the stirrers?"

"Whoops! I'll be right back . . ."

I returned to the kitchen and located a box. On my way back to the coffee bar, I noticed that Moirin had another visitor.

Dressed casually for this affair, the young man wore tight denims—black to match his leather jacket. His hair was dark, too, and rakishly shaggy. It framed a boyish, dimpled face. He was shaking his finger at Moirin, but not in a threatening way. It was more like teasing.

M wasn't nearly as composed as she was with Ross Puckett. Her arms were no longer behind her back in a professional server's posture, but waving madly, and her smile was far from carefree—it looked more like a smirking challenge.

This must be the mysterious Dave, I thought, Moirin's boyfriend.

I remembered her reaction to his call in the shop that afternoon. She said she'd been expecting it, and the look on her face when she got it was one of almost smug pleasure.

Something about that call—including the way she rushed into our back pantry to keep it private—made me think something was up. Whether it was good or bad, I couldn't say.

I was about to go over and introduce myself (i.e., *snoop*) when Esther called out to me. The box of coffee stirrers in my hand reminded me I had work to do. By the time I was free again, Dave was gone.

FIVE

~~~~~~~~~~~~~~~~~~~~~~~~~~~~~~

"**And** you didn't hear any part of the conversations between Moirin and her young man?" Detective Endicott asked. "On the phone or at the party?"

I shook my head. "At the coffeehouse, Moirin kept her call private. At the party, I was too far away, but Moirin was clearly worked up, waving madly, and the young man seemed passionate. Emotional."

"Emotional? How do you mean?" Lori pressed. "Hostile? Angry?"

"More like agitated."

"And you don't know his full name? Where he lives?"

"No, I don't. But her full-time employer might . . ." I gave them Janelle's name, address, and phone.

"All right, Soles, I think we've heard enough from Ms. Cosi," Endicott snapped, silencing us with a backhand gesture reminiscent of a conductor starting a major performance. "Can we begin?"

Lori nodded, pen poised to scribble, and Detective Endicott began to describe the crime scene in a clinical monotone.

"The victim's name is Moirin Fagan. Female. Caucasian. Approximately five feet, five inches tall. I would guess her weight at around one hundred and twenty pounds. Age between twenty and thirty—"

"Moirin is twenty-*five*," I broke in.

"Twenty-*five*," Endicott amended. "According to a bystander. Make a note to confirm from an authoritative source."

"What? Like her driver's license?" I shot Lori a look: *How in the world did this clown get to be a New York City detective?!*

Lori mouthed a one-word reply that reminded me why some municipal promotions are not made of sugar and spice and everything nice: *politics.*

". . . because of an ambient temperature of approximately thirty-three degrees Fahrenheit, the time of death is difficult to determine at this point in the investigation—"

"No it's not," I interrupted again. "The last time I saw Moirin was eight thirty, almost exactly. I'm sure she was killed soon after. And there's a way to determine that, too."

"I very much doubt it." Endicott speared Lori. "You see why I don't trust human witnesses? First this woman claims she was busy working at the party. Now she wants us to believe she can *correctly* recall the *exact* time she last saw the victim."

"But I can."

"Did you see her inside the restaurant, or outside, in the park?" Lori asked.

"Outside. I was coming back from the ice rink."

"And what were you doing outside, Ms. Cosi?" Endicott asked suspiciously. "I thought you were a waitress at this party."

"Actually, I was the beverage service *manager* at this party," I corrected. "And I took a break from my work to go outside for a very specific reason."

"Go on," Lori said.

"My boyfriend was supposed to be at the party to watch his kids. When he didn't show, I asked my employer to step in . . ."

* * *

"**H**OW'S everything going out there?" I asked, behind our beverage station.

"Beautifully!" Madame gushed, accepting my proffered espresso. "Mike's children are having a delightful time on the ice!"

Madame Blanche Dreyfus Allegro Dubois, the owner of the Village Blend, my former mother-in-law, and doting grandmother to my adult daughter, Joy, had been graciously looking after Mike's kids since the start of the party.

I breathed a sigh of relief. "I'm glad they're having fun."

"And I left them in good company," she assured me. "At the moment they're giving Uncle Franco his very first ice-skating lesson."

I nearly dropped a demitasse. "Uncle Franco? You mean—"

Madame nodded.

Emmanuel Franco was a young, former anti-gang detective who now worked with Mike on the NYPD. After Franco and my daughter began a long-distance relationship, he and I became friends. So, when Mike failed to show, I gave him a call.

"I asked Franco to take a turn *watching* Mike's kids," I said. "I didn't expect him to skate with them."

"Don't fret, dear. Both of those children are quite accomplished on the ice. Little Molly likes to glide with her arms positioned just like that famous Russian figure skater, Galina Kulikovskaya, and Jeremy says he's going to skate all winter and try out next year for his school's hockey team."

Madame touched my hand. "I think you should step outside to see for yourself. The sight of Emmanuel Franco surrounded by all those children is well worth witnessing."

"Franco on ice?" Tuck said, peering out from behind the espresso machine. "Sounds like that legendary *Happy Days* episode with Fonzie on roller skates . . . If Fonzie had a badge, a gun, ripped abs, and a shaved head."

With the tinkle of tiny bells, Nancy Kelly set her empty tray on the bar. "Fonzie? Who's Fonzie?" she asked, the peaks of her jingling elf cap bobbing in front of her wide eyes.

"Before your time," Tuck replied. "Like rotary dials, vinyl records, and dinosaurs."

Nancy tossed a wheat-colored braid and shrugged, which made her headgear tinkle like the harnesses of Santa's eight tiny reindeer.

"You should take a break, Clare. Go out there yourself and . . ." Madame winked. "Bring that camera of yours."

At my daughter's request, I'd already filled half my memory card with digital images of tonight's literary cookie displays. But Madame's suggestion puzzled me.

"*You* want Franco's photo? Why?"

"I know!" Tuck snapped his fingers. "She's going to boost next year's donations for the Big Apple Literacy Foundation by selling a beefcake calendar."

Madame offered Tuck a sly smile. "Not a bad idea, my boy, but these photos wouldn't be for me."

I blinked. "Then who—"

Finally I got it, and Madame and I exchanged a scheming look.

A photo of Joy's beau skating with two adorable children might put an idea or two in my daughter's head—like Franco as family man. Like maybe it was time she wrapped up her culinary apprenticeship in Paris and moved back home to New York to settle down, and . . .

With thoughts of grandchildren suddenly dancing in my head, I said—

"Take over, Tuck. I'll be right back . . ."

AFTER pulling off my apron and Mrs. Santa Claus hat, I dug the camera out of my bag behind our counter, picked up my parka at the coat check, and dashed outside.

I passed the TV cameras on the restaurant's patio, where Janelle was finishing up her interview with New York One, and made a beeline for the skating rink, where it wasn't hard to find Franco—

He'd become his own attraction.

With serious expressions, Molly and Jeremy held Franco's hands to keep him upright. Meanwhile, the audience, mostly young nannies, pointed at the muscle-bound cop with giggly, whispering interest.

Clearly, with hunky Ross Puckett gone, the women found a new object of female amusement. Unlike the hockey star, however, Franco was less than comfortable with blades on his boots.

"Slow down, guys, this isn't the Olympics," I heard him plead.

"We *are* going slow, Uncle Franco," twelve-year-old Jeremy patiently informed him. "If we were going any slower we'd be standing still."

Ten-year-old Molly locked eyes with the detective. "Don't feel bad. When I was little, I had to go slow, too."

From the icy wet patches on the man's Yankees jacket and blue jeans, it seemed clear he'd fallen once or twice already—and, no doubt, Mike's sweet-hearted kids had helped him up again.

Fortunately for the sake of Franco's pride (and his posterior), he got the hang of it and began moving more smoothly around the rink, with Molly and Jeremy continuing to spot him like preadolescent training wheels.

I moved with them, around the outside of the rink, shooting picture after picture of the *Franco on Ice* show, taking advantage of the Christmas tree and the twinkling London planes for background.

I even got a few shots of Franco and the kids with the park's famous merry-go-round, La Carousel, as a backdrop.

According to an announcement made during the party, something had gone wrong with the power, and the popular ride remained dark and silent. But I took several shots anyway. The shadowy darkness in the distance, coupled with the Christmas lights around the rink, made the human figures pop, and I was sure I got some great shots.

I was so busy peering through the lens that I stumbled into a pedestrian.

"Oh no, I'm so sorry!" I lowered my camera.

"Think nothing of it," the woman replied with a wave.

I knew when I saw her that she was not a guest. No flashy highlights or elaborate hairdo. In her thirties, the woman wore her mousy brown locks in a severe bun. From the food stains on her sweater, and the bulging fanny pack around her waist, I could see that she was some guest's nanny. A younger woman, also a nanny, stood silently nearby.

"Are those your children?" the thirtyish woman asked.

"Molly and Jeremy? No, I'm babysitting for the party."

She visibly relaxed when she knew she was with a peer. "You work for one of the guests, then?"

"Actually, I'm managing the coffee service for the event."

The woman's attention was diverted by a ten-year-old boy darting among the skaters at twice everyone else's speed.

"Slow down, Adam! You're going to hurt yourself—or someone else!"

The boy slowed, but only until his nanny turned to face me again. Over her shoulder I saw him speed up once more.

"You do the coffees? Everyone's raving about some caramel swirl drink. But I'm not a big fan of caramel." She made a face. "I like peppermint, though."

"We have a Candy Cane Latte."

"Oh, that sounds perfect. I'm going to try one if I get the chance."

Before I could reply, she whirled to face the rink again. "Adam Rayburn, I told you to slow down and I meant it!"

She shook her head and glanced at me. "Spoiled rotten."

I cringed at the hateful tone in the woman's voice. Maybe the kid was a handful, but to hear his own nanny declare it with such venom made me feel sorry for them both.

I could see she was studying me, waiting for me to dish, too. But I had nothing negative to say about these kids, and she quickly shifted gears.

"Duty calls. I'd better go. It was nice to—run into you."

She smiled at her quip and I nodded. "Nice to run into you, too."

The two nannies walked quickly away together, the younger one clearly still interested in watching Franco. But I couldn't any longer. The low battery warning began blinking on my camera. I'd taken enough shots for Joy, anyway. It was time I returned to work.

As I headed for the restaurant, I noticed the TV crew on the patio again. Janelle Babcock was no longer there. Reporter Roger Clark had finished up his interview with the pastry chefs and moved on to celebrity guests.

Singer Piper Penny was now beaming at the camera in a belly-baring metallic pantsuit. I recognized the downtown party girl, who often made headlines for her bad behavior. She'd arrived on the arm of hockey star Ross Puckett. But he was nowhere in sight.

That's when I spotted Moirin Fagan on the park's path. She was in the process of opening a new pack of Lucky Strikes. As M came closer, she was so busy struggling to light the first cigarette in the brisk wind that she didn't notice me. And I was in such a hurry that I didn't call out to her.

We passed without speaking.

Six

~~~~~~~~~~~~~~~~~~~~~~~~~~~~~~~~~~~~

"**My** camera's digital clock is the reason I knew what time I last saw Moirin," I told the detectives. "It was exactly eight thirty when the battery warning light came on, and I headed inside."

"But she could have been out here quite a long time before her murder," Endicott sniffed.

"There's a way to deduce that, too." I met Lori's eyes.

She nodded. "The cigarette."

"It's worth a try," I said, and Lori called out to the CSU team.

"Did anyone find a cigarette butt on or near the carousel?"

"I bagged one up," said a member of the team.

"What brand is it?" I asked. "The name is usually printed next to the filter."

The technician fumbled through the evidence case and located the bagged butt. "It's a Lucky Strike."

"That's her brand," I confirmed. "If the lab finds her saliva on it, then it's clearly hers. And if you time how long a Lucky Strike burns down, then you should come close to the exact time of death."

"Unless she's a chain-smoker, Ms. Cosi. That could very well have been her third cigarette."

"Check her pockets. The new pack should be in there. I saw her open it. If that's the only cigarette missing, then you know she only smoked one."

"So you didn't see Moirin after that?" Lori asked.

"No, I didn't even realize Moirin had gone missing until someone asked after her more than an hour later."

Lori looked up from her notes. "Who asked after her?"

"I didn't get the woman's name. She was a nanny. The same one I'd bumped into outside the ice rink. She said Moirin promised to box up some cookies for her, so I'm not sure that fact is even relevant."

"Did you try to find Moirin after you realized she was gone?" Lori asked.

"No. I didn't . . ." *And I still feel awful about that.* "I thought she cut out on Janelle, that her boyfriend showed and she ditched working the rest of the event to go off with him."

"Enough, *please*," Endicott cried at the end of my account. "Ms. Cosi, thank you for your *extensive* statement. Now, Detective Soles, while we await the arrival of a medical examiner, I would like to dictate my initial impressions of the crime scene. Are you *listening*?"

"Yes, sir."

With a tape measure in hand, Endicott loomed over Moirin's corpse.

"The victim was struck from behind. It appears she received multiple blows from a blunt instrument. There is a significant amount of cranial bone and brain matter mingled with an arterial blood splatter that measures . . ."

For several minutes Detective Endicott measured blood splashes and speculated on the angle of the fatal blow. His graphic testimony became almost too much to bear, but still, I listened, hoping to hear something meaningful in the man's "initial impressions."

"Robbery does not appear to be the motive," Endicott continued. "The victim's purse contains a small amount of cash, a credit card, a MetroCard, a driver's license, and a portable phone—"

"The phone should help you," I cut in. "Moirin's boyfriend Dave calls her regularly, and sometimes she calls him. I'm sure you'll find his phone number in her permanent directory."

"The victim is also wearing a necklace with a sterling silver chain," Endicott continued. "The necklace contains a silver charm in the shape of the letter E—"

"It's not an E," I called. "It's a three."

"My good woman, I know the difference between an E and a three!"

"Untwist the necklace."

Endicott fell silent a moment and frowned. "So it is," he amended. "Do you know of any significance to this number?"

"I asked M about it once; she told me it represented the Holy Trinity."

Lori exchanged a look with me. "She's Irish Catholic."

"Yes."

"Why not just wear a cross?"

"I assumed she had her reasons. But it does seem odd, doesn't it?"

Endicott brushed aside our discussion. "The fact that these items were not stolen and a piece of valuable jewelry is still around her neck strongly suggests that robbery was *not* a motive." He circled the corpse. "The victim's clothes were not disturbed, so this was not a sexual assault, although it certainly could have begun as one and taken an ugly turn when the victim resisted."

Endicott paused. "It appears from the blood splatter pattern that when she was struck, the victim fell onto her stomach. Meanwhile, the bleed patterns indicate that the killer actually turned the victim onto her back, perhaps to make sure she was dead—"

"Or to retrieve something the victim was holding?" Lori suggested.

Endicott waved a dismissive hand. "What's important is

that these injuries are consistent with a blow from a blunt object, which fits the modus operandi in the last attack."

"Last attack?" I said. "You mean there've been others like this?"

Lori frowned, uneasy with my question. "There have been several attacks against women recently, but this is the first fatality."

"Well, do you have any suspects in the other attacks?" I asked, alarmed.

"Not yet." She then gave her head a single sharp shake that seemed to say: *I can't get into that with you. Not now.*

Meanwhile, Detective Endicott went down to his hands and knees. "The weapon was very heavy," he said, examining Moirin's head, "and I'm frankly puzzled by the shape and dimension of the wounds. The damage is extreme enough to have been inflicted by a sledgehammer, or even a baseball bat."

"But someone walking around with a sledgehammer or bat would certainly get noticed," Lori pointed out.

"Unless it was wrapped as a gift!" Endicott pronounced, rising.

Lori exhaled with extreme patience. "Who would go to the trouble of gift wrapping a murder weapon? And they'd have to rewrap it after they used it, unless the weapon got left behind, and I don't see any sledgehammers here."

"What if the killer used something they found in the park?" I chimed in.

Endicott snorted. "Like what, Ms. Cosi? A lawn chair?"

"No, a paving stone."

Lori nodded. "Go on, Clare."

"Well, I was just thinking . . . Before I found Moirin's body, I stumbled over a loose stone near the entrance to the carousel. It's possible the killer saw that the stone was loose, too, and decided to use it as the murder weapon. It's pretty smart, actually. The killer would be able to put the stone back down in the path, hiding the weapon from immediate discovery, and still walk away without holding incriminating evidence."

"Find that stone," Endicott ordered, "so we can eliminate it from consideration!"

The technicians began milling around, eyes to the pavement. But they weren't having much luck finding it because
they didn't know where to look. I did.

"Here it is." I showed them.

Lori dropped to her knees on the cold, wet ground and
bathed the rock in the beam of a tiny flashlight. "Clare's
right. There's blood here."

Three plastic-coated technicians quickly muscled me
aside and surrounded Detective Soles. Endicott, alone on
the carousel, sniffed dubiously.

"Are you sure it's blood and not spilled soda pop?"

"It's blood, sir," one CSU technician confirmed.

With gloved hands, the tech lifted the stone from its slot.
Lori passed the flashlight beam across the dripping bottom.
"I can see brain matter and hair, too."

Using plastic tweezers, a second CSU man pulled
strands off the rock and bagged them. The other technician
placed the paving stone inside a huge evidence bag, marked
it, and sealed it.

"It appears we have recovered the murder weapon,"
Endicott declared.

A technician brought the bagged hairs to Endicott and
the two examined them.

"The victim is a brunette, but these hairs are *orange*,"
Endicott observed.

Lori turned to me. "Do you remember any guests at the
party with this color hair?"

"I do."

"Male or female?"

"Female. I remember when she stopped by our drinking
station. It was close to nine o'clock, about thirty minutes
after I came in from watching Franco ice-skate with Mike's
kids . . ."

Seven

~~~~~~~~~~~~~~~~~~~~~~~~~~~~~~~~~~~~

"So, how's the weather outside?" Tuck asked Madame, who popped back in for another espresso.

"Still delightful," she assured him. "Cold, yes, but no sign of snow . . ."

"Well, I'll tell you what *is* frightful," Tucker whispered after she departed. "Some of the nips and tucks on these celebrities."

Tucker proceeded to regale Esther, Nancy, and me with quiet observations about the night's high-profile guests.

"Far be it from me to pooh-pooh having a little work done. But there's something called moderation. I mean, come now, ladies, stretch that skin any tighter and your eyes might just pop out!"

"I don't think it's that bad," Nancy said.

"And what's with all the spray tans this year? I mean, it's December in New York, Gidget. Paint that skin in Boca, not Manhattan!"

Esther nodded. "It does feel a tad like a science fiction convention. Either that or human airbrushing has created a race of carrot people."

"Like who?" Nancy challenged.

"Exhibit A . . ." Tuck took Nancy's face in his hands and turned it toward an ice blond giant in a five-thousand-dollar suit. "Bad-boy hockey player Ross Puckett. Take note of the bodacious little thing on his arm. That's Piper Penny, the lead singer in Dollahs and Sense, a hot band on the downtown club scene. Notice her tangerine hair? Granted, it's her trademark look, but it's *not* a color that occurs in nature. The same thing goes for a skin tone that's the same hue as the organic citrus they peddle at Whole Foods."

Nancy wrinkled her nose. "She does look kind of . . . unnatural."

"Unnatural!" Tuck cried. "Girl, I know monochrome is in, but that's just pushing it. If that shapely little singer is Ross Puckett's flavor of the month, then the *flavah* is definitely orange sherbet."

"Ross is so cute . . ." Nancy sighed. "What does he see in her?"

"He's a hockey player," Esther said flatly. "The question should be what does she see in him?"

"For starters, he's filthy rich," Tuck noted. "An obscenely large bank account can make even the most vulgar of men suddenly attractive. And Puckett is one of the few hockey players who still has his own teeth—presumably, though they could be implants."

"I saw Puckett flirting with our Moirin a little while ago," Nancy said with a shake of her jingle bell hat. "I nearly butted in and introduced myself."

"Hasn't your libido gotten you into enough trouble?" Esther asked. "Or have you forgotten that incident with the aphrodisiac coffee?"

Nancy pouted. "You two don't understand because you both have boyfriends. New York is lonely without a steady guy. If I knew Ross Puckett liked Day-Glo skin, I would have spray painted myself before I put on the apron!"

"Who'd want to look like her?" Esther said. "Puckett's latest squeeze has skin the shade of a sweet potato, obvious false eyelashes, and fright wig hair. Which actually makes me feel oddly nostalgic because she reminds me of a favorite childhood toy."

Nancy's head bobbed excitedly. "Malibu Barbie, right? She was my favorite, too!"

"Noooo!" Esther slapped her forehead. "*Barbie* is a sexist caricature that bears no relationship to reality! I was referring to Mrs. Potato Head!"

"She may have a sweet potato head but check out those toned arms," Tuck said. "I'll bet she can throw a hockey puck across the Hudson."

"Piper Penny is a singer," Nancy said. "What does her throwing ability have to do with anything?"

"I have it on good authority that Puckett's pretty Penny threw a service tray at a Village waiter last night," Tuck replied. "Only a very big tip kept that story out of the tabloids."

"I'd ask how you got that one," I said. "But I think I already know."

Tucker shot me a smile. "The bistro's owner comes in every morning for *doppio* espressos. He told me on the QT that the tray soared like a Frisbee across a college quad."

Nancy blinked in slight fear. "Oh man. We better keep the demitasse saucers away from her!"

"Hey, look, over there! It's Tommy Bain!" Tuck gushed. "When I was in grade school, he was the Euro-rocker who put the heroin in *heroin chic*."

Esther snorted. "The way he's twitching now, I don't think he can handle the sugar in those cookies, let alone hard drugs."

Suddenly Tuck's eyes went wide. "Look, look! I can't *believe* who's on their way over here. My two all-time favorite housewives, Big D and Little D!"

My assistant manager was beside himself at the approach of two busty women, one petite, the other Amazonian. Both wore skintight animal print dresses, and both were laden with enough gold and diamonds to put the Three Wise Men to shame.

Tuck greeted the pair as if they were old friends, and the women responded in kind.

"Boss, I want you to meet the stars of *TV's True House-wives of Long Island*, Danni Rayburn and Delores Deluca, better known as the Double Ds." Suddenly Tuck blinked. "I'm sorry, I didn't mean to bring up your . . . ah, you know . . ."

"Our breast augmentations?" the tall one (Big Danni) said with a laugh. "I'm not embarrassed. I always say 'If you *bought* it, flaunt it, baby.'"

"They're pretty obvious. Otherwise, what's the point?" agreed Little Delores.

I extended my hand, but the women were both so used to air-kissing like the other celebrities that they'd forgotten how to shake. Little Delores Deluca blinked, and Big Danni Rayburn just looked down at me. (This was a statement of fact, not a rush to judgment. Danni really was big—well over six feet high in her fetish heels, while I was barely five four in my sensible loafers.)

The look-alike blondes had lush figures, flawless makeup, and perfect teeth, but the resemblance ended there. Little Delores appeared reserved, almost bored, while Big Danni's eyes were hungry, expectant, as if she were waiting for me to gush.

"Didn't your show get cancelled?" Nancy innocently blurted.

"Hiatus!" Tuck cried in horror. "The Reality Channel has put the show on *hiatus*. Right, girls?"

"That's right," Big Danni said with a confident smile. "The producer told us there's still a window to revive the show. But we're open to new offers, aren't we, Delores?"

Little Delores nodded, her wide eyes framed by mascara-heavy lashes. "Fame's a bitch, but we are bitches, too. We'll claw our way back if we have to."

Tuck nodded sympathetically. "Being a producer myself, I know how fast the wind can shift. It's no different on Broadway."

"Oh!" Big Danni turned up the wattage on her smile. "You're a Broadway producer?"

"*Off*-Broadway," Tuck replied.

"Yeah, like *way* off," Esther snarked.

Tuck waved his hand. "Pay no attention to that Goth beneath the Grinch Peruvian Beanie. I do two or three revues a year. Right now I'm producing a Christmas drama."

"That's *very* interesting," said Big Danni. Her focus narrowed on Tuck like a peckish predator on a hot lunch. "You know, I can dance, and you heard me sing on *TV's True Housewives*. Don't you think I could star in one of your revues?"

"Actually . . ." Tuck said. "You're already playing a symbolic role in my upcoming cabaret show. After I finish my holiday gig, I'm mounting a musical tribute to *True Housewives*. I was going to cast two female impersonators, but if you and Little Delores want to join the production, I'm *sure* I can reimagine the idea."

Big Danni rested her slim hand on Tuck's arm. "I hope you do! What do you say, Delores?"

Little Delores shrugged. "I suppose it's worth a listen."

Tuck beamed. "From the creative standpoint, I'd love to know. Are you two really close friends?"

Big Danni hugged her little pal. "The closest."

"Aw, that's so refreshing," Tuck said. "I mean, it's nice to know your reality show was somewhat real. Do your kids still have playdates together like they did on TV?"

"Our kids are ice-skating with their nannies right now." Big Danni proudly gestured to the rink. Then she struck a pose, and I almost had to duck to avoid being boob smacked. ". . . although we haven't done a pizza night for months. I'm trying to slim down."

"Good idea," Tuck said with a thumbs-up, "especially for the dance numbers. What do you think of a boozy poolside torch song followed by a pizza playdate kick line?"

"Sounds amazing!"

"Here's my card," Tuck said, handing one to each woman. "The address to the Village Blend is on the back. Come by the coffeehouse. We'll tip some lattes and talk more showbiz."

"See you there," Danni promised, brushing Tuck's face with her manicured fingers. Then Big Danni and her little pal Delores moved on.

"I can't believe how flirty Danni was with you, Tuck," Nancy said.

Esther rolled her eyes. "Talk about barking up the wrong tree. Why would you want to do a cabaret show about those has-beens, anyway?"

"Has-been is better than never-was," Tuck replied. "FYI, Andy Warhol was wrong when he said you only get fifteen minutes of fame. When the spotlight goes out in one place, it goes on somewhere else. I can make those two girls stars again, at least on the Village scene."

"You seem to know all the celebrities, Tuck . . ." Esther said with a tone that implied she had an ulterior motive for asking. "So who's that creepy guy over there? He was openly glaring at you the whole time you were talking to the Double Ds."

Tuck paled. "Oh God. That's Big Danni's famously jealous husband, 'Evil Eyes' Eddie Rayburn."

Eddie stood alone by the windows. His clothes were perfectly tailored and his hair professionally coiffed. What didn't fit with this crowd was the man himself. Short and heavyset, with slightly bulging eyes and an ossified scowl, Eddie Rayburn looked more like one of the small-time hoods involved with my father's bookie operation than a member of the high-society celebrity club.

"Why is he 'famously jealous'?" I asked.

"Over the course of their thirteen episode reality show, he punched out a half a dozen guys who paid too much attention to his wife, Big Danni." Tuck shook his head. "He put one of them in the hospital."

"Remember what Nancy said about 'barking up the wrong tree'?" Esther asked. "You better hope Evil Eyes knows the kind of tree *you* are."

"Coming through!"

Using her elbows as a wedge, a tangerine-haired woman in a two-piece metallic pantsuit pushed through a tight group of latte-sipping society wives. Then she lurched forward, until the navel ring attached to her taut belly scraped against the coffee bar.

Our new customer was club singer Piper Penny. With a smirk, she dropped a half-filled cup of Candy Cane Latte. It splashed across the countertop.

"Hey, Grinch Girl! I need something stronger than peppermint," she demanded. "Now!"

"I'm sorry?" Esther replied.

"Don't front me, Grinchy. Ross Puckett told me you served him an Irish coffee. Make mine a double, and make it *double quick*."

"Fine," Esther said, responding more politely than the woman deserved.

As she fixed the drink, Tuck wiped the mess she'd made. Catching her eye, he gave Piper a sympathetic look.

"Tough night, girl?"

"I'll survive. Provided I get alcohol *in a hurry*."

"Chillax, I'm coming," Esther said, setting the coffee cup on the counter.

"Do you think I could have a saucer for this?" Piper's tone was now suspiciously sweet.

Before we could stop her, Esther gave it over. Then we all tensed when Piper failed to put it under her cup.

"Don't do it!" Nancy cried as she wound up.

Too late. Piper let the saucer fly. Rotating like a Frisbee, it soared over the heads of the crowd, nailing the noggin of the tallest man in the room—ice blond hockey star Ross Puckett.

We all gasped as Puckett turned, rubbing his head. He locked eyes with Piper, who waved at him with an acid grin. Flashing an obscene gesture, he disappeared into the crowd.

Piper shrugged and took a loud gulp. After several swallows, she thrust the cup toward Esther. "Hit me again."

Esther poured another shot from the bottle.

"You're growing on me, Grinchy," Piper said after draining her cup. "That num-nuts jock was right. This stuff is pretty good. Unfortunately it's not the only Irish thing Ross flipped for tonight. So now I'm on my own."

"He dumped you?!" Nancy blurted.

I could see Esther mouthing something to me. *Dropped like a hot Mrs. Potato Head!*

Piper cursed. "The doofus said he just met a cute Irish club girl and needed his space."

Tuck patted her toned, carrot-colored arm. "Men are pigs."

"That one is. Oh, I'm sure he thought he was being decent. He told me I had plenty of admirers here, so I could easily find one of them to take me home." Her gaze narrowed. "That was the first smart thing that dimwit on ice ever said to me . . ."

Piper wore several rings made of actual copper pennies, and she clicked them impatiently on the counter as her gaze swept the crowded room. Finally, she spied Tommy Bain. Like a female raptor sizing up her prey, she studied the fading rock-and-roll legend and turned back to the bar.

"One more taste of blarney, girlfriend." She held out her cup to Esther. "But hold the coffee this time."

Esther glanced at me. I nodded and she poured another shot. Piper swallowed it in one gulp. Then she swiped the back of her hand across tangerine-glossed lips.

"Oh, Tommy! Wait up," she cried, waving her throwing arm.

"She should have brought Tommy Bain down with another hurled demitasse," Esther cracked. "That *might* have been more subtle."

Just then, I felt a tap on my shoulder. I turned to face the nanny I'd met outside. Her bun was a bit more disheveled, and her sweater had a few more stains.

"Sorry to bother you, but do you know who's working the display over there?"

I followed her pointing finger and realized she was talking about Janelle Babcock's table. Several guests were milling around it, but neither Janelle nor Moirin was behind it.

"That Irish girl promised she'd box up some cookies for me, but now I can't find her."

I didn't get a chance to reply. Janelle Babcock rushed up to me.

"Clare! Have you seen Moirin?" She looked a little frantic when she saw the growing crowd around her table. "She never came back from her cigarette break. I checked out front, but she's not there!"

"She'll turn up," I insisted and sent Nancy to lend Janelle a hand for the rest of the night.

THANK you, Clare . . ." Lori finished scribbling in her notebook. Then she brushed away the snow that had accumulated on her shoulders. "Given the color of the hairs we found with the murder weapon, Piper Penny is a very promising lead."

"I agree," Endicott said. "Mitochondrial DNA analysis will soon confirm the perpetrator's identity. The case is as good as solved."

"I know what it looks like," I conceded. "The hairs do implicate Ms. Penny, and she does have a pattern of erratic, even violent behavior. But the motive seems awfully weak. Shouldn't you also be focusing on—"

"Welcome to the twenty-first century," Endicott snapped. "I have millions of unique DNA markers that will definitively establish guilt, and that's where my primary focus should be."

Endicott shook his head. "I know this might come as a surprise to a glorified waitress, but Victorian-era theorizing over clues and motives is a waste of cogitation in the face of modern forensics."

With an expression close to glee, Endicott rocked on his heels. "I have three words for you, Ms. Cosi: *Sherlock is schlock!* As sure as I'm standing in front of you, we'll have the killer in custody in a matter of—"

A harsh mechanical roar drowned out Endicott's words. On a blast of carnival music, the dark carousel suddenly exploded with light.

As Lori and I watched from the footpath, the carousel's platform lurched and began to move. Then a startled Detective Fletcher Stanton Endicott was whisked around the circle and out of sight.

EIGHT

ᘒᘒᘒᘒᘒᘒᘒᘒᘒᘒᘒᘒᘒᘒᘒᘒᘒᘒᘒᘒᘒᘒᘒ

UNTIL I ducked into a warm taxi, I hadn't realized how insidiously the cold had crept into me. My cheeks were chilled, my fingers numb, and the mounting snow that had slipped into my work loafers made my toes feel stiffer than Popsicle sticks.

"Put a frog in hot water," my pop used to say, "and he'll jump out. Turn up the heat slowly, and the greenie won't know he's cooked until he's soup."

Well, tonight, I'd become *frozen* soup; and on the slow, slushy drive from midtown to the West Village, I couldn't stop shivering—and my basal body temperature was only partly to blame.

On top of being grief stricken and incensed over what some cold-blooded monster had done to M, I couldn't help feeling frustrated with Fletcher Stanton Endicott.

The "crime-writing detective" was a smug, shortsighted, and (frankly) silly excuse for a police officer. I felt sorry that a good cop like Lori Soles was saddled with him.

I was shivering for another reason, too. My staff had no

idea that Moirin had been violently murdered, and I was the one who would have to tell them.

In the NYPD, they called this "notification." Mike Quinn had done it countless times. He loved police work, but there was no worse job, he once told me, than explaining to good people how someone they loved was taken from them because of one brutal, selfish act.

First I'll knock back a double espresso, I decided. *Then I'll sit ten minutes by our fireplace.* If that little bit of prayer (and caffeine) time didn't give me the strength to address my staff, then it would at least warm me up.

As the cab moved south, I pulled out my cell and gave Janelle a call.

Lori Soles would be questioning her this evening, and I didn't want to get in the way of that—but I did want to reach out to my friend.

When I got Janelle's voice mail, I hesitated. Certainly, I couldn't leave news as upsetting as Moirin's murder on a recorded message. Instead, I simply told her to call me if she needed to talk.

"First thing in the morning," I promised her, "I'm going to drop by your bakery to see you, okay? And I mean it: call me *anytime* if you need to talk . . ."

When the taxi finally pulled up to my coffeehouse, I was feeling steadier—an adjective that failed to describe the heavyset businessman teetering toward me.

"Hey, honey, hold that cab!"

Topcoat flapping in the wind, the drunk's expensive suit was disheveled, and his maroon tie appeared to be deconstructing at the same rate as his dignity. I couldn't see how he was able to stand on his own, let alone walk, until I spied the brown felt antlers bobbing up and down behind his wide body.

The soft, fleecy horns crowned the shaved head of Dante Silva, fine arts painter by day, espresso jockey by moonlight. With sleeves rolled up, he'd wrapped both tattooed arms around the inebriated businessman.

"I'm going to Tiffany," the drunk declared. "It's important!"

"Why?" asked a second man. This guy, also in a rumpled suit, was half as wide but nearly as drunk as his heavyset pal.

Drunk Man shook his head. "Got to buy the wife's Christmas gift before she grabs the bonus!"

"Tiffany shmiffany," replied the friend between hiccups. "Those few pathetic shekels our company calls a bonus wouldn't buy a shopping bag in that joint."

The drunk broke away from Dante, and I jumped out of the way as he lunged through the taxi door and rolled across the backseat.

"Tiffany, cabbie!" he declared.

"Forget the jewelry shop," the friend told the driver. "We're going straight to Jersey—by way of an all-night drugstore."

"Drugstore?!" cried the drunk. "Why, Fred?"

"Because when it comes to hangovers, diamonds got nothing on extra-strength aspirin—and our two bonus checks together *might* just cover a bottle."

Before sliding into the cab, the friend shoved a twenty into Dante's apron. "Thanks for helping, kid. Buy yourself a ticket to Santa's reindeer games!"

As the cab pulled away, Dante smiled down at me. "You're back late. I thought a kiddie party would end a lot earlier. How did it go?"

"I'll tell you about it later," I said as we crossed the freshly cleared sidewalk. "I see you've been busy shoveling. Thanks."

"I don't mind." He righted his antler hat. "In New England, you grow up doing it. On the other hand, Fred's pal was the third drunk I poured into a cab tonight, and I'm not done."

He paused at the Village Blend's front door, resting his palm on the handle. "Brace yourself, boss. It's like a Bavarian beer hall in there."

Then he swung open the door, and a wall of noise struck us.

Typically, our business would be winding down at this time of night, and the few customers occupying tables would be NYU students or older neighborhood residents, casually dressed.

Not tonight.

It was close to midnight, but every one of our marble-topped tables was occupied by men and women in office garb. A line of customers flowed back from our register like a crooked human river, and behind our counter part-timer Vicki Glockner processed orders while Gardner Evans pulled one espresso shot after another with machine shop precision.

Here we go, I thought, my gaze scanning the mostly middle-aged crowd, *the Great Manhattan Sober-Fest*.

The annual tradition spanned Thanksgiving weekend to New Year's Day. Simple geography was the reason. The Blend sat within spitting distance of a dozen trendy restaurants that hosted holiday parties for private companies all over the city. Every few nights, we found ourselves the pit stop for inebriated office workers before they returned home to their families.

As Dante and I negotiated the crowded tables, conversations ranged from animated, to angry, to post-party confessional: "Did I really *say* that?! Did I actually *do* that? Oh God!"

The intensity of the fussing reminded me of Phyllis Diller's old joke: *"What I don't like about office Christmas parties is looking for a job the next day."*

Dante shook his head. "It's amazing how the myth persists."

"Which one?"

"The one that claims strong black coffee is supposed to sober you up."

"True . . ." I said, although there was some validity in the idea.

Caffeine was an effective stimulant, and a good dose could make an inebriated person a bit more alert. On the other hand, in the words of my ex-husband (the PhD of Partying on a Global Scale): *"If you pump a drunk full of coffee, all you end up with is a wide-awake drunk."*

Right now, my coffeehouse was full of drunks buzzed on caffeine and half shouting to be heard.

That's when it struck me, as deeply and sharply as a chef's knife through a plate of Christmas cookies—

These people and I had something in common. Their day had started out happy, hopeful. It had turned into something else. Just like me, they were upset about something that had happened, something they felt responsible for—even if the consequences were out of their control. Like holiday cookies, we all appeared festive on the outside, but any more pressure and some of us were going to crumble.

Dante called to me over the din. "You need a shot, boss?"

"Make it a triple, thanks. And listen—" I touched his tattooed forearm. "I'm calling a staff meeting tonight, after closing."

Dante cupped his ear. "Did you say staff meeting?"

"Yes."

He nodded. "So that's why he's here."

"Who's here?"

I followed Dante's pointing finger, and there *he* was, my ex-husband, Matteo Allegro, warming the very last stool at the end of our blue marble coffee bar—Detective Quinn's usual seat.

The incongruity of it made me blink.

Initially, Mike Quinn had claimed that perch as my customer. Over time, he occupied it as my friend, my confidant, and finally my lover. With all that had happened tonight, I veritably ached to see him. But tonight he was missing from his usual seat, and I moved to speak with the man now warming it.

Nine

~~~~~~~~~~~~~~~~~~~~~~~~~~~~~~~~~~~~~~

In an ironic twist (ironic for a recovered addict, anyway), my ex-husband appeared sober as a judge tonight amid our half-drunken customers. In his Armani formal wear, he was dressed just as grimly, too. Or maybe black just seemed an ominous color to me, after the disturbing matter in Bryant Park.

On the other hand, not everyone thought Matt looked grim. A table of young urban professionals, three women and one gay man, appeared convinced that James Bond had dropped by to warm up with an espresso. Although their interest in my ex was obvious, Matt thumbed through the overseas market news on his smartphone, completely oblivious to their whispering stares.

Despite my ups and downs with the man, I completely respected Matt's expertise. He was one of the most astute coffee brokers in the country, and the Village Blend was lucky to have him as its coffee buyer. The beans he sourced made us one of the top shops in an insanely competitive market.

Of course, Matt had good reason to work for us—this century-old concern had been started by his great-grandfather and was now owned by his mother. She planned on leaving the business (and the landmark Federal town house it occupied) to us both. And since we intended to bequeath it to our only daughter, he and I had plenty of incentive to keep our relationship civil and our coffeehouse thriving.

I approached the coffee bar and patted his muscular shoulder, draped in expensive fabric. "If you're here to help Dante eject holiday drunks, you're overdressed."

He smiled. "While that sounds like loads of fun, I'm actually here for a midnight snack."

At my questioning look, he set aside his smartphone and opened a brown bag on the counter. Savory aromas wafted over me: grilled beef, caramelized onions, and *pomme frites* fresh from the fryer.

A little gurgle of yearning taunted my stomach. Ignoring it, I took over the stool next to him and made a not-so-wild guess: "Given your designer monkey suit, I assume you came straight from a Christmas party?"

"An entire *round* of Christmas parties. I told Breanne I needed *real* food, and she let me loose for a take-out run. We're hooking up at one o'clock. Some music executive's throwing a Jingle Bell-a-Palooza at Daddy-O."

Letting Matt "loose" was the perfect explanation for the health of his second marriage.

During the better part of his year, he trekked the unglamorous Third World, sourcing coffee via small farms and community cooperatives. When he was away, he played. He'd done it when he was married to me—and after he was divorced from me. Wedding Breanne hadn't put a crimp in his style, which (to most women) came off smoother and cooler than my barista Gardner's jazzy Christmas playlists.

It was no mystery to me why Matt's matrimonial calculus had a better result with Breanne. The willowy blonde was not some poor, young wife trying to run a small business while raising a baby, virtually alone (i.e., *me*). She was the high-powered editor in chief of *Trend* magazine and an international, jet-setting fashionista who took first-class tours of European cities, entourage in tow.

Bree didn't share my "provincial" view that marriage vows were sacred. She fully accepted Matt's hound dog nature, allowing him "off leash" for limited periods. She was also gorgeous enough to keep him happy at heel, and she footed the bills for their high living, which made my ex-husband amenable to wearing a diamond-studded collar while on her turf—at least in small doses. When the collar got too tight, he'd be gone again, heeding the call of the wild.

And speaking of wild . . .

As Matt unwrapped a ginormous patty melt, I got the distinct impression I was about to watch a gleeful hunter consume his hard-won prey.

"That looks like an awful lot of beef," I said.

"Angus. Ten ounces."

"I don't understand. You were escorting Breanne to a night of holiday parties that *didn't* serve food?"

"They served things that *passed* for food."

"Come on, how bad could it be? They were catered parties, weren't they?"

"Yes, but the first shindig was thrown by Lite Bite Cuisine, one of Breanne's advertisers. Their corporate chef microwaved up an entire line of frozen diet dishes. Ever tasted a 'Skinny Mung Bean Alfredo'?"

"Not lately."

"How about a 'Lactose-Free Parfait with Flaxseed Granola'?"

I shook my head.

"Then we were off to the *Get Fit* get-together at Cooper Union. Do you know what a braised leek-wrapped water chestnut tastes like? *Nothing.* That's what it tastes like."

Matt picked up half his patty melt and offered it to me. At the Bryant Park party, I'd scarfed a baker's dozen of

Christmas cookies—sugar, buttercream, chocolate, and caramel—which (come to think of it) didn't add up to "real" food, either. When the aroma of freshly cooked beef hit my nose, my protein-adoring saliva glands kicked in.

Once again, I ignored them.

"I plan on eating with Mike," I stated firmly. "When he gets in . . ."

"Suit yourself," Matt said, and then he shrugged, as if aloof, but his expression was more telling. Like the alkie who abhors indulging alone, he was obviously miffed by my sniffing rejection.

With off-putting gusto, he tore a big, sloppy bite from his beef-a-palooza snack, which proceeded to ooze juice onto his whiter-than-white dress shirt.

I pointed. "Your wife won't be happy if you show up like that."

"I have another shirt in the SUV."

He began reaching for a fry, but stopped. Well aware of my hungry stare, the man dumped the entire cone of shoe-strings onto the patty melt's wrapping paper, sending a fresh wave of caramelized potato air my way.

Next he opened a small plastic container. Like a sadistic foodie Picasso, he drizzled ruby red ketchup over the golden brown canvas, while shooting me a taunting smile.

"Are you *sure* you don't want some?"

My mouth was really watering now. Swallowing hard, I started to shake my head—but the fries were too much! Breaking down, I snatched three and shamefully shoved them into my mouth. As they hit my buds, I closed my eyes.

Oh God . . . The ketchup is homemade; the chef even smoked the tomatoes!

Matt saw the look on my face and didn't ask again. He simply slid the untouched half of his sandwich my way. The artisan bread oozed with a thick layer of melted white cheddar. *Oh man . . .*

With a sigh, I succumbed.

"Just one word of caution, Clare," Matt smugly warned

as I took my first juicy, meaty, cheesy bite. "You heard of the Five-Napkin Burger? Well this is an Eight-Napkin Patty Melt."

"Eight?" I mumbled, mouth embarrassingly stuffed.

Matt smirked at the dribbles now running down my front and pointed to the pile of paper napkins. "Since you're eating *half*, you're only entitled to four."

"Oh?"

He blinked. "I'm *joking*."

I stared and he frowned, pausing to study me.

"Clare? What's wrong?"

"What do you mean?"

"Something must be wrong. I could always make you laugh."

"No you couldn't," I said, waving his comment aside.

"Sure I could. I even made you laugh the day we signed our divorce papers."

"I was giddy."

"You were *crying*."

He was right. I was crying, all those years ago. And given this evening's sad discoveries, I was close to crying now, but what good would it do anyone?

Matt studied me after that, shook his head, and set the rest of his sandwich aside. "What's wrong? Tell me."

"I don't think this is the time and place to—"

"What's *wrong*, Clare?" His tone was steely, but his brown eyes looked worried. "It's not our daughter, is it?"

"No, nothing like that. As far as I know, Joy is fine . . ."

Lowering my voice, I finally spilled it—the grim news about poor Moirin Fagan, the manner of her death, my attempts to help the assigned detectives, even my guilt over assuming she was shirking work, instead of being beaten to death with a footpath stone by some crazy predator.

"I should have done more than cover for her—"

"You can't blame yourself," Matt insisted. "Moirin was working at your friend Janelle's display, not yours."

"You don't understand: Moirin was working for both of us. Janelle and I had a special arrangement."

"What kind of arrangement?" His voice had gone from supportive to tense.

"Janelle agreed to bill me a 'service charge' along with her weekly cookie dough invoice. That charge was based on the hours that M spent at the Blend, helping the baristas with cookie and pastry sales."

"So you took a shortcut; found a way to hire a seasonal worker without going through the hassles of officially adding a new person to our staff?"

"I couldn't afford to hire another worker, even a part-time one, to do the fresh-baked cookies for us; the whole thing was an experiment, anyway. I didn't know if the revenue would offset the costs. The arrangement benefited Moirin, too. She was grateful for the chance to earn extra cash." I frowned and rubbed my eyes. "I just wished she hadn't been working *tonight*."

Matt touched my shoulder. "Clare, just because she worked part-time for you doesn't make you responsible for what happened to her."

"When she went missing, I didn't look for her, Matt. I didn't even try."

A blast of pop music suddenly filled the coffeehouse, much louder than the mellifluous holiday jazz that had been barely audible over the noisy customers.

"I'm gonna dance, dance, dance, and shake my boo-ty. / Oh, the boys, they say it's my national du-ty . . ."

The brash singer was popular on the downtown scene, and a few of our younger female customers squealed and sang along.

"There's a problem here, it's very near, / and it can only be solved by shakin' my rear . . ."

Gardner thrust his head out from behind the steaming espresso machine. "No way, Vicki," his deep voice boomed in that stern but controlled monotone. "You are not playing Piper Penny on my watch, especially that inane song."

"Fine! I'll turn her off, *after* it's over," Vicki said, dancing in place.

When the song played out, she switched back to Gardner's

playlist. A smooth jazz rendition of "Blue Christmas" began, but Piper's voice continued to echo in my head, and I rationally considered the theory of the lead detective on Moirin's case: did the popular club singer really beat M to death?

My mind called up the memory of tangerine-haired Piper in her belly-baring metallic pantsuit, throwing that demitasse at Ross Puckett's head. The outburst was incriminating, but I'd noticed the singer before that.

The first time I saw Piper Penny was during her TV interview in the front of the Bryant Park Grill. It was also the last time I saw Moirin alive.

I closed my eyes and tried to conjure the image of M coming toward me on the park's path. For some reason, my mental painting refused to depict her alive. In my mind she was a ghost, ethereal, like the pearl gray plume that had spiraled up from her cigarette.

"Oh my God," I murmured.

"What's wrong?"

I gripped Matt's arm. "The cigarette! Before she was killed, Moirin came toward me lighting a cigarette!"

"What are you talking about?"

"A smoke signal!" I gathered up my parka and purse. "I just have to test my theory before I tell the police . . ."

"Test what theory? Where are you going?"

"To the convenience store. I need a cigarette and I need it *now*."

Ten

~~~~~~~~~~~~~~~~~~~~~~~~~~~~~~~~~~~~~~~

"**I** still don't understand," Matt groused as we stepped onto our icy sidewalk. "Why are we out here?"

The snow was coming down faster now. Nearly two inches had accumulated on the cleared walkway since I'd last seen it.

"I'll explain in a minute. Be right back!"

"*Now* where are you going?!"

My damp loafers were no match for this weather, so I ran up to my small office, switched to snow boots, and rushed to rejoin Matt, who was buttoning up his black cashmere topcoat.

"Let's go," I said.

"Where, Clare?"

"To buy cigarettes," I reminded him. "And it has to be a Lucky Strike."

"Since when did you start smoking, anyway?"

"Who said I was smoking?"

"Okay, fine. I'll just watch and learn?"

"Good idea."

The frigid wind kicked up, pelting my cheeks with stinging kisses. Matt groaned, feeling it, too. He lifted his scarf to cover his face, and I flipped up the hood of my white parka.

While Dante had dented the accumulation around the Blend, the adjacent shops weren't open this late, and a good five inches had piled up on their stoops. The sparkling white layers were pockmarked with pedestrian shoe prints, but those indentations were filling up fast.

Matt and I linked arms to keep from slipping in the drifts, which glowed softly under streetlamps, half muted by the swirling snowflakes.

"I'm dying to find out what you're up to, so I hope this place is open," he said against another gust of winter.

"Saheed's Deli never closes," I assured him. And I was right.

The tiny convenience store announced itself amid the landmark town houses like a blasting glass jukebox in a quiet cathedral, its bright windows a beer-and-chips beacon in the storm—which was not an exaggeration. The shiny storefront had attracted a number of the storm's stragglers, including a threesome of NYU students huddled under the awning and an elderly man cradling a Chihuahua too tiny to negotiate the deepening snow.

Saheed wasn't on duty, but one of his male relatives stood behind the counter.

"I'll take care of this," Matt said, drawing his wallet as the man passed me the cigarette pack.

"You better buy a lighter, too," I said. "Unless you're carrying one."

Matt grabbed one from the Bic display. "My Ronson is with my travel stuff."

Back outside, I tore the cellophane off the Lucky Strike package and shook one cigarette out.

"I hope you're telling the truth about not having a smoking habit," Matt said, tucking his wallet in place. "At eleven bucks a pack, I can see why you'd have trouble meeting the payroll."

"It's the sin tax, Matt, and sins are costly." I arched an eyebrow. "You, of all people, should know that." I displayed the cigarette. "Are you going to light this thing, or what?"

Matt blinked. "Me?"

"Yes, Mr. Global Trekker. You've sampled practically every drug known to man—"

"And I enjoyed some of them, too. But I never liked tobacco."

"And yet you've smoked enough contraband Cubans."

"Fine," Matt said, snatching the white cylinder out of my hand. "Do we *have* to do it outside in the cold?"

"That's how Moirin did it."

"Did what?"

"Smoked what I believe was her last cigarette. When I saw Moirin Fagan for the final time, she was leaving the Bryant Park Grill and walking in the direction of the carousel. That's where I found her body."

Matt frowned, studying my face. "Okay," he said and struggled to light the Bic in the stiff wind.

"The police found orange hairs on the footpath stone the killer used as a murder weapon. Piper Penny had reason to be furious with Moirin tonight, and the singer has orange hair. But I think Piper has an alibi. We'll know for sure after this experiment."

Matt cursed and stepped behind a snow-covered Dumpster to dodge the stubborn wind. "Go on," he said, and I heard the Bic flick several times.

"As Moirin passed me, she opened a fresh pack of Lucky Strikes. She was so busy lighting her cigarette that she didn't notice me. And at the same time, I saw Piper—"

"Following Moirin?"

"No. She was in front of a New York One TV camera. Roger Clark was just starting his interview. I'm sure it went on for at least five minutes, maybe more. He seemed quite taken with her."

"She's photogenic, then?" Matt said.

"Oh yeah."

Matt cursed again and the Bic clicked.

"The butt of Moirin's Lucky Strike was found beside her body. So, right now, you and I are going to figure out whether Piper Penny had enough time to finish her interview, track Moirin down, and bash in her head before the poor dead girl finished that cigarette—"

A choking cough interrupted me. Finally, Matt just waved the Lucky Strike to show me it was lit and I checked my watch.

"You smoke, I'll time. How often do you think a smoker hits a cigarette, anyway?"

"You"—*koff, hack*—"tell me!"

The phone in my bag beeped loudly. "Oh, thank God!" I cried, sure it was Quinn, calling at last. But it wasn't.

"Esther just texted me. She marked it urgent."

Matt puffed on the cigarette. "What"—*koff, keck*—"does it say?"

"'Worst News Ever. Must talk 1st thing in AM.'" I sighed. "She must have heard about Moirin's murder. I still have to break the news to Dante, Gardner, and Vicki tonight—and I'll have to call Tuck and Nancy so they don't hear it on the Internet. And on top of this tragedy . . ." I took a breath, then finally said it out loud. "Quinn has gone missing on me."

"What do you mean *missing*? It's the age of smartphones. Nobody goes missing unless they want to." Matt caught my stricken look. "I'm not suggesting that the glorified flatfoot is dodging your calls. I know how he feels about you."

"He's traveling," I said.

"In this weather?" Matt scowled. "I'm rethinking a ten-block drive to the Meatpacking District, and your thick-headed detective is trying to get to New York from DC?"

"On an airplane."

Matt slapped his own forehead. "Bad idea, Clare. You don't—"

"Mess with the weather," I finished with him. "I know. I learned that lesson well enough from you."

"Honduras?" he said, and I nodded.

Back then, Matt had still been my husband and Joy a little

girl. He'd thought he was "bigger than mother nature"—
that's how he put it to me after a hurricane nearly killed him.

Eighteen inches of rain fell in the first twelve hours, followed by hazardous flooding, and finally a mudslide. Despite
all the warnings, Matt had attempted to travel across the
country and ended up stranded in some nameless village in
the Copan district, just as the worst of the monster swept
ashore.

Trapped by sixteen feet of rushing water, on the second-
floor balcony of the only brick building for miles, he'd
spent the entire night helping a retired Honduran cop with
a flashlight haul people out of the raging water.

The next day, trees the size of boats washed down the
mountain and slammed into the building, one after the other.
The structure held together, but not the town or its people . . .

"We couldn't save them all," he'd told me in a hollow
voice, after returning home. A week later, waking from a
nightmare, he finally shared his guilt about the innocent
victims he saw slip away—an old man, two women, and a
small child.

Matt fell silent at my mention of that memory. A minute
later, he waved his cigarette. "This thing is about finished."

I checked my watch. "Eight minutes. You were sucking
pretty hard there, so let's add one more minute." I brushed
the snow off my eyelashes. "Even nine minutes isn't long
enough. There's no way Piper Penny killed Moirin. She
didn't have the time."

ELEVEN

~~~~~~~~~~~~~~~~~~~~~~~~~~~~~~~~~~

"**W**AIT a second," Matt said. "Aren't you jumping to conclusions? Moirin could have been chain-smoking . . ." He paused to cough again. "God knows why."

"The Crime Scene Unit only found one butt at the scene."

"She could have tossed the first butt, or even a second, before she reached the carousel. Seems to me you have to know how many cigarettes were missing from the pack that they found on Moirin's body."

"That's exactly right." I pulled out my cell phone.

Matt displayed his own butt. "Are we keeping this as evidence or something?"

"Of course not."

Matt tossed the smoldering cigarette into the snow-choked gutter, and I dialed the number of Detective Lori Soles. She picked up on the first ring.

"You're still at the scene?" I asked.

"The precinct. Transcribing Endicott's notes," she replied flatly. "What's up?"

I told Lori about my timeline issues. ". . . so I'd like to

know. Was there more than one cigarette missing from Moirin's pack?"

Lori hesitated, and I knew why. Sharing information like that with a witness wasn't exactly kosher procedure.

"Come on, Detective. I'm only trying to help. You know that."

For the next few seconds, all I heard was a city garbage truck rolling by on Hudson, plow scraping the pavement. Then Lori spoke again, her voice much quieter.

"According to the CSU team's preliminary notes, only one cigarette was gone from the Lucky Strike pack found on Moirin's body."

Only one! I mouthed to Matt in triumph.

"Listen," I told Lori, "when Moirin lit that cigarette, Piper Penny was being interviewed by New York One. You can find the raw tape of it and time it for yourself, but I highly doubt Piper had time to complete that interview, throw on a coat to shield her clothes from blood splatter, track down Moirin at the park's carousel, and beat her to death."

"I don't know, Cosi. We have orange hairs on the murder weapon. We have a motive and witnesses to Ms. Penny's violent temper that night, for which she has an established pattern on previous occasions. Timewise, it still might be possible—"

"But smoking a Lucky Strike takes under ten minutes, and Moirin's cigarette wasn't even completely finished before it was snuffed out by her own blood—"

"Dear God," Matt muttered next to me.

Lori exhaled hard. "How do you explain her very unique color of hair on the murder weapon?"

"I can't. Unless . . ."

"What?"

"The captain of the New York Raider's hockey team, Ross Puckett—he was Piper's date, remember? Well, Puckett was nowhere in sight when Moirin was killed—"

"So he decided to accost or sexually assault Ms. Fagan, and it ended in murder? That's your theory?" Lori's tone was skeptical. "It would mean Ross planned ahead and brought some of his date's hair to frame her."

"I can't explain the orange hairs, only the timeline."

Lori sighed. "I don't know about Puckett, but I'm going to push the hair analysis to the front burner. We'll probably know something by midday tomorrow. I'll get back to you."

"Thank you!" I said and ended the call.

Matt adjusted his collar. "Let's head back to the Blend. This storm seems to be getting worse."

My mood was buoyed by Lori's response, but then I glanced at the murky sky, crowded with cascading flakes, and my spirits fell.

"I wish Mike would call."

"Maybe he did. Check your messages again."

I did and shook my head. "Something must be wrong. Before I left the Bryant Park Grill, I tried calling the airline. They said information on Quinn's flight was pending. His ex-wife won't return my call, and he has yet to return mine. *Pending?* What does that mean? Honestly, I don't know what to do . . ."

Matt reached for his own phone. "Maybe I can help. I downloaded a dozen airline apps into this thing. Give me his flight info."

"It's a commuter airline. Capitol Express, Flight 324 out of Baltimore. It was supposed to take off a little after five . . ."

Matt paged past screens until he located the right app. "Here we go. I'll find your boyfriend for you." His thumbs went into action. "The flight took off two hours late, and it landed in LaGuardia at . . ."

Matt paused, then swallowed.

"What?"

"Nothing . . . I mean it's probably nothing. The plane didn't land, that's all."

"Didn't land? But it's a one-hour flight, and it took off over five hours ago!"

Matt's thumbs repeated their keyboard dance. "I can't

get anything more. The real-time schedule just says Capitol Express Flight 324 has not yet arrived."

"Can it be circling that long?"

"I doubt the plane had that much fuel. It was probably diverted because of the weather."

"Then why doesn't it *say* that?!"

Matt looked up from the screen. "What the hell was Quinn doing on an airplane tonight, anyway? Did you pressure him to come home?"

"Just the opposite! I begged him to stay put. It was his ex-wife who bullied him onto that plane. That's why we . . . well, we had words."

"You and the redheaded underwear model went at it again? Who brought the handcuffs this time?"

"Not funny."

"Well, what exactly did she tell you?"

I went through the entire play-by-play: How Leila Quinn dropped off their kids at the Cookie Swap with an "update on Mike" for me. According to her, he couldn't get a flight out of Washington National, so he called her to apologize for missing the party. She went nuts and guilt-tripped him so badly about "letting his kids down" that he changed his plans again and drove for an hour to BWI, which was just fine with her.

"When Leila Quinn smugly told me how she 'convinced' Mike to drive to Baltimore to get a flight to New York in time for the party, I told her a thing or two, and she left the Cookie Swap in a hissy fit."

"Sorry I wasn't there. I do enjoy a good catfight."

Off my irritated look, Matt raised an eyebrow. "Don't be modest. I personally think you could take her at mud wrestling."

"Again. Not funny."

"It's a little funny . . ." He shrugged. "Seriously, Clare, don't feel bad. What's the holiday season without a family squabble?"

"We're not family."

"Not yet. But the flatfoot gave you that cereal box ring, didn't he?"

"The Claddagh is a friendship ring."

"It's more than that," he said quietly. "And you know it."

"I do, but . . ." I closed my eyes. "For five months now, Mike's been commuting from Washington . . . and I miss him so much, especially at night . . . and I'm here, and he's not, and he *must* know that I'm worried sick about him . . . yet he never even bothered to call!"

I stopped and met my partner's gaze. "What if he can't call? Didn't you once tell me that when a plane goes down, airlines never say so? They simply list the flight as never arriving . . . Matt, what if . . ."

My voice caught, and I hated myself but the tears finally came. I could feel my nose running and my body shaking.

"Oh crap," Matt whispered. "Clare?"

He moved to take me in his arms, but stopped—and in a monumental moment of growth, Matteo Allegro actually made an effort to respect my boundaries.

"Do you need a hug?" he asked sheepishly.

I shook my head no, but like my embarrassing *pommes frites* breakdown, something inside me crumbled. My arms groped for something to hold on to, and before I knew it, my face buried itself in his strong shoulder, where it proceeded to ruin his exquisitely woven cashmere topcoat.

Twelve

~ ~ ~ ~ ~ ~ ~ ~ ~ ~ ~ ~ ~ ~ ~ ~ ~ ~ ~ ~

That night I discovered something far worse than notification—*waiting to be notified.*

After (literally) crying on Matt's shoulder, he offered to stay with me, but I wiped my eyes and insisted he rejoin his wife.

"I'll let you know if I hear anything," I assured him.

"You do that, Clare, because putting you through this was completely unnecessary on Quinn's part, a total dick move; and if that flatfoot actually turns up alive and well, you better let me know because *I'd* like to kill him."

"I appreciate your loyalty, Matt—I do. But I think there's been more than enough killing tonight . . ."

We walked me back to the coffeehouse in silence. The historical district had gone silent, too. Few vehicles attempted to negotiate the slippery streets, which were becoming impassable, and the tops of every parked car looked like some wedding cake designer went mad with whipped cream frosting.

By the time we reached the Village Blend, the shop was emptying out. I bade Matt good night and brushed the snow off my parka. As my night shift served the last stragglers, I made private calls to Tucker and Nancy.

Then I politely cleared the shop and locked the front door. Gathering my kids together around the fading fire of the shop's brick hearth, I broke the news about Moirin.

Gardner Evans bowed his head with stoic sadness, Dante Silva cursed like a Bronx cop, and Vicki Glockner burst into tears, her crumpet-colored curls breaking free of their loose ponytail.

"I'm so sorry," I said. "I'm very upset, too."

"I was Moirin's Secret Santa!" Vicki shared between sobs. "I already put her gift beside Bing Crosby in the pantry. I couldn't wait to see her reaction when she opened it!"

"What did you get her?" Gardner gently asked.

"Tickets to see Purple Lettuce."

I blinked in confusion. "You got her tickets to see radicchio?"

Vicki shook her head and began to sob again.

Dante caught my eye. "Purple Lettuce is an indie band."

Whoops. "What a thoughtful gift," I quickly assured Vicki. "Moirin really liked those downtown club bands, didn't she?"

"They're actually from Long Beach in Nassau County," Vicki informed me. "They've gotten really big now, but Moirin said she's followed them from their first dive appearance on the Island."

Dante cursed again. "Who would *do* that to an innocent girl?!"

His outburst was so sharp and loud that Gardner, Vicki, and I started.

Clearly, Dante was the angriest, and I shouldn't have been surprised. Most days, he was an easygoing, "space music"–loving, live-and-let-live kind of dude. But like most artists, he had rivers of passions that ran deep; and when heated, those depths boiled up with ferocity.

Suddenly, he was peppering me with questions about who did it, or who the police *thought* did it. And the look in his eyes said he was ready to go out into the storm by himself and bring the killer to justice with his bare hands.

I could have mentioned Piper Penny, but since I firmly believed those orange hairs either didn't belong to her or were placed there to frame her, I simply said—

"The police have a number of leads."

"Come on, boss. Don't give me that official baloney. Who are they looking at for this?"

"What happened to M was awful," I replied levelly, "but we have to control our emotions. We have to trust the police to bring M's killer to justice."

Dante exhaled hard on that, and I bit my own cheek.

As far as "trusting" the police went, I certainly trusted Mike, and I trusted Lori Soles; but I did not (for one nanosecond) trust Fletcher Stanton Endicott. Unfortunately, he was the lead detective in Moirin's case.

Where did that leave me?

Frustrated, that's where—which was why I began questioning my staff about Moirin's life, specifically about her boyfriend, Dave.

Like Tucker and Nancy, none of them had ever met Dave. They didn't know much about Moirin, either, for that matter. All they knew was that her family was back in Ireland. Other than that, she'd kept her private life just that—private.

"Let's finish our work and call it a night, okay?" I finally said.

"Gardner and Vicki should get out of here," Dante insisted. "They have the longest commute. I can just walk home."

"Are you sure?" I asked.

"Yeah. I need to burn off my fumes," Dante said. "You might as well head upstairs, too, boss. I just want to put on my music and try to chill."

I glanced at our French doors, framed in tiny white Christmas lights, the casement panes half coated with shaggy frost.

"You know what, Dante?" I said with a sigh. "I think we all need to chill. And given tonight's weather, it won't be a problem."

Thirteen

~~~~~~

"**Java!** Frothy!"

The sight of my two furry roommates bounding into my apartment's kitchen didn't allay my worries about Quinn, or lift my spirits about Moirin, but they did make me feel less alone.

Java was my big coffee bean brown lady with attitude; Frothy, my sweet little ball of white fluff. As I popped a juicy can of Salmon Supreme, their purring bodies circled my legs like a yin and yang of feline gratitude.

Out of habit more than hunger, I opened the fridge to scan the contents and spied the medium-rare pepper-crusted roast beef. It was perfectly cooked, all ready to be sliced razor thin for wraps and sandwiches. I'd made it special, to welcome Mike home.

I slammed closed the fridge door. *Okay! Enough of this waiting, I need a pro . . .*

I found my cell and placed a call to Sergeant Emmanuel Franco. Holding my breath, I prayed he would answer and not his voice mail.

"What's up, Coffee Lady? Isn't it past your bedtime?"

"Have you heard from Mike?"

"No, should I have?"

"He's missing . . ."

I explained the situation—including my extreme frustration at not knowing *who* the heck to call on the Washington end of Quinn's life because he would never tell me *anything* about his work in Washington.

Franco's reply was cop-calm. "Try not to worry, okay? I have a contact with LaGuardia security. I'll find out where his flight was diverted . . ."

If it was diverted, I thought, swallowing hard.

After ending the call, I trudged up the short flight of stairs to the duplex's second floor, rubbing my arms as I moved through the chilly gloom of the hall to the master bedroom.

During the decades Matt's mother ran the Village Blend, she'd lived in this two-floor apartment above the coffeehouse. Over the years, she'd furnished the place with lovingly preserved antiques, many of them museum-quality pieces.

An array of paintings and sketches graced the walls, each from an artist who'd patronized her shop at one time or another—Hopper, Krasner, Warhol, Keith Haring. She even framed a doodle on a napkin by a half-drunk Jackson Pollock.

None of it cheered me now; and then I saw it, a blinking light on my bedside phone! Someone had left a message on the landline! I literally lunged for the button, hoping I'd hear Mike's voice, but as the recording played, my spirits bottomed out.

"Boss," Esther said, "I can't believe the news I came home to . . ."

I know, I thought, expecting her to unload about Moirin.

"Boris lost his job today!"

What? I blinked in confusion, until it hit me. Esther's "Worst News Ever" text message was about her boyfriend, not Moirin.

"Boris can't believe it," she went on. "That Brighton Beach bakery has been in Brooklyn for four decades! Today the owner comes in and announces he's closing the business and moving to Florida! Everyone's out of a job, just like that! It's maddening . . ."

Esther went on for another minute, ending with a desperate plea for me to give her boyfriend a job.

Boris Bokunin was smart, funny, and artfully offbeat. The Russian-born aspiring rap artist would fit in well with my oddball family of baristas, and I had no doubt he'd be a good worker. I simply didn't have the budget to hire him.

Now I felt even worse—and I didn't have the emotional energy to make another notification call.

I'll talk to you in the morning, I mentally promised Esther. Then I peeled off my work clothes, threw on my oversized Steelers' T-shirt, and collapsed into the antique four-poster.

The master bedroom's cold hearth made me especially sad tonight. A fire would dispel the chill in the air, but I didn't have the heart for it. Mike was the expert at kindling blazes in this room (yes, in more ways than one), and I always left it to him.

Frustrated with the winter-night silence, I reached for the remote and flipped on the television—a new addition to my bedroom. (With Mike in DC so often, my evenings had gotten too quiet.) Turning to one of the twenty-four/seven cable news channels, I hoped for an update on the storm and got it. The blizzard was the lead.

". . . ten to twelve inches in the New York City area," a perky weather girl forecasted, "with heavier accumulation north and west of the city. Now back to our Storm Tracker desk!"

"Thanks, Carol . . ." said the more serious-faced female anchor. "The Northeast was slammed tonight with the first deadly storm of the season. Airports from Virginia to Massachusetts are closed and travel advisories are now in effect until eight AM. New York's Mayor Stanton held a press conference earlier . . ."

"There's no reason to put your life and others' lives in danger," Stanton's slightly nasally voice advised from behind a podium. "Stay off the roads. Our plows will be working all night, but secondary and tertiary streets may be impassable until midmorning. Remember, our heat hotline is 311, but for life-threatening emergencies dial 911 . . ."

As the anchorwoman's voice came back, I felt the light movement of cat paws on the bed, then the warmth of two furry bodies curling up beside me.

". . . and reports are coming in from all over the Northeast. Dozens of car and truck collisions, some fatal, and—as we first reported thirty minutes ago—we have an unconfirmed report of a commuter plane, which had been diverted over the Atlantic, going down off the New Jersey coast . . ."

A plane went down?

"Meroow!" Java complained as I bolted upright.

"To find out more, let's go live to Bob Morris in Trenton. Bob, what can you tell us?"

"Well, Joan, emergency crews are mobilized on what sources say is a commuter plane crash off the coast of New Jersey . . ."

I listened closely for any mention of an airline, a flight number, even an origin city. But "Bob" mentioned none of it! Was he actually in the dark? Or did the authorities ask him to hold back details, until next of kin were notified?

I lunged for the landline handset and dialed Capitol Express. The airline was a small company with an automated operator who asked me to hit 1 for *yes* and 2 for *no* about ten times before I managed to get a live operator.

"Capitol Express, how may I direct your call?"

"Your automated system continually says that information about Flight 324 is *pending*. Can you *please* tell me if it actually took off from BWI—and if it did, when and where it landed?"

"Ma'am, are you a family member of a passenger on board that flight?"

"Actually, I'm a . . ." *Just say yes, Clare!* "Yes, yes! I'm a family member."

"Family members should call this 1-800 number . . ." recited the woman. "Leave your name and a contact phone number and one of our special agents will be in touch within the hour. Would you prefer I connect you?"

"Yes, connect me!"

My cell went off just then, and I quickly checked the caller ID.

Dante Silva.

I exhaled hard. Whatever Dante wanted to discuss could wait. I let his call go to my voice mail, dropped the cell in my robe's pocket, and turned my attention to the airline's recorded message.

"If you are a family member of a passenger on board Flight 324 . . ."

When the line beeped, I left my name and two numbers as instructed. Then I hung up and stared blankly at the cable news. A commercial flashed across the screen followed by a sports report. But I couldn't make sense of it.

Outside my dark window, big, wet snowflakes tumbled from the clouds, and I imagined an airplane falling among them, hitting the dark sea and going down. That's how I felt, like I'd hit something hard and was sinking.

I could have phoned Matt or Madame. I could have tried to reach Franco again or returned Dante's call. But the gears in my mind had frozen in place; my thoughts went numb, save a primitive prayer, recited over and over . . .

Please, God . . . don't take him from me. Please . . .

I'm not sure how long I sat there, staring and praying, but at some point, through the surreal fog, a noise began to register. A distant banging . . .

Bam! Bam!

Someone was pounding on my apartment's front door. The noise was loud and strong—*Bam-Bam-Bam!* I pictured Franco's thick fist, swinging away.

"But why didn't Franco just call?" I whispered.

Unless his news about Mike had to be conveyed in person—the way a cop delivers . . .

"A notification," I whispered numbly into the chilly bedroom air.

Slowly, stiffly, I pulled on a robe and forced my legs to move. Across the bedroom. Down the stairs. My hand was shaking as I unbolted the lock and pulled open the door.

FOURTEEN

~~~~~~~~~~~~~~~~~~~~~~~~~~~~~~~~~~~

A tall, broad-shouldered man stood on my landing, larger than life. His topcoat was open, plaid scarf hanging loosely around his neck. His caramel brown hair was sparkling with half-melted snow. His square jaw was ruddy, his nose redder than Rudolph's.

"About time, sweetheart."

"Mike?" I rasped.

Quinn's cobalt eyes smiled. "Who else were you expecting? Santa Claus?"

"I thought you were *dead*!"

The smile in Quinn's eyes vanished. "What?"

"I thought you were—" I couldn't say the word again.

"Aw, don't be silly, come here . . ."

As he pulled me against his long, hard body, sobs of relief racked my small frame, ending on a less-than-romantic case of the hiccups.

"Take it easy," he murmured into my hair. "Everything's okay."

But it wasn't okay. After my wave of relief ebbed, an irrational anger began stirring inside me—*irrational* because my logical self knew Mike Quinn to be the most patient, considerate, brave-hearted man I'd ever met. A man like that would never have meant to put me through this terror. He had to have an explanation.

But as his strong arms loosened their comforting hug, my logical self went AWOL. Fury rose in my veins like boiling mercury up a thermometer. My hands balled into fists, and those fists began pummeling Quinn's chest.

"How could you"—*hiccup!*—"*do* that to me? How!"

The cop in him reacted instinctively. His fingers clamped on my right wrist, swinging it fast around my body; then he grabbed the left, sweeping it back to join its mate.

"Let me go!"

"No."

He had me facing away from him now, slightly bent over, my arms pinned behind my back—and I realized what he'd done. *He used his powercuffing maneuver on me!* So, okay, he hadn't actually clamped on the metal cuffs. But the very idea that he was restraining me with a cop technique made me even angrier.

I struggled to free myself, failing miserably. Quinn's build was solid as a skyscraper. Moving the Empire State Building would have been easier. I felt him bending over me, his chest pressing my back.

"Calm down," his cop voice warned in my ear.

"I can't! I'm really, really"—*hiccup!*—"pissed!"

"I noticed."

Quinn had never seen me like this; and, honestly, I hadn't seen me like this since I'd been married to Matteo Allegro!

We stood there for a good minute: me hiccupping, refusing to relinquish my righteous fury; and Quinn unwilling to let me go. If the landline's extension hadn't rung, I'm not sure what the man would have done with me.

"Let me answer that," I demanded. "I'm expecting"—*hiccup!*—"two emergency calls."

"You're done assaulting me?"

"For now."

He released me, and I moved quickly into the living room, rubbing my bruised wrists as I went. Still breathing hard, I snatched up the handset on the fourth ring.

"Ms. Clare Cosi?"

"That's . . . right," I said, suppressing the hiccup, and trying my best to swallow the rest.

"I'm calling as an official representative of Capitol Express to respond to your inquiry about your family member, Mr. Michael Quinn."

"Yes, I—"

"Although he purchased a ticket for Flight 324 out of BWI, he did not board the plane."

Obviously! "I know that now. Thank you."

"If Mr. Quinn failed to board the plane, his luggage would have been taken off the flight. He can recover it through our baggage claim office at BWI. Do you understand?"

"The flight really did crash then? It's in the Atlantic?"

"I'm sorry, Ms. Cosi, but I cannot officially reply to your question at this time. You have all of the information that I am authorized to give you . . ."

When the call ended, I turned to face Quinn. He looked stunned.

"My flight *crashed*?" he asked quietly.

"They won't confirm it, but the news reported a commuter plane went down, and—"

The phone rang again. This time it was Franco calling back.

"Clare," he said, tone grim. "I'm heading for the door now. I'm on my way over to see you."

"No, Franco. Turn around. You don't have to come. Mike is—"

"I *do* need to come. Listen to me. You better sit down. There's been an accident."

"Mike's here! He's with me. He's okay!"

"Oh, geez Louise . . ." The young sergeant blew out air. I heard a noise. It sounded like his big body had collapsed into a small chair. "Thank God."

"Believe me, I did . . ." Then I thanked the young sergeant for his help.

"No problem, Coffee Lady. You need anything else, just call, okay?"

"Okay."

Quinn cursed. (*Finally*, it seemed the guy was putting it together!) "Didn't Leila *call* you?!" he asked.

"I called your ex-wife to ask if she'd heard from you," I assured him. "She didn't pick up, so I left a voice mail message. And she never called me back."

Quinn's expression darkened. "She *never* called you, never even left a message?"

"Why? Did she know something?" Before he could answer, the cell in my pocket went off. I checked the caller ID. "Uh-oh . . ."

"Who is it this time?" Quinn asked.

I hit the connect button. "Hello?"

Matt's voice came over the line: "I saw the news. Have you heard anything?"

"He just showed up."

"Alive?"

"Yes."

"In one piece?"

"So far."

"Put him on."

I held my phone out. "It's for you."

Quinn met my gaze, didn't ask who it was, just put the phone to his ear. "Yes?"

Even standing a foot away, I could hear Matt shouting. There were expletives—in several languages—bald-faced insults, and a few threats.

"You stupid flatfoot! How could you do that to her? . . ." He said something in Spanish, finishing in Portuguese, and then . . . "If you *ever* put her through anything like that again . . ."

To Quinn's credit, he stoically took everything Matt dished out. Then he surprised us both. "Yeah, you're right, Allegro," he said.

This time Quinn held out the phone. "He wants to talk to you again."

I put it to my ear. "Matt?"

"Say the word and I'll break him in half."

"Go to bed, Matt—and take a few aspirins, okay?" (Clearly, he'd consumed *a lot* of alcohol at that last holiday party.)

Quinn rubbed the back of his neck. "I hope that's the last call."

"I got one from Dante earlier. He might call back."

Quinn shook his head. "That was me downstairs, trying to reach you. Dante let me in the shop, and I borrowed his phone."

"What happened to yours?"

"Ran out of juice hours ago. My adapter was packed in my luggage."

"What happened to your key?"

"It's on a ring, with all my other New York keys, inside my luggage . . ."

"Which is still in Baltimore?"

He shook his head. "If that plane is at the bottom of the Atlantic, then so is my Pullman."

"That's not what the airline rep told me."

"That's because I violated TSA protocol."

"What?! Mike, what in heaven's name *happened* to you?"

"I'll be glad to tell you," he said. "But can we sit down first? Like civilized people?"

I took a deep, calming breath, and studied his face. "You look exhausted. Are you hungry?"

"Starving."

I remembered that beautiful eye round in my fridge, sitting there in all its pepper-crusted perfection—completely untouched.

"How does a roast beef sandwich sound?"

"Like Christmas dinner."

Fifteen

∾∾∾∾∾∾∾∾∾∾∾∾∾∾∾

"**T**ALK," I commanded, waving my knife in the air.

The eye round was on my cutting board, ready for surgery. Warily eyeing the blade, Mike shed his coat, scarf, and suit jacket. Then he folded his tall form into a cane-backed chair at my kitchen table and began rolling up his sleeves.

"Where do you want me to start?" he asked.

"At the beginning," I said. "Why didn't you take my advice and stay put in Washington?"

"Believe me, I was ready to. But then I called Leila to tell her I'd be missing the party, and she pitched a fit. I felt bad, like I was letting my kids down."

"Your kids had a great time at the Cookie Swap, Mike. I'm sure they would have loved to have you there, but it wasn't worth risking your life, for heaven's sake. Leila played you, don't you see that?"

"I do now."

"Well, I'm thankful you didn't get on that flight, but how in the heck did you get to New York? And what did you mean about violating TSA protocol?"

"I checked my bag at BWI, and I was waiting to board

at the Capitol Express gate when the airline announced a two-hour delay. I went to the bar and saw another guy from Justice. He was trying to get to New York, too, and we agreed to ditch our flight plans and drive up together. We estimated the flight would take an hour anyway, add in the delay time, plus a taxi ride from LaGuardia to Manhattan, and driving looked like a straighter shot—"

Except for the weather, you blockhead!

"Nobody at the gate seemed to know how to get our bags to us inside of an hour, so we flashed our credentials and got an okay to keep our bags on the flight. We knew LaGuardia baggage claim would hold them, and I'd have them delivered here in the morning. No problem."

"Only there was a problem. You thought you could drive two hundred miles during a *blizzard*?"

"Stupid, I know."

"You and your friend had a few drinks and thought you were supermen? That's your excuse?"

Mike folded his arms. "It was a bad call."

Gritting my teeth, I turned to the beef. The pepper-crusted eye round was medium-rare, a gorgeous shade of dusty rose at the center, and I wanted the slices razor thin for buttery tenderness. But I was still so agitated I had to force my hand to stay steady as I cut.

I shook my head. "You know what your problem is, Quinn? You've spent too many years in the city. Talk to Allegro sometime; he'll set you straight."

"I seem to recall he did that already."

"Matt was buzzed, that's why he let loose on you—and believe it or not, he cares about you, too. He also learned how to respect the weather, the hard way."

"Well, we were making good progress until we hit south Jersey. Between the snow and a multicar accident, 95 slowed to a crawl. My colleague's car didn't have GPS, but our smartphones did, so we—"

"Let me guess. You got off the turnpike and tried to navigate secondary roads?"

"Yes, and it was okay until—"

"Your phones died, and you didn't bother to bring a paper map or compass. Am I right?"

Mike grunted and folded his arms, obviously annoyed with my correct assumptions. "Our rechargers were packed away in our luggage, which were still at the airport."

"So you got lost?"

"Very lost. And the road conditions were getting worse. We ended up in the New Jersey Pine Barrens, out of gas. A state trooper saved our asses. Helped us get gassed up again and onto the Garden State Parkway. Then it was slow going, but we made it."

"Mike, what if that trooper hadn't found you? You could have died from exposure?!"

His eyebrow arched. "Better than a plane crash."

"You should have stayed put!"

"Yes, obviously. We're going in circles now, Cosi. Can't you forgive me?"

"Not yet. I was up here thinking the worst. Why didn't you call?"

"I knew you'd be busy working at that party. I didn't want to bother you, worry you, or, frankly, *argue* with you, so I called Leila instead, gave her the update about driving, and asked her to tell you. I assume she was at the party?"

"She dropped off the kids, but we fought—about you— and she stormed off."

"You fought with her?"

"Yes, and I'm *not* sorry I did . . ." I stared him down. "I was right about the danger of traveling tonight, and she was cruel to keep any information about you from me. She did it deliberately because we fought. She wanted me to suffer."

"I know that now. And it's my fault. I'm truly sorry, Clare. The fact is . . . I thought I was sparing you worry."

"Mike, listen to me. I'm not the kind of woman who's content to be kept in the dark. I want to know—I need to know—the absolute truth. Tonight, when I didn't know what was happening on your end, I didn't even know who to call in Washington."

"Clare, I've told you already, this isn't like my squad

work in New York. The things I'm doing now are classified. I can't tell you who I'm working with."

"I don't care if you're working with the Joint Chiefs of Staff! What if I lost touch with you again? Who would I contact? That is *it*, Quinn. I have *had* it!"

For a moment, he looked stricken, and I realized that he misunderstood. He thought I was breaking up with him. But it was just the opposite!

I waved my knife. "You are *not* leaving this duplex again without giving me two names and numbers in DC."

Mike exhaled, clearly relieved that contact numbers were all I wanted. Then he sat back, eyed the blade, and gave me a little smile.

"And if I don't?"

I put down the knife and lifted the dish with his mile-high roast beef sandwich. I'd layered the tender slices on a crusty Italian roll, kissed it with the creamy tang of home-made horsey sauce, and finished it off with baby spinach and a sprinkling of sea salt.

"Didn't you say you were hungry?"

"Give it."

"Names and numbers. At least two."

Mike went silent a moment, then he pulled out his smartphone and tossed it on the table. "It's dead. But when I get it recharged tomorrow, I promise, you'll have them."

"And I'm supposed to trust you?"

"I'm starving, Cosi. And I survived a blizzard and a plane crash. You want me to die of malnutrition?"

"I'm still angry with you, but . . ." I set the plate in front of him. "I do love you, despite that."

"There's no despite about it," Mike said and tore into the sandwich, closing his eyes and moaning like a man in the throes of long-denied ecstasy.

Still standing, I stared down at him. "What does that mean? No *despite* about it?"

Mike took another bite, answered as he chewed. "Back when I was on the street, coming up in the ranks, my job . . . well, it wasn't the safest."

"That's an understatement."

"Do you know when I knew for sure that Leila didn't love me anymore?"

I shook my head.

"When she stopped getting angry if I didn't call."

"You're kidding, right?"

Mike put down his sandwich; met my gaze. "How could she love me when she couldn't care less if I lived or died? Clare . . . your anger is what assures me of your feelings."

"So you want me to pummel you more often?"

"You pummel me again, Cosi, and you'll feel cold steel around your wrists."

"Promise?"

He reached around his belt, pulled the cuffs clear, and slapped them on the table.

"Try me."

"No. I don't think so . . ." I folded my arms. "As I recall, there are plenty of other ways to express passionate feelings . . ."

"Oh, yeah?" A slow smile spread over Mike's face. Then he hooked his arm around my waist and pulled me close. "Show me."

WE abandoned the dishes and climbed the steps to the master bedroom. Mike's kisses brought sweet warmth to my chilled skin, and I returned the favor. Then we shed our clothes and put our quarrel to bed.

As the snow piled higher, the outside world became quieter, more distant, but it didn't make me feel cut off anymore. With Mike's steady heartbeat beside mine, the frozen silence outside made me feel all the more tucked in and safe.

Soon, I was sinking again, but not into a numb and terrified state. I was relaxing into a dream and wishing I could stop the clock and stay like this, in Mike's arms, for all time.

"Oh damn . . ."

Hearing Mike's soft curse, I stirred.

"What is it?"

He stroked my hair. "I was just lying here, thanking God I'm alive—and remembering my Pullman is at the bottom of the ocean . . ."

I closed my eyes. More than luggage had been lost tonight, but I'd been too self-focused to consider it. I recited a silent prayer for all the victims of the storm, including the families and friends who would be grieving with the news.

Moirin's family in Ireland would soon be grieving, too, but her death wasn't caused by a storm. Another person had brutally beaten that poor girl; a killer who was walking free, a monster who could strike again.

That's when I remembered—Janelle Babcock never called me back tonight. I wondered if the police had contacted my friend yet. Would they wait until morning? No matter when she heard the news, it would be hard to take, and I didn't want her to face it alone.

First thing in the morning, I'll go to see her . . .

There was nothing more I could do tonight, so I swallowed hard and said one more prayer, a thank-you to heaven for sparing the man lying next to me.

"You know," Mike was saying, "every item in that Pullman is easily replaceable, except one."

"What?"

"I ordered something specially made for you, even had it engraved. I was going to put it under the tree. I'm so sorry, sweetheart. There's no time to replace it. Your Christmas gift is lost."

"Oh, Mike, no it's not . . ." I turned in his arms. "My gift is right here."

Sixteen

~~~~~~

The *urgent* beeper on my cell phone went off early the next morning. Quinn, exhausted by his trip, didn't even budge. There was nothing in the world I wanted more than to cling to the warm body beside me and drift back to sleep.

But that was not to be. I rolled over to check my phone's messages. There was only one, a text from Janelle.

"Come over ASAP, we need to talk."

Yes we did. The police had likely questioned her by now, and I wanted to find out what she told them, including what she knew about Moirin's mysterious boyfriend, Dave. So I reluctantly left Quinn snoring in my bed and braved the chilly morning.

I set off for Janelle's West Side bakery as the first rays of dawn broke through a fog that rolled off the Hudson River. The snow was piled high; there was no traffic, and hardly anyone on the narrow neighborhood streets. Yet despite the desolation, I got the eerie sensation that I was being watched.

I saw no one, of course, but the feeling rattled me. Hailing a taxi was out of the question because there weren't any.

So my only choice was to pick up the pace, no easy task on the slippery, snowy sidewalks.

I'd convinced myself I was just being paranoid, until I noticed a man in a bright blue parka lurking in a doorway of a closed shop across the street. Eyes hidden behind dark glasses, he held a smartphone to his ear. When he realized I'd seen him, he quickly gave me his back.

Oddly suspicious behavior, I thought, considering I was too far away to eavesdrop on his conversation.

I let it go and continued on, crunching through the ice-crusted blanket and hopping clear of white drifts. Every once in a while I peeked over my shoulder to make sure the man in blue wasn't stalking me.

The character of the neighborhood I was entering didn't allay my paranoia. Not much traditional West Village charm could be found this close to the river: no perfectly preserved Italianate row houses, quaint bistros, or secluded gardens; no flickering faux gaslights or wrought iron fences. This neighborhood was dominated by former factories that once serviced the busy waterfront but had since been converted into apartments, lofts, and co-ops.

As I approached the retasked warehouse where Janelle rented a ground-floor storefront, I heard footsteps. Yet when I turned, there was no one, which spooked me enough to practically lunge for the golden light shining from the tiny bakeshop. My gloved fingers frantically jammed the doorbell until Janelle peeked through the caramel-colored blinds and buzzed me in.

"Clare!" she cried. "You scared the life out of me, girl. Are you okay?"

"Are you?"

Her teary brown eyes met my green ones. Then she threw her strong mocha arms around my neck, and I reached my arms around her well-worn baker's jacket.

"Who did this to our poor girl?" she sobbed.

"That's what I want to find out."

"I should have gone outside and searched for her last night! Why didn't I? I should have known that girl was too responsible to duck out on me. But I've had so much bad luck hiring assistants, I assumed she'd let me down like the others."

We stepped apart and she dabbed her eyes. "If only I'd gone looking, I might have found her in time to call an ambulance or something. But I didn't, and now M is dead . . ."

I'd known Janelle Babcock since she was the pastry chef at the five-star restaurant Solange, long before she struck out on her own, but I'd never seen her so distraught.

"There was nothing you could have done," I insisted. "Detective Soles told me Moirin was killed outright. There was no saving her."

"I'd like to find the SOB who did this before the police do," Janelle said, folding her fingers into a fist. "I still have my daddy's knuckle-dusters around here somewhere. But if I can't find the dang things, my rolling pin will do just fine!"

Janelle suddenly froze and sniffed the air, then she cried out. I followed as she raced to the eight-burner stove.

I'd expected to encounter a host of lovely holiday scents at Janelle's shop this morning. And while the dominant aroma inside the bakery was sweet and delightful, it was also completely unexpected.

"Is that root beer?" I asked.

"That's right," she replied, stirring a pot of simmering brown liquid with a silicone spoon. "I was contracted to develop recipes based on soda flavors. Right now I'm reducing root beer to create a simple syrup to flavor cakes, cookies, and frozen desserts."

"Why not use extract?" I asked.

"Because I'm creating this recipe for the New York Beverage Company website, and they don't make extract. They want home cooks to use their bottled soda."

"Got it."

Catering was only one aspect of my friend's expanding business. Janelle, who'd grown up on Creole French cooking in New Orleans and earned a scholarship to study at Le

Cordon Bleu in Paris, also sold her premium baked goods wholesale to shops, boutique food stores, and coffeehouses like mine.

In the past year, she'd taken on developing original recipes for food and beverage companies, too.

"I honestly don't know how I'm going to get everything done without an assistant," Janelle said. "I have yet to bake cookies for the next Swap, and there are three catering jobs on my schedule. Plus these soda pop recipes are due next week!"

Janelle pointed to a cooling rack. "At least one recipe turned out well. You should try those root beer whoopie pies. I have some coffee with chicory I brewed up fresh, too."

I fetched the treats while Janelle watched her bubbling pot. Near the cooling rack, next to a tempting sheet pan of brownies iced with pretty pink candy-cane frosting, I spied a large traditional-looking cream pie smothered in meringue. A single slice was missing.

"Mmm . . . what's this cream pie? Looks delicious."

"Looks can be deceiving, girl. Didn't your grandma teach you that?"

"What's wrong with it?"

"My auntie used to make a sweet potato pie with maple syrup that was heavenly. I thought substituting root beer syrup for the maple might be worth a shot. But the thing turned out downright nasty. Slightly slimy instead of creamy, and with a medicinal tang, like something they'd force down your throat at a hospital."

"Aw, too bad about the cream pie fail, but you certainly scored with these whoopie pies. The old-fashioned root beer flavor really comes through. They're amazing."

When the whoopie pies were reduced to a few crumbs, I set my empty coffee cup aside. "Did the police visit you last night?" I asked.

Janelle nodded. "A woman, Detective Soles, and some dude in a plaid jacket and a Ward Cleaver sweater vest. They asked a lot of questions."

"Did they grill you about Dave?"

"M's friend?" Janelle shook her head.

Crap. I couldn't believe they hadn't followed up with that lead. But then Endicott believed Piper Penny was their murderer—and was waiting for forensics to confirm it.

I cleared my throat. "I told Lori Soles about the young man who was speaking with Moirin at the Cookie Swap. The way they were arguing, I'm sure it was her boyfriend, Dave."

"I couldn't say," Janelle replied. "I never met Dave. And I don't put much faith in the police, anyway. I just know they're going to look in all the wrong places, and I'll be the one who ends up in hot water."

"You? But you didn't do anything wrong."

Janelle shook her head. "The last time I checked, hiring an illegal immigrant and paying her under the table was against the law. Several laws, in fact."

I blinked, hoping I'd misheard. "What are you saying?"

"It's been a real struggle, Clare, keeping this business going. I've had financial setbacks. A couple of clients went under before they paid their bills, and lately I've had employee troubles, too. *Expensive* employee troubles. When Moirin came along last year, she was perfect for my shop, except—"

Janelle paused, her expression guilty. "Except she had no green card or social security number, at least not legit ones."

"M was an illegal?"

"She had to be. The girl's IDs were obviously forgeries. I used to buy better dang fake IDs back in high school."

I was floored. I'd never had to worry about Moirin's immigration status because technically I wasn't paying her salary. But if the government came knocking, Janelle and I would both be in hot water.

Janelle knew what I was thinking and tried to reassure me. "Don't worry, girlfriend. If I get busted, I won't say anything about our deal."

"That's the least of my worries. I assume you kept this information from Detectives Soles and Endicott?"

"They didn't ask, and I didn't tell. But I'm sure they'll figure it out soon enough."

"And you're certain Lori didn't ask you about Dave?"

"His name never came up, and I couldn't have told them much, anyway. I don't even know his last name."

"Neither do I."

"And I don't think M was all that sweet on him, anyway. Moirin and Dave might have dated, but they weren't exclusive. A lot of guys called my assistant while she worked in this kitchen. There was a Benny and a Tony. They called almost every other day." Janelle offered me a sly smile. "Our girl was playing the field, and it was a *big* dang field."

Janelle had just outlined one of the most basic recipes for domestic violence. If Dave wanted more than Moirin was willing to give, her murder could have been a crime of passion.

"The police have Moirin's cell. They may have followed up with Dave already. I wish I could talk to him. If only I had his phone number, too. Or even his last name. Something to go on—"

"Wait!" Janelle cried. "A couple of months ago, Moirin asked me to send a few dozen cookies Dave's way. I probably have the delivery address in my computer."

Janelle thrust the spoon in my hand and ordered me to keep stirring, while she went to a laptop on the corner table. As she searched, I stirred the simmering brown liquid. The spicelike aroma of sweet root beer syrup was heady, nearly overwhelming.

"Found it," Janelle cried. But she quickly frowned as she scribbled on a Post-it. "I'm sorry, Clare, but this can't be Dave's address. Now I remember. Moirin told me this is where he works."

"Better than nothing." I read the address. "'Evergreen Retirement Community, Recreation Center . . .'"

A retirement community? Hmmm . . .

An idea began simmering—not as cloying as Janelle's root beer syrup, but just as heady. If I wanted to meet and question Dave, I had the perfect plan, as long as I could secure my favorite partner in snooping: Matt's mother, Madame Blanche Dreyfus Allegro Dubois.

Despite her advanced age, Madame was a dynamo, and she was never busier than the holiday season. My biggest obstacle would be scheduling her time.

The front buzzer interrupted my plotting. Through the blinds in the front door, I saw a looming silhouette and frowned in alarm, until Janelle glanced at her watch and said, "That's probably my supplies. Turn off the syrup; let it cool. Let's go say hello to the deliveryman."

But when we opened the door, three men were standing there—and they'd come to deliver an ugly surprise.

Seventeen

〜〜〜〜〜〜〜〜〜〜〜〜〜〜〜〜〜〜〜〜〜〜〜

"I'M Dick Belcher, Channel Six News at Eleven . . ."

An assertive blond in a navy blue blazer, Belcher had perfectly coiffed hair, Marlboro Man looks, and a face I'd seen hundreds of times. On either side of him stood men in blue parkas with photo IDs hanging around their necks. One carried a video camera on his burly shoulder. The other still clutched the smartphone he was using when I caught him spying on me from that doorway.

"This is my cameraman, Ned," said Belcher, "and my producer, Lou . . ."

Before I could head him off, he homed in on a startled Janelle. "You're Ms. Babcock, is that correct?"

Janelle nodded mutely.

"Perhaps you'd like to give us a statement about your former employee, Moirin Fagan?"

Dick Belcher's tone was borderline polite, but he didn't wait for an invitation. He barged into the shop, his cameraman in tow, while producer Lou brought up the rear.

Overwhelmed by the man's aggressiveness, Janelle stepped back. The man with the camera gently elbowed me aside and pointed the lens at Janelle. Dick Belcher gave his cameraman a silent nod, and the tape began to roll.

"According to a source at the NYPD, your employee, Moirin Fagan, was the first murder victim attributed to a string of serial attacks the police are calling 'the Christmas Stalkings.' Do you believe the police commissioner should have warned the public before this perpetrator turned to murder?"

Belcher shoved his microphone into Janelle's face.

"I . . . I didn't know about any stalker," she stammered.

But I did, I realized, as my mind raced back to last night's crime scene in Bryant Park . . .

Standing on the carousel, Endicott had described Moirin's injuries as being consistent with blows from a blunt object. "Which fits the modus operandi in the last attack," he'd said.

"You mean there've been others?" I'd asked Lori.

My question had made her uneasy. "There have been several assaults against women recently" was all she'd say.

"Do you have any suspects in the other attacks?" I'd asked.

Lori gave me a look that said she couldn't reveal more. Now I wondered why. Was she the "source" who revealed it all to Belcher? Was Endicott?

The newsman looked directly into the camera. "The public has the right to know, and we're here to inform. News Six has learned that there have been four attacks since Thanksgiving. The victims, all female, escaped serious injury. But as of last night, the authorities fear that the Christmas Stalker's reign of terror has turned deadly."

Impossible, I thought. *There was no way some random predator was going to lure Moirin onto the carousel by brandishing a paving stone!*

On top of that, I heard Moirin on the phone yesterday afternoon, setting up a rendezvous. She must have known her attacker.

If this "serial attacker" was the theory the detectives

were pursuing in Moirin's case, then her killer would never be caught.

Finished with his monologue, Dick Belcher faced Janelle again.

"What would you like to say to this predatory serial attacker who took the life of your assistant in such a brutal fashion, Ms. Babcock?"

Too distraught to speak, Janelle's eyes filled with tears and she turned away.

This is cruel, I thought, but the newsmen obviously didn't agree.

The shared look between Lou and Belcher told me this was exactly the reaction they'd wanted—emotional footage for their lead tragedy of the evening.

Stepping up, I wrapped protective arms around Janelle. "Please leave her alone now," I warned them. "Give her some privacy."

"Just a few more questions," said Belcher.

"Didn't you hear me?" I said as Janelle continued to cry. "You and your news team need to turn off your cameras and get out of here *now*."

I let go of Janelle and moved toward them, my arms outstretched to shoo them away. Instead of retreating, the cameraman refocused the lens on me, and Belcher thrust the microphone under my nose.

"Would *you* like to make a statement, Ms. . . ." Belcher glanced at his producer who nodded. "Can you state your name for the record?"

"Cosi. Clare Cosi. And I made my statement. I asked you and your team to leave."

"Not without a comment from you," Belcher insisted.

"Fine, you want a comment? Here's your comment: Whoever killed Moirin Fagan is a sick, sad excuse for a human being—a monstrous coward who thinks slinking away into the night is cover enough after taking an innocent life. Well, justice will be served when that worm is caught and punished. I'll do everything in my power to see that happen, and that day can't come soon enough to suit me!"

"One more question for Ms. Babcock."

The camera swung back to Janelle.

"No! No more!" my friend cried, hands raised to shield her face.

"Ms. Babcock, please tell us . . ."

How can I make this jackass leave? What do I have to do, hit him with a—

I almost smiled. Janelle's failed pastry experiment sat on a table a few feet away, and before the News Six at Eleven team could react, I walked over to it, snatched it up, and threw the meringue-topped root beer sweet potato monstrosity right into Dick Belcher's startled face.

The newsman howled, dropped his microphone, and began frantically swiping the goopy root beer–flavored mess off his formerly perfect hair and natty blazer.

"Now will you go?" I calmly asked.

"I-I'm going to sue you for this!" Belcher sputtered. "My cameraman caught your whole assault on tape!"

I folded my arms. "Just be sure you show the footage at trial. Your competition at Channels Two, Four, Five, Nine, and Eleven will get great ratings out of broadcasting it, over and over again."

Eighteen

~~~~~~

By the time I got back to the Village Blend, I was frozen to the bone from my crosstown walk. I shed my parka and approached the espresso machine for some much-needed caffeine reinforcement.

I found Esther there, her eyes red from crying. I immediately hugged my sad-faced barista, and the Dark Queen of Goth hugged me right back.

"Nancy told me what happened to M. Do the police have any clue who did this?" she asked.

"Not yet. Which is why they're going to be looking for answers—and so am I."

Esther broke our embrace. "What do you need to know, boss?"

"For starters, more about M's personal life."

"Well, she lived in Brooklyn, I'm not sure where. She had a boyfriend named Dave, but Dave *what* I don't know. M went clubbing a lot, but never mentioned which clubs." Esther paused. "I guess I don't know squat, either."

"Don't feel bad. It seems Moirin was a private person. Not even Janelle knew much about her."

Esther shrugged. "Who really knows anyone, anyway? I mean, look at my poor Boris. He put his trust in a boss who threw him under the bus!"

"I think I can help your boyfriend," I said.

Esther's zombie-chic eyes went wide. "You're going to hire him?" she cried hopefully.

"Janelle's going to hire him. The poor woman is distraught, overworked, and at the end of her rope. She needs Boris as much as he needs a job."

"You're talking about Moirin's job?" Esther said, crestfallen.

"Don't think of it that way. See it from Janelle's point of view. She just lost her assistant baker in the middle of a busy week of catering events, and on top of all that, she has to prepare for the Global Goodies Toyland Cookie Swap next Friday. Janelle is desperate for someone who can hit the ground running, and knows his stuff well enough to hit it right out of the ballpark with the first swing."

"Baseball metaphors aside, nobody works harder than Boris," Esther said. "And my boyfriend is smart enough to run a bakery himself. But are you sure about this?"

"I broached the subject with Janelle before I left her bakery this morning." (*After* I chased the obnoxious Dick Belcher and his News Six at Eleven team out the door.) "She told me she's met Boris, she's aware of his resume, and she'd be grateful for his help."

Esther threw her arms around *me* this time. "I'm going to call Boris right now—"

"No, first, you're going to pull a pair of double Americanos for Mike and me. Then you can deliver the good news to your boyfriend."

I managed to open the duplex door, step over lounging furballs Java and Frothy, and make it to the bedroom—all while juggling a plate of Eggnog Crumb Muffins and two ginormous cups of wake-up juice without spilling one drop.

Mike was an unmoving lump under the sheets, and I wondered if he'd stirred at all while I was gone. I set the cups and muffins on the nightstand and reached out to touch his shoulder.

That's when Mike clamped onto my sore wrist for the second time in twelve hours. But I didn't mind. Helpless in the man's firm grip, I yelped as he dragged me onto the bed and used his body to pin mine.

"Mike! Let me up!"

He silenced me with soft lips and roving hands, and I soon confirmed something *had* stirred under those sheets.

"Come on," I said, squirming. "I've got a long day and so do you. Have some coffee. Not that you need perking up, apparently!"

Smiling, Mike released me and sat up. The sheets fell away, baring his powerful chest. His sandy hair, tousled from sleep, was longer than I'd ever seen him wear it, and he finger brushed it back before taking a big swallow from his cup. He followed that with a colossal bite of my special holiday eggnog muffin, accompanied by some amusing guttural sounds of male satisfaction.

"Where have you been?" he asked. "I thought you had Saturday mornings off?"

"A text message from Janelle. She asked me to come over. She's understandably upset and needed to talk."

"Upset about what?"

I was silent long enough for Mike's expression to cloud. "Clare? What's wrong?"

"Something happened that I didn't mention last night . . ."

I gave Mike a severely truncated version of the tragedy, starting with my discovery of Moirin's corpse and ending with Lori Soles being assigned to the case. At some point in my retelling, Mike pulled me close. When I was done, I stared up at his grim, hard-lined face.

"Damn, sweetheart," he said quietly. "No wonder you freaked out on me last night."

"I didn't 'freak out.' I *reacted*."

Mike took another gulp of his coffee. "So that's why you went to Janelle's?"

I nodded. "Something weird happened on the way over, too. I felt like I was being followed, and after I arrived, a news team showed up on Janelle's doorstep to badger us with questions."

Mike frowned. "Which news team?"

"Channel Six."

"Dick Belcher? That guy's a real pain. Specializes in ambush journalism."

"He sure ambushed Janelle and me."

"What did you say?"

"What's the difference? What bothers me is how this Belcher guy found out about me, about Janelle. Our names weren't in the papers. The news stories didn't even mention the Village Blend. So how did Mr. News Six know enough to bother Janelle and me?"

Mike scratched his stubbly jaw. "That is funny, considering you're dealing with Lori Soles and Sue Ellen Bass. They're pretty tight-lipped, and they would never talk to a jerk like Belcher."

"Sue Ellen is on medical leave. Lori has a new partner."

Mike straightened. "Who?"

"Detective Fletcher Stanton Endicott."

"Oh no. Not Mr. DNA."

"I take it you know the man?"

"I know him."

Mike drained his cup, pulled off the sheets, and slipped into his terrycloth robe.

"You *were* being followed, Clare," he said. "That's Endicott's style. Big stories make big cases, and he likes to be in the middle of a big case. Makes him look like a superstar, and it helps his literary career, too."

"Great. Now what?"

Mike offered me a sympathetic shrug. "Expect more leaks."

I sighed. "I wish someone would leak something about Moirin's personal life."

"But you worked with her. Don't you—"

"That woman's a mystery. And Moirin wasn't even born in the United States, so there's a limit to what I can find out."

I stepped up to Mike.

"Now that you're a bona fide Federal agent, maybe you can help?"

"You want background on her?"

I nodded.

"I suppose I can reach out to someone at the Immigration and Naturalization Service. I have quite an impressive"—he arched an eyebrow—"*Rolodex* now."

I let out the breath I'd been holding. "Thank you."

"No guarantees," he cautioned.

I smiled. "You know, I'd really love to get my hands on that Rolodex of yours sometime . . ."

"I'll bet you would."

The phone on my nightstand rang. After the string of calls last night, I was wary and checked the caller ID. "Oh God. It's your ex-wife."

"Good. I have a few things to say to her." Mike scowled as he snatched the phone. "Hello."

His features softened immediately, and I knew it wasn't his ex but Jeremy and Molly on the other end. Mike chatted with his kids for about ten minutes, while I finished my own coffee and made the bed. When he hung up, Mike was no longer scowling.

"I'm going to take them for the afternoon," he said. "We're going to see a movie called *Santa Claus, Zombie Hunter*—can that be right?"

"That's the title. It's a hit with the pre-teen crowd."

"What ever happened to *Rudolph the Red-Nosed Reindeer*?"

"These days little Rudy would have to be a robot who transformed into a supersonic spacecraft complete with laser beams, missiles, and microwave oven."

"Kids today . . ." Mike smiled. "We're also having frozen hot chocolates at Serendipity. You're welcome to join us. In fact, Molly was insistent."

I shook my head. "We'll all do something tomorrow. Today I've got an errand to run with Madame." (And we'd be running all the way to a retirement home in Brooklyn—if I could persuade her to help me.)

Mike seemed suddenly distracted. "With my luggage lost, I hope I have something to wear."

"You left lots of clothes here. I'm sure you'll find something."

Mike loosened his robe. "I'd better hit the shower."

"Shave close, please. It's cold outside, my skin is delicate, and I don't need beard burn on top of frostbite."

"That would mean you have future plans to kiss me?"

"Yes."

"Good. Something to live for."

Mike closed the bathroom door just as my smartphone beeped, announcing a text message from Lori Soles.

"On the QT, U were right. Hairs definitely NOT from Piper Penny. Will be in touch."

I looked up from my screen. *Now how can those forensics guys know that so soon?* I wondered. *DNA analysis takes days, sometimes weeks . . .*

The answer came to me when I ran through the facts—and it almost made me laugh. But I couldn't laugh for sure until I spoke with Lori Soles.

Nineteen

~~~~~~

An hour later, with Quinn off to see his kids, I headed downstairs to the Blend.

Janelle's famous Lemon Sugar Cookies were in our pastry case, and I planned on boxing up a baker's dozen and delivering them personally to Matt's mother at her Fifth Avenue luxury apartment.

The cookies were delicious—sweet-tart perfection. They were also one of Madame's favorites, and I hoped they'd be a suitable bribe to enlist her help.

To my surprise I found the woman already in our shop, relaxing beside the Blend's fireplace and sharing a plate of those very same cookies with Sergeant Emmanuel Franco of the NYPD.

I fixed myself a French pressed cup of our Ethiopian Sidamo. The beans were superb. Matteo had sourced them in the Gera Woreda, and their bright citrus notes made a coffee that paired excellently with Janelle's cookies.

Franco rose when I arrived at their table, and the handcuffs on his belt rattled. "That was some night, eh, Coffee Lady?" he cracked.

"Emmanuel told me all about your *nocturne horribilis*, my dear," Madame said, pecking my cheek.

Madame looked stunning in a holiday red bouclé jacket with loop buttons, over an embroidered blouse of white silk—both pieces custom made for her by a legendary fashion designer (and longtime friend of the Blend). Black thin-legged silk pants, matching half boots, and an adorable necklace with a gold mistletoe charm completed her seasonal ensemble.

Franco was the flip side of the fashion coin in black denims, rugged work boots, and a scuffed leather bomber jacket over a sweatshirt. It wasn't even noon and he already had the beginnings of a five-o'clock shadow.

"Are you enjoying the cookies, Emmanuel?" Madame asked.

"They're okay, I guess. A little girly, though. What is it with women and lemons? Lemon cake. Lemon cookies. Lemon pie. Lemon bars. I'd mention lemon tarts, but I wouldn't want you ladies to get the wrong idea."

"I was reminding Emmanuel of his promise to deliver our Christmas gifts to Joy when he goes to Paris in two weeks," Madame said.

Franco nodded. "I'm happy to do it. But make sure you don't wrap those gifts, because airline security is only going to open them up."

"You'll wrap them for us when you get to France, won't you?" Madame asked.

"Me and my two left thumbs. I'll do my best," he said then raised his index finger. "Here's a tip, ladies. If you want a bow, make it a stick-on."

"Is that why you're both here? To plan my daughter's Christmas?"

"I'm on duty in an hour," Franco said. "I just stopped by to see how you were after your exciting evening."

"And I'm waiting for my wayward son," Madame replied. "We're off to Brooklyn. I'm treating him to lunch at a lovely little Williamsburg bistro that's now serving our beans."

I sighed. "Well, I hope I can change your mind about those plans with Matt. I need help and I need it today."

Madame tilted her head. "What is it, dear?"

"Actually, it's right up your alley."

I explained about Dave and the Evergreen Retirement Community in Brooklyn where he worked, and how I planned to gain access to its recreational center to meet him—provided Madame was willing to help.

Madame broke one of the sweet-tart cookies with her long, elegantly manicured fingers, took a bite, and chewed thoughtfully. "Perhaps I will visit this community. Incognito, of course."

"I'm counting on your acting chops to get us inside."

Franco snorted. "Blanche is going to need more than acting skills, Coffee Lady. Nobody from Brooklyn dresses like her."

"You know, Franco makes a cogent point. You'll need a disguise." I checked my watch. "We can find something at the Salvation Army shop on 14th Street and be back before Matteo arrives."

"The Salvation Army? Isn't that rather . . . extreme?" Madame replied. "I could have my driver take me back uptown, change into something more . . . casual."

"I don't think you own anything 'casual' enough for this. And we need to be here to meet Matt."

"Maybe I should reschedule the lunch?"

"No. Matt's useful. Dave is probably a charming, cooperative young man with nothing to hide, but it's also possible he's a handsome young murderer who could go postal when confronted. Matt should come—as our muscle."

"You're right, dear. Even with a questionable wardrobe, this adventure will be much more fun than seared scallops in a bistro."

"Well, I hope your son doesn't object to my plan. You know how he dislikes our doing these sorts of things."

Madame patted my hand. "He'll come around. All it takes is a little deception on our part. Just enough to string him along—until he has no choice in the matter."

Twenty

~~~~~~

"**EVERGREEN** *Retirement Community. Where Life Begins Again.*"

Matteo Allegro almost did a double take when he read the sign over the entrance to the ten-story glass and steel building.

He brushed back his rakish dark hair. "I thought we were going to lunch in Williamsburg? Mother said something about a new restaurant that's serving our coffee beans to their customers?"

"We'll be dining at Durango's soon enough," Madame replied. "I told you I needed to make this little side trip first."

"*Little*?" Matt shook his head. "If this side trip were any longer we'd be in the middle of the bay, not on the shore looking at it."

As if summoned by his words, a sharp wind blew off the white-capped waves, and we were pelted by stinging ice. We redoubled our steps to the front doors, and Madame tugged at the collar of her dowdy brown coat to mitigate the chill.

Matt noticed her discomfort and snickered. "Are we missing our cozy-warm sable coat, Mother? I should have known something was up when I saw those odd clothes you're wearing. Where did you get them? The Salvation Army?"

Madame made a show of checking her shabby wool coat, her dun brown polyester pants, and the tan-colored sneakers on her feet.

"There's nothing inappropriate about my attire," she proclaimed.

"Sure there is," Matt replied. "You forgot the shapeless floral print muumuu."

"You exaggerate, my boy. I'll admit I've dressed down—"

"Dressed down? Looking at you makes *me* feel old."

And that was my Peter Pan ex-husband's real problem with Madame's disguise. With his youthfully energetic mother still a vibrant force in his life, he never had to think of himself as getting older.

"Okay, I give up. Why are we here?" he asked. "And please tell me we're visiting one of your friends."

"I'm looking for a change," Madame replied. "I'm lacking a sense of community in my life. Clare is so busy at the shop. Joy is living in Paris. You're traveling all the time."

She paused, touched the corner of her eye, and sniffed loudly. "Sometimes I get lonely—"

Matt was unmoved. "You have more friends than you have time for." He whirled to face me. "You put her up to this charade, didn't you?"

"No comment," I said as we entered the glass-walled lobby.

"I'm rather tired of my old apartment, too," Madame continued. "Many of my favorite haunts are gone, so even Manhattan has become a bit of a bore. I could use a change of venue to perk things up."

"Uh-huh," Matt said.

"Look around, my boy. The scenery outside is lovely. The beach, the ocean, that strip mall across the street."

"Oh, sure," Matt smirked. "And with the added charm of that view of the Cyclone roller coaster at Coney Island, the aesthetics here rival the south of France."

"Matteo Allegro! Where did you learn to be so snide?"

"In this town? It's a survival skill."

While Madame and her son bickered, I noticed a staff directory posted on the wall. A "David Brice" was listed as activities director—and that cinched Janelle's claim that Dave worked here.

"Well," Madame was saying, "you have to admit this facility *is* very modern. Each suite has its own balcony with an ocean view. It's quite civilized."

Matt scanned the utilitarian lobby—linoleum floor, off-white walls, plastic chairs. "Mother, I don't accept the premise that you're going to give up a Fifth Avenue penthouse crammed with original art and valuable antiques for an efficiency apartment in this Bauhaus-By-the-Sea monstrosity. Which means you, or more likely *Clare*, are up to something sneaky, hazardous, and potentially illegal."

Matt sighed. "But now that I'm here, I'll play along with whatever your stupid game is, provided you eventually feed me—" He glanced at the Breitling on his wrist. "Even if lunch ends up being dinner."

His mind made up, Matt strolled to the front desk.

"I'd like to speak to someone in admissions, please. I think my mother might require supervised confinement . . ."

"WELCOME to the Evergreen Retirement Community. I'm Ellen Beesley, head of admissions. It's a pleasure to meet you."

The impossibly slender, modestly dressed middle-aged woman rose from behind a cluttered desk and extended her hand—to Matt, of course.

After a polite shake, Matt shed his camel hair topcoat to reveal a formfitting hunter green cashmere sweater over tight black chinos. Matt pushed his sleeves back to expose his tanned, hard-muscled forearms.

Mrs. Beesley's eyes appeared to pop, and her slim fingers instinctively primped her straight black bangs.

"Please, have a seat," she said, maneuvering it so that

Matt landed in a chair right beside hers. "Now how can I help, Mr. Allegro—"

"Matt, please," my ex insisted. "Short for Matteo."

"Matt-aay-ooh . . ." She drew out the pronunciation, savoring the syllables. "How exotic."

"And may I call you . . . ?"

"Nellie," she replied, touching those black bangs again.

"Well, Nellie, this is my mother, Blanche. She's getting on in years and I need to find her a new place to live, where she can have the proper . . . supervision."

"Blanche is alone?" Mrs. Beesley asked.

"Widowed," Matt replied.

Mrs. Beesley nodded sympathetically. "I'm thrice divorced myself, but I can certainly understand her anxiousness. As the weeks wear on, the lack of companionship becomes oppressive. Does Blanche reside with you and your wife?"

"My ex-wife," Matt corrected.

Mrs. Beesley's excited smile at the "ex" news was fleeting, but I caught it. I also noticed how she slid her chair even closer to Matt's.

"Clare maintained her emotional bond with my mother after our marriage ended," he continued. "Though lately she's been busy with her career, and a new romantic interest. Now Clare feels she can't take care of Mother the way she used to."

Mrs. Beesley addressed Madame in a loud voice. "How are you feeling, Blanche? Was your trip taxing? Is there anything I can get for you?"

Madame frowned. "You may decrease your volume, young woman. There's absolutely nothing wrong with my ears."

"Oh, very good," the admissions administrator replied in a normal tone. "Would you like some tea?"

"Actually, we'd love a tour of your facilities," I said, jumping in. "Especially your recreation center. Recreation is very important to Blanche . . ."

Mrs. Beesley frowned. "All in good time. But first I'd like to make sure that our community is the right fit."

"I'm sure she'd fit in anywhere," I replied. "Provided there's a *recreation center.*"

"How is your mental acuity, Mrs. Dubois?" Mrs. Beesley asked.

"As sharp as a tack," Madame shot back.

Matt caught the administrator's eye and shook his head. Mrs. Beesley diplomatically cleared her throat.

"You feel you've noticed some decline in your mother's mental condition, Matt?" she asked.

He nodded. "You can tell by looking at her that she's completely lost her fashion sense."

"Ridiculous!" Madame sniffed.

"As well as her sense of humor," Matt added.

Mrs. Beesley touched her chin. "I'm not sure these are mental health issues, clinically speaking."

"Blanche is bored easily and requires constant stimulation," I interjected. "That's why we're terribly interested in your *recreational programs and facilities.*"

This was my third-time mention of the recreation center, and I hoped Matt's thick head would take the sledgehammer hint this time, because clearly Mrs. Beesley was paying no attention to me. Thankfully, my ex finally got a clue.

"Clare is right," he said. "Mother can be quite manic. ADD, if you know what I mean? She's constantly on the go, and we're never sure quite where. She says she's going to her quilting circle, but we find her at a high-stakes bingo game. Last week we found her playing slots at the Queens Racino at the Aqueduct Racetrack."

"Oh my," gasped Mrs. Beesley.

"By the way, how lively is your recreation center, Nellie? Does your facility sponsor activities like quilting and bingo, that sort of thing?"

"Oh yes. There's an entire array of activities. No slots, I'm afraid."

"Posh. What am I supposed to do without slots?" Madame muttered. "I suppose you don't allow betting on the ponies, either?"

Mrs. Beesley leaned close to Matt and laid a lingering, sympathetic hand on his. "She gambles often?"

"Too often. She'd lose the house if we didn't supervise her every move."

Mrs. Beesley leaned even closer, until she was practically nuzzling his neck. If her chair tipped over she'd probably end up in Matt's lap—not that she'd mind.

"It sounds like Blanche's gambling habit has become a challenging issue," she said softly. "We should certainly discuss this before we consider placement at Evergreen."

"I'd be happy to discuss anything at all with you, Nellie," Matt continued in an exaggerated whisper. "But not with Mother present. Why don't you and I chat alone, while Clare escorts Mother on a tour of your recreation center."

Mrs. Beesley's face lit as brightly as the LED lights on her desktop Christmas tree. "Why that's a splendid idea, Matt-ay-oh."

Twenty-One

~~~~~~~~~~~~~~~~~~~~~~~~~~~~~~~~~~~~~~

The Evergreen Recreation Center was a supersized play-room with a wall of glass sliding doors that faced Lower New York Bay. A wide deck of polished wood led to a beach of snow-covered sand glazed with a crust of ice, its distant shoreline foaming with frigid, crashing waves. If I could have scooped that view into a latte glass, I would have made a fortune.

"This is quite pleasant," Madame said, checking out the room.

In contrast to the chilly winter panorama, the scene inside the recreation center was quite warm. Golden sun-light streamed into the space, where a gas fireplace flick-ered on one wall, its mantel adorned with a colorful line of hand-knitted Christmas stockings.

An antique silver Chanukah menorah graced a table on one side of the hearth. On the other, an eight-foot spruce twinkled with multicolored lights, its piney branches heavy with white tinsel, red bows, and dozens of handmade orna-ments, including a host of soapstone-carved angels.

Although the big-screen television played on another wall,

few were paying attention to its closed-captioned images. The billiards table and indoor shuffleboard court were quiet, too. Only two of the many card tables lined up along the windows were occupied; one by a group of men playing poker, another by four women working on a large quilt.

The real action appeared to be at the far end of the room, where a group of residents and staff members had gathered around an upright piano. The piano sat on the floor, next to one end of a small, low stage. Most of the group stood, some leaned on canes and walkers, and a few occupied wheelchairs.

I couldn't tell what the group was discussing, but the conversation was curious—hushed tones followed by a loud eruption of surprise and agitated buzzing.

"I wonder what that little gathering is about," Madame whispered. "Do you think we shou—"

Suddenly she yelped and rubbed her polyester-covered posterior. "My word!"

"What's the matter?" I asked.

"Someone pinched me!"

We both turned to find an elderly man wearing a rascally grin. A sky blue jogging suit hung on his scarecrow frame, and a brown fedora topped his silver head. The hat was cocked at a jaunty, Sinatra-style angle. As we stared, he touched the brim.

"You pinched me!" Madame cried, shaking a manicured finger at him.

"You're darn right, babe," replied the man with an old-school Brooklyn wink. "That's some *koo-koo* carriage you're pulling. I'm looking forward to bouncing a quarter off that rear bumper some night real soon."

The Rat Pack wannabe touched the brim again. Then he strolled out of the room, pushing through the double doors as if he owned the place.

"Well, I never." Madame sniffed.

I stifled a laugh. "Sure you have."

She smirked. "So I have. But never in a place like this! And you know, Otto would be far from pleased to hear—"

Pausing abruptly, she gripped my arm and pointed. "Clare, look at that!"

I followed her finger to a large cork bulletin board. On the left side, a banner read: *First Friday Follies, 7:30–8:30 PM. This Month's Folly Fotos!*

Beneath were a number of photos of residents in costumes performing comedy skits, improvisations, or singing together at standing microphones. But it was the right side of the cork board that caught Madame's eye:

CHRISTMAS EVE SPECIAL!
"OLDIES AND NEWBIES CHRISTMAS KARAOKE"
HOSTED BY MOIRIN FAGAN
SIX TO NINE O'CLOCK
OPEN TO ALL RESIDENTS AND THEIR FRIENDS
AND FAMILIES

A red-letter Postponed banner slashed diagonally across the poster like an open wound.

"We came to the right place," I whispered.

That's when I spied a young man with dark hair replenishing the long snack table with carafes of hot water beside bags of tea, Sanka packets, and bowls of fresh fruit.

The man's back was turned, but from his silhouette, I had almost convinced myself this was Dave. I took a single step toward this stranger before Madame yanked me backward.

"Don't forget, Clare, our 'muscle' is back in the admissions office charming the business suit off that scrawny man-eater."

"Not literally, I hope."

"I mean it; you cannot confront this young man alone. You told me that yourself. He might be a vicious killer."

"You're right. Let's split up. I'll keep an eye on Dave, and you fetch Matt."

Madame hurried through the double doors and down the hall. But I knew she would have to cross the entire length of the ground floor to reach the administration offices. I just hoped Dave wouldn't disappear in the meantime.

As the minutes ticked away, I kept my gaze trained on the youth's back. Finally, he turned and walked away, pushing through the double doors and out of the recreation room.

I followed him quietly—until he slipped a card key into a door marked Employees Only.

Darn it! I can't lose him. I've got to risk it—

"Excuse me, Dave?" I touched his shoulder.

He whirled, a startled look on his young Latino face. *"¿Puedo ayudarle?"*

"Oh, please forgive me," I said. "I was looking for Dave."

Smiling, he politely switched to English. "Dave's in there . . ." He pointed back to the recreation center. "He's the dude sitting at the piano."

The door lock clicked, the young man pushed through it, and I headed back into the playroom.

Twenty-two

∿∿∿∿∿∿∿∿∿∿∿∿∿∿∿∿∿∿∿∿∿

If David Brice sat at the piano, I couldn't see him. The thick knot of residents and staffers gathered around the upright was as good as a human curtain. Luckily, as I crossed the room to get a closer look, their little meeting began to break up.

A tide of rolling wheelchairs and creeping walkers swarmed slowly toward me. Only one woman in a wheelchair rolled the other way. She pushed right up to the piano bench. I moved closer, as well, until I caught my first glimpse of Dave—and halted in surprise.

I'd been expecting a boyishly handsome, dark-haired guy of middle height, age no more than early thirties. In short, I thought I'd be meeting the same man I'd seen Moirin arguing with at the Cookie Swap.

But this Dave, specifically David Brice, Activities Director according to his name tag, was pushing sixty, hardly the age-appropriate boyfriend I would have expected for a twenty-five-year-old club girl like Moirin.

On the other hand, Dave Brice was not unattractive. His face, though etched with lines, sported a Kris Kristofferson–

esque beard. His tawny shoulder-length hair was shot with gray, and pulled into a short hipster ponytail; a small loop of gold glinted in one ear; and his clothes consisted of distressed jeans, a denim shirt, open at the collar, and a navy blue sport coat.

"Oh, Dave!" wheelchair woman called.

"Yes?" Dave replied.

"Just one more thing!"

"You know," Dave said, "from the expression on your pretty face, Edith, I knew you had something up your sleeve besides Kleenex . . ."

In any given workweek, I heard hundreds of voices in my coffeehouse, but the timbre of this man's voice gave me pause. Deep, smooth, and uncommonly resonant, it was the kind I used to hear on late-night FM radio, and I could just picture the man sitting behind a mike, sipping two fingers of Scotch between LPs.

"If M can't host the Christmas Eve party," Edith continued, "then can you at least tell me when she'll be doing her next 'Take it Back' session? My daughter wants to bring my granddaughters to the city, and I want them all to enjoy it with me . . ."

From the sound of Edith's questions, the news of M's brutal murder hadn't yet reached the residents here. *Does Dave even know yet?* I wondered. *Or is he in the dark, too?*

As Edith talked, I studied the man. A shadow crossed his amiable expression. I could see that discussing M was upsetting him, and I concluded that he likely *did* know what had happened to the girl. But why was he keeping the truth from the residents?

"Everyone has such fun in M's sessions—young and old. I know my Sally and her girls will just love it, too," Edith said. "So you'll let me know?"

Dave hesitated before replying. He swallowed hard, and when he spoke again, his voice was much weaker, its dulcet magic subdued.

"I'll let you know, Edith."

"You're a good one, Dave. And I must compliment you

again; last night's First Friday Follies was one of your very best!"

At the mention of the Follies, I realized Dave Brice was the man sitting at the piano in almost all of those bulletin board photos. Clearly, one of his duties was to help the seniors put their show on every month.

As Edith backed away, Dave closed the piano cover, and stared into space, absently cracking his knuckles.

I was eager to talk to him, but Matt and his muscles had yet to make an appearance. I checked my watch. *For heaven's sake, Mrs. Beesley's grip must be harder to slip than Quinn's powercuff hold!*

Suddenly Dave snapped out of his stupor. He swept up a small pile of sheet music into a blond leather messenger bag and fastened it. Then he stood—and I frowned.

The man was tall, at least six feet with long limbs and a sturdy chest. Despite his age and thickening middle, the guy didn't look like anyone's pushover. Of course, Matt had twenty years on him, but that was about it.

He noticed me then, and gave me a polite nod—as if I were a family member here for a visit. In a few long strides, he was across the playroom and pushing through the double doors.

As he moved down the first-floor hallway, I shadowed the man, hoping he'd stay in a public area. Instead, he turned a corner and went through a heavy fire door marked *Exit*.

Oh crap, he's leaving the building!

Thinking fast, I untied the thin decorative scarf from around my neck and draped it over the door's handle. Then I moved through the doorway and found myself in a service stairwell.

Footsteps clanged on the metal stairs below me, and I knew Dave had gone down. I did, too. Descending the short flight, I spotted him moving toward an exterior door. In another few seconds, the man would be out of the building and off to heaven knew where.

"Excuse me!" I called from the stairs. "May I speak with you?"

Dave stopped at my call, his hand stilling on the door's metal crossbar.

He turned, offering a weak smile of interest—it was practiced, slightly plastic—but his amber gaze grew sharper as I approached, making me suddenly conscious of my appearance.

In all my life, I had never been what one might call *slender*. In the eyes of New York's fashionistas, I was a total fail. In the eyes of most men I encountered, however, my curvy pieces apparently fit together just fine.

Ever since my late teen years, when I'd finally shed the baby fat of my nonna's home cooking, my carved-out Italian curves seemed to magnetize male gazes. According to Matt, my figure was "lush." In Quinn pillow talk, I was "temptingly ripe." Less than comfortable with the attention, I discouraged it daily by tying on my Village Blend apron.

At the moment, however, I was sans apron, and Dave Brice seemed to be considering my topography like a man mildly suspicious of newly presented terrain. His gaze traveled up my charcoal gray slacks, moved over the bend in my hip, made a switchback-like return to my nipped-in waist, ascended and descended the generous gradients in my butternut sweater, and arrived (finally) at my face.

"And who might you be?" he asked, his tone friendly yet guarded. "Do you have a relative here or are you new on staff?"

"Neither . . ."

Okay, Clare, your former mother-in-law put on Salvation Army clothes to look the part. The least you can do is turn on the charm . . .

While *young and innocent* had expired for me about two decades ago, my heart-shaped face, framed by softly wavy, dark-roast hair, offered an innocuous enough impression; and I pushed it, tilting my head and widening my green eyes.

"Actually, the reason I came here was to speak with you . . . It's about M . . . Moirin Fagan?"

Dave's affable expression instantly vanished. The *trust*

me, I have no ulterior motive ploy was a bigger bust than
Janelle's root beer sweet potato pie.

"Are you from the police?" he hissed quietly, glancing
behind me to make sure no one was around to overhear.
"Because I already spoke with the detective who raided
Moirin's apartment last night, and I'm not about to put up
with harassment, understand?"

"I'm not a cop."

"Then you're from the press, and I want nothing to do
with you."

Before I could stop him, Dave's hand smacked the metal
bar and he slammed through the back exit.

"I'm not the press, either!" I cried. "Please come back!"

Of course he didn't. Dave Brice continued to stride
away, leaving me holding open the building's heavy back
door. A frigid gust of air whipped around me, tossing a
curtain of hair across my eyes. With determination, I raked
it back.

I've come this far. I can't stop now.

Given the photos I'd seen upstairs, there was no way
David Brice could have murdered Moirin Fagan. Still, I
didn't know this man—or what he'd do to me if I pushed
him too far.

You know what? I don't care!

Moirin Fagan *knew* her killer. I was certain of it, yet I
knew next to nothing about her life. Finally getting some
answers was worth taking the gamble, so I made a split-
second decision: I would chase down my murdered employee's pissed-off boyfriend into a desolate employee parking lot.

Twenty-three

~~~~~~~~~~~~~~~~~~~~~~~~~~~~~~~~~~

Fearing the thick metal door might auto-lock behind me, I cast about for something to prop it. I spied an old umbrella stand in the corner and dragged it over, positioning it against the frame. Then I hurried outside.

The air was freezing with frequent bone-chilling gusts sweeping in off the water. The previous night's snowfall had been cleared, but the frozen pavement beneath my low boots felt slippery, and I nearly fell trying to catch Dave before he reached his car.

"Please talk to me! It's important!" I assured him, but nothing I shouted would slow the man's single-minded retreat.

Out of desperation, I grabbed his arm.

Bad idea.

The second I initiated physical contact, Dave felt justified in doing the same. Wheeling, he took hold of me by my poor, tortured wrist, and not gently.

"What do you want?"

He spoke low, through gritted teeth, and his hold on my

wrist was expert, just enough pressure and torque to fold my arm and force me against the front of his car.

We were the only two people in this back parking area, which had slots for maybe two dozen vehicles and only five or six actual cars—including the sporty silver convertible directly behind me.

"Listen," I pleaded. "I do not work for the NYPD or the media. I'm a friend."

He considered my claim for a moment before smirking. "Okay, *friend*, come with me."

Yanking my wrist, he dragged me to the sports car's passenger side. As pangs of pain shot down my arm, I heard a distinctive *click-clock* sound, saw the keys in Dave's other hand, and realized he'd remotely unlocked his car's doors.

"Get in."

Oh God. Confronting this man without backup hadn't been the safest gamble, but I was certainly smart enough to keep myself from being driven off alone by a man who had no qualms about painfully restraining me.

"I'm not going anywhere with you."

"You want to talk? We're doing it on my terms."

A below-zero gust howled off the water, sending a nasty shiver through my frame. Climbing into the car would shield me from the biting wind, but I shook my head.

"I am *not* getting into your car. Forget it."

He frowned down at me in silence, obviously considering his next move.

Well, I didn't have to consider mine. If David Brice tried to push me into his Mazda Miata, I was going to act like a drunken Rockette, kick him in the coconuts, and run like mad.

But Dave didn't force me into his car, although the steel grip on my wrist remained annoyingly tight.

"Talk then," he finally said. "Who are you?"

"My name is Clare Cosi. I'm the manager of the Village Blend coffeehouse in Greenwich Village. Moirin Fagan worked for me."

"Show me an ID."

"I don't have a wallet on me. It's in my bag, in Mrs. Beesley's office."

"Then find another way to make me believe you."

I considered a half dozen, but any obvious identifiers involving Moirin would have been known by the cops and possibly the press. That's when I remembered what Vicki Glockner had mentioned last night.

"One of M's favorite bands was Purple Lettuce. A barista of mine bought her tickets for their concert in January. It was going to be her Secret Santa gift . . ."

Dave exhaled hard, his posture deflating. *Finally*, he believed me!

"Hey, you! What are you doing to her?!" The angry male voice was howling with more force than the wind across the lot. "Let her go!"

It was Matt, following my crumbs—he'd seen the scarf I'd left on the first-floor door handle, then the propped exterior door. Now he was moving toward us, sans coat (like me). His fists were balled beneath pushed-up sweater sleeves, and every few steps, his dress shoes slipped on the icy concrete.

Dave glanced up at Matt, then back down at me. "You know this joker?"

"He's my business partner. I brought him to watch my back—in case you turned out to be a murderer."

Dave blinked, looking confused. "You think I killed M?"

My ex-husband's heavy hand landed hard on Dave's shoulder. "I said, *let her go.*"

The man released me so suddenly I fell back against his car.

"I didn't kill M," Dave loudly proclaimed, palms in the air.

"I know that," I said, righting myself and rubbing my poor wrist.

"You *know* that?" Matt's head nearly spun on his neck. "Clare, are you crazy? You're going to believe this guy, just like that?"

"It's not a matter of believing him. He has a rock-solid alibi."

Dave's eyes narrowed on me, his expression suspicious again. "I thought you said you weren't with the NYPD."

"I'm not."

"Then how do you know I have an alibi?"

"A person doesn't need a degree in astrophysics to add two and two, and I don't need a badge, a law degree, and a forensics lab to tell time." I pointed to the building. "I saw the recreation room bulletin board in there. You were in enough of those photos to convince me that you sat at that piano at last night's First Friday Follies from seven thirty to eight thirty, and I know exactly when M was killed. There is no way you could have traveled from South Brooklyn to Bryant Park in the time it takes to smoke a Lucky Strike."

The look in Dave's eyes changed after that. Not that he suddenly thought of me as a best friend, but his amber gaze certainly stopped spearing me as if I were going to serve him with a desk appearance ticket.

Another frozen gust whipped off the water, and I fought against a shiver as I turned to Matt. "That's why the detectives didn't ask Janelle Babcock about Dave. They already knew he couldn't have killed Moirin . . ."

As I spoke, I felt a cloak of warmth being draped over my shoulders. Dave had lent me his sport jacket.

"Thanks," I said, pulling it tighter around me.

"Sorry I was rough on you," he said quietly.

"It's okay." The garment still carried the warmth from his body heat, along with a pleasant citrusy whiff of male deodorant. "Now can we go back inside and talk?"

"Please," Matt added flatly, rubbing his own arms for warmth.

But Dave shook his head. "No, I can't do that . . ."

What?! I followed the man as he moved to the trunk of his Miata, pulled out a black leather jacket, and slipped it on.

"I don't understand. Why won't you talk to me?"

"I'll talk to you," he said, "but I'm not discussing M in that building. One of the residents might overhear, and we haven't broken the news to them yet."

"Look, I'm really sorry to inform you of this, but the local stations will have the full story, *with Moirin's name*, by tonight's broadcast. At least one station is out there trying to get exclusive interviews. And—"

"There he is!"

I looked up and gasped. *Speak of the devil*, my pop used to say, *and hell will deliver him*.

A pair of men emerged from the building's back door wearing blue parkas and press credentials. One of them carried a video camera on his shoulder; the other held a cell to his ear and pointed directly at David Brice.

Bringing up the rear was the blond Marlboro Man in his Channel Six News blazer. The hair, I noticed, had been freshly washed and recoiffed—clearly a necessity when some crazy Village coffeehouse manager throws a pie in your face.

"Who in hell is that?" Dave asked.

"Dick Belcher, Channel Six News," I replied. "And it looks like he's here to ambush you."

"Oh man, I hate paparazzi. Always did . . ."

Always did? I stared at the man. He said that like he'd once been famous. My mind raced, but I couldn't place him. Clearly this Channel Six News crew could.

"Brice! Brice Wildman!"

Brice Wildman? Was that David Brice's stage name? It still didn't ring any bells, but the news crew rushed forward, shouting for the "Wildman" to stop.

Dave jumped behind the wheel, and I gripped Matt's shoulder.

"I need your cell phone . . ."

"What?" he cried as I picked his pocket. "Why?"

"I'll use it to keep in touch," I said, yanking open the sports car's passenger door. "My cell is in my bag in Mrs. Beesley's office."

"You're not going with him!" Matt's eyes were close to popping.

I pointed to the advancing news crew. "It's better than dealing with them again!"

"Again?" Matt said. "You mean they're the ones who made Janelle cry?"

"Yes!" I said, diving into the passenger seat. "Just take your mother to lunch, okay? I'll see you later!"

Dave revved the engine. "*Now* you want to get in?" he quipped.

"Belcher and I have history." I slammed the door. "Drive!"

Twenty-Four

〜〜〜〜〜〜〜〜〜〜〜〜〜〜〜〜〜

As we peeled out, I peered into the side mirror. The little round glass reflected a curious spectacle—Matteo Allegro trying to buy us time.

Shouting like a New York nut, he rushed the newsmen, arms waving madly. The pavement was so icy that avoiding contact with my (seemingly) half-crazed ex was impossible without slipping.

Dick Belcher and his crew slid like penguins and crashed into one another, two of them going down. The cameraman managed to stay on his feet. Lucky for Belcher, the producer broke his fall.

Thank you, Matt!

He waved at our car and flashed a thumbs-up of triumph. I rolled down the window and returned it, just before Dave hung a left and blasted us out of the parking lot.

We stopped at the end of the drive and he made a turn onto the public road. There were two directions to go, left toward the bay or right toward the parkway. He went right.

"Where are we going?" I asked.

"Lunch," he said, adjusting his mirror. "You like Italian?"

"How do you think I got these hips?"

He smiled. "Italian it is. And it's on me. Consider it an apology for the manhandling."

"Thanks, I will."

We began driving—at normal speed—through the neighborhood. This part of Brooklyn was mostly middle-class and residential with close-packed brick apartments and strips of shops and markets, nail salons and phone stores, bars and restaurants. I sat quietly for two full blocks, but I couldn't wait until lunch to talk. I was way too curious—

"So you're famous?"

"Was. Past tense." He glanced at me. "It's ancient history."

"Not to Channel Six. According to them you're *Brice Wildman*. What were you? An actor? A musician?"

"Musician is something of a stretch. Performer is more like it. I was the lead singer and founding member of a band."

"Which band?"

He shook his head.

"Oh, come on. You can't leave me in the dark. What was the band?"

"The Infernal Machine."

I searched my little gray cells, but . . . "I don't think I know that band."

"That's because you weren't a teenage boy in the late seventies."

"Excuse me?"

"We were an unsuccessful heavy metal band, Clare."

Heavy metal? I blinked, wondering how a person went from hair-head screamer to retirement home activities director. And if Dave's band was so "unsuccessful," then why did those news guys call him by his stage name?

"Did you have any hits?"

He shrugged. "Three in the Billboard Top 100."

"That sounds pretty successful to me."

"Oh, when we were hot, the money rolled in—and, man, it was great. I had a luxury home in Malibu, a flat in London . . ."

My mind tried to paint that picture—Dave thirty-plus years thinner in skintight leather pants and a black fishnet muscle tee, wrinkles erased, along with those salt streaks on his tawny head. I shaved off his full beard, made the ponytail longer and set it free. The man did have an amazing voice, and I didn't doubt he was a rock star back in the day. Yeah, I could see it.

"What happened?"

"I let our manager handle the money, and a lot of other stuff, too. What the hell? I was in my twenties and just wanted to party . . ."

He shook his head. "The guy put the titles to my properties in his name, embezzled a lot of our income, too. I fired him. He evicted me. I heard the bastard's still got his mistress living in my London flat."

"That's awful. Did you sue?"

"Of course . . . and the lawyers took the rest of my money. The outcomes netted me very little. By then, my career was kaput. You know what *kaput* means, Clare? Finished. Utterly defeated."

"You retained your music rights, though?"

Dave laughed. "I was the lead singer, the front man. I had the looks so I became the face of the band. When your kisser is on all the album covers and posters, the groupies are great. But when the party's over, if you don't write the songs, you don't get music rights."

"After all that success, you really ended up broke?"

"What do you think you're sitting in? This is a Mazda, not a Mercedes."

"There's nothing wrong with this car, Dave. I think it's a very nice car."

"Yeah, well, let's just say it's not the driver's seat I imagined for myself. Then again, it was my own damn fault."

"Seems to me your manager should have gone to jail. How is that your fault?"

A horn blare interrupted us and our attention was drawn to a commotion ahead. The city's snow plows had cleared the messy streets, but plenty of parked cars were still buried under drifts. One of those cars blocked our way, its wheels working to gain traction. With vehicles behind us, we were trapped.

Dave sat back and sighed. There was nowhere to go.

"I got taken for a reason, Clare . . ."

"Why? Was it a vendetta, something like that?"

"No . . ." He folded his arms and smoothed his beard. "As a kid, I wanted fame and fortune so badly that was all I thought about; and when I got it, I assumed—like every stupid kid who hits one out of the park on luck—that easy street had arrived for good and things would only get better. I wasn't paying attention, so I got screwed. But the reason my career crashed and burned wasn't because some gonif of a manager stole from me; it was because I had nothing else. And fires built on nothing flame out fast."

"Not always."

"*Always*." He met my eyes. "If you want a long creative life in the arts, you have to build on a stronger foundation than a juvenile lust for fame and fortune. That was something it took me too long to figure out. It was a lesson I tried to impress upon M."

"On Moirin? Why?"

"She was an aspiring songwriter and recording artist." He glanced over. "You didn't know?"

I stared, slack-jawed for a moment. "She never mentioned anything like that to me—or the pastry chef she worked for. I don't think my staff knew, either."

"I can't say I'm surprised. That girl had a lot of firewalls."

"What does that mean?"

"The residents at Evergreen didn't know about her vocal aspirations. The people who hired her for singing jobs didn't know she made rent money baking cookies. And nobody—including me—knew much about her life back in Ireland."

"So let me get this straight. You tried to help her? With her singing and songwriting career?"

"I did what I could for her, with the limited connections

I still have . . ." The traffic ahead was finally moving. Dave put the car in gear.

"Can you be more specific?"

"I'd give her advice, call her whenever I heard about a gig. She landed a few recording jobs. Backup singing, studio stuff. The jobs didn't pay much, but she was starting to get attention."

As we drove through the next block, I considered Friday's timeline. "Tell me something. Did you happen to call Moirin yesterday afternoon?"

He shook his head.

"Well, did you set up a rendezvous for someone else to meet her? Or maybe she had an appointment to meet with someone?"

"Neither. I hadn't spoken with Moirin since Tuesday night, when we had a dress rehearsal for last night's show."

I sat back and stared blankly out the front window as I tried to think it all through. Whoever called Moirin Friday afternoon had been making plans to meet her. If it wasn't Dave, then who was it? And was that person her killer? Before I could ask more questions, Dave pounded the steering wheel.

"What's the matter?"

"Check your mirror," he advised.

We were now sitting at a red light in a four-way intersection with apartment buildings flanking us and a cargo van idling behind with lettering across its front—X-I-something or other.

A single red-faced man was working at the side of the road behind us, attempting to dig his parked car out of a city-plowed wall of ice-packed snow.

"What is it?" I asked. "Do you know that guy?"

"Not the man shoveling. Look *behind* us. The van."

I looked again, bending down to see more of the van reflected in the mirror, and realized the idling vehicle wasn't just any cargo van. It had a microwave dish on the roof and a pissed-off-looking man behind the wheel in a snow-dusted blue parka.

Oh crap. Mirrors reverse lettering!

I turned in my seat to reread the van's front inscription and confirmed the ugly development: News Channel Six!

That crew was on an ambush mission, and the second we got out of this "Wildman's" Mazda, I knew Ned the cameraman would start rolling, and Dick Belcher would begin firing hardball questions—one of which would certainly be why this former rock star, who'd just lost his too-young girlfriend in a brutal murder, was tooling around in a sports car with the dead girl's shapely employer.

"You want a free lunch?" Dave asked. "Help me get out of this."

"How far is the Belt Parkway?"

"Maybe a quarter mile."

Well, I thought, snapping on my shoulder harness, *I am hungry.*

"I have a few ideas how you can lose them," I said. (Actually, given my years with authority-loathing Matteo Allegro, I had more like a dozen.) "To start with, don't go anywhere on the green light. Wait right here for it to turn red again."

Dave looked puzzled a moment then nodded. "Oh yeah, I remember that trick. Okay, I'll give it a try . . ."

The traffic light flipped from red to green, and we just sat there.

Traffic behind us became impatient and the honking began. Dave glanced at me. "Are you sure you're up for this? I mean, managing a coffeehouse, you probably aren't used to high-stress situations."

"Are you kidding?" I said as our green light went from warning yellow to angry red. "Floor it!"

Twenty-Five

∿∿∿∿∿∿∿∿∿∿∿∿∿∿∿

DAVE'S sports car shot through the intersection on the solid red light with the oncoming traffic barely missing us. Horns blared at our audacity. But we made it across. And News Channel Six didn't.

From my side mirror, I saw the van attempting to lurch forward, Dick Belcher leaning over the driver's seat, shaking his fist. But there was no way for Ned to move without getting smacked. So they were forced to sit and watch as we sped away.

"That felt good," I said.

"Yeah . . ." Dave smiled. "It did."

The apartment buildings were flying by us now—red brick then yellow brick then red again—their sizes dwindling down with each block we traveled away from the bay.

"Didn't you say something about having a 'history' with that news guy?" Dave asked, manually shifting from third to fourth.

"That's right—a very short history."

"Love affair?"

"Let's just say it involves loud threats and cream pie."

Dave arched an eyebrow. "Kinky."

"More like *hinky*."

"I don't follow."

"Some jerk in the NYPD leaked names in Moirin's case file. This morning, Dick Belcher used that information to ambush me and my friend Janelle. When he wouldn't let up, I asked him to leave her bakery. He ignored me, so I threw a meringue-topped root beer–laced sweet potato pie in his face."

"You're kidding?"

"Extreme, I know, but—"

"No buts," Dave said. "You were protecting your friend."

"Yeah, well, pie or not, it was an assault."

"At least it was an edible one."

"Actually not. According to Janelle, the filling had all the appeal of slimy hospital medicine. It's no wonder the man threatened to sue me."

Dave shot me a half-amused glance. "In my day, I did far worse."

"With that wrist hold you put on me, I can believe it. Where did you learn that move, anyway?"

"When you play concerts on the road, you have a lot of downtime. I learned it from a bouncer."

Three blocks later we hit a red light. No big deal, except that when it turned green again a long gasoline tanker truck was stuck in the middle of the intersection, "blocking the box," as we say in New York. By the time the truck driver swung his big rig around the bend, the light had gone to red again and we were stuck.

That's when a familiar microwave dish appeared in my side mirror. News Channel Six.

Dave cursed.

"You can't sit through the light and go through the red this time," I said. "They won't fall for the same trick twice."

"I couldn't do it anyway. Look at the traffic, Clare. There's no way to shake them on these streets."

"Then we'll shake them on the expressway. I'm sure

your sports car goes faster than their van. As a last resort we can outrun them."

"I'm in," Dave said, eager to punch the gas.

"But take it *slow* this time," I warned. "We want to make them think we've given up."

"Okay . . ." Dave downshifted into second. Moments later, we rolled up the ramp, the News Channel Six van hugging our bumper. In my side mirror, I could actually see a victorious smirk on Dick Belcher's face.

When we merged onto the busy four-lane highway, News Channel Six backed off a little, but continued to dog us.

"So, Clare? Do you have a plan besides breaking the speed limit? I'll go there if I have to, but . . ."

"Drive casual. Just let them follow us for a while."

"Then what?"

"When we get close to the Brooklyn–Battery Tunnel, I'll let you know."

Dave nodded and settled in for the ride. "Answer me another question."

"If I can . . ."

"Why is a Greenwich Village coffeehouse manager tracking an ex-hair-head all the way to the tip of Brooklyn?"

"Short answer or long one?"

"Let's try short."

I glanced in the mirror, at the news van stalking us. "Honestly? It comes down to one word: *guilt*."

"Guilt?" He pursed his lips. "You better give me the long answer."

I did, explaining what had happened at the Cookie Swap. How I saw Moirin go out for a cigarette break and never come back. How I assumed she was shirking work, and led Janelle to think so, too. How neither of us bothered to look for her.

Dave's hands tightened on the steering wheel. "The cops told me she was killed instantly. What could you have done? Found her body sooner, maybe? She'd still be dead."

"Maybe I could have seen the killer. Maybe even stopped the murder. But I'll never know. And I have to live with that."

"So what do you want from me, Clare? Absolution? I'm not a priest."

"I just want information. The police . . ." I paused, wondering how to avoid sounding grandiose (or delusional). "Look, I found Moirin's body. I was there when the Crime Scene Unit arrived, and a pair of homicide detectives, too. One of those cops is a regular at my coffeehouse. I know and trust her, but the other . . ."

"What about the other?"

"Well, he's senior to my detective friend, and he has city hall backing. He's also the lead on the case, but I think he's leading the investigation in the wrong direction. Meanwhile, with every hour, every *minute* that goes by, M's case gets colder, and the chance of catching this killer slips further away. The officers who frequent my coffeehouse tell me that most murders—"

"I know," Dave said, nodding. "Most are solved within twenty-four to forty-eight hours. That was my hope. That the killer would be caught quickly, so that when I delivered the bad news to the residents, there would at least be some closure with the pain."

"Well, there won't be any closure if the investigating team doesn't get their act together. Believe me, Dave, I want closure, too. Frankly, I'm not going to stop until I see Moirin's killer brought to justice."

Dave's face hardened. "What can I do to help?"

"M was a very private person. I didn't know much about her. I'd like you to help me fill in some blanks about her life." I straightened in my seat when I saw the sign for the Brooklyn–Battery Tunnel. "But first let's lose these losers, shall we?"

"What's the plan?"

"Dick Belcher knows I'm with you. And he knows my coffeehouse is in Manhattan, so let's make him think that's where we're going. I want you to drive *past* the entrance to the Brooklyn–Battery Tunnel, then speed up like you're heading to the next East River crossing—the Brooklyn Bridge. Got it?"

I held on as Dave shifted from third to fourth and we blew by the Tunnel exit.

"Now what?" he asked.

"Look for a way to hide. We need a big vehicle, something to cut off Belcher's line of sight long enough for us to slip off the exit just before the bridge. Like I said, he knows I'm with you. If he can't see us, chances are he'll assume that we're heading to Manhattan. Their van will continue on the expressway, trying to catch up to us—but we'll be gone."

"There's our camouflage," Dave said a few moments later. "I'll slip around that mattress delivery truck. That thing's big enough to cut off Belcher's view."

Without warning, Dave grimaced and punched the gas, shifting to fifth. I was jerked back in my seat as the Miata went from fifty to seventy-five in what felt like three seconds.

"Nice pickup," I said with faint bravado.

The tires squealed and I was thrown against my harness as we moved into the left lane. When we slipped around the truck, and came back in front of it, Dave nearly clipped the safety wall. I straight-armed the dashboard and watched the News Channel Six van disappear from sight. It may have been a trick of the light, but I swear Dick Belcher's face turned purple.

We continued to fast-forward, moving around an SUV, another delivery truck, and a van. As we guessed, the Channel Six team couldn't keep up with us. All they could do was stay on the expressway and hope to catch us down the road.

Finally, the last exit before the Brooklyn Bridge came and we flew down its ramp. Near the bottom, Dave hit a patch of dirty snow and the car fishtailed. I had visions of a rollover, but he managed to regain control before we were dumped out onto a neighborhood street.

We pulled over, waited, and watched, but the van didn't follow. They took the bait, driving past the exit, assuming we were going over the Brooklyn Bridge.

"By the time they realize we gave them the slip, they'll be in Manhattan."

"Should we loop around?" Dave wondered, his face a

tad pale. "Get back on the expressway in the other direction and take the Battery Tunnel?"

"I have a better idea. This is Cobble Hill. I know a little restaurant off Court Street. Nunzio's specializes in Sicilian seafood, and they make a mean pizza, too. Best of all, they have parking behind their restaurant. So even if Belcher and his team figure out what we did, they'll never find us because your car won't be on the street."

"Sounds good," Dave said. "And pizza sounds even better."

Twenty-six

〰〰〰〰〰〰〰〰〰〰〰〰〰〰〰

An hour earlier, Nunzio's would have been packed, and they certainly would be again for dinner. But this late in their lunch service, their dark-paneled dining room was quiet, and we were given a very private corner booth, *away* from the window, as Dave requested.

We ordered quickly on my suggestions. Then Dave leaned back and rolled up the sleeves of his denim shirt. I could see why he'd have to wear long sleeves on the job. Tattoos heavily covered both arms—I caught a glimpse of scarlet chains on one forearm, the elaborate bottom of a Gothic cross on the other.

"So what were your Top 100 hits, anyway?" I asked.

"Let's see . . . 'Hard as Steel' made it to the top fifty. 'Bones to Dust' went higher . . ."

He reached for the bottle of Valpolicella the waiter opened for us and poured wine into my glass. It was early in the day for me to have alcohol, but I'd learned a thing or two over coffee talks with Detective Mike Quinn.

In unofficial interviews, you used what you could to

loosen tongues. Like Mike (not to mention Pliny the Elder), I believed in *in vino veritas*.

Unfortunately, the vino portion of our program was mine alone. Dave set down the bottle after filling my glass. Then picked up the bottle of sparkling water, twisted off the cap, and filled his glass.

"What was your third hit?" I prompted.

"That was the biggest, by far. We were in the top ten for three whole weeks."

"The title?"

"'A Fine Line Between Heaven and Hell.'"

My gray cells spun again—and this time they hit three cherries. "I think I actually heard of that one."

"You don't have to humor me, Clare. I have no ego about it. Not anymore."

"Wait, I can remember." I held up a finger. "When your planet's spinning madly / on a burning white-hot core . . . Right?"

"You got it."

"You can scream in rage and fury. / You can beat, beat, down the doors . . ."

"I'm impressed."

"Then how does it go? Something about a tale to tell."

"If no one upstairs hears me / won't heed the tale I tell. / Then down below they'll fear me / I'll turn heaven into hell . . ."

"That was a great song—I mean, I admit heavy metal was never my thing, but when I was growing up, the boys on my block really connected to it. You expressed something there for them."

"Yeah," he said flatly, "adolescent anger."

I shifted, unsure how to read him. "What are you getting at?"

Dave sipped his sparkling water. "I used to scream those lyrics without giving them a thought. Most teenage boys do. Believe me, they hold a lot more meaning after your career crashes and burns. There really is a fine line between feeling on top of the world and having it all go to hell."

"You don't have to be a failed rock star to understand that . . ."

The previous evening's events had illustrated that enough for me: The heavenly party followed by the hellish murder. And then that awful scare with Quinn. All week long, I'd been aching to shower him with kisses the moment I saw him. Then what did I do? Thrash him with angry fists when he walked through my door.

I studied David Brice and made a simple deduction. "I take it your fall included addiction?"

"Are you fishing?"

I shrugged. "In vino veritas, in aqua sanitas."

"Excuse me?"

"In wine there is truth, in water there is health. So, either you're trying to make sure I speak the truth while you stay sober, or you're a former alcoholic." I pointed to his glass. "People on the wagon don't drink."

He nodded. "That's right. We don't."

"How long?"

"Thirty years, give or take the occasional slip."

Our Caesar salads came with a basket of garlic knots, and Dave finally connected the dots for me, explaining how a heavy metal headbanger becomes a retirement home activities director.

Drug and alcohol addiction was the first step. After his band's third Top 100 hit, nothing clicked again. The new album tanked, and the new manager was honest but not nearly as competent as the previous manager in getting them booked. The band members fought, and they finally broke up.

Dave landed hard with little money. An overdose of drugs and drink landed him in an ER, then a detox program where a social worker and man of the cloth began the long process of getting his head straight again.

It was an AA program that turned Dave around, helped him "get up and grow up," primarily because of the relationship he'd forged with his sponsor, John Macardle.

"Jackie, that's what he liked to be called," Dave said.

"The guy was a former marine, Golden Gloves champ, and tough-as-boot-leather father figure—one I'd never had . . ."

Dave had never formerly studied music, and Jackie, a high school phys ed director and wrestling coach, helped him apply to colleges.

"I taught music after that, middle-school level. It was a solid, respectable income while I kept trying in the music scene—some backup singing until the voice went, then record producing, songwriting. Small-time stuff. Nothing ever broke out again, not like my early years, but I did all right for myself. Got married, had a beautiful girl. My wife died of cancer about ten years ago; my daughter got married, moved to Indiana; she teaches music theory at IU . . ."

"How did you end up at Evergreen?"

"Jackie ended up there. He's in another wing now, pretty much bedridden—and I visit him as often as I can. But a few years back, he asked me to help him find someone to play the piano for a holiday party. Hell, I did it myself, was happy to. The activities director job opened up a month later, and he called me about it, knew I was looking to retire—I loved the kids at school, but PS budgets were being cut, especially for music programs, and I was ready for a change anyway."

"So how did you meet Moirin?" I asked, finishing off my salad. "At a downtown nightclub?"

He shook his head. "I travel a lot these days, visiting my daughter, friends around the country and Europe. My Park Slope house is small, but it's also technically a two-family, and I never liked the idea of leaving the property empty, so I decided to rent the first floor as a furnished one-bedroom. Moirin was my tenant."

"How long was she living with you?"

"Since she moved to the city? Maybe two years? She answered one of my flyer ads on a studio board, struck me as an honest girl—honest enough to mention that she could barely scrape together a security deposit, and that she had no references at all."

"You rented to her anyway?"

Dave shrugged. "As a former musician, I like to help strug-gling young artists when I can, so I let her have the place without a security deposit. I never had cause to regret it."

The "struggling young artist" line confounded me, and I wondered if maybe Moirin had played the man to get close to him. Or had David Brice really been looking for a pretty, young tenant who'd be a potential bedmate?

Though M was gregarious and quick-witted, she seemed more of a party girl than someone with artistic sensibilities. So I asked him, quite frankly, whether she had any real talent.

He blinked, surprised. "Moirin had one of the most beautiful voices I ever heard. Haunting, you know? She claimed she was untrained, but she had amazing range and control. When Moirin sang, it was like . . ."

Dave's eyes misted and he paused. He took a sharp breath and finished his thought. "Moirin Fagan sang like the angel she was . . ."

The waiter came to clear away our salad dishes. When he left, I reached across the table to squeeze Dave's hand.

"I'm sorry," I whispered. "And I believe you about M. I do. It's just that . . . I had no idea she was a serious musician."

"Well, she *was* serious. She kept up with the music scene. Went to clubs, networked, studied trends, practiced daily—I helped her out with voice coaching, exercises, per-formance tips, that sort of thing. She even quit smoking twice. Tobacco and weed are hard on a voice. She fell off the wagon both times, but I know what that monkey is like, so I couldn't fault her."

"I have an important question for you. It might be painful."

"Go ahead."

"Last night, I saw Moirin speaking with a young man at the party, shortly before she was killed. He was good-looking, late twenties maybe early thirties, boyish face, brown hair. Did she know anyone like that?"

"Not that I know of."

"You're sure she wasn't . . . stepping out on you? Seeing another man?"

"Excuse me?"

I locked eyes with him. "You're not going to play games with me, are you?"

He stared for a long moment. "Wait, wait . . . you think? No! Look, Moirin rented a place in my house; we became friends. Yeah, okay, the girl had a crush on me, an obvious one, but I kept her out of my bed."

I gave him a look—an *obviously* skeptical one.

"There was nearly a forty-year age gap between us," he went on. "I saw a lot of relationships like that in the music business; and they all ended badly—or as de facto father-daughter marriages. That's not what I wanted."

"You're telling me that you and Moirin never once . . . ?"

"No. And frankly, I was never tempted."

"You expect me to believe that?"

"Believe what you like! Picking up a bedmate is child's play for me, especially in this town."

"At your age?"

"Listen, honey, if I wanted you, we'd be making it right now. You'd have your pants off and your panties down for me faster than I could finish this sparkling water . . ."

I stilled at his words, stunned that he'd gone that far. "Let's leave me out of this, if you don't mind."

"You ask me personal questions and get touchy if I get personal? Baby, I'm telling you the truth. If you can't handle the truth, get up and call a cab."

And that's when I saw it—the bad boy rocker. Cocky, angry, sexually aggressive. The flame was vintage, but it still burned with vivid, dangerous heat at the core of David's amber eyes.

Twenty-seven

~~~~~~~~~~~~~~~~~~~~~~~~~~~~~~~~~~~~~~

I took a hit of wine—a long one—and reminded myself what Mike Quinn once said about police work in interview rooms.

"You're trying to locate the right string to pull, the one that unravels the subject's social clothes; and when you find it, you yank without mercy, as hard as you can . . ."

That's what I'd just done, I realized. I'd mentally stripped the guy down. And despite the ugly turn of our conversation—actually, *because* of it—I knew that I was making progress, getting good information behind this particular firewall in M's private life.

On the other hand, Dave and I weren't sitting in a police precinct; and I didn't have a badge, a gun, or any sort of backup. Pushing "Wildman" Brice any further on the question of whether he and Moirin were more than platonic friends would have been a very bad idea.

Time to change the subject. "How about we talk about something else?"

Dave continued to glare, and I half expected him to get up and storm off. But he didn't.

In a gesture of peacemaking, I reached for his bottle of sparkling water, refilled his glass, and then (thank goodness) our pizza arrived.

In my experience, any "truth" in the drinking of vino couldn't hold a candle to the honest sharing that often came when eating good food. Or as my nonna put it: *"Il pane apre tutte le bocche." Bread opens all mouths.*

And Dave and I both opened wide for this.

New York City possessed the best water in the nation for making pizza crust; so perfect, in fact, that pizza-makers all over the country famously imported it to mix up their dough.

This crust had the hallmarks of the best in the city. Thin but not too thin. Chewy but not before the slightest snap of crispness—like that slender crust of ice that had formed on the snow outside. Biting down gave you the satisfaction of al dente crunchiness; then almost immediately came the softness, that chewy goodness of fresh-baked, hand-thrown dough.

The fresh tomato sauce had the aromatics of local pizza-makers: oregano, rosemary, basil, and garlic. Its sweet, smooth flavor carried only a hint of bright tanginess, which meant the acidity had been tamed by the kind of long, slow cooking my nonna used to do for her customers—with pride and love.

The sausage and mushrooms had been chopped finely and sautéed in olive oil before being sprinkled in all their caramelized glory over a sweet white blanket of shredded cheeses—fresh mozzarella, young provolone, and aged Asiago—melted to a bubbly, warm pond of gooey, creamy, slightly salty goodness.

"How do you like it?" I asked, midchew.

He nodded, mouth just as busy. "Not bad, Cosi."

Okay, progress, I thought. *A few bites of Nunzio's famous pie and I've gone from "honey" and "baby" to "Cosi." Now let's get me back to "Clare"* . . .

"Can you tell me more about the Evergreen Recreation Center? How did M come to work there?"

"We were short on help last year," he began, pausing to wipe sauce from his mouth. "I offered her a hundred bucks out of my own pocket if she'd 'volunteer' to lend a hand at Evergreen on Thanksgiving Day. She did."

Dave sat back, and I was relieved to see him relaxing again. "Turned out M missed being around family. She liked the old folks; she made them laugh and they made her feel like she belonged, so I got her a part-time paying position."

"And when did that start?"

"Last January. She started this whole off-the-wall program to bring modern music to the residents."

"You mean club music?"

"All kinds of music. I thought the whole thing was brilliant, and a lot of the residents loved it, especially the i-Grannies."

"The what?"

"The Internet Grannies—that's our in-house computer group. They talk to their grandchildren through social networks, and a few months back Moirin had a brilliant idea about helping them connect to their grandkids through music."

"How?"

"She'd start with an artist or group that the kids today are into and she'd play it for the folks here, and then 'take it back'—that's what she called her sessions. She'd show them where the artist's influence started so they'd have a more personal connection to it, you know? Feel better equipped to listen and talk about it. Adele, for instance."

"Adele who?"

"She just goes by Adele. She won a boatload of Grammys and young people love her. M showed the i-Grannies how her style dates back to Aretha Franklin and back even further to Billie Holiday. She did the same thing with Maroon 5, a pop band out of LA, and One Direction—a British-Irish boy band. She played sample songs and then connected them back to the Jackson 5 and back even further to Frankie Valli and the Four Seasons."

"Did she introduce them to that Long Island group she followed? Purple Lattice?"

"Purple *Lettuce*." He arched an eyebrow. "They're like the Dawes, Clare."

"The who?"

"*The Who* is another genre."

"You're kidding with me, right?"

He smiled. "I'm talking neo-folk rock—M showed how the current movement can be traced back to Crosby, Stills and Nash."

Finally! "I've heard of them."

"Well, M would have given you one of her psychedelic star stickers—and showed you how they're related to the Byrds, the Kingston Trio, and Woody Guthrie."

"I wonder why, with that kind of passion for music, she worked as a baker's assistant."

"Easy money. She could do the work in her sleep." Off my look, he explained, "Her family owned a bakery in Ireland."

That brought another fact to light. "M never told me much about her Irish life. From the few remarks she made, I assumed she grew up in a rural area and moved to a more populated city, where she worked in a pub. She said something about a whacker of a manager, making all the girls on the waitstaff wear short skirts."

Dave smiled, but it was a sad smile. "I heard that story, too."

He sipped his water again, then knocked back the rest of the glass. "Lately, Moirin started hosting karaoke shows. She even uncovered surprising talent among our own residents. Thanks to her, we have an in-house Elvis—his real name's Ben Finkelstein. We've got a married couple that do Sonny and Cher. We've even got our own Rat Pack."

"The Rat Pack doesn't surprise me. My former mother-in-law met 'Frank' when he stopped to admire her *koo-koo* carriage."

"Guy with a fedora?"

I nodded, and Dave chuckled. "Yeah, that's Tony. Our karaoke Sinatra. He's pretty frisky."

"What did Moirin earn for this work?"

"Very little. With this economy, our funding is drying up fast. Now that Moirin's gone, we'll probably have to suspend the extra programs, which will break a lot of old hearts at Evergreen."

"You say you didn't check Moirin's references. How did she sign the lease? Did she put a previous address down?"

Dave shook his head. "I don't do leases. I rent on a handshake."

I sat back and my chair creaked. "Did you ever see or hear anything that seemed odd? Anything that distressed Moirin, upset her? *Really think*, okay?"

"Well . . . there was something that always bothered me . . . about this time last year. It was around midnight, and I was hauling my garbage to the street. When I passed her door, I heard Moirin crying—"

"Crying?"

"Absolutely sobbing, you know. I knocked on the door, but she wouldn't talk to me."

"She didn't say anything about why she was crying?"

"No. And I respected her privacy."

"Well, a girl crying is fairly normal."

"Yeah, but here's what was odd about it: The next morning, she's at my door, bright and early, asking if she can borrow two hundred bucks. She says she needs money to buy a little black dress to impress some date. I figured her crying was about a boyfriend breaking up with her. Maybe she was looking to win him back with a sexy dress. Or she was thinking, 'screw him,' and wanted to get dolled up and find a new man."

"She paid you back?"

"Hell, I just gave her the money. I didn't regret it, even though I found out later she was lying."

"Lying about what?"

"M lied about a lot of things, Clare. Okay, maybe *lying* is too strong a word. Let's say she was full of contradictions."

I leaned forward. "Name one."

"I'll name two." He smoothed his beard and leaned forward. "Look, I don't expect you to believe me, but M had too many beers at some club one night, and she came knocking at my door. I answered and she threw her arms around my neck. I sent her back down to her room, told her I didn't think of her that way, and it would just mess up both our lives. She said it was just as well, something had happened in Ireland that had put her off romance."

"What? Like a bad breakup?"

"Worse than that, she said, but she refused to tell me anything more. And then there was that dress. The little black dress I gave her two hundred bucks to buy wasn't bought to impress any date. I saw it hanging inside a dry cleaner's bag. It was black, but the dress had long sleeves, a longish skirt, and a high collar. It even had a lace veil. It wasn't a party dress. It was the kind you wear to a funeral."

"And she never mentioned anyone dying?"

"I asked if everything was okay, and she sang me a verse of 'Don't Worry, Be Happy' . . ."

We finished our pizza and continued talking over cappuccinos, but I didn't learn much more. As I crunched a hazelnut biscotti, I wondered about the people M met in the music business—especially the men.

"Dave, those studio jobs you mentioned, the backup singing Moirin did? Did she have any of those jobs recently?"

"Her last job was about six weeks ago. She was making so much cash during the holidays, working for Janelle and you, she said it was worth the time off singing. She planned to start looking to audition again in January."

That's when I remembered what Janelle had said. "Are you sure she didn't mention two male friends? Janelle said she overheard calls from men named Tony and Benny."

"Tony and Benny?" Dave laughed. "Weren't you listening?"

I closed my eyes. *Of course, that's right . . .*

"Tony's our karaoke Sinatra," Dave reminded me. "And Ben is Elvis."

"So M was taking calls from eighty-year-old men?"

"They liked to kid around with her," he explained, "run new karaoke ideas by her. On the other hand, it could have been more serious, which should finally convince you why Moirin and I were never lovers."

"Why?"

"Isn't it obvious? I was too young for her."

Twenty-eight

〜〜〜〜〜〜〜〜〜〜〜〜〜〜〜

DAVE drove me to Manhattan, dropping me off a few blocks from my coffeehouse, just in case the Channel Six van was staking it out. They weren't, thank goodness. Belcher had moved on to his next "breaking news" target.

By now, it was very late in the afternoon. With December days so short, shadows were already gathering in the snowy canyons of Manhattan. A winter-night cold had descended, making my shop's shining windows feel like a welcoming beacon of warmth and cheer.

I pushed through the beveled glass door to find my coffeehouse absolutely packed with holiday shoppers. Bags and boxes covered nearly every table and half the floor. This was nothing new, of course; every year, they flowed into our neighborhood from Jersey, Long Island, and Westchester, jamming the Village streets. I was very happy to catch the business.

With care, I maneuvered my way through the crowded café tables, smiling and nodding hellos, and finally moved around the counter.

Jingling bells greeted me. "Ho, ho, ho, Mrs. Boss. Happy Crazy Saturday!" Nancy said as she adjusted her jester-elf cap.

"It's been this busy all day?"

"Not so bad now," she replied. "You should have seen it three hours ago; it was standing room only, with a line out the door—and baby it's cold outside!"

I moved to our coat hooks and hung up Dave's sport jacket, making a mental note to return it soon. He'd chivalrously insisted I keep it around me for the few blocks I had to walk, and I didn't argue. Now I slipped a blue Village Blend apron over my sweater and dress slacks.

This was my day off, but clearly my staff could use an extra pair of hands. "So, what needs to be done?"

"Before anything else, you need to talk to the lady cop," Nancy said, waggling her eyebrows.

I followed my barista's jerking thumb and spied Lori Soles with one of our Fa-la-la-la-latte cups in her hand. "Okay, it shouldn't take long. Then I'll start spelling you guys for breaks. You've been working so hard, I'm sure you can use them."

"Thanks," Nancy said. "Much appreciated!"

I pulled an Americano for myself and arrived at Lori's table in time to see her tear the head off a helpless gingerbread man. Three more crispy little cookie men lay on her plate, all of them beheaded in the same grisly fashion.

"Are you reenacting the Reign of Terror? Or are these decapitated cookies stand-ins?"

"They're *gingerbread* men, Cosi. The only thing suffering here is my waistline."

I sat across from her. "Were you waiting long?"

"Ten minutes. Long enough to regret coming."

Impatient much? "So, how was your day otherwise?"

"Brutal," Lori replied. "Yours?"

"Chock-full of fun surprises. For instance, I started the morning with an *ambush* by newsman Dick Belcher. Any *clue* how that might have happened?"

Lori cursed.

I smirked. "You know something about that leak in your boat, do you?"

"I had nothing to do with it. Beyond that I cannot comment." Lori bit the right arm off another gingerbread man and chewed it up with gusto.

"I talked the incident over with Quinn this morning. He thinks Endicott might be Dick Belcher's Deep Throat."

"Quinn's a smart guy. That's all I can say."

"Oh no, it's not. You're going to say *a lot* more before you go. You owe me that. Do you have any solid leads on Moirin's murder?"

"None that I think will pan out."

"In other words, Endicott's got a hunch you think is way off target?"

"Exactly."

"Well, I got your text message," I said. "Those orange hairs that Endicott was so excited about? They were dog hairs, weren't they?"

"A Nova Scotia Duck-Tolling Retriever—mature, in good health, although we don't yet know what sex." She shook her head. "How did you guess?"

"I knew they weren't from Piper Penny. And that park is open to the dog-walking public."

"Well, thanks to Mr. DNA's rush to judgment, the precinct's entire detective squad is in stitches over it."

"He's a laughingstock?"

"Someone left a pooper scooper on his in-box."

"I'm beginning to get the picture. Endicott freaked, am I right? When he found himself humiliated, he leaked Moirin's case file to Dick Belcher. He's trying to make M's murder look like it's part of the Christmas Stalkings—not because he has any hard evidence, but because his 'hunch' connection will make the general public think that he's on top of the highest profile crime of the holiday season. Am I warm?"

Lori exhaled. "You're hot as a steam wand."

"Well, now Endicott's really stuck, isn't he? I mean, if a lab technician can't solve his case for him, what's he going to do? Interview witnesses? Dig into the victim's background? Sounds absolutely *Victorian*."

"Touché, Cosi."

I leaned across the tabletop. "I think Moirin knew her killer. Did your forensics team find anything else?"

"The victim's saliva on the cigarette butt, assorted gum with assorted saliva that doesn't match the victim, a few drops of dried blood of a type that doesn't match the victim, either." Lori shook her head. "Mr. DNA demanded further analysis on everything CSU scooped up, but so far there's no breakthrough on that front."

"That's the second time you called Endicott 'Mr. DNA.' Quinn used that nickname, too. Coincidence or something more?"

"You never looked up his books, or you wouldn't have to ask. Anyway . . ." Lori broke a headless gingerbread man in half, dunked his legs into her coffee, and glanced around. I waited for her to finish her cookie. Instead, her eyes suddenly got wide.

"Dammit," she whispered.

"Look, I know what you're thinking," I said, misinterpreting her angst. "You regret coming here because you've got something you *want* to tell me. Something you feel you *should* tell me. But you aren't *supposed* to tell me, am I right?"

Lori's voice dropped an octave. "You're right. And *if* I tell you, you can't tell anyone. Now, listen closely to me. If you want to hear more, you have to do as I say."

"What? You want me to swear an oath or something?"

"When I tell you to laugh, *laugh*."

"What?"

"Act like I told you the funniest cop-walks-into-a-bar joke ever."

"Are you feeling okay?"

"Knock, knock, Cosi . . . come on, *laugh*."

"A *knock, knock* joke? Really? What am I, five years old?"

"No, you're being watched by the NYPD, and so am I. Now do what I say and *chortle*, at least."

I did. Loudly.

"Good," Lori said, lowering her voice again. "Now I'm only going to say this once. I don't believe Moirin's murder has anything to do with the Christmas Stalkings. I agree with you. I don't think Moirin's murder was random. I think she knew her killer. *Laugh*."

I did, not quite as loudly this time.

"Well, Endicott is the lead investigator, and Mr. DNA has got his own theory. Unfortunately, he *does* have a shred of evidence to back it up."

"What theory? What evidence?"

Lori inhaled before she dropped the bomb. "All four of the Christmas Stalker's assaults are connected to this coffeehouse. That's an irrefutable fact. Three victims were assaulted shortly after leaving the Village Blend. Moirin worked here, and was murdered at Bryant Park at an event catered by the Village Blend. Now *laugh*."

I did as Lori commanded, but I felt more like crying. *The Christmas Stalker was attacking my customers? The fact that innocent women were being preyed upon was bad enough, but hearing that my coffeehouse was involved? It was almost too horrible to contemplate.*

I ended my laughing act with a desperate gulp of my Americano. It had gone cold.

"There's an undercover cop watching us right now, isn't there?" I asked.

Lori nodded. "She walked in and spotted us immediately. I thought I had a window before . . . But I guess I should have called you instead."

"We can go upstairs for more privacy."

"That would look even worse, Cosi. And there's no reason to panic. Everyone I know comes here for coffee, so keep pretending we're simply having a casual conversation. Smile, okay? Good."

"Does Endicott have any suspects?" I asked, a silly grin plastered across my face.

"Yes. And that suspect is under surveillance, twenty-four/seven. The undercover cops are just waiting for him to make the wrong move, so they can scoop him up for interrogation."

"Who is he?"

"One of your employees, Clare. Endicott believes the Christmas Stalker works right here, at your Village Blend."

Twenty-nine

~~~~~~

One of my baristas was the lead suspect in the case of the Christmas Stalkings. My reaction to this news?

I spilled my cold Americano all over the table.

I dabbed frantically at the mess with a paper napkin, then gave up and fetched a roll of paper towels from behind the counter. Lori rose to help me tidy up the area.

"Is Endicott crazy?" I whispered. "What evidence does he have?"

"Not much," Lori confided. "The barista in question phoned Moirin three times in the past week. No messages were left and none of those calls were ever returned by the victim, indicating to me that she didn't want to speak with him. The fourth and final call came at five fifty-five yesterday afternoon—"

"At that time, we were at the Cookie Swap inside the Bryant Park Grill, waiting for the doors to open."

"This time Moirin spoke with the caller. The call lasted for six and a half minutes."

"I already told you that Moirin also received a call yesterday afternoon, here at the Blend—"

"Dead end," Lori replied. "We traced it to a disposable phone, bought with cash, first activated in midtown Manhattan."

"I heard Moirin talk with the caller, set up a rendezvous. Can't this information clear my barista?"

"Not by a long shot, and you know it."

My knees felt wobbly and I sank back into my chair. Lori sat again, too, and we kept up the happy-talk act.

I tried to flag Nancy down to bring us more coffee, but my young barista was having a lively conversation with a middle-aged male customer. I recognized him as Eddie Rayburn, the man Tucker called "Evil Eyes" at the last Cookie Swap. A tough guy with a violent reputation, Eddie was also the husband of reality star Danni Rayburn.

Oh man, what does he want? I'd have to ask her about their conversation, but now I had more important things to discuss, like—

"Who is Endicott's suspect?" My face had the silly grin again, but my tone carried very little patience. "Which of my baristas has he put a tail on?"

Lori's grin was more like a tigress baring her sharp white teeth. "I'm very sorry, Cosi, but I can't tell you."

"Then at least tell me what you found in Moirin's apartment. I spoke with Dave, her landlord. He told me you were there."

"Endicott sent me out to Park Slope alone. He can't be bothered with 'grunt work,' as he puts it. Between transcribing the man's notes and going through Moirin's mail, I feel like a glorified secretary."

"What did you find?"

"A lot of CD-Rs with Moirin singing. We confiscated her tablet computer, too. I spent the better part of this afternoon going through her digital diary."

"Diary!" I leaned forward. "Go on."

"Moirin called it 'My American Journey.' She talks about coming to New York City, finding a place in Brooklyn with an ex–rock star. Her daily travails—pretty banal stuff. There's a lot of poetry, music lyrics, I guess. The tenor of her diary changed three months ago. That's when Moirin received a letter, probably in the mail because we couldn't find anything in her e-mail account of any importance."

"What's this letter about?"

"Sure you don't know? Did she ever mention anything like that on the job here—to you or fellow workers?"

"Nothing. I'll ask my staff, just to be sure . . ."

"The diary never says what's in this letter or who it's from, but she writes about how the letter brought 'terrible news.' Later she says, 'the letter changes everything.' Three weeks ago she wrote about how the *Letter*—she began to capitalize the word at this point—would help her 'build a better future for herself, and for others.'"

"No sign of this Letter in her apartment?"

"I searched her place thoroughly, found junk mail, bills, but nothing that seemed out of the ordinary. Oh, and one more thing."

"Yes?"

"Laugh, please. One last time . . ."

I did. Meanwhile, Lori rose and donned her coat. Finally, she stooped low and pretended to peck me on the cheek. "You know most of what I told you is confidential," she whispered. "None of it came from me, you understand? It could cost me my career."

I continued my laugh-track imitation until Lori was out the door.

I sat in silence for a moment, my neck prickling, uncomfortably aware that I was being watched. Finally I rose, bussed the table, and moved behind the counter. I kept walking until I reached the dishwasher. I put the cups and plates inside.

The Village Blend's time clock was mounted on the wall near our tiny Christmas tree. I snatched the stamped cards and leafed through them, checking the hour and minute every employee reported to work last evening—the night Moirin was murdered.

It didn't take me long to identify Endicott's prime suspect.

Shaken by the revelation, I let the cards slip from my hands, and they scattered over the Secret Santa gifts. As I gathered them up, I set off our plastic Bing Crosby, who launched into his battery-powered song.

I replaced the cards, washed my hands, and went up front again. Fingers shaking, I pulled an espresso. When I turned I came face-to-face with a bright green Grinch Peruvian Beanie.

"Aaah!" I cried.

Esther put her hands on her hips. "What's wrong?"

"That hat of yours! It's too creepy."

She grinned. "That's the effect I was going for."

I sipped my espresso and closed my eyes. Calm again, I addressed Esther. "What's up?"

"You're up, boss. Way up. Boris totally owes you for his job at Janelle's. And my boyfriend is like an elephant. He never forgets."

"I'm glad it's going to work out."

"For sure! He's helping at her bakery already, and sometime next week, Boris will start taking M's old shifts, baking cookies for us."

"Okay, but no smooching in the back with your boyfriend," I teased. "You two keep things on a professional level."

"I'll try, boss, but you know men. Boris can't keep his hands off this sweet bod of mine!"

"Listen, on my time, the only *sweet thing* I want that boy to be heating up is cookie dough!"

Jingle, jingle, jingle . . .

I caught my youngest barista by the arm as she breezed by. "Nancy, I have to ask you something."

"Sure."

"You were speaking with Eddie Rayburn a few minutes ago. What were you two talking about?"

"Nice guy, Mr. Rayburn. He just asked me about Tucker's schedule. He wanted to know when Tuck would be here. I explained that he wasn't due in until Tuesday. Mr. Rayburn thanked me, and he even gave me a tip!"

"Blood money!" Esther shrieked.

Nancy pouted. "Did I do something wrong?"

"Wrong?!" Esther held her head. "You only told the famously jealous Evil Eyes where and when to find his next victim!"

"I don't get it," Nancy said.

"It's obvious. Evil Eyes must have found Tuck's card in his wife's purse and flew into a fit of jealous rage. Now he's looking to give our Tuck a severe beat down, just for chatting up his wife!"

"Call Tucker," I told Esther. "Give him fair warning. Then get that 'sweet bod' of yours back behind the counter. A new wave of holiday shoppers just came through the door—and they're headed our way."

THIRTY

~~~~~~

LATER that evening, I was dragging a plastic container of marinated chicken out of the lower shelf of the refrigerator when a shadow fell over me. Suddenly a strong hand gently squeezed my rump.

"Mmm, prime . . ." murmured a deep voice.

"Hey!" I cried, straightening. "Is that any way to say hello?"

I set the chicken on the counter beside the diced onions, chopped mushrooms, and uncorked bottle of dry Marsala imported from Sicily. Mike Quinn slipped out of his coat and tossed it over a chair.

"I can do better. How's this . . ." He spun me around and covered my mouth with his. I smiled through his teasing then ardent kisses—until I heard the olive oil sizzle in the skillet.

"You want to burn the place down?" I asked, reaching over to reduce the fire.

"Just trying to warm you up," he said, holding on to me.

"It's working. Hungry?"

"For food?"

"Don't get cute."

"I'm famished, Cosi. All I've had to eat today is popcorn, hot dogs, and Goobers. I need real food."

As I broke free, Mike affectionately squeezed my wrist. I yelped, and he frowned down at the angry purple bruise that had blossomed on my lower forearm.

"Damn, did I do that?"

"Let's just say you started the trend."

He scratched his head, but I didn't elaborate.

Never a casual dresser, Mike always wore a suit and tie on the job, and since moving to DC for his stint with the Justice Department, he'd been dressing more formally on weekends, too.

Because he'd lost his luggage, he'd thrown on the blue denims and casual sweater that he'd left here after our fall foliage–watching trip in Shenandoah National Park.

For three glorious days in October, we'd driven the thirty-four-mile stretch of Skyline Drive between Thornton Gap and Swift Run Gap, exiting the car now and then to view the fall colors from a mountain trail. We ended our outing in an adorable bed-and-breakfast near the park. Then Mike drove us back to New York City, donned his suit again, and hopped a train back to G-man land.

Mike hadn't worn those jeans since that weekend—which was a shame because he looked very good in tight denims, maybe because when he wore them, he shed some of his worries and even a few inhibitions, along with the suit and tie.

I was delighted with him looking so relaxed, and told him so. His reply was a remark about relaxing even more, and he stepped around me to rummage the refrigerator. I knew what he was looking for—a bottle of beer—but I slipped him a thermos instead.

"What's this?"

"A frozen eggnog latte," I said, passing him a frosted glass from the freezer. "Tuck came up with the recipe. It's delicious."

Mike poured and sipped, then smacked his cream-moustachioed lips.

"I hope you enjoyed the movie that much."

He sat at the table and crossed his long legs, ankle over knee. "I wish. I just don't get holiday movies these days."

"You liked *Elf* when we rented it."

"Until they cast the Central Park Rangers as the Four Horsemen of the Apocalypse—that's where they lost me."

"Well, I hope you had *some* fun."

"Jeremy enjoyed the action. Molly covered her eyes during the scary parts, but she liked the musical numbers."

"How on earth did they fit song and dance into a movie called *Santa Claus, Zombie Hunter*?"

"The same way they fit in the zombies. Absurdly."

"And this film had a plot?"

"Sure, as plots go."

"Enlighten me, if that's the right word . . ."

I was finished flouring the chicken. Now I lay the flattened, tenderized, Marsala-and-garlic-marinated fillets in the hot oil. While I sautéed both sides to a golden brown, Mike recapped the film.

"It starts when zombies attack the North Pole, trapping Santa and his elves inside their workshop. Mrs. Claus is bitten by a zombie and infected with zombie-itis."

"How awful."

"Don't worry. These zombies can be cured; all you have to do is rescramble their brains with a successive frequency of specific audio tones—"

"Hence the musical numbers? Christmas carols, no doubt."

Mike paused. "Did you see this film already?"

"No, but I raised a daughter, which means I have an advanced degree in kiddie film studies."

"Well, Santa doesn't know Mrs. Claus can be saved. So he decides to put her out of her misery."

I'd already removed the chicken and added the onions to the hot oil. Now my eyes were tearing. "God, don't tell me any more. I'll have nightmares."

"It all turns out okay. Thanks to the computer brain inside Rudolph the Red-Nosed Supersonic Robo-Rocket."

"You're joking."

"I'm not." Mike crossed his heart. "Rudolph figures out

the zombies are part of an elaborate plot by an evil toy manufacturer who can't compete with Santa's operation. Santa invades bad-guy headquarters, takes down the zombie ninjas, cures all the folks infected with zombie-itis, rescues Mrs. Claus, and saves Christmas—all in an hour and a half."

"Wow," I said. "All they needed was a cliff-hanger ending that leads to a sequel."

Mike blinked. "You have seen this movie, haven't you?"

"You mean there actually was a teaser ending?"

"The film finishes with a shot of Santa's Workshop under a full moon—"

"Don't tell me. A werewolf howls?"

"You should dream up this stuff yourself, Cosi."

By then the onions were sweet and brown, all their bitterness gone. I added a yin and yang of mushroom slices—half clean white buttons, half earthy dark portabellas—along with a pat of butter. I added chicken stock, and was measuring the wine when Mike wrapped his arm around my waist and nuzzled my neck.

"How about a sip?" he asked.

"Marsala is a wonderful wine for cooking and marinating. But for my taste, it's too concentrated for anything else."

I was glad when Mike heeded my not-so-direct hint. I knew how he'd been dealing with stress in DC—happy hour cocktails. But I wanted him sober and lucid when I discussed Lori's visit.

So Mike grudgingly returned to his eggnog latte while I tossed the mushrooms in the wine, scenting the kitchen with sweet and savory aromas. When the liquid was reduced by half, I returned the chicken to the skillet, then rolled it in the thickening brown sauce until the meat was warm and buttery.

Mike's stomach rumbled. "That smell is going to turn *me* into a flesh-eating zombie."

The table was already set so I prepared the sandwiches. Chicken Marsala can be served over pasta, rice, or roasted potatoes, but Mike's visit with his kids ran overtime. It was almost nine o'clock—too late for a full-blown meal. A chicken Marsala sandwich with a crusty, fresh-baked semolina roll was a perfect compromise.

"Eat," I said, "before you get zombie-itis."

I presented the succulent sandwich and no comprehendible sounds came out of Mike for the next ten minutes. Only oohs, ahhs, mingled with the occasional grunt of animal satisfaction.

I had a sandwich, too—half the size of his—and when the plates were cleared, I started water simmering for the French press. Then I set a slice of my Apple Spice Crumb Pie with Warm Custard Sauce in front of the man. Once again, all conversation ceased as he slipped into an enraptured food trance.

When dessert was over and we finished our coffee, I sat down and finally recounted the details of today's visit by Lori Soles. I didn't hold anything back—because if you can't trust a hand-selected member of a U.S. Attorney's special anti-drug task force, who can you trust?

"Lori was leaking to you for a reason, Clare. She's enlisting your help the same way Endicott got Dick Belcher to help him out after his humiliation over those dog hairs."

"Endicott was desperate. He's the guy who got humbled."

"Lori's humiliated, too," Mike pointed out. "Think about the way Endicott is treating her. Like a glorified secretary. She told you that herself."

"There's one more thing Lori told me. She said that one of my baristas is the prime suspect for Moirin's murder and the Christmas Stalkings. He's now under twenty-four-hour surveillance."

Mike's face turned grim. "Do you know who it is?"

"I checked last night's time cards. Dante Silva came in almost two hours late, so this job doesn't provide an alibi for the time Moirin was murdered."

"Maybe he was delayed by the storm."

"Dante usually walks to work, he lives so close."

"Did you ask him about it?"

I shook my head. "Dante came in shortly after Lori left.

I knew by then he was the suspect, but I didn't feel right mentioning it."

"Good call. If Dante is innocent, he has nothing to fear. If he's guilty, then he should be locked up."

"He's innocent."

Mike surprised me with his reply. "What makes you so sure?"

"Come on. Dante has an Italian temper, yes, but he's not violent."

"Clare, you have an Italian temper, and you don't look violent, either. Yet in less than twenty-four hours you assaulted a police detective, threatened that same officer with a knife, and assaulted a television reporter with a cream pie."

"Meringue-topped sweet potato, actually."

"I stand corrected—but you take my point?"

I closed my eyes. It was true, all of it. I had to admit that my own reactions, when pushed too far, were very like David Brice's when I'd pushed him at lunch today. The cocky, angry, sexually aggressive rocker in him had shown itself, and I found it disturbing to witness.

Is that what happened the night of M's murder? I couldn't help wondering. *Had there been a man in her life like David—a man in the music world, but one much younger and angrier? A man who was slick, even charming on the surface, but unstable at his core? A man capable of murder? Was he this Stalker, too? Or were they two different cases?*

One thing I was certain of—whoever killed M, it was not the young man Endicott suspected.

"I know Dante Silva, Mike. He's a passionate artist, but his heart is so good. He's one of the sweetest people I know. He's absolutely innocent!"

"You're probably right. Dante could have a good reason for being late. It could be coincidence."

Mike was humoring me now, "blowing sunshine" as Franco would say. I knew because of what Mike really thought about coincidence. In a criminal investigation, it was not an adequate answer for anything.

Before I could reply, I glanced at the antique wall clock and realized *News Six at Eleven* had just begun. I grabbed the remote and switched on the small television on the counter.

Mike gave me a quizzical look.

"I want to see how much of my press ambush gets aired," I said, and fell silent when I heard the smarmy voice of Dick Belcher.

". . . A former employer and friend of the victim was obviously distressed by the murder . . ."

The edit didn't include Belcher's aggressive questions, only a quick shot of Janelle melting into tears and backing away from the camera.

". . . Clare Cosi, manager of the Village Blend coffeehouse in Greenwich Village, reacted with anger to the news of this brutal murder."

Suddenly I was staring at my own florid face glaring back at me.

"Whoever killed Moirin Fagan is a sick, sad excuse for a human being," Television Clare said. "A monstrous coward who thinks slinking away into the night is cover enough after taking an innocent life. Well, justice will be served when that worm is caught and punished. I'll do everything in my power to see that happen, and that day can't come soon enough to suit me!"

I heard Mike groan.

Dick Belcher moved on to another story, and I muted the television.

"What's wrong?"

"I know your outburst was heartfelt, Clare, but you shouldn't have done that. You sounded like you were threatening the Christmas Stalker."

"I was threatening Moirin's killer. So what if I was threatening the Stalker, too? Whether the Stalker killed M or not, the man *is* targeting women in my shop. I want him caught just as much as M's killer!"

"And that's my point. Throwing down the gauntlet isn't a smart move given that the Stalker is working out of your coffeehouse. I'm worried that a public scolding could influence the selection of the Stalker's next target, or even how violent the attack is."

All the anger drained out of me. Mike had pulled the right string. He knew I would never knowingly endanger any member of my staff any more than I would risk a member of my family.

"You're right," I whispered. "I was just so angry."

"A natural response to a crime so brutal."

I massaged my forehead. "You've seen so much of this over the years. How do you deal with your anger?"

"First of all, I try not to get angry. Anger on the job doesn't accomplish anything or help anyone. But I'm human, and I do get angry." He paused. "When that happens, I ask God for patience."

"But I don't *want* patience." I met his eyes. "I want these monsters caught as soon as possible. I want them brought to justice."

"That will happen. I guarantee you, this Stalker—and Moirin's killer, whether they're two different people or not—isn't smarter than Lori Soles. He's probably not even smarter than Endicott. He'll be apprehended."

"In the meantime, I have to take precautions. Protect my staff."

"Come here . . ." Mike took me in his arms. "I know you'll do all you can. But for now, try not to worry."

I rested my head on his broad chest. "And how on earth am I supposed to do that?"

"Focus on something else."

"Like what?"

"Like us. I'll be back in DC this time tomorrow, and we won't be able to touch each other again for at least a week."

"You're right," I said. "These days, the clock is always ticking."

He took my hand and gently tugged. "So let it tick— upstairs."

Thirty-one

꩜꩜꩜꩜꩜꩜꩜꩜꩜꩜꩜꩜꩜꩜꩜꩜꩜꩜

I spent Sunday with Quinn, Jeremy, and Molly, but I was only going through the motions. For the kids' sake, I put on a good face, and at the end of the day, I put Quinn on a train. Then I headed back to my suddenly lonely duplex; and on Monday, it was back to the holiday grind.

The first thing I did was call a meeting of my staff—the entire staff, even employees who weren't scheduled. I closed the store early and opened my 6 PM summit by sharing what Lori Soles had told me about the Christmas Stalker's MO. The man was prowling for victims at our coffeehouse.

I warned them that undercover police officers could be planted among our customers, but that shouldn't cause them to let down their guards. They needed to watch for any suspicious behavior, and take precautions when coming or leaving work—especially the females.

Finally, because there was safety in numbers, I announced that no one would close the Village Blend alone until the Stalker was apprehended.

When the meeting was over. All of us headed out to

Brooklyn in a caravan of cabs for Moirin's memorial service. The evening event was organized by Dave Brice and held at the Evergreen Retirement Community.

WHEN we arrived, we were ushered to the recreational center. The large room was filled with flowers, most sent by families of the residents. Beyond the wall of sliding glass, the beach looked bleak, the ocean blacker than a silent night.

A priest and a rabbi who serviced the senior community presided over the solemn event. Emotions ran highest when Dave Brice delivered a moving eulogy, followed by a recording of an original bittersweet ballad of love and loss, sung by Moirin herself.

Though production values were slight, the raw emotion in M's voice shined through, and I found my gaze wandering to the view again, where I saw lights flickering in the dark distance—holiday decorations near Coney Island. I hadn't noticed them before. They twinkled in the night like nearby stars, lifting my spirits.

On the way out, I saw the poster Madame discovered on our first visit. The special holiday sing-along that Moirin was scheduled to preside over had a brand new banner: *Postponed* had been changed to *Cancelled*.

My spirits sank again.

Nancy saw the sign and tears sprang up. "What a shame!" she cried. "Now all these nice seniors won't have a Christmas Eve party. It's so sad when the holidays come and you're left out of the celebration, when everyone else is having fun but you."

By the time I returned to my chilly apartment above the coffeehouse, it was after midnight, and my quilt-covered bed and two purring felines were calling to me. But I had good reason to resist.

The evening's heart-wrenching service had stirred my emotions, and my mind couldn't stop drifting back to Bryant Park, the Cookie Swap party, and that young, handsome man with whom Moirin was speaking—the one I thought was Dave.

My mind's eye saw that Mystery Man so vividly that I grabbed my sketch pad and drew his portrait. It took three tries before I was completely satisfied, but the final sketch was as perfect a likeness as my recollection allowed.

It was nearly 4 AM before my head hit the pillow, cats curling up close. Fortunately my assistant manager opened every Tuesday, so with the knowledge that the Village Blend was in the capable hands of Tucker Burton, I slept late.

When I finally opened my eyes, it was close to noon.

I barely had time to feed Java and Frothy, shower, and throw on jeans and a sweater before I was due to check in downstairs. With no time to brew a morning cup, I descended the service staircase, muttering my need for caffeine like one of Santa's Christmas zombies.

"ROUGH night?" Tuck asked, pulling an emergency espresso.

I nodded without comment, having entered the coffeehouse on unsteady legs, my laptop under one arm, my sketchbook under the other.

After downing the shot, I thanked him. "What about you?" I asked. "Any sign of 'Evil Eyes' Eddie Rayburn?"

Tuck made a face. "Everyone's making a big deal about this, but I'm sure it's nothing. Just in case, I *do* have backup."

"Who?"

He jerked his thumb toward the end of the counter, where a lean, young Latino sat on a stool, scanning a computer tablet.

"It's nice to see Punch again," I said. "I don't think he's been here since last week."

"He's been pulling double-duty for the holiday season, my children's production on the weekends and a cabaret weeknights—an all-male revival of one of my all-time favorite movies, *White Christmas*. Punch is reprising Vera-Ellen's role. You should see him perform 'Sisters'!" Tuck said proudly. "Danny Kaye wasn't nearly as graceful when he tried it in drag."

I scratched my head, trying to recall the number. "Bing and Danny did it together, right? How did that song go?"

Tuck smiled, belting out an Irving Berlin line.

Punch glanced up (never one to miss a cue) and completed the phrase.

"Very pretty. But can he fight?" I asked (pinching a line from one of Quinn's favorite movies).

"Listen up, honey," Punch called down the bar. "If you want to be a drag queen in this town, you'd better learn to defend your honor. And FYI—I'm a fan of *The Dirty Dozen*, too."

He jumped out of his seat, dropped into a martial arts crouch, and threw a half dozen superfast punches, tight brown muscles rippling on his biceps.

"I'm impressed," I said, then turned back to Tuck. "Since you have everything in hand—*and* your back appears to be sufficiently watched—I'll grab a table. I need to review our supply list for Friday's Global Goodies Cookie Swap."

I barely sat down before the first crisis of the day erupted, and it involved Detective Endicott's favorite suspect: my barista Dante Silva.

"Happy friggin' holiday!" a drunken voice bellowed. "Only some of us don't get a holiday. Some of us get *bupkis*!"

A portly middle-aged man in a natty suit stood in the center of my coffeehouse, waving a sheaf of papers.

"It might be Christmas for all of you, but not for me!"

I rose from my seat, ready to intercept the man, but Dante was faster. My barista had just arrived for his afternoon shift, Village Blend apron still slung over his shoulder.

"Come on, friend, let's take it outside."

Dante's voice was calm but firm. In response, the drunk hurled his papers in my barista's surprised face. The loose sheets flew into the air and fluttered down around my startled customers like angry birds.

Dante's face flushed red, but he immediately got control of his anger. "Dude, you're acting crazy. And that's not going to do *you* any good—or anyone else. So let's talk this over on the sidewalk."

Suddenly the hostility drained out of the poor man, and he allowed Dante to guide him to the exit without resistance.

"You don't know the pressure I'm under," he said plaintively.

"You can tell me all about it once we're *outside*."

As he physically herded the stranger, Dante called out to a man sitting alone near the shop's entrance. "Hey, Fred, could you help me out?"

The man nodded and jumped up to open the door.

As soon as he reached the sidewalk, the boozy stranger broke away from Dante and took off down Hudson Street. Coatless, my barista stood in the cold, watching until the man disappeared around a corner.

When Dante came back through the door, he thanked Fred for his help.

"Did your pal Larry get home okay?" Dante added with a smile. "He sure seemed determined to raid Tiffany at midnight on Friday."

"Oh yeah, I got him home." Fred quickly donned his coat. Then he paused to tip his hat. "Have fun at those reindeer games."

This time Dante opened the door for him. "Happy holidays, Fred!"

The entire incident didn't last longer than two minutes, but it was long enough to remind me of Dante Silva's value as an employee.

Polite to a fault, he not only took the time to remember a regular customer's name (during a crisis, no less), he managed to exchange a few friendly words with the guy. And I was willing to bet Dante knew Fred's favorite drink, too.

Of course, we all knew that Dante was popular with the ladies. But he was *always* a gentleman when flirting with them—warm, funny, kind, and just plain sweet.

This young artist, who could pull a near-perfect God shot, and deliver an Italian barista experience to the males and a thrill to the ladies, was a cherished member of my extended family.

And this was Fletcher Endicott's fingered prime suspect? It was hard to take. Yet I couldn't deny that Endicott did have reason to suspect Dante—and I had questions of my own.

As Dante joined Tuck in gathering up the scattered papers, I moved to help, aware an undercover officer could be watching us.

"Dante," I said quietly, "when you're done here, go up to my office and wait for me there. We need to talk."

As I moved away from the pair, I examined one of the scattered pages. It was a resume, professionally printed.

Our angry customer was a forty-seven-year-old bank executive. His out-of-control behavior was very wrong, but it wasn't without reason. According to the dates on his resume, he'd been laid off almost exactly one year ago.

Thirty-two
~~~~~~

"**W**HAT'S up?" Dante asked as I entered my small office on the Blend's second floor.

I shut the door, sat down at my scuffed wooden desk, and cut to the chase: "I need answers from you, Dante. Be as honest and accurate as you can. You called Moirin several times last week. She didn't return your calls—until a few hours before she was murdered. What were those calls about?"

Dante's expression was a mixture of surprise and embarrassment. "Did she tell you about my call? Did she say I was harassing her or something?"

"She didn't tell me a thing." I let my answer hang, and after a pause, Dante spoke.

"I asked her out to a gallery show. She said she was busy, so I pressed it a little, asked her to chill with me after work some night. That's all."

"And she . . . ?"

"Shot me down. M was blunt. She said something ugly happened back in Ireland when she dated someone from work, and she wasn't interested in dating a coworker *ever* again."

"What did you say?"

"What could I say? She wasn't interested."

"You weren't angry? Hurt by her rejection?"

He shrugged. "Sure, I was disappointed. But that's life, right?"

"Tell me why you came late for your shift that night? Two hours late."

"I was on a tear. I'd painted all night and most of the day. I was so keyed up after that, I couldn't lie down. So I called Moirin."

"You wanted to tell her about your painting?"

He nodded. "I was hoping she'd want to see it for herself. Instead our chat kind of lowered my energy so I took a nap. I didn't set the alarm and woke up late. But I made it up to Gardner and Vicki. You remember? I sent them home and stayed after closing to clean up alone."

Dante frowned. "Wait a minute—you don't think I had anything to do with Moirin's murder?"

"Not *me* . . ."

He studied my face. "It's the police, isn't it?! I'm a suspect because I made a few calls?" Dante shook his head. "Dude, I can't believe this!"

"Listen to me carefully. I know you're not a killer. And Mike says if you're not the Christmas Stalker, you have nothing to fear, either."

"What!? The cops think I'm the Stalker, too!"

Happy he "guessed" that, as well, I lowered my voice. "The police are following several leads. But those calls you made to Moirin sent up a red flag."

Dante rubbed the back of his neck.

"I want you to look at something." I slid my sketchbook across the desk. "Have you ever seen this man here at the Village Blend?"

"Good sketch . . ." Dante studied the image a minute before he answered. "I never saw the guy. Did a police artist do this? Is this man M's killer?"

"I drew it. From memory. I don't know if he's the killer or not, but I saw them speaking shortly before she was murdered. He wasn't dressed formally for the party, and he appeared to be very familiar with her."

Dante took a second look, then shook his head. "I suppose he could have been here, but I don't remember him."

"Keep your eyes open. If you *ever* see this man—"

"I'll know what to do," Dante said, balling his fists.

"You'll *tell me about it*, that's what you'll do."

Dante nodded and I sent him back downstairs.

When he was gone, I closed my sketchbook, waited ten minutes, and followed. I hit the Blend's main floor in time to hear Nancy's ever-cheerful voice greeting a new customer.

"Hey, there, Mr. Rayburn! Are you here to see Tucker?"

Oh great. Just what I need—another angry middle-aged man.

ᴛHIRꞆy-ᴛHRᴇᴇ

~~~~~~~~~~~~~~~~~~~~~~~~~~~~~~~~~~~~~

EDDIE Rayburn, the guy known across reality TV–land as "Evil Eyes" Eddie, jealous husband with a short fuse, scowled as he scanned the coffeehouse. Finally, he spied Tucker at the register.

With deliberate care, he raised his arm, pointed a stubby gloved finger at my assistant manager, and cried—

"You! You're just the angel I came here to see!"

Flashing a huge smile, Eddie surged forward, arms outstretched.

Tucker moved around the counter, meeting the human fireplug in the center of the coffeehouse, where Eddie bear-hugged my assistant manager.

I'd frozen in place the moment Eddie arrived, expecting Tuck to be hospitalized. But the pair began talking like long-lost buddies.

I shot a perplexed glance at Punch. He simply shrugged.

"Look, Tucker . . . I can call you Tucker, can't I?" Eddie asked.

"Call me Tuck, Mr. Rayburn!"

"And you call me Eddie. All my friends call me Eddie! Can we sit down?"

Tuck glanced hopefully at me. "Actually, I'm on duty—"

"No worries," I interrupted. "Sit down at the counter, Tuck. I'll take over."

Tuck guided Eddie to the stool beside his boyfriend, and made introductions. I served up White Chocolate Snowflake Lattes, and lingered close enough to shamelessly eavesdrop.

"Let me be straight with you, Tuck," Eddie said in a gravelly voice. "My Danni hasn't been the same since her *True Housewives* show was cancelled. You guys are in showbiz, too, so you know the score. One minute you're on top of the world with a big-ass television hit, an appearance on Leno, a sit-down with those dames on *The View*, even a cook-off with that extra virgin *EV-oh-oh* what's her face?"

"Rachael Ray?" Punch guessed.

"That's the one! Then suddenly the show's over, the lights are out, no more cameras following my Danni around, recording every minute of her life like she's queen of—whatever. Lately, her producer stopped returning her calls . . ." Eddie paused, shook his head. "The show did a number on Delores's marriage. Her husband left her. Now even the paparazzi have lost interest. Danni and Delores didn't even get mentioned in the Cookie Swap gossip column coverage. Danni cried her eyes out for two whole days."

I sighed at what sounded like another David Brice cautionary tale about instant fame. How did David's FM-smooth voice put it? *"There really is a fine line between feeling on top of the world and having it all go to hell."*

"That's terrible," Tuck said with genuine sympathy. "Danni. Delores. They're both so charming and vivacious. Fame's a fickle boy, but he won't abandon them forever. Your wife and her little buddy may have hit a speed bump on the road to stardom, but they'll make a comeback."

"That's what I tell my wife every day, but Danni doesn't believe it coming from me." Eddie poked his thick index finger into Tuck's chest. "She believed it from you, though."

Tuck swallowed as Eddie gulped his latte and smacked his lips, ignoring his foamy milk moustache.

"So tell me about this show you're gonna do? The one with the girls in it . . ."

Tuck and Punch exchanged uneasy looks.

"Well, to be honest," Tuck said, "I haven't exactly written it yet."

"What do you mean you haven't written it yet?"

"Well, I, um . . ."

Eddie drew himself up. "You weren't pulling my Danni's chain now, were you?"

Suddenly, the scowl was back.

Uh-oh . . .

Thirty-Four

~~~~~~

"You have to understand," Tuck quickly chattered, "it started out as this little idea for a cabaret show. We were going to do the whole thing in drag. Well, maybe not the whole thing. A big, strong guy like you, well, we'd have to cast somebody who's really butch. Anyway, since Delores and Danni want to be involved, I envision something much bigger."

"Yeah, so do I," Eddie said.

"Of course, like I said, I haven't written it yet. In fact, I just started rewatching your latest *True Housewives* season On Demand. And we still have to find the proper venue, and a backer, of course."

"Never mind that . . ." Eddie waved his beefy hand. "I'll find you all the backing you need—all the way to Broadway."

Tuck and Punch gasped, and then exchanged wide-eyed stares.

"That's how I roll, gentlemen," Eddie promised. "I'm a professional promoter. That's what my firm does. I have a lot of diverse clients—from hip-hop to hockey teams—and

I have access to real whales, investors with big money who are always looking for new high-profile projects. Just don't let my Danni or her little buddy know I'm involved. I want the call to come from you."

Tuck couldn't contain his excitement. He might have been Danni's angel, but Eddie was Tuck's Santa, granting his Christmas wish for a really big show, maybe even on Broadway.

"Will you be at this week's Cookie Swap?" Eddie asked. Tuck nodded.

"Perfect. I want you to hook up with the girls there. Tell them about your big plans, that you're lining up backers, a theatrical space, the whole thing."

"Are you sure about this?" Tuck asked.

"Here's my cell number," Eddie said, sliding his card across the counter. "Whatever you need, I'll supply. Dream up that big show for Danni and Delores. And I'll make it happen."

With that promise, Eddie downed the rest of his drink and finally wiped his milky upper lip.

"So, Danni mentioned you have a show running now?"

"Just a little production at the Manhattan Children's Theatre," Tuck said. "A limited-run holiday show. It's an adaptation of a Christmas story by O. Henry—"

"Sure, sure. I know O. Henry," Eddie said. "*Gift of the Magi*, right?"

"Well, *Magi* has been overproduced, so I chose to adapt a lesser-known story. I call it *The Christmas Stocking*, although the title of O. Henry's original story was 'Whistling Dick's Christmas Stocking.'"

Eddie's eyebrows practically hit our tin ceiling. "Whistling what?!"

"Dick is the name of the story's hero. And he whistles. Nevertheless, given modern argot, I felt we should change the title. I mean, 'Whistling Dick'? Think of the children!"

"Smart move," Eddie replied. "Shows you got good commercial instincts."

Tuck gestured to his boyfriend. "Punch here is the star

of the piece. He plays a jaunty hobo named Dick. After surviving a harrowing set of circumstances, Dick saves a kindly family from robbery and ruin on a chilly Christmas Eve."

"It's a lovely part," Punch said. "But it does have its challenges."

"He's talking about Dick's big climax," Tuck explained (and he actually said it with a straight face).

"Go on," Eddie said, nodding with interest. "What does Dick do to climax?"

Oh good heavens.

"Well, Dick is a hobo, and he's learned that other hobos—bad ones—are planning to break into this nice family's home and rob them during the night. A little girl inside was kind to him, and he doesn't want to see her hurt. But the bad hobos learn Dick is going to warn the family, so they hold him prisoner at their bad hobo camp."

Eddie was on the edge of his seat. "Go on!"

"Well, Dick can see the family's house on the hill, so he writes a note, warning them of the robbery, attaches it to a rock, and uses a lady's stocking that he's been carrying around to shoot it through their window when his hobo guard isn't looking."

"I don't get it?" Eddie said. "How does a lady's stocking help you hurl a rock?"

Tuck turned to his partner. "Punch, show Eddie how it's done."

Punch shook his head. "I don't know—"

"Come on," Tuck coaxed. "Your costume and props are in your backpack."

"Okay, okay." Punch leaned over and rummaged through his bag, coming up with a red-and-white-striped woman's stocking and a rock roughly the size of a tennis ball.

"Here's how Whistling Dick saves the day . . ." Punch dropped the rock into the stocking and began to spin it over his head. The rock pushed against the toe of the sock, stretching the material in a colorful display. The rock literally began whistling around his head.

"When I let go, it flies all the way to the other side of the theater, where it breaks a false window. Fake glass rains down and everything. It's amazing. A real show stop—"

With a sudden snap the stocking flew out of Punch's hand. Like a candy cane firework, it sailed in a red and white arc across the landmark coffeehouse and right through a pane of glass in our wall of French doors.

Shattered shards crashed to the hardwood floor, thankfully near no customers. Outside, there was a bang, and a car alarm began to wail.

Oh crap.

For a moment, everyone gaped at the broken window.

Then Eddie Rayburn broke into peals of laughter. "I hope you have better control in front of an audience, Whistling Dick," he said, chuckling. "I mean, think of the children!"

Eddie grabbed his hat and buttoned up his coat. "I'll see you people on Friday!" Still laughing, he walked out the door.

"I'll get the broom," Nancy said.

"Oh goodness, Clare. I'm so sorry!" Tuck cried.

"Me too," said a contrite Punch.

"Don't worry about it. We're insured." *With a five-hundred-dollar deductible* . . . I sighed. *Making that one very expensive climax.*

Tuck slumped in his chair. "Maybe I should have staged 'The Little Match Girl.'"

"Why didn't you?" Nancy asked, broom and dustpan in hand.

"I wanted to, but the producers at the Children's Theatre found the story of an abused little girl, trying to avoid going home on Christmas Eve, only to freeze to death instead, was just *a tad* depressing for a young holiday audience."

Nancy looked up from her sweeping. "You're right, Tuck. 'The Little Match Girl' is really depressing. But at least *she* wouldn't have made such a mess for me to clean up!"

⊥HIRⱫY-FIVE

⟰⟰⟰⟰⟰⟰⟰⟰⟰⟰⟰⟰⟰⟰⟰⟰⟰⟰⟰⟰⟰

⊥HE rest of the week went by without further incident (or broken windows, thank you very much). Then Friday rolled around, bringing another party.

True to his word, Eddie Rayburn attended. The Double Ds came, too, along with hockey star Ross Puckett, and a few more suspicious guests.

Much of this would be recounted to the responding detectives because, in the end, another poor young woman would be killed by repeated blows to the head, just like Moirin. And like the previous Cookie Swap, the timeline for this bash held the clues to the basher.

Oddly enough, the key events began, as they did the week before, on the subject of coffee stirrers . . .

"I *said*, do you have enough?" Matt yelled.

"Enough what?" I called from behind the red and white counter. "Come around, so I can hear you!"

Matt struggled through the buzzing crowd to my side of the café counter.

We were swamped with customers—girls in pretty party dresses, boys in tiny suits, adults in designer evening wear, and full-grown men in elf tights and felt hats.

The location for tonight's fund-raiser was the most famous toy store in the world. Catering to the pampered and privileged, this legendary Fifth Avenue establishment featured high-end merchandise displayed across three vast floors, personal shoppers, a private party room, and an event consultant.

My staff and I were located in the rear of the first floor, where we'd taken over the store's little café.

"Last week, you told me that everyone at the first Cookie Swap wanted a swirl-it-yourself Caramel Latte," Matt said. "So are you short on stirrers again?"

"No. Tonight, we're about to run out of—"

"Plastic swizzle sticks!" Tucker and Esther finished together, hands busy filling orders.

"Our Gumdrop Spritzers have been *flying* out of here," I explained to Matt. "We're offering every flavor a gumdrop comes in: cherry, lemon, lime, orange, mint, grape—"

"And we slide an actual gumdrop onto each drink's swizzle stick before serving it," Tuck added.

While Europeans routinely added high-quality coffeehouse bar syrups to sparkling water, most Americans had never seen baristas blend them with anything but espressos and steamed milk. But freshly made sodas carried remarkably bright and powerful flavor. There was really no comparison to a pre-bottled or canned soda, and many of tonight's guests were getting their first taste of them.

"We're even mixing the drinks to order," Esther jumped in, "and kids are suggesting some fun combos, too— cinnamon-orange, cherry-vanilla, and mint-chocolate."

"Who knew a simple Italian-style soda could beat out a caramel latte?" Matt said.

"I did," Tuck smugly replied.

"That's true, you did," I conceded.

"And how did he know?" Matt asked.

"Tucker Burton's Death of Popularity theorem," Esther declared.

"A little philosophy I have about customer behavior," Tuck explained, handing out a smile with another gumdrop drink. "When Thing A catches on, the mere whiff of its popularity makes it even *more* popular; but soon A becomes *so* popular that it's considered common, humdrum, and consequently dropped like a pet rock in exchange for Thing B. Then B becomes so popular, it's dropped for Thing C, and so on down the variable alphabet."

"That's not just customer behavior," Matt said. "That's human behavior." He turned to me. "So you need a hand?"

Esther cackled. "You're going to pull shots and texture milk in that outfit?"

I patted his shoulder. "Sorry, Matt. She's right. You're not dressed for the part. But I must say, you *do* clean up very well." (A serious understatement . . .)

Matt's fitted Armani jacket draped like flowing black water over his muscular frame, and the whiter-than-white dress shirt, worn with a fashionably open collar, was pressed to perfection. (No burger grease stains tonight.)

As for the rest of him, in recent months, Matt's flirtation with facial hair had him swinging from goatee to trendy scruff to mountain-man beard and back again. Tonight he'd shaved close and clean, reacquainting me with the strong line of his jaw. His raven locks appeared trimmed, too— still long enough to look rakish, yet neatly brushed back, giving him an air of relaxed elegance.

The man looked good enough to eat, and I told him so (although not in those *exact* words).

"Thanks." He grinned. "But Bree should get the credit. She dressed me."

"She *dressed* you? What? Like a life-sized Ken doll? Hey, doesn't this place sell those?"

"Wrong floor." Matt jerked his thumb up. "Barbie and Ken are on the mezzanine. *You*, however, are located on the first floor, which features stuffed animals and Muppets."

"The perfect shopping floor for you. I've met a number of your 'extracurricular' lady friends. Stuffing-for-brains pretty much describes them."

"Very funny."

"Oh, come on, admit it," I said. "Tuck's Death of Popularity theorem sums up your love life."

"It does not." He folded his arms. "For one thing, I don't do anything alphabetically."

"You mean your little black book is arranged *phonetically*?"

"Okay, okay . . ." Matt formed a time-out T with his hands. "I didn't come here to discuss my little black book. I came here to relieve you."

"Excuse me?"

"I'm losing my jacket and rolling up my sleeves," he said. "Just take off your apron, hand it over, and then you can, well—take off."

"Why would I do that?"

"Because Janelle Babcock wants to talk with you."

"Janelle? Can't it wait?"

"Apparently not. She grabbed my arm and said she needed to see you, ASAP. She's very upset with you, Clare."

"With me? Why?"

"She says you betrayed her."

"What?" I cried. "I'm Janelle's friend! How could I betray her?"

Matt showed me his palms. "She wouldn't say, and her display table was swamped so she sent me to get you."

"Give it ten minutes," Tuck called over to us. "Her mob scene will disperse—and so will ours."

"What happens in ten minutes?" Matt asked.

"A surprise floor show in the grand entrance," Tuck said. "I heard it from one of the personal shopping elves—an actor friend." He filled us in. "Every kid will rush to see *this* show when they announce it, and the parents and their camcorders won't be far behind."

"Just go, boss," Esther insisted. "Mr. Boss can go, too. Tuck and I got this covered."

"You're sure?"

The two nodded, and I pulled off my apron.

"Brace yourself, Clare," Matt warned. "It's a madhouse out there."

"Then by all means—" I extended my arm.

ⲦHIRTY-SIX

~~~~~~~~~~~~~~~~

Dodging kids, nannies, elves, and flying gumdrops, we maneuvered our way through the open café area, which flowed right into the store's colorful candy shop. That's when Matt got bonked by a balloon bouquet and I was pelted by a hail of jelly beans.

"We can make it!" Matt assured me, and I followed his end run around the Necco Wafers display and onto the toy industry's equivalent of a jam-packed main street.

At the other end of this crowded center aisle the grand entrance rose up with three stories of spotless plate glass, forming a massive Fifth Avenue storefront. Matt gestured toward the impressive lobby.

"Did my mother give you the rundown on what's going on up there?"

"Too busy—both of us. What's the deal?"

Matt briefly described the red-carpet treatment for tonight's guest families.

"Two living toy soldiers greet them at the door, then four Nutcracker ballerinas dance them to the coat check and usher them to the 'photo-op area,' where their pictures are supposed to be taken with the stars of some new hit kiddie movie: *Santa Zombie* something?"

"*Santa Claus, Zombie Hunter.*"

"That's the one. And, of course, right next to the faux Hollywood set, the store is displaying its entire line of toys from the movie . . ."

Of course! I thought. *And so convenient for purchase.* But then that was the draw for tonight's location: one-stop holiday shopping.

The kids had the run of the place all night. They could play with the display toys, enjoy interactive exhibits, munch on free cookies, all while making up their gift lists for Santa Claus.

An army of personal shoppers, dressed as Santa's elves, kept track of these lists. And every elf knew *just* how to process a titanium credit card.

It was a dream come true for any child (at least the ones whose parents could afford it).

Matt looked a little like a child himself as he gawked at the floor-to-ceiling displays of toys and games. "I think it's been like fifteen years since I was last in this place. I was trying to buy new ice skates for Joy."

"Except this toy store doesn't sell ice skates."

"Yeah, I figured that out—after about an hour of screwing around." He shook his head. "You have to admit, this is one cool place."

"Oh sure, especially if you're in the market for an eight-thousand-dollar stuffed giraffe or twenty-five-thousand-dollar Barbie Foosball table."

"Aw, come on, Clare. I know you're down about what happened to Moirin. I am, too. But it's not like you to be cynical. Aren't those gumdrop drinks of yours bringing back a few good memories? When Joy was little, didn't you show her how to make her own gumdrops?"

"I'm surprised you remember that."

"Of course I do . . ." He paused, then said, "It wasn't all

bad. Our little family had a lot of good times, didn't it? You even made Gumdrop Cookies out of those homemade gumdrops. They were one of Joy's favorites."

"But not yours." I gave him a weak smile. "You always asked me to make my—"

"New York Cheesecake Cookies. I remember!" He nodded then sighed. "I haven't had one of those in years. Too bad Bree doesn't bake."

"Your wife's here tonight, isn't she?"

"Not yet, but there are so many tall, thin salon-blondes at functions like this, I may have trouble locating her."

"Why don't you stand at the door and watch for her fur?"

"Furs are out this year." He waved his hand. "She's been wearing that new Fen reversible coat. It's all the rage this season, or so she says."

"She's right. I saw it on a few women last week." *Can't afford it, but I saw it.*

"Red, black, who knows what side she'll show the public," Matt griped. "I told her to text me when the cab pulls up."

"Speaking of texts . . . did you get the one from Desdemona in Crete? Something like next time she'll bring the grappa?"

"You know what? I'd appreciate it if you *didn't* read my text messages."

"Believe me, I didn't mean to. I thought you were trying to reach me."

"No. But I have a suggestion. The next time you jump into a sports car with an ex–rock star, bring your own cell phone."

"So I assume you'd prefer I not mention Desdemona to Bree?"

"Hey, listen, just because I shared a bottle of grappa with a socialite whose father happens to own a chain of cafés across Greece doesn't mean anything nonkosher went on."

"So Breanne knows about Desdemona?"

"Does Quinn know you shared a pizza with 'Wildman' Brice?"

"Let's drop the subject."

"Yes, let's . . ."

During our barbwired trek through the crowded store, we were continually passing bakers' stations. Their tables were positioned to the right and left of the center aisle, around elaborate toy displays.

Tonight's Cookie Swap theme was "Global Goodies: Holiday Cookies from Around the World," and once again the participating bakers provided delicious delights. There were holiday treats from Norway and the Netherlands, the Ukraine and Poland, Italy, Ireland, Great Britain, and the Middle East. (I was so stressed-out, even this dazzling variety of cookies couldn't tempt me!)

"Are you sure you don't know why Janelle is upset with me?" I tried asking Matt again.

"I swear I don't."

"It's not like her . . ."

At last, near the shop's grand entrance, we came upon Janelle's French-themed table. The spread was stunning. She not only filled her display with cookies but bite-sized masterpieces of French pastry.

My eyes went wide, my saliva glands awakened, and (stress be damned) my rumbling stomach announced it was time to start sampling!

Thirty-Seven

∿∿∿∿∿∿∿∿∿∿∿∿∿∿∿∿

Given her culinary training, I expected Janelle's table to be a Gallic delight, but her New Orleans roots were on display, too, and I was pleased to see it.

During her years in the Big Easy, Janelle had created impressive desserts for minor then major restaurants. But her contributions to the city's famous "Reveillon" dinners were what earned her national attention.

Reveillon, derived from the French word for "awakening," was a Creole holiday feast dating back to the 1700s. Families returning from Midnight Mass on Christmas Eve dug into this lavish meal. The tradition fell out of favor until NOLA's restaurants revived and transformed it into a citywide prix fixe dinner—multiple courses of spectacular dishes that would "awaken" the holiday spirit.

Once, in my coffeehouse, over late-night lattes, Janelle recounted some of her past holiday dessert courses to me. I swooned at her descriptions of Eggnog Crème Brûlée served with Pecan Brittle; Cherries in Snow Vol-au-Vent; and "New Orleans Gingerbread" (aka spiced Cajun *Gâteau de*

Sirop) plated with warm Caramel Bourbon Sauce and cane syrup–sweetened Crème Fraiche.

She served Bananas Foster Tarte Tatins; White Chocolate Pots de Crème with tiny Candy Cane Cookies hanging off the rims; Pain Perdu Holiday Bread Pudding (a dish that inspired my own plans for Mike Quinn's Christmas morning breakfast); and finally a Spiced Pumpkin Roulade with Cream Cheese Filling.

(Rolling cake was a tricky technique, but Janelle's description sounded so festive that I adapted it for my coffeehouse customers into a much simpler Cream Cheese Swirl Pumpkin Bundt Cake—sold by the slice!)

"This is an amazing spread," Matt gushed.

"And clearly we're not the only ones who think so . . ."

The table was so crowded with guests that Janelle didn't notice our arrival. She stood at the far end of the display in her colorful Mardi Gras chef's jacket and toque. A group of women in elegant party dresses had gathered around to hear her explain the difference between a French praline and a New Orleans praline—both of which were represented on her table.

Closer to our end, Janelle's newly hired assistant, Boris Bokunin, was busy replenishing the stock. As fast as some little hand grabbed a doily with a pastry, Esther's boyfriend refilled the empty space.

Wiry and tightly wound, Boris was a sweet guy at heart with perceptive gray eyes. He wore his blond hair in short, scary spikes and sported tattoos under his white baker's jacket, yet his manner was always respectful.

Though no taller than Esther, Boris typically vibrated with the compacted energy of a firecracker. But tonight he seemed tired, and I knew why. He'd been working around the clock to help Janelle prepare for this Swap.

I also noticed the usually loquacious young man (aka "Russian émigré, slam poet, and urban rapper"—in Esther's words) was staying *unusually* quiet tonight. He nodded affably at each guest, but if anyone asked him a question, he pointed out Janelle.

"Miss J, she has no problem with my accent," he explained when I asked why no spontaneous rapping tonight. "But I do not wish to confuse the people."

"You mean because you're serving at the French table?"

"*Da*." He nodded. ". . . though a Russian chef at a French table is not so strange. Of noble traditions, I *could* explain of Catherine the Great and dishes invented on Franco-Russian plates—" (He wasn't kidding—beef Stroganoff was a classic of this marriage, and one of my faves.)

But he shrugged. "Why bother? These kiddies have no patience for learning such things. They *want* their goodies and their little kid *bling*."

"I understand," I said. "On the other hand, I always enjoy your rapping."

"You are a sweet lady, Clare Cosi. So for *you*, the boss lady of my beautiful Esther . . ." He leaned close. "Clare Cosi, Clare Cosi / a fresh urban posy / have a taste of these treats / a miraculous feat / of butter and cream / and sweet pastry dreams."

Now *there* was the Boris I knew—and Esther loved.

I smiled. "Don't mind if I do . . ."

Then I dug in, and Matt joined me.

We started with Janelle's miniature Yule Logs, what the French called *la bûche de Noël*, a rolled cake made of chocolate and chestnuts, representing the special wood log burned on Christmas Eve. Then we moved on to her bite-sized triple-chocolate Mille-Feuille.

Literally translated, these "one thousand sheets" of buttery, crisp chocolate puff pastry were layered with mocha pastry cream, topped off with ganache, and sliced into small sampler squares.

Both of us tried the petite Red and Green Macarons (pistachio meringue cookies with raspberry buttercream) and tiny *Budino Blancs*—Janelle's clever white-chocolate-dipped marzipan version of the traditional French Christmas sausage *boudin blanc*.

Then Matt gobbled three Mendiant Cookies. These were

my friend's take on the traditional French Christmas candy. (Instead of tempered chocolate, she smoothed ganache over the surface of buttery French sablés, using the chocolate icing as her canvas for the traditional studding of nuts and candied fruit.)

Finally, I sampled the Tuiles . . .

No doubt Janelle added these light, crisp French cookies after last week's brush with the perpetually dieting models and actresses. *(Smart!)* Even I felt zero guilt scarfing her three varieties of sweet, delicious curls—orange-pecan flavored with Grand Marnier; mocha with chocolate and Tia Maria; and traditional almond with a hint of Amaretto.

"Ladies and gentlemen!"

I stilled, midcrunch on my Mocha Tuile, as the announcer's deep voice blared over the store's public address speakers.

"Rudolph the Red-Nosed Supersonic Robo-Rocket is about to land on our plaza with a special gift for you! So come to the front of the store to watch from our grand lobby or bundle up in your coats—and come outside to watch the show and meet Robo-Rocket Rudolph in person!"

Matt and I blocked our ears as every child in the store shrieked with excitement. Then the stampede was on. Party dresses and little suits flung themselves down the center aisle, their elegant parents hurrying to catch up, personal shopping elves bringing up the rear.

Matt got bonked again by flying balloons, and I was shoved so hard by some man trying to film his excited child's sprint that I literally leaped behind Janelle's table to avoid crashing into it!

When the pixie dust settled, you could practically hear crickets chirp. Up and down the now-empty aisle, bakers glanced around in a kind of daze, wondering what, in the name of Santa, had just happened.

Matt, Boris, and I now stood completely alone. At the other end of the table, Janelle finally realized I'd come by. Turning, she locked eyes with me, and her smile turned upside down.

"You!" she cried, stabbing the air with her finger. "I have a bone to pick with you!"

"For heaven's sake, Janelle, what did I do?"

"I'll tell you what you did!" she cried, barreling close enough to bite my nose off. "You took a big ol' carving knife—and stabbed me right in the back!"

Thirty-Eight

~~~~~~~~~~~~~~~~~~~~~~~~~~~~~~~~~~~~~

I stood bewildered, mouth gaping. "Janelle, what are you talking about?"

"How could you not warn me that St. Nick was here!"

"St. Nick?"

Fearing for Janelle's sanity, I exchanged confused looks with Matt. Was she working too hard?

"What's your problem with Santa Claus?" I asked.

"Not Santa Claus!" She threw up her hands. "*St. Nick Bacque*!"

"Who?"

She tried again to explain, and I assured her: "I have *no idea* who you're talking about. Who is 'St. Nick' Bacque?"

"Do you remember my mentioning my 'expensive' employee problems? Well, Nick was it! He comes off sweeter than praline—he'll *yes* you to death, smooth talk you, tell you anything you want to hear. Then you find out he's a thieving snake!"

"But what does that have to do with me?"

Janelle's powerful baker's hands went to her ample hips. "Your employer—and former mother-in-law—is on the board of this thing, isn't she? I figured you and she knew all about it. And you didn't even warn me that he'd be here! How could you let a snake like him wrap himself around potential high-end customers at a function like this?"

"But I've never even met this St. Nick!"

She froze, staring at me, finally thinking it through.

"Oh my gosh . . . you never did, did you?"

The fury seemed to drain out of her and she shook her head. "Nick worked nights, baking for me, eleven to seven. I guess you never did have cause to come by my shop during those hours . . ."

"We're friends, Janelle. Why didn't you ever mention the problems this man caused you?"

She looked away and her body slumped even more. "Nick came to me as a friend from home—a cousin of a gentleman chef who gave me one of my first big breaks. Well, I was happy to do the same for him, but he turned out to be a real piece of work. He cost me plenty."

"You could have shared some of these details with me."

"I was embarrassed by the whole thing. It showed my stupidity as a new business owner, and I didn't want you thinking badly of me. You're a friend, Clare, but you're also a good customer, and I didn't want to shake your confidence in my ability to run my bakery well . . ."

My mind began working. "Janelle, when this St. Nick worked with you, did he spend any time with Moirin Fagan?"

"Of course! M was one of my two part-time girls, and after I fired him—for sexually harassing my other girl, who quit on me—I promoted M. She jumped right in and started doing double shifts. She was like an angel to me."

"Where is this guy?" I peered down the first-floor aisle.

"He's on the mezzanine," Janelle said. "I haven't seen him yet, but half an hour ago, a customer asked me about the *other* chef here who got his start in New Orleans. She handed me his business card, and Boris had to hold me back from storming up there and strangling the snake!"

Matt broke in. "I think I know who you mean, Janelle.

And I think I know why the organizers put him on the mezzanine." He smirked. "Boy Toys and Barbies."

"What do you mean?" Janelle and I asked in unison.

Matt checked his watch. "That kiddie show is supposed to last forty minutes. Why don't we go upstairs right now? Boris can watch Janelle's table, and you two ladies can *see* what I mean."

THIRTY-NINE

WE hurried down the deserted main aisle, took the escalator up to the mezzanine level, and I stopped dead at the top. Unfortunately the stairs kept moving and Matt crashed into me.

"Clare! What are you—"

"It's him," I whispered.

"Him who?" Matt asked.

"The Mystery Man!"

"Another superhero?" Matt quipped, glancing at the action figure display. "I can't keep track."

"Mystery Man isn't a toy . . ." I pointed. "He's the man I thought was Dave. The one I saw Moirin talking with right before she was murdered!"

Janelle followed my finger and smirked. "That's no man, honey. *That* is St. Nick, my former assistant baker, and a sneaky varmint in sheep's clothing!"

"That's Nick Bacque?" I faced her. "Why didn't you tell me he was the one who spoke to Moirin at the last Cookie Swap?!"

"Clare, I had no idea that man was even at the last Swap!

The only guy you asked me about was Dave, and you never described him to me!"

Matt frowned. "Whoever he is, ladies, the guy's a real operator."

I glanced back across the mezzanine and saw what Matt meant. It appeared Nick was taking full advantage of the deserted floor. He'd left his own baker's station in the Boys' Toys section and moseyed over to Dolls to hit on the beautiful honey-blond baker positioned there—Rita Limon.

I remembered Rita from the last Swap. Her "Little Match Girl" table was incredibly clever, especially those edible matchsticks—Cherry-Topped Brandy Snaps, the ones that hockey star Ross Puckett tried to get a buzz from by sucking out the fillings.

It was clear to me now why the party organizers stationed this attractive pair up here. Nick Bacque was the perfect boy toy: a young raven-haired Ken doll in black formal wear and black silk shirt.

Rita Limon was a vivacious young Barbie. Even from this distance, I was impressed with her South American–themed display table. And I could understand why the opposite sex would find her physical charms even more appealing than her pastries.

In her short, pencil-thin dress of gold glitter, Rita was a striking vision with salon-colored hair that flowed like honey in a stylishly smooth ponytail down to her narrow waist. Fit and young, she projected an air of approachable elegance.

Nick Bacque was certainly captivated. We watched while he attempted to nuzzle Rita's neck—until she roughly shoved him away. From that gesture, and the unhappy expression on her harried face, she needed someone to run interference.

"Let's help her out," Matt said, stepping forward, but I held him back.

"No. I don't want you to rattle this guy, Matt . . ." *Not before he answers my questions about Moirin.* "Let Janelle and me handle him."

Matt folded his arms. "Are you sure?"

I scanned the mezzanine. "Tell you what. Be our backup. You go left, circle around through the Boy Toys display. Janelle and I will move straight in and confront him head-on in the Barbie section. You can come up behind him, and if we're in any trouble you can jump in."

"Got it!"

With our battle plan set, Matt took off through the super-hero aisle.

And just in time, too. Nick's advances were becoming more aggressive, and Rita was losing control of the situation. I paused to decide on the best approach, but Janelle was not nearly so cautious.

"Take your slimy hands off that woman, you skeevy little skunk!" she bellowed, storming forward.

So much for not rattling the guy!

FORTY

~~~~~~~~~~~~~~~~~~~~~~~~~

NICK saw Janelle's determined charge and backed off, but only a little. Janelle continued her blitz, rolling right up to him, hands on hips.

"Well, well, if it isn't my old straw boss," Nick said with a smarmy smile.

"Straw boss?!" Janelle blinked at the terrible insult, obviously hurt. "How could you call me that? I gave you a valuable apprenticing opportunity, taught you, worked side by side with you. I was no straw boss. I was a *real* boss, and you stole from me."

By now, I'd caught up with the bickering pair, and Rita Limon exchanged surprised glances with me. Together we watched the two go at it.

"I stole from you?" Nick scoffed. "You are either confused, or stupid."

"Neither," Janelle replied. "I was naive. Trusting. But I caught up with your tricks. You were double ordering everything, only I never saw the other half of those deliveries, did I?"

Nick smirked and folded his arms. "You signed off on

every order I placed. If there were errors, you should have caught them earlier."

"There were no errors!" Janelle cried. "The stuff came in the front door, and went out the back—and always when you were on duty."

Nick practically laughed through Janelle's rant. "There is nothin' you can prove. I got you pegged right, darlin' . . . *Stupid*."

"Excuse me, Nick," I interrupted. "But I saw you talking with Moirin Fagan at the last Cookie Swap. What were you two discussing?"

Nick seemed to notice me for the first time. He ran his eyes along my body, from my simple black dress to my work-ready ponytail and low-heeled pumps. Certainly, I was no Rita, but that didn't stop the man from switching on the smarmy charm.

"Why do you need to know, sweet thing? Were you jealous?"

"I want to know because she's dead."

"I know she's dead. I read the papers. You think I killed that little thing?"

I met his gaze head-on. "I don't know what you're capable of. Answer my question."

"Sure, sugar. Come closer. I'll whisper it into your cute little ear."

Nick snaked his arm around my waist. Janelle exhaled in disgust as I quickly slipped his grip.

"You told Moirin what?" I demanded.

"I asked Moirin if she wanted a raise. I wanted to hire her for my new bakery." Like a stage magician, Nick flicked his fingers and a business card appeared between them.

"Give me a call," he purred. "I'm hungry for business, and I cater to . . . *every* need."

He tried to tuck the card into my cleavage. I slapped his hand *hard*.

"Why, you're a little spitfire, Clare Cosi. I like that!" He grinned wide, as if this was a game—one he enjoyed playing.

"How do you know my name?" I demanded.

"I know lots of names in this town, sweet thing. The ones that count. And I can provision your little ol' landmark coffeehouse, too."

"Over my dead body," I replied boldly. (To be honest, I was bolstered by the sight of Matt skulking behind Nick, near a display for radio-controlled cars.) "And I'd like to know just how you managed to wheedle your way into the Cookie Swap with a barely opened bakery?"

"Last week, I dropped by the Bryant Park Grill to let the Swap director know I'd be happy to help out at the last minute—if any of her other bakers let her down. Well, Sobel's Bake Shop . . . you know the joint? On the Upper East Side? Poor Sam had a fire on Monday, a real bad one. I once did a little part-time work for him, so I stepped in to pass out *Lebkuchen*, *Pfeffernüsse* . . ." He snapped his fingers; another card appeared there. "And a whole lot of business cards."

He offered it to Janelle this time. She ripped it to pieces.

"You prefer my cell phone app?" he quipped.

"What else did you and M talk about?" I demanded.

Nick shrugged. "I might have warned Moirin to be real careful with the recipes she 'shares' while she's working for Janelle."

"What are you saying?" Janelle cried, bewildered.

"How many dang recipes did I come up with? Recipes that you peddled to food companies? To websites and magazines? Where do you get off calling *me* a thief, straw boss? I'm the guy who got cheated!"

"I paid you good money for those recipes," Janelle shot back. "And you knew the score. Everything you created belonged to me."

"Produce a contract that states that in writing and I won't call you a damned liar."

Janelle's face softened, as she tried to understand Nick's betrayal.

"I hired you as a colleague, Nick, and a friend. We did business on a handshake—"

"In writing," Nick said, expression hardening.

Janelle's expression soured, too. "You knew the score, Nick."

"And you're a cheat, Straw Boss—"

"¡Ay Dios mio! Will you shut up already?"

The command came from an unexpected source: Rita Limon, and it was followed by a string of Spanish invective that began with "¡Tonto de burro estúpido!" and ended with something that, accompanied by a hand gesture, seemed obscene enough to make world-traveling, multilingual-cursing Matt Allegro blush.

"You're just like my ex-husband," Rita continued. "All charm and big talk, which slowly turns into intimidation and lies. You are nothing but a con man, Bacque."

Rita's verbal assault was unexpected. It embarrassed Nick while killing any hopes he may have harbored for hooking up with her tonight. It was enough to melt down his Cajun cool.

"You wetback bitch," he bit out. "Who you callin' a con man—"

Nick physically lurched toward Rita. I was sure he was going to strike her, but before Janelle or I could stop him, he was cut short by a huge, radio-controlled outback jeep that somehow slammed right under his legs.

With a howl Nick flew backward, crashing over the toy and into a display of limited-edition Prince William Ken dolls. Boxes covered with colorful Union Jack packaging rained down on the sputtering Cajun.

I whirled in time to see Matt toss aside a remote control, then hurry forward to help Nick to his feet.

"Sorry about that, old sport," Matt said, affecting a fairly convincing upper-crust, yacht-cap-wearing, lockjaw tone. "Can't imagine where that toy came from! Perhaps you should get back to your table before something else happens?"

Nick, livid and sputtering curses, tried to break away from Matt.

"Now, we don't want any trouble," Matt warned. "Or I'll

be forced to report you to Mother, an influential member of the Cookie Swap board."

In a fraction of time that defied particle physics, the furious, violent Nick Bacque was replaced by the charming St. Nick.

"Oh my! Please excuse my off-color remarks, sir. And thank you so much for your assistance," he said, gushing oilier than a well of Texas crude. "Perhaps I can give you my business card?"

"A capital idea!" Matt declared, throwing me an eye roll as he led the jerk away.

FORTY-ONE

⚬⚬⚬⚬⚬⚬⚬⚬⚬⚬⚬⚬⚬⚬⚬⚬⚬⚬⚬⚬⚬

WITH a firm hand on Nick's shoulder, Matt guided the Cajun boy toy back to the Boys' Toys.

"I think he'll behave now," Matt said when he rejoined us.

"Thank you, *amigo*. I can't stand men like that!" Rita confessed. "Probably because I married someone just like him. I was young. *Estúpido*."

Rita spoke with a Latin lilt, but her English was perfect.

"Can you believe that *puto* wanted to hook up in that little kid's party room after the Swap?" She gestured to a frosted glass door beside the store's giant floor piano. "He suggested we have a *little party* of our own."

"Ooooo, yuck!" Janelle and I cried together. (The toys must have been getting to us. We were starting to sound like little girls at a slumber party.)

"Your table is awesome, Rita," Janelle gushed.

"Totally," I said, nodding in agreement.

"Thank you! *Please*, sample anything you like!"

Matt grinned and rubbed his hands together. "I think I'll start with a *Brigadeiro*."

Rita laughed. "Nostalgia?"

"Yeah. We both know they're not exactly haute cuisine," Matt replied, accepting the tiny paper holder from Rita's manicured fingers. Inside was the simple, chocolate-sprinkle-covered truffle.

"What is that?" I asked.

Rita smiled. "Try one! No children's party in Brazil is complete without it."

"I've been to enough of them to know," Matt replied and popped the tiny, sweet ball into his mouth.

I bit into mine and my taste buds were instantly drenched in creamy fudge deliciousness. An extra depth of flavor told me coffee also lurked somewhere in Rita's unique recipe.

"I'll have one of these eight-pointed stars," Janelle said. "They're made of puff pastry, I see." When she bit into the treat, the crust crumbled all over her chef's jacket.

"My bad," Rita said, passing Janelle an extra napkin. "I'm still new at this. Serving *Pastelitos de Cajeta* at a party like this was a big mistake."

"Don't sweat it, honey," Janelle replied. "You'll learn. That's why I cut my napoleons into bite-sized pieces. We all make mistakes. But at least yours is a delicious mistake!"

"Aw, thank you!"

Janelle finished her star and brushed the mess away. "And the *cajeta*—it reminds me of penuche! You make your caramel from goat's milk, right?"

Rita nodded. "And a bit of rum. So yummy."

I reached for a simple shortbread cookie from a tray of them, shaped like stars, bells, and angels. As I suspected, the cookie melted in my mouth like butter—or, more precisely, lard.

The New York's food police might not approve, but animal fat was a staple of Latin American cuisine. Anise tickled my nose, and from the sugary sweetness of the cinnamon, I guessed this was a Mexican delicacy.

"New Mexican," Rita explained. "*Biscochitos* are a favorite at Christmastime. You'll find them all over the Southwest, too. I saw them in Arizona, when I worked as a cook at a resort spa." She laughed. "I couldn't serve them, though. Not at a health spa!"

"How long have you been at this, girl?" Janelle asked, as impressed as I was by her skill.

"My sister and I both baked all of our lives. When I first came to America, I worked at the resort. One of the ladies who went there liked my dishes so much that she brought me here to New York, and I became a personal chef to her wealthy family. The pay was good, and I saved up enough money to bring my sister Linda to America. Then I caught a little break with some TV exposure. It helped me find backers, and I was finally able to quit my personal chef's job and partner with my sister to open our dream bakery."

Matt's yummy sounds were interrupted by a sharp buzz. "Damn," he said, checking the text message. "Breanne is outside, waiting."

Matt extended his hand. "Wonderful to see you again, Rita."

"And you, *amigo*," she replied, her smile as radiant as it was genuine. "Come visit us sometime! All of you! The main shop is near Columbia University, and we just opened a kiosk in Grand Central's food court."

Matt promised he would and departed.

I invited Rita to stop by my Village Blend, and she said she looked forward to it.

"Well, I'd better go, too," I said.

Rita, Janelle, and I shared hugs. Then we headed our separate ways, and my mind started working.

When this party is over, I'm calling Lori Soles . . .

Nick Bacque was bad news, and she needed to hear all about him.

I also planned to catch Rita before she left tonight. Once I got her away from Nick's line of sight, I'd ask her about the first Cookie Swap. Last week, her station had been near the front doors. She might have seen Nick follow Moirin outside or even heard a conversation between the two—

A simple statement from Rita Limon to the police could help begin to close Moirin's case.

"Is Rita still up there?"

The question interrupted my thoughts. I was just step-ping off the escalator when a woman approached me. It took a moment, but I recognized her.

She wore makeup tonight, and her mouse-brown hair had been styled to curve perfectly around her chin. She wore a red party dress, too. But even if I hadn't remem-bered her from our brief encounter at the Bryant Park ice rink, I would have known her by tonight's two nanny iden-tifiers: a utility tote bag over her shoulder instead of a designer purse; and the cheap, flat shoes. (You can't wear designer heels when you're tasked with three solid hours of chasing after high-energy children.)

"Oh, hello," I said. "How are you enjoying this week's Swap? Did you ever try our Candy Cane Latte?"

The nanny seemed puzzled a moment, then smiled brightly. "Oh, that's right! I remember! Yes, yes, that latte was delicious."

"Tonight, I recommend the Gumdrop Spritzers. If you're not too busy you should definitely try one."

She nodded. "Caught a break just now. The little Ray-burn kids are watching the show." She touched my arm. "So do you know if Rita Limon is up there now?"

I nodded. "On the mezzanine. Look straight down the main aisle to the Barbie section. You can't miss her display. It's wonderful."

"Yes, I've really missed her cookies," the nanny called over her shoulder as she headed off.

Forty-two

~~~~~~~~~~~~~~~~~~~~~~~~~~~~~~~~~~~~~~

As I arrived back at the store's café, a deafening whoop erupted from the audience crowding the front of the store. The fireworks had begun.

According to Tuck's showbiz source, the Robo-Rudolph show began with sing-along songs by Santa; then came fireworks on the plaza; followed by Rudolph emerging from a life-sized Red-Nosed Supersonic Robo-Rocket.

The plucky robot reindeer would pantomime a prerecorded song and dance number called "Don't Die On Me, Christmas." Then he'd greet the children while his army of elf-helpers handed out promotional T-shirts—which meant my staff and I had roughly fifteen minutes of relative calm before we were mobbed again.

Tucker was making the most of his downtime, icing glasses for a new round of Gumdrop Spritzers while Esther gleefully impaled innocent gumdrops with swizzle sticks.

"The whole thing is just *weird*," Esther was saying to Tuck. "And I usually like weird. I'll even admit, when I see some of the holiday shoppers who stumble into the Blend, they actually resemble zombies. But mashing up the walking dead with the most festive season of the year? I just don't see it."

"The zombies that Santa Claus battles in the movie aren't dead. They're simply under an evil spell," Tuck explained. "Also they don't eat flesh; they gobble up all the holiday sweets they can find. Plus these zombies can be cured by the right song, which is being piped in here even as we speak."

Esther listened for a moment, then shrugged. "So the only drawback to zombie-itis is bad movie music and possible type 2 diabetes?"

Tuck fixed her with his gaze. "Admit it, Snark Grinch. Those are two scary propositions!"

Before Esther could reply, I noticed something just as frightening: a pair of ruby-sequined predators moving through the sweetshop's candy aisles like lionesses through a rainbow veldt.

Big Danni Rayburn burst from cover first. She bounced on tiptoes as she approached our counter, her bustier-clad chest thrust out so aggressively that her "enhancements" seemed more like helium balloons holding her aloft.

"Hiii-eeeee," Big Danni squealed. "Remember us?"

"Of course Tucker remembers us," Little Delores Deluca purred. "Who doesn't remember 'spectacular'?"

It was then I noticed Big Danni's husband hanging back in the candy shop. Eddie Rayburn waved and smiled at Tucker—but that smile didn't reach those "evil eyes." The gesture looked more like a threat than a greeting.

Tuck audibly gulped then quickly welcomed the women.

"Wow! Girls! I'm so glad you're here," he cried, moving around the counter to air-kiss them both. "I was hoping to catch up with you. I have a very important offer to make the Double Ds!"

"Sounds delicious," Danni said with wide, heavily made-up eyes.

"Should we alert our agent?" Delores asked.

"Do, because that little cabaret show I told you about—"

Big Danni cocked her head. "The one where we get to play ourselves?"

"That's the one. Only the size of the project has ballooned out of proportion—"

"Kind of like their *enhancements*," murmured Esther before I elbowed her into silence.

"In fact," Tuck continued, "the show has gotten so big the whole production may be headed to Broadway."

Danni and Delores let out whoops loud enough to rival the cheers on the other side of the toy store.

"Can we sit?" Delores asked. "Talk about this?"

Tuck gave me a sidelong glance and I nodded once.

"Sure, here's an out-of-the-way table," Tuck said. "Let me get you something to—"

"You're not moving, sugar daddy," Delores declared as she slung her red Hermes Birkin bag across the table, into an empty chair.

"Girl? Hey, girl?" she called in my direction. Then Delores snapped her cougar-length fingernails. "Hello!"

I blinked. "Sorry. Were you talking to me?"

"Who else? Fetch me one of those gumdrop drinks. Strawberry. Make it a double."

Tuck reacted. I signaled that it was okay, boorish customers in this town were nothing new—and I was being inattentive. (Though in my defense, it's been a few years since anyone addressed me as "girl.")

"And what can I get you, ma'am?" I asked Big Danni.

"Whatever Delores is having," she said with an impatient wave.

I pushed Esther in front of me as we both made the spritzers. "Are you delivering, or am I?" she asked when the drinks were made.

"I'll spare you the pain," I said, lifting the tray. *Besides, I want to hear this conversation for myself!*

"What sort of acting have you done?" I heard Tuck ask the Ds as I approached the table.

"I appeared in an episode of that serial killer cable show *Wexler*," Danni said. "I played a girl named Emily. I knew my lines, but I always missed my cue."

"Bad direction?" Tuck asked.

"No, it was my fault. The other actor would say, 'Hey, Em,' and I'd be waiting to hear 'Hey, Danni.'" She rolled her eyes. "Sometimes I'm such a ditz. But it won't matter in your show because I'll be playing myself."

Tuck faced Delores. "How about you? Any thespian experience?"

"Last month I auditioned for the role of a police assistant on that network show *Criminal Intent*. I even got tips on how to play the part from my sister, who really *is* a PA for the police commissioner's office. I dressed all dowdy for the audition, too, just like my sister."

Little Delores sighed. "I didn't get the part, but my agent told me to look on the bright side. A girl like me just can't hide her glam."

I'd served the drinks and was about to depart when Danni screeched at me.

"This is strawberry! I hate strawberry!"

Danni then waved her spritzer in the air until some of the liquid sloshed onto her own Birkin bag—much like her friend Delores's, only pink instead of red. And she kept hers tightly slung over her shoulder.

O-kay, I thought. *So much for "I'll have what Delores is having."*

"How about lemon-lime?" I suggested. "Or cherry?"

"Whatever," she said, whirling to face Tuck again.

"You only have to be your vivacious selves and this show will be a hit," Tuck declared. "And you know what that means? Instant fame, all over again."

The Double Ds squealed and Danni bounced in her chair.

As I headed back to the counter, I thought about all of those privileged children who'd come to the party tonight. They pointed to the toy they wanted, and no matter the cost, Daddy or Mommy sent their personal shopper off to process the credit card.

The Double Ds fit right into that paradigm. They didn't

know it, but a Secret Santa was holding the credit card for them, willing to shell out the cost of making their dreams come true.

But the vast majority of struggling actors, writers, and artists didn't have it so easy, and I saw examples of it daily in my own coffeehouse: fine arts painter Dante Silva; jazz musician Gardner Evans; Goth poetess Esther Best. And then there was poor Moirin, who'd worked so hard as a baker's assistant while trying to scale the ladder of singing success. It just didn't seem fair—or right.

"Let's try a lemon spritzer this time," I told Esther as I set the tray on the counter.

She arched her eyebrow. "Not lemon-lime?"

"This one should be sour." *To match the lady's personality,* I nearly added, but didn't have to.

Esther winked with understanding. "I got you, boss. And I think—uh-oh . . ."

"What?"

She lifted her chin and lowered her voice. "Here comes that lunkheaded Ross Puckett."

"The hockey player?" I asked without turning. "You serve that spritzer. I'll serve the lunkhead." *Because this time I've come prepared . . .*

Forty-three

〰〰〰〰〰〰〰〰〰〰〰〰〰〰〰〰

A minute later, Ross Puckett approached the toy store café counter. Looking dashing in his extra-large formal wear, he grinned stupidly—until he came face-to-face with his worst nightmare.

"Whoa! Not you!" he cried, clearly remembering our last encounter. "Keep back, Coffee Lady. I just had my Bruno Maglis polished this morning. They were plenty scuffed from our last meeting."

"That's terrible. I'm really sorry about that," I said, pouring on the charm. "How about I make it up to you right now?"

Puckett's eyes narrowed suspiciously. "How are you going to do that?"

"Easy. I'm going to prepare something really special for you: a cherry cordial latte with a mix of kirsch, crème de cacao, and Kahlua. I guarantee it will give you a happy holiday buzz."

To my surprise, Puckett shook his shaggy blond head. "I'll take one of those Gumdrop Spritzers instead. Make it a cherry, now that you got me thinking about it."

I added the syrup to the icy club soda, dropped one of our dwindling supply of swizzle sticks into the glass, and handed it over. I was about to compliment the hockey captain on trying to stay dry tonight, when Puckett drew a flask out of his jacket pocket and poured a clear liquid into his glass.

I arched an eyebrow. "I see tonight you've come prepared."

He smirked. "Fancy drinks can't beat the punch of pure vodka."

As he returned the flask to his pocket, he brushed at the telltale crumbs still clinging to his black lapels. They were pieces of Rita's *Pastelitos de Cajeta*, and I knew he'd visited—and very likely hit on—the beautiful Latina in the Barbie doll section. Once again, I remembered how much he'd liked those Brandy Snap Matchsticks from the first party. They'd been Rita's, too.

Ross Puckett flashed me a flirtatious smile. "Got to go," he said, adding a wink. "Maybe see you later."

He sauntered off, turning for a final wave before vanishing among the sweets. I scanned the candy shop and realized Eddie was gone, too.

When did he disappear?

That's when I got the shivery feeling of being watched. I turned to find Delores Deluca staring hatefully at me.

What did I ever do to you, lady? I silently wondered.

"How did it go with the lunkhead?" Esther asked.

"He was his old charming self, which is more than I can say for the Little D over there." I leaned closer to Esther. "Is it my imagination, or was that woman glaring at me while I was talking to Ross?"

"She was," Esther replied. "The whole time."

I shook my head. "Maybe she was jealous that a celebrity was giving a cheesy wink to me instead of another celebrity like her. Anyway I can't take the stares. Hold down the fort. I'm going across the street."

"Where?"

I pointed to the recessed glass door on the exterior wall

of our little café. "I'm using that door to slip outside. I'm going to that bar, see it? Vintage 58."

Typically, this side door was used to give the public access to the café before the store opened. During the party, however, the door was locked from the outside. But I could go through it now and have Esther let me back in.

"Why are you going to a bar, boss? If you need a drink, I can pour you a kirsch-laced Kahlúa!"

"We need swizzle sticks, dear. I know Vintage 58 has them, emblazoned with their logo. I'm going to talk the manager into gifting me a couple of hundred, for which he will get a massive amount of free promo with this VIP crowd."

Esther gave me a thumbs-up. "Problem solved on the cheap. A-plus!"

On the way to the side exit, I passed Tuck and the Double Ds. Tuck was telling the girls all about the rock-in-the-sock stunt in his Children's Theatre production. Noting the large windows along the wall, I was grateful he resisted the temptation to provide an actual demonstration this time.

FORTY-FOUR

~~~~~~~~~~~~~~~~~~~~~~~~~~~~~

TWO hours later, the guests were gone, and much of the staff, too. Other than four security guards and a manager—all of them gathered near the front doors—only a few bakers were still packing up their things, and that's what I was counting on.

Before one particular baker left, I had questions for her. Tucker had departed already so I asked Esther to finish packing up while I headed for the store's escalator.

The vast space felt strangely empty and eerily quiet as I walked by the stuffed animals and toy soldiers. When I reached the mezzanine, I moved to the Barbie section, but Rita Limon was gone.

I stepped closer. On the shelf above, a line of beautiful plastic dolls looked down at me with unseeing eyes, and I realized—

Rita's not gone. Not yet . . .

Her cookie table hadn't been packed up and broken down, which meant she was still around here somewhere. The restroom was the likeliest place to look, so I moved past the $25,000 Barbie Foosball table, the $1,500 jeweled

Etch A Sketch, and the giant floor piano, and entered the store's private party room.

Countless parents had rented this space over the years to celebrate their children's birthdays. The room was cheerful with kid-sized tables and chairs, jumbo stuffed animals, and tall windows that overlooked Madison Avenue.

Tonight the party had been throughout the store, so this room was set aside for use by the participating bakers and party staff to hang coats and keep personal items.

Another door, inside the room, led to the restrooms, and I expected to find Rita there. I pushed the door with the little girl silhouette and found the room dark and freezing cold.

I almost left, but something didn't seem right. An odd, metallic smell hung in the air, and I had a very bad feeling about the chilly temperature. So I flipped on the lights. Nothing appeared out of the ordinary, until I moved inside.

Dark liquid had been spilled on the tile floor at the far end of the room. I moved closer to examine it, pushed open the last stall door—and screamed.

Rita's body was crumpled in a corner stall, blood pooled around it. Like Moirin, her head had been bashed in at some point during the festivities. An open window let the winter air in, a smart move on the part of the killer to mask the time of death.

I was shaken, angered, and finally outraged over this savage crime. Those emotions would lead me to put myself in danger later this very night (a decision I would not regret, given the outcome). But first the homicide detectives would have questions for me, and I was more than ready to provide answers.

FORTY-FIVE

~~~~~~~~~~~~~~~~~~~~~~~~~~~~~~~~

THIS was my second NYPD crime scene in a little over a week. Like Tucker Burton's repertory company, the costumes were different, but the cast was pretty much the same.

Detective Sergeant Fletcher Endicott was here, in paper booties, milling around a Ken doll display. Mr. DNA was dressed ludicrously formally for a murder investigation. Beneath his clear plastic "clean suit," he wore a black tux, white tie, and burgundy silk vest.

Instead of a digital recorder, the man was speaking into a smartphone while watching the white-suited CSU team walk in and out of the children's party room area, plunking on keys of the giant floor piano as they combed for clues.

Endicott was forced to speak loudly to be heard over the discordant floor-piano concerto (which, for me, made eavesdropping that much easier).

"Yes, Captain! I have the situation well in hand!" Endicott declared. "My prime suspect has been under surveillance for days. He's finally made his next move, and I'm certain we shall be taking him into custody this very night!"

I blanched. *Surely he isn't referring to my barista?*

"Mobile communications is about to patch me through to my undercover tail. She's been posted at the coffeehouse where our suspect works . . ."

Oh God, I realized, he *was* talking about my barista, which meant the man's prime suspect for Rita Limon's murder was again Dante Silva—the very young man he believed bludgeoned Moirin Fagan to death last week as part of a serial string of Christmas Stalkings.

"I have no doubt our undercover followed the suspect to *this* location within the time frame of the murder . . ."

I cast about for someone sane and spotted Lori Soles.

Like Endicott, Lori fit right into the Barbie aisle with her red and black evening dress and pearl earrings. Her short blond curls were sleekly slicked down this evening. Her bright red lipstick matched the holly berry red in her dress; and with her high-heeled pumps on her already long legs, she literally loomed over a uniformed officer, who was giving her an update.

When Lori finally saw me frantically waving, she approached, heels clicking.

"If this crime scene is formal, I'm underdressed," I told her.

"Thank the stars you are . . ." She stepped closer: "As a member of the suddenly high-profile Stalker Task Force, I was 'invited' to the Mayor's Holiday Gala: a formal dinner followed by a performance of *The Nutcracker* at Lincoln Center." She checked her back and lowered her voice. "I was coerced into attending as Fletcher Endicott's dinner partner. Honestly, Cosi, I was relieved when the evening ended early."

"You were Endicott's date? What did *Mr.* Soles think of that arrangement?"

"He's still laughing."

Meanwhile, Endicott continued his conversation with his superior: "No, sir. It pains me to report that the toy store's security cameras are useless on this floor . . . Yes, they do have them. But it seems they were focused on the rather costly Barbie Foosball table, jeweled Etch A Sketch, and the like and not on the stacks of cheap plastic dolls where the victim was stationed. And though the private party room has cameras, they are only made active during private parties—"

Endicott was interrupted by the beep from his police radio.

"Pardon me, Captain, but I have vital business to attend to! I shall give you my update straightaway!"

Oh good heavens . . .

Endicott lowered his smartphone, snapped up the police radio, and barked into it: "Officer Chen? Are you hard of hearing? Did I not order you to report in if the suspect left the coffeehouse during his shift?"

As he listened to the reply, Endicott massaged his forehead, as if in pain. "What do you mean he never left? Perhaps he slipped by you while you were in the little girls' room?"

Endicott listened again—to an earful, apparently. "Yes, yes, I understand. You're looking at him right now. Fine. *Keep* looking. He might not be guilty of *this* murder, but I am convinced that espresso jockey is our Christmas Stalker!"

Espresso jockey?

As Endicott tucked the radio back into his pocket and turned around, I didn't hesitate.

"Dante Silva is not the Christmas Stalker," I loudly called from behind the police tape. "You're chasing the wrong suspect!"

Every uniformed officer and CSU detective stopped what he or she was doing to give me a blank stare. With pursed lips and squinting eyes, Endicott looked as if he just sucked on a candy shop sour ball. With righteous vigor, he strode up to me.

"If you recall, Ms. Cosi, I chased *your* suspect the first time around. I'm referring, of course, to Piper Penny—"

"What you chased were a few hairs!" I corrected. "And I *tried* to tell you that I had doubts about her, that the timeline was off, but you refused to listen. Then you fixated on my employee instead of looking for viable suspects."

He folded his arms, considering his options. "Fine. We're in a toy store. I'll play your little armchair detective game. Whom do you think is a 'viable' suspect?"

"Certainly not my barista."

"Maybe not for this murder, but I'm keeping a tail on him."

"Why?!"

"For one thing, he remains my prime suspect in last week's case—and in our series of Christmas Stalkings."

"Dante Silva would never bludgeon a girl to death. You're wasting valuable time thinking he could. And if your stalker really is working out of my coffeehouse, I'll tell you who you should be looking for and why . . ."

Endicott was still scowling, but I could see he was curious. "Go on."

"Times are tough right now and the holidays make it feel even tougher. I've overheard plenty of complaints after this season's office parties and seen outbursts from drunken customers, especially middle-aged men."

"So what are you saying?"

"That your Christmas Stalker is probably a male commuter who doesn't have an apartment in Manhattan, someone who's been using my shop to stay warm, stew, and consider victims to follow so he can get his pervy jollies bashing her. As for the reason . . . I'm sure he has some undiscovered mental problems. And the attacks are misplaced rage over feeling helpless about what's happening to him. If he hasn't been laid off, he's probably been marginalized in some way, demoted or passed over. I'll even bet you his boss is—or was—a woman."

"You're reaching, Ms. Cosi," Endicott said with a dismissive wave. "Some anonymous, angry office worker has no connection to last week's murder victim. Your barista does."

"And you're still assuming the two cases are connected. I'm telling you they're not. The Stalker's victims were random. And it's clear that Moirin knew her killer."

"She knew your barista. If he's the Stalker, that explains it."

I wanted to scream. But before I could, a white-suited CSU detective came out of the party room and tapped Endicott's shoulder.

"We've got something," he said.

The look on Endicott's face told me he was thinking the same thing I was: *I hope it's better than dog hairs!*

Forty-six

~~~~~~~~~~~~~~~~~~~~~~~

LORI joined them, and the three stepped away from me (which didn't stop me from moving along the crime scene tape until I could overhear).

"The killer tried to clean up after the murder," the CSU detective explained. "We found a single fingerprint in the victim's blood on the back of the hot water faucet. It's not legible enough to be admissible in court, but it's clear enough to point to, or eliminate, a viable suspect for this homicide—if you have one."

An uncomfortable silence followed. Endicott said nothing. But Lori spoke up in an animated whisper. She gestured in my direction, and Endicott's frown deepened. Finally, all three detectives approached me.

"All right, Ms. Cosi," Endicott began. "You found the victim. We've reviewed your statement with the uniformed officers. Now tell us . . ." He let his words trail off as he shook his head.

Lori jumped in. "Cosi," she said plainly, "we want to know what you think."

Finally! I took a deep breath and admitted: "I didn't witness Rita Limon's murder, but I did eyewitness a threat against her earlier this evening. The other baker stationed on this floor during the Cookie Swap was smitten with Rita. He suggested they hook up in that very party room after hours. When she rejected him, he swore at her and menaced her with physical violence—and I wasn't the only one who saw this. There were two other witnesses."

Endicott nodded. The sour ball was gone. "Clearly, this is its own particular case!" he declared. "That would explain the barista's lack of involvement—and the discrepancy."

"What discrepancy?" I asked.

"Rita Limon's skull was cleaved, not bashed," Lori said.

"Well, I can't explain the changing MO," I said. "I mean, I don't know why this killer used a rock last week and some kind of bladed weapon this week, but this person I'm telling you about was at the last Cookie Swap, too. I saw him talking with Moirin Fagan shortly before she was killed. His name is—"

The smartphone vanished from Endicott's pale fingers, and the digital recorder reappeared. He waved it under my nose.

"Nick Bacque," I finished, reaching in my pocket for his card. I recited the address of his bakery. "But I doubt you'll find him there. Nick left this toy store fifteen minutes before I found Rita's body. If you're lucky, he's still in that bar across the street."

Lori blinked. "Vintage 58?"

I nodded. "When the bakers were finished here, they left through this store's 58th Street exit, which means they had to walk through the café I was managing. Nick even caught my eye as he left and fired off a smirk. I saw him cross the street and go into the bar."

"What was Mr. Bacque wearing when you saw him leave?" Lori asked. "And was he carrying bags? Boxes?"

Though it was Lori who asked the question, both she and Endicott seemed to be hanging on my reply.

"All the leftover cookies are sent to homeless shelters, so Nick didn't have to haul anything away—"

"What was he wearing?" Endicott repeated.

"He dressed in a tux for the event, and he was wearing a long charcoal gray topcoat when he went out the door. He was also carrying a large green tote bag. Big enough to contain a change of clothing, if that's what you're getting at."

Endicott faced Lori. "I have to report in, but I want you to take two . . . no, *four* uniformed officers . . . take them over to that bar and pick this guy up. If that saloon has a back door, I want two officers covering it."

"He's had time to change his clothes, maybe even dump the bloody stuff somewhere," I warned.

"Maybe," Endicott said. "But he can't change his fingerprints, and he probably didn't change his shoes, either. Even if he did, we can examine his skin for traces of blood or other indicators that he bludgeoned Rita Limon to death—"

"Other indicators? You mean defensive wounds, that kind of thing?"

Lori nodded as Endicott's smartphone buzzed and he waved us all to be silent—though the CSU techs were still playing their plunky concerto.

"Captain? Yes, I'm moving to apprehend a suspect as we speak!"

With a silent wave, Endicott dismissed me and sent Lori off to marshal her four-man arresting force.

I hurried to catch her. "Will you check in with me again? Tell me if that bloody print can be matched to Nick?"

"I'll update you when I can, Cosi. But do one thing for me, okay?"

"What?"

"Stay out of sight during this arrest. If this Bacque character is as violent a scumbag as you claim, you don't want him knowing you had anything to do with fingering him."

Nice sentiments, I thought. *But the moment Nick Bacque arrives in an interview room, he's going to hear how an "eyewitness" heard him threaten Rita this evening.*

Two and two was four, and Nick would add up another obvious clue. He saw me watching him leave the store. He'd know I sent the police to pick him up. But given the violence of the crime, bail would be set impossibly high. I doubted Nick would have the cash or collateral to post it.

As I headed down the escalator, I was sure my endless night was over. Unfortunately I'd forgotten my grade school astronomy: this was December, the month with the longest nights of the year.

I'd have to get through plenty more darkness before dawn.

Rᴇᴛᴜʀɴɪɴɢ to the toy store's café, I found Esther and Janelle waiting for me. They rose for a group hug, then Esther poured me a cup of the French roast that she and Janelle had been sharing. I spied a plate of leftover pistachio and raspberry macarons, downed the treats, and gulped the coffee.

Reinvigorated by the caffeine and sugar, I told them everything that had happened upstairs. As I got to the part about Nick Bacque's imminent arrest, Lori Soles clicked through the café.

We all watched the Amazonian detective in dinner dress and cover girl makeup lead her small blue army of uniformed men out the 58th Street exit.

"Whoa," Esther whispered. "It's NYPD Barbie. 'Comes with *two* outfits, *and* her own badge, cuffs, and pepper spray!'"

"I can't understand how Nick could set up a bakery business so quickly," Janelle said.

"I think we both know how he did it," I said. "While he worked for you, Nick double ordered everything, then moved half the stuff to his own bakery."

"But that's just it," Janelle countered. "Nick didn't have a bakery, and he would have had the same trouble renting one that I had. With no prior history of retail rental, I had to jump through lots of hoops. Credit checks, stuff like that.

Nick could never manage it. His financial situation was shakier than mine."

I handed Nick's card to Janelle. "Maybe he partnered up with someone, or maybe Nick got a special deal for a run-down dump—"

Janelle released a string of obscenities, the more colorful ones in Creole French.

"I know this address! Nick and I checked out this retail space together when I was searching for a place to expand— back when I trusted Nick and *thought* my books were in good shape. It's a third-floor commercial kitchen. The previous tenant installed a giant dumbwaiter that ran from the basement to make deliveries easy."

Janelle shook the card in her hand. "I almost leased that space, too, but Nick convinced me the rent was too high for the inconvenience of a third-floor walk-up."

"He talked you out of it, only to grab the space behind your back." Esther shook her head. "That's a special kind of cad."

Outside, loud voices were shouting. "What's happening?"

Janelle moved to look out the glass door. "A bunch of cops just led Nick Bacque out of the bar across the street. I do believe that man is in handcuffs, too."

A minute later, a siren wailed, and faded just as quickly.

I finished my coffee in a single gulp. "Janelle, how would you like to prove Nick Bacque ripped you off? Nail him to the wall harder than he is now."

Janelle's smile doubled in size. "I'm game. But how?"

"Where there's a dumbwaiter and a camera, there's a way."

Forty-seven

∿∿∿∿∿∿∿∿∿∿∿∿∿∿∿∿∿∿∿∿∿∿

A shivering Esther whispered to Janelle through nearly blue lips. "The last time we tried something this radical, she had to climb a fire escape!"

"No fire escapes tonight," I said. "But we do have to convince one of the residents to buzz us in."

"Leave that to me," Esther said with confidence.

The four-story brick building was located in the Village, not far from my coffeehouse but on an unfashionable corner of Sullivan Street. The ground floor was occupied by Sherpa, a Himalayan restaurant, which was shuttered for the night. Above the eatery there were three floors of dark windows. Janelle led us around the corner, to a quieter, more shadowy side street.

"That's the kitchen," she said, pointing to a high window beside a neat row of aluminum-hooded oven vents.

"Looks like the only way in is through the front door," Esther said as she led us back around to the front and up a short flight of granite steps to the building entrance.

"How are you going to get us in?" I asked.

"Watch and learn, grasshopper . . ."

Esther moved her hand to the twin rows of intercom buttons next to the door. Each button had a name listed beside it, but she didn't bother reading any of them. Instead, she ran her finger down the left column, hitting every bell.

Inside of ten seconds the intercom crackled. "Yeah?" said a male voice.

"It's me," Esther whispered into the speaker.

The door beeped, and we pushed through.

We moved quickly down the hallway to a battered stairwell door and took the stairs down to the open basement. Esther found a switch and harsh fluorescent lights flooded a large, damp room with a dingy concrete floor.

"There it is," Janelle called. She moved to the large dumbwaiter embedded next to a sidewalk chute in the front wall. I could see how deliveries would be made. The locked doors above the chute would be opened up, and goods would be sent down the chute and loaded into the dumbwaiter. Then the baker could activate the little elevator, lifting the deliveries right up to the kitchen.

Esther twisted the dumbwaiter's handle and the door popped open. The boxy inside was about the size of your average dishwasher.

"Somebody's got to crawl in there," I said.

Janelle frowned at Esther's ample bosom and generous hips. Esther stared back at Janelle's expansive waistline and well-padded posterior. Then they both turned to face the comparatively short and slender me.

"I have an idea!" Esther chirped. "Janelle and I will both squeeze in there. But I doubt we'll have the space to bring the camera along, too."

"Okay, I get it. I'm the only one small enough to fit."

"Have a fun ride, Sherlock."

"If it nails Nick Bacque, I will. Here, hold this—" I handed Esther my large shoulder bag. "And help me inside . . ."

They did. After I was squeezed in there, camera case tucked under my chin, I told them to send me up—

"And when this thing stops, you two go outside and

around the corner. Wait three minutes. If you don't see me, it will mean the third-floor exit doors are locked, and I can't get out—so come back in and bring this thing back down."

"What if you do get in?" Esther asked.

"I'll open the window that Janelle pointed out and wave. Then I'll take pictures while you guys keep watch. Yell up to me if you see a nosy cop, a curious building super, or Nick Bacque—in the unlikely event the skunk is kicked loose by the NYPD."

"Yell?" Esther said. "You never heard of a cell phone?"

"The signal could be iffy up there, depending on his appliances. I think my way is better."

Janelle nodded. "It's a plan, then."

I fumbled around the inside of the box. "Where's the up button?"

"This isn't an elevator, sugar, and it's not electric. I'll have to reel you up."

"What?"

As Janelle gripped a flywheel embedded in the wall, Esther closed the door and plunged me into total darkness.

"Make sure you throw the brake when you get to the top!" Janelle called, and with a squeaky lurch, the car began to ascend.

The creepy ride through the narrow aluminum shaft seemed eternal. Finally the box bumped to a halt. Thankfully, Nick hadn't locked his dumbwaiter doors. They burst open and I literally rolled out.

For a good ten seconds I laid on the linoleum floor of the darkened commercial kitchen, just listening. I heard the tick-tick-tick of a wall clock, the hiss of a gas jet, a muffled voice in another apartment.

I pulled the phone from my pocket and opened it. As I feared, with all these metal machines, my cell signal was weak. Meanwhile, my eyes grew accustomed to the darkness and I could discern shapes around me: A pair of commercial ovens. A sink. A large stove. Rows of cabinets. A massive refrigerator. I spied a wall switch and flipped it. Overhead fluorescence came to life.

I crossed the room and opened one of the large windows. There was no screen so I stuck my head out and waved to Janelle and Esther on the sidewalk below. I was about to duck back inside when I spotted movement on the sidewalk.

A woman strolled along the boulevard a half a block away. I soon realized this woman in a powder blue ball gown and matching topcoat was blissfully unaware that a man was following her.

With his face wrapped in a black scarf and a fedora hat pulled low, the man increased speed until he caught up with her.

Before I could shout out a warning, the man seized the woman by her arm and spun her. I heard a startled cry, and a struggle ensued. That's when a wooden club appeared in the man's gloved hand!

"Oh my God!" I screamed to Esther and Janelle. "The Stalker is attacking a woman up the block." I pointed. "Go! Both of you! Help that poor woman now before she gets bashed!"

FORTY-EIGHT

〜〜〜〜〜〜〜〜〜〜〜〜〜〜〜〜〜

As Esther and Janelle ran off toward the struggling pair, the woman in the ball gown broke free. But instead of fleeing her attacker, she lashed out with flying fists.

One, two, three punches slammed into the Stalker's face in quick succession. Reeling, the thug dropped his club. A fourth blow knocked his hat off; a fifth smashed his nose flat.

A final high-heeled kick to the groin laid the Stalker low.

As he sank to the icy pavement, Esther dived onto his back, pinning the Stalker to the ground. Janelle arrived seconds later, cell phone in hand.

The woman adjusted her ball gown and tried to fix her frazzled blond wig. With an exasperated cry she gave up and tore the hairpiece off. That's when I recalled where I'd last seen those fighting moves—*and* that lovely powder blue dress.

"Punch!" I heard Esther cry. "I thought you were a woman. Are you okay?"

"I broke my heel," Tuck's boyfriend shrieked. "And these shoes are freakin' expensive!"

The man on the ground shifted, and Esther applied more pressure, eliciting a yelp of pain.

Janelle, speaking to a police dispatcher, gave me a thumbs-up. I ducked back inside the kitchen.

What a night, and it isn't over yet . . .

I unpacked my camera and double-checked the batteries. I had plenty of power and an entire digital card to fill, since I never found the time to take pictures at tonight's Cookie Swap.

I started my photo diary with a pile of cardboard appliance boxes stacked in the corner. Most had delivery labels, and the addresses on them were Janelle's.

Gotcha, you skunk!

I snapped away, getting close-up shots of some packing invoices, too.

It took a few moments to locate the appliances themselves—two blenders on a stainless steel counter, sheet after sheet of expensive silicone trays and baking pans on shelves, a commercial mixer beside a steel table in the center of the kitchen.

Strike one.

Next I rummaged through drawers. I found the expensive knives attached to a box with Janelle's address on it, plus a set of stainless steel baking utensils. I ignored small stuff, but the fourth drawer yielded a bonanza: three manila envelopes, each one clearly marked.

The envelope marked Keys contained just that. Different sets, including keys for Janelle's bakery (which I pocketed), and a set marked Sobel's.

This second set brought back a memory. At tonight's Cookie Swap, Nick had mentioned working for Sam Sobel, and stepping in when the old baker's kitchen was damaged by fire. *Coincidence? With Nick Bacque involved?* I was starting to have doubts.

The third envelope was from a property company and contained the lease for this bakery space. I thumbed through it, looking for any partners. I gasped when I saw the name of his supposed cosigner: *Janelle Babcock* was scrawled on the dotted line.

Nick had forged his former boss's name to help him acquire the lease.

Strike two.

I was feeling more confident now (after all, with Janelle's name on this legal document, I wasn't even breaking and entering!), and I took my time photographing every page of the lease.

Next my nose alerted me to a cloying but familiar smell oozing from a metal cabinet. I opened the door and found the source—three cans marked *Acetone.*

Colorless and flammable, acetone was used in most nail polish removers. It was also used in lacquers and varnishes, and some paint removers, too. But I didn't see any fresh paint or varnish jobs here.

So why would a baker store it in his kitchen? Because acetone was one of the top twenty accelerants used to start illegal fires—and this baker also happened to be an arsonist!

Strike three and you're out, Nick Bacque!

I snapped and snapped, making sure to include the pair of scorched asbestos gloves sitting beside the cans in my compositions.

I moved on to the pantry, where I found other cans. And I was sure these cans didn't come from Janelle's bakery, either. *I can't wait to tell her about this!* The potentially criminal contents of these cans gave me a sense of satisfaction, too—even if it was just a culinary crime.

Finally my camera beeped, warning me the digital card was out of memory. I removed the tiny card from the camera, tucked it into a holder, and slipped it into my coat pocket. I fumbled through my camera case for another card, but came up empty, which meant it was time to go.

Why not quit while I'm most definitely ahead?

For the first time in days I'd accomplished something, brought a little bit of justice into this unjust world. I'd gotten the goods on Nick Bacque, and with Janelle's forged name on the lease I could expose him without facing trespassing charges myself.

Better still, from the view outside the window it appeared the Christmas Stalker had been apprehended at last—and, just as I told Mr. DNA, the culprit was not my barista.

With a dozen police cars filling the narrow street, and a New York mob of the curious appearing out of thin air, my escape would be easy.

Why leave by the dumbwaiter, when all I have to do is walk out the front door and mingle with the crowd?

With a self-satisfied sigh, I tucked my camera into its case as I headed for the exit. But as I reached for the doorknob, I realized I couldn't open the door. The dead bolt was the kind that required a key from the inside as well as the outside.

The moment I had that realization, I heard the bolt being thrown and watched the door yawn open. The man standing on the threshold looked as surprised as I was, but he recovered fast.

"Well, well, darling," Nick Bacque purred. "I was just daydreaming about all the *nasty* things I wanted to do to you—and now here you are, like my own little Christmas wish come true."

Forty-nine

~~~~~~

He lunged so suddenly that he might have grabbed me, if I had been his target. But Nick had spied my camera case and guessed what I was up to. Now it was the camera he wanted.

With both hands, he yanked the case, and I howled because my right arm was tangling in the strap. As he dragged me closer I tried to kick him, but my foot struck the wall.

"Taking pictures?" he hissed, hot breath on my cheek. "Maybe we should look at them together—"

With a snap the strap broke. As I stumbled backward, Nick spiked my camera into the linoleum, dashing it to pieces. Then he slammed the front door and locked the bolt into place.

Now I was Nick's prisoner, and I half expected him to take his sweet time. Maybe take off his coat, taunt me. Instead he lunged again, eyes flashing with rage, mouth set in grim determination. I eluded his grasp by rolling across the kitchen's steel table and landing on the other side.

What followed was something out of a French bedroom

farce, where a man chases a woman around a bed. Except this was no bedroom. I was being chased around a steel baking table, and there is absolutely nothing funny about running for your life.

After a few laps, Nick positioned himself between me and the window. This was strategic, I realized. On his way here, he must have seen the police on the street. Clearly, he wanted to prevent me from calling for help.

Now I was without a rescue, and I couldn't escape through the door unless I managed to knock him unconscious and rifle his pocket for the key. That left me only one way out. The way I came in. Fortunately I'd left the door to the dumbwaiter open. All I had to do was wait for the right moment.

It came suddenly, when Nick flew across the table instead of around it. I felt his powerful fingers grip my wrist and twist. Crying out in pain, I swung my other arm around, slamming him in the side of the head.

Breathing hard, his topcoat open, Nick grunted but wouldn't let go. Finally I grabbed a can of condensed milk from a shelf and brought it down on his forearm.

With a cry of pain, he released my wrist, and I dived into the dumbwaiter.

I fumbled for the brake before I realized I didn't need to. I'd forgotten to lock the car in place, as Janelle had instructed. As a result, my descent was *way* faster than the ride up!

The wooden car landed so hard it broke into pieces. My teeth clacked together from the jolt, and dust rained down on me. But amazingly, I was okay—well enough to hear Nick Bacque yell down the shaft.

"You got nothin', bitch! Nothin'!"

Yeah, that's what you think . . . As I felt the reassuring square of the digital card holder, still in my coat pocket, I knew I'd nailed him.

I pushed the door open and rolled out, tearing my coat on the shattered wood before hitting the concrete floor. I just wanted to lie there for a moment and catch my breath, but I didn't dare. Nick could still come down here looking for me.

I raced up the basement stairs, down the building's hallway, and out the front door.

THE cold air was bracing, especially with the huge tear in my parka. But it took me under a minute to reach the Sullivan Street crime scene, where I was surrounded by uniformed officers.

Janelle spied me and hurried over. "Esther and Punch are giving statements to the police. Did you know the Christmas Stalker was one of your customers? Some guy named Fred—"

"Listen," I said, breathless, "we've got to get out of here. Nick Bacque was released by the NYPD. He showed up and nearly killed me!"

Janelle blinked. "He's loose?!"

"And dangerous!" I noticed a cab turning onto Sullivan and waved madly to flag it down. "We're going to your place, *now*."

"You don't want to report that he attacked you to these cops?"

"The NYPD released him once already. I have a better plan. Get out of town tonight—and let Lori Soles arrest him *again* tomorrow."

Janelle nodded, then broke away to inform Esther, who told us to go on without her. Punch would walk her back to the Blend.

As Janelle shoved me into the cab and gave me back my shoulder bag, I explained my hasty change in travel plans.

"I was supposed to visit Mike in DC this weekend, anyway. All I'm doing is moving up my train ride by twelve hours."

"Leave right from my place, girl. Nick knows where you live so no going back to your apartment." She examined my torn parka. "I'll lend you a new coat, and see your cats get fed."

"Esther will do that. The weekends I'm with Mike, she takes care of Java and Frothy. She already has a key."

"So what evidence did you get on that skunk?"

"Plenty. I'll download my digital photo card to your computer. Then I'm calling Detective Soles . . ." Despite my throbbing wrist and aching arm, I suddenly felt crazy laughter bubbling up.

"What's so funny?" Janelle asked. "Or are you having some kind of post-traumatic stress reaction?"

"No. I was just thinking: Nick is one piece of work. Arson, forgery, theft—*these* weren't enough for the guy?"

"What do you mean?"

"I saw cans of partially hydrogenated oils in that jerk's pantry. I'll bet you didn't know he's using trans fat to make his cookies."

She gasped, shook her head, and joined in on my stressed-out laughing fit. "Yeah, girl, last I checked, *that* was against the law in this town, too!"

Fifty

⌒⌒⌒⌒⌒⌒⌒⌒⌒⌒⌒⌒⌒⌒

I hit the café car the second we pulled out of Penn Station. Turkey sandwich in hand, I returned to my train seat to find my cell phone vibrating the heck out of my plastic pull-down tray.

I couldn't answer fast enough.

"It's Soles. I got your message on what you found, and—"

"Why, Lori? Why did you let Nick Bacque go free?"

Her voice was steel. No apologies, just the facts: "The man was clean, Cosi. No blood, no residue. And none of his prints came close to matching the bloody fingerprint we found on the faucet."

"Okay, I get it. He didn't kill Rita . . ."

I took a breath, hoping my risk tonight wasn't in vain. "What about the message I left on the incriminating evidence in Nick's bakery: the keys to Sobel's, the accelerants that point to arson, the forged signature on the lease, and all those stolen goods?"

"I've got a call in to the fire marshal on Sobel's case. And I'll get together with Janelle in the morning. I'm sure we'll have Nick back in custody soon—and I have no doubt he'll do time."

I collapsed back in relief against the cushioned headrest. "Tell me about Fred. He's the stalker you were looking for, isn't he?"

"He is. Fred Allman confessed to every one of the serial stalking incidents. And his profile is eerily close to what you described. Jersey home, divorced, disgruntled, demoted at work, passed over for a younger woman, and he's on medication. Good call, Cosi. Endicott even admitted it— said you 'trumped' him."

Trumped? I gritted my teeth. *This is not a game. It's people's lives!*

"Has Fred confessed to killing Moirin? Or Rita?" I pressed.

"So far he denies killing anyone. He's got an alibi for Rita and there's no match on that bathroom faucet finger-print. He's still in the interview room, and claims he has an alibi for Moirin, too, something about an office party. He hasn't lawyered up yet, so we may still get something."

"You'll get nothing . . ." I told Lori what I'd witnessed last Friday. When my taxi rolled up to the Village Blend, Dante had been helping Fred and his friend into a cab. Both men had come from their office party.

"I'm sure Fred's alibi will check out," I said. "He may be the stalker, but it's like I've been saying all along, the stalker didn't kill Moirin or Rita. So where does that leave you? Back to square one?"

"Not on Rita," Lori said.

"Really? Well, please tell me who you suspect. Remember, I was at that party. Maybe I can help you with an observation . . ."

"Rita Limon was involved in a very ugly divorce. Her husband was seeking half ownership of her assets."

"That's motive but hardly opportun—"

"Opportunity knocked, Cosi. Victor Limon caused a scene at the front door of the Cookie Swap. He didn't have an invitation and store security turned him away. But we're speculating that he slipped past security after the stage show outside. They say it was possible. The kids and parents flowed in so fast after some Rudolph show that if someone wanted to gain access to the party, they could have done it then."

"Have you picked him up?"

"Not yet. We're looking. The murder weapon is also a question mark. We can't find or even identify it."

"You can't identify it? What do you think it was?"

"The medical examiner says it appears that her head was cleaved with some kind of axlike weapon."

"An ax?! How could her ex-husband have gotten an ax into and out of a toy store? Without anyone noticing!"

"I don't know, but even CSU is stumped. They're looking at a whole range of bladed weapons that might fit into those wounds—axes, machetes, even a bayonet."

"A bayonet!"

"They have yet to find a match."

How incredibly odd . . .

"Okay," I said. "Apart from the murder weapon, it sounds like you actually do have a viable person of interest on Rita's homicide, but what about Moirin's? Who's going to bring her killer to justice?"

The pause was deafening.

"Got to go," Lori said, and the line went dead.

My body was exhausted, but my brain kept running . . .

Did Rita's ex-husband actually sneak into a toy store, cleave her head with an ax—or some other odd weapon— during a public holiday party, and then sneak out again, *with* the weapon?

The mind boggled.

Maybe Rita's ex-husband was trying to create a Cookie Swap crime scene like last week's, so the police would blame the serial basher. But why use an ax—or any kind of bladed weapon? That wasn't even the basher's MO!

Gazing out the murky train window, I couldn't see

much, other than the reflection of my own exhausted face, and I eventually nodded off, sleeping like a corpse for much of the train ride until—

"Ma'am? Wake up. Last stop!"

Yawning, I pulled on the coat Janelle lent me and reached for my shoulder bag. Then I trudged across Union Station's majestic marble floor, pushed through its glass doors, and headed for the cab stand.

Fifty-one

ﾟｧｳﾟｧｳﾟｧｳﾟｧｳﾟｧｳﾟｧｳﾟｧｳﾟｧｳﾟｧｳﾟｧｳﾟｧｳﾟｧｳﾟ

WHENEVER I came to Washington, I always thought the air smelled fresher than New York. Its plazas and parks gave it a much more spacious feeling, as well. But at four in the morning on a freezing December night, it felt a little *too* spacious.

Columbus Circle was completely deserted. The lack of traffic spooked me, but I had no intention of waking Mike Quinn. The man was a workaholic, who ran on very little rest. I wasn't about to rob him of even more.

Besides, his apartment building was located right here on Capitol Hill, which meant the taxi ride would be under ten minutes, *and* I had keys to let myself in—so I waited.

By the time a cab rolled up, I was shivering.

The air wasn't just cold, it was raw and gusty. Janelle's swing coat was stylish, but the material was thin compared to my thick parka, and it was way too big for me. By now, I'd flipped up the giant hood, and hugged myself, trying to get the loose fabric tighter around me.

On the short taxi ride along Massachusetts Avenue, I

imagined myself slipping into Quinn's nice, warm, king-sized bed—and cuddling up to the nice, warm, king-sized man.

He'd been expecting me to arrive in the early afternoon, but I knew he'd be happy to wake up and find me next to him in bed. I would have saved him a trip to pick me up—*and* I could make us breakfast, first thing.

After a hot pot of coffee and a fresh stack of my buttermilk pancakes, the gears in my brain would surely start turning again, and I'd be better able to think things through. My stomach began to rumble as I imagined those warm, fluffy pancakes flipping on the griddle.

Oh man. I wish I hadn't thought of that . . .

Now I tried to remember if I'd stashed frozen blueberries in Mike's freezer on my last trip. If I did, I'd make us blueberry syrup. If not, my maple-butter syrup would have to do.

As the cab pulled up to the modern brick apartment building, I paid the driver then headed inside. The man at the front desk gave me a friendly wave. For going on five months now, I'd been coming here every other weekend, so he knew me well.

Mike was fifteen floors up, high enough for his small balcony to boast a view of the Capitol Dome and Washington Monument. He was also close enough to the Justice Department to walk to work if he wanted—and close enough to the National Gallery to give me a pleasant way to pass the time on those days (yes, even Saturdays and Sundays) when some urgent matter might pull him away for a few hours.

As the elevator doors opened, I dug around for my big ring of keys. His apartment door had two locks. Yawning, I undid the dead bolt first, but my fingers were so cold that I fumbled the keys, loudly dropping them twice in the hallway before locating the second key for the lock on the knob.

Finally, I opened the door.

The apartment was shadowy, but enough ambient light spilled in from the living room's windows for me to see the key ring when I loudly dropped it, yet again!

I let the heavy door swing shut behind me. As I bent down, I came to three important realizations in less than two seconds—

(1) A very large person had been hiding behind the door and was now surging toward me. (2) I was not wearing my own white parka but Janelle's too-large black coat with the hood still up. And (3) one exhausted coffeehouse manager plus one half-awake G-man added up to sleep-deprived stupidity!

"Aaaaah!" I cried as Quinn powercuffed me for the second time in a week. Only this time, he wasn't so gentle—because he didn't know it was me. Some unknown perp was gaining access to his apartment at an ungodly hour and his street cop reflexes kicked in.

In one fluid motion, the cold steel of Quinn's handcuffs bit my wrist with painful force and jerked my right arm backward to meet my left. With a loud click, my wrists were shackled together. Nearly simultaneously, my right leg was swept out from under me, and I landed with a thud, both of my cheeks kissing the area rug.

Crap. Not again . . .

Honestly, I was lucky he brought me down on a luxury floor covering with very deep pile—*and* that he didn't break my wrist—although for a moment, it felt like he had.

"Aw, no," he murmured as he rolled me over and yanked back my huge hood. "Don't tell me . . ."

I blinked at the man's bewildered face—and the dangling butt of his very large gun. He wore pajama bottoms (and not much else). His caramel brown hair was mussed from sleep, his blue eyes tired and bloodshot. Barefoot and bare chested, he'd shrugged into his shoulder holster in what had to be record time.

The way the leather straps hung off his broad chest, the guy looked ready for a role in the next *Rambo* movie. All he needed was a shaggy black wig, rip cord headband, and knife in his teeth.

"Clare?"

"Hi, Mike."

Fifty-two

~~~~~~~~~~~~~~~~~~~~~~~~~~~~~~~

I woke up alone in Quinn's bed, wearing his pajama top (and not much else). Late morning sun peeked in through the closed mini blinds. Still groggy, I couldn't decide.

Did we make love? Or did I dream it?

I vaguely became aware of something cold on my arm and realized my poor, bruised limb was propped on a towel-covered pillow. A makeshift compress of ice in a tube sock had been secured around my swollen wrist.

"Mike?"

"You up?" he gently called, moving into the bedroom.

Still holding a section of the *Washington Post*, he peered at me over the rim of his reading glasses—a new addition since he'd begun work in DC. (Only Quinn could make librarian half-glasses look sexy.)

He appeared much more relaxed this morning, too. No holster, no gun, no cuffs, just a pair of worn blue jeans on his long legs and a New York Raiders sweatshirt over that powerful torso. And that's when I knew for sure: I hadn't dreamed it. Mike had made love to me.

"I'll start the coffee," he said.

"I can do that—"

"Don't you move, Cosi. I mean it." He whipped off his glasses, shaking them like Rambo the Librarian. "You're not going anywhere . . ."

Smiling, I leaned back on the pillows, my eyes moving over the bedroom. The Justice Department had provided these digs for Quinn's temporary special assignment.

As corporate complexes went, it was nice enough, with luxury amenities like a fitness room, rooftop pool, and business center. The place came fully furnished and even boasted hardwood floors and an appliance-filled kitchen. But the decor was hotel homogenous, the art on the walls bland and corporate—pasty landscapes and framed splotches of color to match the carpeting.

With his East Village one-bedroom being sublet to another cop, Quinn displayed very little of himself here: a few snapshots tucked in his dresser mirror (his kids, some family members, and me), personal toiletries, clothes, shoes. That was it.

I did my best to bring in more touches of homey-ness— hand-thrown pottery and quilted pillows from our outings in Maryland and Virginia; some fun posters from the Folger Shakespeare Library; and a few framed pictures I'd taken of his OD Squad downing muffins and red eyes in my Village Blend.

"Here we go . . ."

Mike was back fast with two steaming NYPD mugs. The coffee was my Holiday Blend. (I sent him freshly roasted bags on a regular basis.) By now, the man knew the drill on grinding and brewing, and the rich, nutty, slightly spicy aroma was heaven-sent.

I sipped and sighed as he presented me with a white paper bag.

"I got us some breakfast. That little French place around the corner . . ."

Inside the sack were freshly baked croissants—chocolate, cherry, almond, and apple. *Oh, nice, they're still warm!*

As I used one hand to stuff my mouth with flaky pastry and cinnamon apples, he took tender hold of the other and removed the ice-filled athletic sock. It was then that I realized he'd secured the thing by linking his cop handcuffs around it.

"So were you *trying* to be funny?" I asked. "Or is this one of those 'hair of the dog that bit you' remedies?"

"Whatever works." He smiled. "And this did. The swelling's down . . ." But his smile faded as he examined my arm's exhibition of the color purple. Now he looked burdened with guilt.

"Mike, please don't feel bad. I should have called you. And honestly . . . most of these bruises didn't come from you."

It took him a second to process that. "Someone *else* did this to you?"

I nodded.

His expression went stony. "Who?"

"It's kind of a long story . . ."

Now his blue eyes were blazing. "Tell me."

I did, bringing him up to date on everything that had happened and finishing with the assurance that because of my discoveries, Lori Soles would have "St. Nick" Bacque *back* in custody, hopefully by the time I returned to New York.

Quinn's expression—or rather, his lack of one—failed to change as I talked. I could guess what he was thinking, but frankly I didn't want to.

This was what he'd been like early in our relationship. The man's "cop-curtain" would come down, he'd clam up, and I'd play twenty questions with myself on what was going on behind his interview-room stare.

As our time together progressed, I lost patience with the guessing games and insisted he open up, trust me with what he was feeling.

"So . . . ?" I said, giving him *the look*—the one that said, *Tell me what you're thinking or I'm going to scream!*

He folded his arms. "You really want to risk wrecking a pleasant weekend by knowing what I think?"

I flopped back on the bed and stared at the stucco ceiling. "You think I was stupid to risk going into Nick's bakery."

"Not stupid, just—"

"Reckless. Wrong."

"Yes. Both."

I sat up and met his eyes. "But do you think I'm wrong about Rita's killer? Do you think her homicide was simply her ex-husband, making it look like the basher? Do you really think it has no connection to M's murder?"

Mike rubbed the back of his neck. He hesitated before answering, and in the silence, the words *M's murder* began to echo through my brain, bringing back a memory from last night's party . . .

> TUCKER: *What sort of acting have you done?*
> DANNI: *I appeared in an episode of that serial killer cable show* Wexler. *I played a girl named Emily. I knew my lines, but I always missed my cue . . . The other actor would say, "Hey, Em," and I'd be waiting to hear "Hey, Danni."*

Hey, Em, I thought. Or *Hey, M* . . .

I grabbed Mike's shoulders. "Oh my God! *Moirin* isn't M's real name! I'm sure of it!"

"Oh?"

I explained my theory, starting with the thespian-challenged Danni Rayburn and ending with one of my staff meetings.

"Last Friday, before the first Cookie Swap, Esther, Tucker, and I sat around a café table, discussing funny holiday hats. When Esther called her Moirin, she didn't react. Then I addressed her as *M*, and she realized we were talking to her. It wasn't the first time I'd seen that happen."

"So what's your conclusion?"

"Her real name must have been something like Emily,

Emmaline, or Emma. She was clever to ask people to call her M. She could maintain a false name while being called something that sounded like her real one."

A tiny, amused smile lifted the corners of Quinn's mouth. "Mike?"

He rose without a word, went into the next room, and came back holding a cardboard shirt box with a stick-on bow.

"What's this?"

"An early Christmas gift," he said. "Something you asked for."

I blinked, trying to remember. "I didn't ask you for any—"

"Yes, you did. Open it."

Fifty-three

࿙࿚࿙࿚࿙࿚࿙࿚࿙࿚࿙࿚࿙࿚࿙࿚

I lifted off the box lid, confused at the stack of typewritten pages. From the first paragraph, I could see it was a transcript from a police interview.

"What is this, Quinn? Don't tell me you're writing your memoirs. Is this DC assignment going to your head?"

"Zip it, Cosi—and keep reading."

I did and, after a few pages, my jaw dropped. "*Where* did you get this?"

"CARIN."

"Excuse me? Carin *who*?"

He smirked. "Jealous?"

"Should I be?"

"Not unless you think I want to share French pastry in my bed with an international network of asset-tracing experts."

"Excuse me?"

"CARIN is an acronym for the Camden Assets Recovery Interagency Network. I have a friend there who hooked me up with a CAB contact."

"And when we say *cab*, I take it we're not talking about a taxi driver?"

"CAB stands for Criminal Assets Bureau. They work out of Dublin."

More alphabet soup. "Boil it down, Quinn, or we'll be in this bed all day."

He arched an eyebrow. "Promise."

"We'll see. Talk to me . . ."

He did.

Mike's years of working on narcotics crimes had put him on cases with tendrils that reached into international jurisdictions. Because drug dealers moved money and assets around the world, members of CARIN sometimes asked Quinn for help.

Now, because of me, he asked them for help.

First he phoned Lori Soles, requesting e-copies of M's fingerprints. He sent the prints to his contact at CARIN, who put him in touch with an agent at CAB, a division of the Irish police—also known as the Garda. Within days, Quinn was sent a confidential police interview transcript from a Dublin "Book of Evidence" procedure over five years before.

"But this transcript is not about Moirin Fagan . . ." I continued to page through it. "It's from an interview with a woman named Emma Brophy."

"That's right. It's like you just told me, Cosi." That little smile was back. "M's real name wasn't Moirin. It was *Emma.*"

I scanned the paperwork, trying to glean what crime M had been charged with. "This police interview is about stolen property, but she wasn't the one who stole it."

"That's right. Keep reading."

I did, and the whole story came together. M (aka Emma Brophy) had been working in a late bar, what the Irish call their nightclubs. The place was a magnet for the young, wealthy set.

There was also valet parking, and one of the club owners,

who had family connections to an organized crime network, set up an international car-theft ring.

When a luxury car was parked, a copy of the key was
made. Someone in the ring followed that car for a period of
days, waiting for a chance to drive it straight to a dock,
where it was shipped to another country for resale.

A low-level member of that ring was also a bartender at
the club and played in a local band. This young man began
dating Emma (M), who had no idea about his criminal
activity.

Cormac began giving M things—a flat-screen television, electronics, designer dresses. She had no idea they
were stolen. And the club owner had no idea Cormac and
his valet buddy were making copies of more than just a car
key. When they got their hands on a house key, they started
letting themselves in and taking pricey items. This sloppy
greed is what got them caught.

Close to Christmas, Cormac came by Emma's place. He
handed her a wrapped gift and told her not to open it. He
said this wasn't a gift for her, and she should put it under
the tree and leave it there.

By now, Emma suspected that her boyfriend was into
shady dealings. So, after he left, she did open it, and found
a handgun.

She rewrapped the gift, pretended everything was fine,
but pressed her boyfriend for answers. He'd had a lot to
drink that night and—*in vino veritas*, Cormac confessed
his criminal activities, and she let him have it.

Emma told Cormac she was shocked and disgusted. She
demanded he quit breaking the law. While she didn't want
to rat out her own boyfriend to the police, she was sickened
by what he'd done. She went to bed conflicted and woke up
in a terrible jam.

On a tip, the police raided her place, and Cormac fled,
climbing a trellis to the roof. He got away clean and is
believed to be at large in Eastern Europe.

In the meantime, the police arrested Emma Brophy as

the receiver of stolen goods. She spilled everything that her boyfriend told her about the criminal ring, including how it operated, and who was involved.

The recovered gun was connected to a murder. When M learned that, she knew what she had to do. She forged a deal with the Garda, agreeing to wear a wire and get people in the ring to admit guilt, including Cormac's older brother. She would also testify against them.

In exchange, she asked for the police to help her and her younger cousin, who worked at a Dublin bakery. The girls were best friends, and they wanted to relocate to America. According to Quinn, officials helped Emma and her cousin with the proper paperwork to begin a new life across the pond.

"So where did they set her up?" I asked, flipping through the pages.

"It's not in there," Quinn said. "And my contact wouldn't tell me. I got the impression no one in the Garda ever recorded that information. After Emma agreed to build a case for these officers, they dropped all charges against her and got her out of the country clean."

"Okay . . . so Emma came to America about five years ago. Yet her landlord, David Brice, told me she came to the city to live with him only two years ago. Where was she for the other three years?"

"Does it matter?"

"I'm just trying to get a picture of her life. A timeline . . ."

Mike shook his head. "The picture is clear enough. What you want to know is here." He tapped the papers. "Cormac got away clean. He's still at large."

"You don't think . . ."

"I do."

I stared at the papers and understood the logic of it.

"The violence of M's murder does fit a crime of passion," I admitted. "And Lori Soles told me M wrote in her diary recently about some *Letter* changing her life—a letter Lori has yet to find. Maybe this Letter was from Cormac.

M must have known her killer, and what you're suggesting does fit all the evidence, except . . ."

"What?"

"Why would Cormac kill her in a public place like the Cookie Swap? Why risk it? And why use a rock from the park, for heaven's sake? It's so stupid."

"Given the guy's stupid moves in the past, I wouldn't put too much stock in his suddenly getting smarter."

"But what would killing M get him? Revenge? Seems to me it would just increase the likelihood that he would get caught."

"Revenge killings are common enough. The Garda agree."

"So they're looking for Cormac now?"

"Not just Cormac. The Garda is also looking at known associates of people whom Emma Brophy testified against. If any of them traveled to America over the last six months, they're going to be looked at, maybe questioned."

"Then there's nothing more I can do to help."

"No, Cosi. But it's *because* of you we have this lead. I'm sending a copy of what you're holding to Lori Soles. She and Fletcher Endicott will likely work with Irish officials on pursuing leads on this side of the ocean. You did a good thing, asking me to get involved. Lori and Endicott may have dug this up eventually—but your curiosity saved the investigation valuable time."

I nodded. But feeling "good" about anything connected with M's brutal murder wasn't in the cards for me. Mike seemed to sense it. He leaned closer, his voice softened.

"You know, what I said to you earlier, about what you did last night—it wasn't entirely fair."

"What do you mean?"

"You may have been wrong to risk your safety, going into that scumbag's bakery. But you were right about Nick being a criminal."

"Thank you."

"And you may have been reckless going up in that

dumbwaiter, but you were also brave and self-sacrificing when you sent both of your backup ladies to help Punch."

"What are you getting at?"

"Just that . . . down deep, there's something in you, something I've struggled with myself over the years. You're dogged when it comes to finding the truth, but you're a little too impatient for justice."

"Is that such a crime?"

"No." He held my gaze. "It's one of the reasons I love you. One of the many reasons."

I smiled at that.

"But if you're not careful," he added in quiet warning, "that impatience is going to get you into real trouble. Do you hear me?"

"I do."

Quinn's lips twitched. "You know, Cosi, I like hearing you say those words."

"Oh really?"

"I know this separation of ours hasn't been easy, but I still look forward to the day we say those words to each other, in front of a witness or two."

"You do?"

"I do."

My spirits lifted at that, and I wanted to return the favor. "I have something for you . . ." I said, reaching for my handbag on the nightstand. I fished inside and pulled out a surprise. *Jingle, jingle, jingle . . .*

"What's this?" Quinn asked.

"A little holiday spirit, courtesy of the Village Blend."

The jingle bells were attached to a long wool scarf of Village Blend blue with a beautiful pattern of white snowflakes.

"I'm giving these to all my baristas as a Christmas gift this year."

Quinn laughed. "You expect me to wear a scarf with little sleigh bells? To the Federal Triangle?"

"Yes," I said. "It represents the happy, jingly spirit of

Christmas, something to keep you comfy through the months of winter."

He smiled as I wrapped the soft material around his neck. It jingled merrily as I gently tugged both ends, pulling his lips against mine, and for the next two days, we spent our time kindling the kind of heat that could keep us warm through another lonely week of nights apart.

FIFTY-FOUR

❧❧❧❧❧❧❧❧❧❧❧❧❧❧❧❧❧❧❧❧

By Tuesday afternoon, I was back on the job—the coffee job. With Quinn's revelation about Irish gangsters, I assumed M's case was beyond my help. But I assumed wrong.

Espresso in hand, I had just taken a seat with my laptop when Madame swept in, swinging two colorful holiday shopping bags. She charged right up to my table with an accusation—

"My great-great-grandmother was quite an accomplished matchmaker. I had humble aspirations in that direction, but you, my dear, are thwarting them!"

"Me?"

"Yes, you! I am trying to instill visions of marital bliss in my granddaughter, but how can I do that when you have yet to send Joy those photos you took of Emmanuel Franco skating in the park?"

I blinked. "Somehow the words 'marital bliss' and 'Emmanuel Franco' refuse to add up in my mind, and you know what? I am positive they wouldn't in your son's, either."

"Oh poo!" Madame spat, sinking into a chair. "Who cares what Matteo thinks?"

"Because *you're* desperate for a great-grandchild?"

Madame grinned. "Or maybe *two*. A boy—and a girl. Perhaps at the same time! Oh, wouldn't twins be a delight!"

"I'm not sure my daughter would agree with that, but . . . I'm game. I'll send the photos to Joy right now."

As I opened the Bryant Park photo files on my laptop, Boris delivered fresh espressos and a dish of newly baked Chocolate Candy Cane Cookies. After he served, he pointed to the screen.

"Ah, so cute! She is like a tiny Galina Kulikovskaya!"

"That's Molly Quinn, my boyfriend's daughter," I explained as I displayed more pictures, in quick succession.

Boris pointed. "There! You see . . . Molly imitates *Sleeping Beauty*, Galina Kulikovskaya's famous ballet on ice. For years now, she skates in worldwide show to music of Tchaikovsky. See the way the little girl makes a pillow with her hands then rests head on it? Very nice . . ."

"Clearly, Molly's a fan of the former Olympic skater."

Boris nodded. "She must love you then."

"Me? I haven't ice-skated in at least a year—"

"But you look just like Galina."

I rolled my eyes. "Please."

"You do!" he insisted. "She is about your age now. After I take next batch of cookies out of oven, I will show you." Boris disappeared behind the counter and went to work.

"Where are the photos of Franco?" Madame asked.

I jumped to the next image.

"Oh yes, that's lovely," Madame cooed.

I glanced at the image—but it didn't make me coo. The shot of Franco holding Jeremy's and Molly's hands was adorable enough, but a bad memory spoiled it. In the background loomed the darkened carousel, where I'd found M's body.

Madame touched my arm. "Clare? Did you hear what I said?"

"Sorry, I got a little sidetracked." I tapped the screen. "That's where M was murdered. I took this picture shortly before she was killed."

Madame frowned. "Have the police made any progress?"

I brought her up to date on what Quinn had discovered, including a very basic revelation: "Moirin Fagan's real name was Emma Brophy."

"Hmmm . . ." She tapped her chin. "Have you tried searching the girl's real name on the Internet to find out more about her?"

I nodded. "The hits were astronomical. Over eight hundred thousand. Facebook pages. High school yearbooks. Twitter. Dating services. I still want to find out where M spent those three years in America—before she came to New York City, but . . ."

I shrugged. "I'm trying to take Quinn's advice and let it go. Lori Soles is on the case in New York. The Garda is working the Irish angle. Quinn's probably got his Fed friends looking for Cormac and associates by now. What can a coffeehouse manager accomplish that the pros can't?"

I stared at the image again. This time I looked beyond the human figures, at the shadowy carousel.

"What's this?" I blinked, leaning closer to the screen. Madame did, too, and we clunked heads.

"Either I'm seeing stars or that's a speck of blue!" Madame declared.

I moved the photo to the Edit Picture program and magnified the image. The blue speck turned into a blue blob. Another magnification and the blob became a familiar bright blue logo—the symbol of the Raiders hockey team.

"It's an ice skate bag," I said. "See, it's shaped like a triangle. Someone hung it on a wooden horse inside the carousel." I turned to Madame. "That bag wasn't there when I found M's corpse! Do you know what this means? That bag must have belonged to the killer, who was waiting there to meet M!"

"Is it possible you snapped an image of the murderer?" Madame asked.

I expanded another section of the photo, then another. "There!" I tapped the screen. "A silhouette!"

Madame shook her head doubtfully. "It *might* be a silhouette."

"You're right. Even if that is a person, there are no details. It could be a man or a woman. But Ross Puckett skated for the kids that night. That could be his bag."

"Too easy a conclusion, dear. I'm afraid there were a lot of Raiders fans in attendance that evening. I saw several young men with Raiders backpacks. Parents and nannies carried Raiders skate bags, too."

"You're right, but this must mean something—"

The tinny sound of Bing Crosby singing "White Christmas" echoed through the quiet coffeehouse. I looked up to see Vicki Glockner emerging from our pantry area.

"Someone placed a Secret Santa gift under the tree," Tuck announced.

"No, the other way around . . ." Vicki said with a sigh. "I'm taking one back. Those Purple Lettuce tickets that I was going to give to M? I'm sending them to my cousin on Long Island instead. He's a huge fan."

So was M, I recalled.

On the night of her murder, Vicki had mentioned how M had followed Purple Lettuce since their start on Long Island.

Wait a minute. Since their start on Long Island!

"Vicki!" I called. "When did Purple Lettuce start performing?"

She shrugged. "At least four years ago."

I looked at Madame. "Let's search 'Emma Brophy' and 'Long Island' together and see what we find . . ."

"Did you know there's another gift addressed to M on the Secret Santa shelf?" Vicki was saying to Tucker as I frantically typed.

"It's probably from Dante," Tuck replied sadly. "Just leave it there for now . . ."

There was no 'Emma Brophy' that seemed relevant, but I refused to give up. Broadening the search to simply 'Brophy' and 'Long Island' did the trick.

We struck sleuthing gold.

Fifty-five

~~~~~~

For vanity's sake, Madame had "forgotten" her reading glasses, so I read the *Long Island Newsday* article out loud.

"'Baker's Assistant Dies in Fiery Late-Night Crash' says the headline," I began. "It's dated last December."

According to the story, the victim was Kaitlin Brophy, twenty-two, a recent Irish émigré who was sleeping in her apartment over a local bakery when a late-model BMW convertible slammed into the building, igniting the gas lines feeding the ovens. The owners didn't live on the premises, so they survived. But there was no saving the young assistant. The unknown driver fled the scene."

A follow-up story proved even more explosive.

"Look at this!" I cried. "The car that struck the building belonged to Raiders hockey captain Ross Puckett!"

Madame nearly dropped her demitasse. "Was he driving?"

"Puckett reported the car stolen shortly after the accident occurred. He must not have been charged with anything, because I can't find anything else. The whole story just disappears."

I caught Tuck's attention and waved for another round of caffeine.

My mind raced. "Kaitlin died almost exactly a year ago. I remember something David Brice said. He heard M bitterly crying in her apartment around this time last year. He said the next day M borrowed money to buy a black dress. A *funeral* dress!"

I faced Madame again.

"Kaitlin must have been the unnamed 'cousin' who was mentioned in Quinn's transcript from Dublin—and she was killed by Ross Puckett's car! Then Ross turns up again, right before M dies? Whether the car was stolen or not, this is too much of a coincidence . . ." (And I knew how Quinn felt about coincidences.)

"But what about Rita Limon?" Madame asked.

"Lori Soles believes that was a different killer. Right now, Rita's estranged husband looks guilty as sin."

Madame arched an eyebrow. "But how does this fit with your man's Irish criminal theory?"

"Back in Ireland, M's troubles started when her boyfriend began stealing cars. And when she turned on him, he fled. Maybe this guy Cormac is in America now, seeking revenge."

"So this Irish hoodlum came to America and stole Ross Puckett's car to kill Kaitlin? Then he attacked M, a year later, pretending to be the Stalker?"

"I know," I said, shaking my head. "That theory sounds far-fetched. But here's something that doesn't. What if Cormac or his friends came to America to do more than take revenge and jack cars?"

"Like what, dear?"

"What if they came to set up some kind of sports betting operation? Maybe Ross Puckett got involved with it. Maybe he threw a game or two, changed the point spread for a payoff?"

"You're thinking like your father," Madame said disapprovingly.

"Maybe I am . . . but I'd love to have a long talk with that hockey captain, peel away a few layers of jock armor, and get to the truth."

"I believe he's invited to the next Cookie Swap," Madame suggested.

"That's days away, and he might not show. Anyway, a kids' party isn't the right venue. Ross has a weakness for the hard stuff. If I could get him good and loaded first, who knows what that genius would admit."

I pulled out my cell phone. "I better tell Lori Soles what I found . . ."

She answered on the second ring. "What's up, Cosi?"

"I found something . . ." I told Lori about my digital photos and about my suspicions concerning Ross Puckett and the manslaughter of Kaitlin Brophy. She took it all in without comment. The pause was so long, I finally asked—

"Well, what do you think?"

"I'm taking notes . . ."

When she said nothing else, I asked, "What have you been working on, detective?"

She exhaled. "The forensics people are driving us all mad. They're still testing bladed weapons, trying to find a match to Rita Limon's head wounds. Last time I checked, they were on a Gurkha knife."

I glanced again at the image in the corner of my computer screen, the magnified photograph of the triangular bag with the Raiders logo, and said—

"Try an ice skate."

"An ice skate? Why do you think the murderer used an ice skate?"

"It's just a hunch, based on my photos. I'll e-mail them to you . . ."

"Good. And good enough for me, Cosi. I'll suggest an ice skate."

"Great, then—"

"Hold on. I have a question for you."

Lori surprised me by mentioning Danni Rayburn's nanny. She described the woman, and I realized it was the same one I'd encountered on the toy store escalator last Friday, after I'd left Rita.

"Have you had any contact with that woman since the Cookie Swap?"

"No. Is she a person of interest?"

"I can only say the NYPD wants to question her, but it seems she has turned up missing."

"Missing or presumed . . . ?"

"Presumed *missing*, Cosi. Thanks for the tip. Got to go."

The line went dead just as Tucker showed up with our espressos. Boris arrived, too, waving an issue of *Sports Illustrated*.

"Cookies are cooling. Now I want you to look at the cover," Boris insisted. "See? You *do* look like Galina Kulikovskaya."

The woman on the cover was beautiful, but the headline and subtitle were more intriguing. They said:

GALINA, WE LOVE YOU

Why Do Filmmaker Brian Kelly, the House of Fen, and Hockey Pro Ross Puckett All Think Galina Kulikovskaya Is the Hottest Thing on Ice?

"And here," Boris said, flipping pages. "Galina at practice."

I hardly glanced at the photo. I was too busy reading the breakout text:

> *"I'd give up hockey and turn to figure skating if I thought I could get into Galina's leotards," says Raiders captain Ross Puckett . . .*

Suddenly Madame's nearsightedness miraculously cleared up and she read that line over my shoulder.

"My word, Clare . . . Perhaps *you* could fool Mr. Puckett into thinking you're Galina Kulikovskaya."

"Certainly not!"

Tuck nodded excitedly. "Oh, I could pull that transformation off! A little makeup, a convincing wardrobe, some body shifting—"

"Body shifting!"

"I could teach you some moves, too. Like that *Sleeping Beauty* thing Galina does," Tuck went on. "It's a cinch."

"So I just show up at the Barclays Center disguised as the great Galina and ask to see Ross Puckett?"

"As a matter of fact, my Matt and his Breanne are attending a party at the Barclays Center tonight," Madame said. "I do believe my son mentioned that it's sponsored by the Raiders. I can't say for sure whether our Mr. Puckett will be there, but it is worth a thought."

I felt Tuck's hand on my shoulder. "It's destiny, CC."

"But I can't skate," I protested. "Not like an Olympian."

"Oh, for heaven's sake," Tuck said. "It's a holiday bash. Nobody will expect you to skate!"

"But I can't speak Russian!"

Madame grinned. "Boris does. He can teach you."

"Better idea. I can be translator!" Boris declared. "Then I, too, can go to this fancy-shmansy hockey party."

"Matt would never agree," I stated with absolute certainty. "And Breanne? Forget it."

"You won't know until you ask." Madame rose. "I'll pressure him from my end, too, and you'll have to let me know how it all turns out."

"You're abandoning me?" I wailed.

"Otto has his own holiday party this evening, and I simply must attend. Busy, busy, busy . . . *au revoir!*" Madame gathered up her packages and strolled out the door.

I stared up at Tuck and Boris. They grinned back expectantly.

"Fine, I'll call Matt. But I'm telling you, he'll never, *ever* go for it."

Fifty-six

∽∾∽∾∽∾∽∾∽∾∽∾∽∾∽∾∽∾∽∾

Thε tension inside Breanne Summour's stretch limousine was so thick you could cleave it with an ice skate.

The fashion maven hadn't spoken a word since we climbed into her car, and her sullen silence pretty much set the tone. Resplendent in a silver sheath and pashmina stole, Breanne sat beside a sour yet dashing Matt Allegro, who was just as nonloquacious as his wife. I sat facing the couple, so Breanne kept her eyes focused on the scenery during the entire trip from her East Side apartment to the Barclays Center in Brooklyn.

Boris, my "translator," seemed to be the only person having any fun. In Fen formal wear, he grinned as he adjusted his gold cuff links for the tenth time.

"I feel handsome as *Yames* Bond," he'd declared when he first saw his reflection in the full-length mirror. I hoped Esther would get a chance to see his Cinderella transformation before he had to return the borrowed duds.

The lead-in to my masquerade was something out of a reality show.

Breanne agreed to produce *Clare's Total Makeover* once

Matt convinced his wife to go along with our deception. What she demanded in exchange, I didn't ask. A special favor? A tighter leash? A devil's contract signed in Matt's blood? All I know is that she absolutely insisted the disguise be convincing. To that end she spirited Tuck, Boris, and me to her Sutton Place penthouse apartment, where a hairdresser, two wardrobe specialists, and a fashion editor waited to advise us.

Despite the presence of Bree's experts, it was Tucker, wielding years of theatrical experience, who took command of this production. With a showman's eye he made every decision, from the proper hair color to suitable attire.

But it began with everyone staring at my discount sweater and stonewashed denim–clad form. Hands thoughtfully placed on chins, Tuck and his staff offered a critical head-to-toe appraisal of what they saw. (It wasn't pretty.)

"Boris is right about your face being a mirror image of Kulikovskaya's, but the resemblance ends there," Tuck declared. "Your figure is much more . . . shall we say *lush*? And Galina could have used your *rear padding* during all those falls in ice dance training."

"Oh, *that's* a tactful way of putting it."

The hairdresser leaned close, his fingers caressing my chestnut locks.

"Nice color, healthy ends, *much* too light for Galina," he declared. "We'll give her a fast raven wash. And her emerald eyes are all wrong. Miss Kulikovskaya has brilliant sapphire *blue* eyes."

Tuck nodded. "No time for a contact fitting. We'll have to go with snow-blind."

"Pardon me?"

"'Galina Kulikovskaya suffered from snow blindness twice in her life,'" Tucker said, reading from her *Sports Illustrated* profile. "'First when she was a teen and practicing on the frozen banks of the Kura River in *Tbilisi*. The second time during the run-up to the Olympics where she won the Gold.'"

Tuck faced the fashion editor. "We need sunglasses. Stylish, but large enough to hide Clare's eyes."

The woman scurried off, while the others went to work. Two hours later, I stared in awe at my own reflection.

My hair was darkened and twisted into a bun; a ribbon of blue silk encircled my neck (to make it appear "swanlike," apparently); and my "lush" breasts were taped practically flat. They'd blanched my olive skin to a snowy white, using a pound of foundation; painted my lips redder than cherry pie filling; and squeezed my hips into a pair of Spanx. Over my weak protestations, they'd actually double wrapped me with a bikini girdle *under* the spandex panties.

Swathed in a Fen gown of shimmering blue, I barely recognized the freshly painted, severely flattened, and torturously slenderized me.

"*That* should attract Ross Puckett's attention," Tuck declared. "You're the perfect bait for Number 88. He'll skate right to you!"

I hoped so, because I intended to mentally probe the man once I got him alone. Puckett had flirted with Moirin before she was killed, he'd visited with Rita before she was murdered, and he'd had his BMW convertible "stolen" and used as a weapon to kill M's cousin almost exactly one year ago.

Did it all add up to anything?

I wasn't entirely sure. But knowing a vicious killer was still walking around out there scot-free, I was absolutely ready to *try* doing the math. I intended to draw Ross out for answers, but I'd have to draw him in first, and there was no better bait to attract a serial playboy than a pretty, famous, and *famously desirable* woman.

Despite the need for sex appeal, I protested the dress's skimpiness. It had nice long sleeves (to hide my bruised arms), but an obscenely short hemline.

Tuck insisted the length was appropriate "to show off your toned skater's legs."

"I don't have skater's legs!"

"No, but you do have toned legs. They're very shapely with well-developed calves, not surprising given the hours you spend on your feet at the Blend, plus the daily New York walking."

"But, really, it's ridiculously short. If I were to bend over—"

"Take my advice—and don't."

"But—"

"Listen, honey. We have to do something to make up for your lack of cleavage. You're wrapped flat as a hockey puck and covered up everywhere else. Don't forget, your goal is to *attract* this jock's attention."

"Are you sure it's not to catch pneumonia? I *am* going to an ice rink."

"We have a solution for frostbite!" Tuck announced, stepping aside.

The fashion editor approached, offering me a pair of Kazuo Kawasaki sunglasses and Breanne's own ankle-length sable coat. "Ms. Summour suggested you borrow it. Galina Kulikovskaya should be swathed in fur."

I was wrapped in the sable's warm embrace right now, as the limo rolled up to the Barclays Center. An usher opened the door and cold night air washed over us. Matt climbed out first.

I took a deep breath—cut short when an iron grip closed on my stocking-clad thigh. Breanne leaned close and hissed into my ear.

"If you are exposed as the fraud you are, I am going to claim you fooled me, too. Make no mistake, Clare Cosi. If this masquerade goes south, you're on your own."

Breanne released her killer grip, and with a practiced smile she took Matt's hand and exited the car.

I slipped on my sunglasses, barely rattled. After all, Matt's new wife was running true to form. When coerced, she was there to help. But when the "fit hit the shan" as my pop used to say, she was "outta there" quicker than a cornered Dublin hood.

"You are Galina Kulikovskaya," Boris sternly reminded me. "Speak *Russian*, or not at all."

The rapper had tried to teach me a few phrases in his native language, but I had trouble pronouncing what was supposed to be my name. Boris suggested I turn my V's into W's as Russians do when speaking English. But my decision about my Russian accent had already been made.

"I told you before. I'm sticking with *da* and *nyet*. At least until I interrogate Ross Puckett."

Boris nodded. Then, in a perfect imitation of Matt—or perhaps *Yames* Bond—he extended his hand to help me exit the limo.

Fifty-seven

~~~~~~

Because this was a private party for a few hundred guests, there were no paparazzi or press lurking at the doors. The only indication of an "event" taking place was a gathering of ushers at the arena entrance. While we checked our coats inside the vast foyer, I whispered to Matt—

"I'm sorry about all this."

"Sorry? Why?"

"Breanne does *not* look happy."

"She'll get over it. And believe me, I want to catch Moirin and Rita's killer as much as you do. Besides—" He threw me a reassuring wink. "This little stunt might prove to be *a lot* more fun that the deadly dull holiday parties I've been forced to attend."

We next descended a flight of stairs and entered a long tunnel. Moments later we exited in the middle of the arena, right beside the ice rink. The arena blazed with lights. Hundreds milled around the buffet table, the wet bar, the children's snack table.

Nearly invisible in the gloom, thousands of empty seats rose up in tiers under a lofty, steel-framed roof. I was still gazing in awe at the brand-new section of the arena when a familiar voice called my name—well, Galina Kulikovskaya's name, anyway.

"Evil Eyes" Eddie Rayburn, a fireplug in formal wear, took my hand and graciously kissed it. "A pleasure to meet you," he cooed.

"*Da*," I replied.

For the crowd, I gracefully mimicked the real Galina's signature gesture, the graceful arm pillow that evoked her famous *Sleeping Beauty* ballet on ice routine. The move was greeted with excited applause.

"A shame you didn't let us know you were coming," Eddie said. "I'm the promoter for this venue. I could have arranged something special with the press."

Shaking my head, I muttered one of the phrases Boris taught me. (I believe I said, I want a bowl of soup.)

Eddie shot Boris a puzzled look.

"Galina, she say no camera," Boris explained, thickening his Russian accent. "The champion, she have snow blindness. Bright lights and flashbulb *werry* bad for eye. *Werry, werry* bad."

Eddie nodded. "Ah yes—"

Suddenly an exuberant ten-year-old boy rushed among us, shoving Boris aside and stepping on my designer pumps.

"Adam! Behave like a gentleman!" Danni Rayburn cried as she chased after her son. Huffing, she paused to apologize.

"I can't control him," Danni said. "My nanny just disappeared on us, and we haven't hired a new girl yet!"

There was a crash, and all eyes faced the rink. Little Adam, sans ice skates, had rushed onto the ice, slipped, and slammed into a rack of hockey sticks, scattering them.

"Adam Rayburn! You get back here this instant!" Danni yelled.

In response, her son crawled to his feet and slide-skated away on his loafers, brushing ice dust from his little suit.

Meanwhile, Eddie Rayburn assembled the guests and

made introductions. While I shook hands and listened to "translations" of everyone's effusive greetings, I finally spied the other half of the Double D team.

Delores Deluca stood alone near the bar, champagne flute in hand. She observed the guests mingling, and her friend's frantic attempts at parental control, with bemused disinterest. Then her gaze found me and her disinterest fled. The look on her face turned almost hateful.

She rose from the bar and began to approach. As she neared, however, her nasty expression morphed into one of suspicious curiosity.

Oh crap.

Delores seemed somewhat smarter than her ditzy friend—not to mention more prickly. I still recalled the glare she gave me last Friday.

Did she recognize me from the toy store Cookie Swap?

Luckily, I was saved by the hockey captain. Before Delores could get closer, Ross Puckett shouldered through the crowd to speak with me, a look of fanboy adoration on his typically blank face.

"Oh, gee, Ms. Galina . . . I mean Ms. Kulikovskaya. It's really an honor to meet you. I'm a big fan."

"*Da, da,*" I replied, neck craning to address the giant. I extended my hand. Unfortunately Puckett didn't kiss it in the manner of an Eddie Rayburn. He shook it hard enough to jar my bruises.

Because this invitation-only event was billed as "practice and party," Ross was in his Raiders uniform, including the famous Number 88 jersey. It was the first time I'd seen him in his natural habitat, and he seemed even larger and more imposing—*and*, yes, physically scary enough to be a multiple murderer.

"Excuse me," Eddie cried, rushing up to us. He held something in his beefy hands: a faded pair of pink ice skates. "Remember these?"

Boris pretended to translate. I shook my head.

"Why, these are the skates you wore while performing *Sleeping Beauty* at Madison Square Garden a few years ago," Eddie said, loud enough to attract everyone's attention. "How about you put them on, give us a demonstration."

Yikes!

Excited applause broke out. Ross joined the chorus, and even insisted on donning his own skates to join me. Boris leaned close, pretending to translate.

"Vat za heck am I supposed to do-sky?" I whispered.

Boris sat me down and pulled off my pumps. As he laced up the skates (which mercifully fit!) he gave me a way out, through rap! "If your back's to the wall / and there's no one to call / don't whine, don't bawl / just take the fall."

Off my puzzled look, Boris gestured toward the hockey sticks on the ice.

"Trip," he said. "And make it look good."

Fifty-eight

~~~~~~~~~~~~~~~~~~~~~~~~~~~~

I glided onto the ice to cheers and applause, grateful that my nascent skating skills came back in a mental rush. But twirling and swirling were well beyond me, so I faced the audience, faking them out, yet again, with another signature Galina arm move.

I continued to skate, one foot smoothly in front of the other, which was about *all* I could manage out here. I couldn't even use a toe pick! So I swallowed hard and braced myself for some necessary pain.

I turned, gliding backward a bit, as if I were considering which Olympic-level jump to show off. I wanted my fall to look convincing, but I needn't have worried about verisimilitude, because I'd misjudged the distance to the hockey sticks, and collided with them much sooner than expected.

One second I was moving along, and then I was airborne, staring in shock at the pink ice skates on my feet—only those feet were framed by the lofty ceiling lights high above, not the ice below.

I landed with a jarring thud that bruised my tailbone.

The audience whooshed in a collective gasp. I let fly

with a convincing howl of pain—convincing because it *really hurt*.

Eddie Rayburn paled, as visions of an Olympic-sized lawsuit danced in his head (it *was* his hell-spawn who scattered those hockey sticks in the first place)! I felt strong but tender hands gather me up, and lift me off the hard, cold ice. Encircled by a pair of powerful arms.

Then a shadow fell over me. I looked up, into the concerned, starstruck face of Ross Puckett.

The guy was built like a Roman god and the skates on his feet flew like Mercury's wings as he rushed me across the rink's ice. Before I knew it, we were through a nearly invisible door—a first aid room, I realized.

Inside the brightly lit space, he set me down on an examination table. Then he closed the door and twisted the lock.

"Where does it hurt?" he asked.

"My ankle," I moaned, though it was really my tailbone that was smarting!

Ross gently removed the ice skate and ran his callused hands along my ankle and up my calf. "There's no swelling. Let me ice it."

He tugged off his own skates, crossed to a small freezer, and retrieved a segmented ice pack. He carefully wrapped the cold compress around my lower calf. Then his eyes met mine; well, my *sunglasses*.

"Better?"

I nodded. "You are *werry* kind."

He chuckled. "It's cute the way you talk."

Here comes the playboy I knew—and counted on.

I flirtatiously batted my eyelashes before I remembered he couldn't see them behind my sunglasses. I reached out and touched his hand instead.

"*Tank* you. For everything," I said softly.

That was all the encouragement Ross needed. Suddenly I was fending off an octopus.

"*Nyet, nyet,*" I protested. "Am married *voman*."

"Don't let a little thing like *that* stop you," he insisted.

Panting, Ross nuzzled my neck. I pushed him away. *Back off, big boy!*

"Maybe you need to relax, have a drink," Ross said, producing a familiar flask. He thrust the container under my nose, but I shook my head and pushed it away.

"Am training."

"Hell, I'm training every day, and it never stopped me. Come on, give it a try. It's good stuff. Smirnoff."

"I drink too much *wodka*, I *womit*." *Ooh! That didn't come out right!*

Ross shrugged and took a gulp himself. The alcohol had an immediate effect on his libido and he renewed his assault on my virtue.

"*Nyet*, my husband *werry* jealous!" I cried.

"You don't know jealous," he replied with a sly laugh.

"*Da*, I do," I said. "My husband keel to keep me. And he has dangerous friends who watch my every move. Irish gangsters who do terrible, violent things. Irish gangsters *werry* bad. Do you know Irish gangsters?"

Ross shrugged again. "I saw *The Departed* once. I liked *Scarface* better. Remember the ending?" Ross formed little guns with his fingers and thumbs.

"Bang! Bang! 'Say hello to my leetle friend!'"

"*Nyet*. Not Hollywood gangsters. *Real* gangsters. Irish men who steal cars and like to bet on the ponies and the sports. Crazy, jealous men like my husband."

Ross scowled and swallowed another snort. "So your husband's real jealous, hunh?"

I nodded, rolling with his question. "*Da*. Once husband got behind wheel of BMW convertible. Try to run Galina's trainer over. He miss, wreck car. He run away, say car was stolen to get insurance."

"What a coincidence," Ross said after another toot. "I had my BMW convertible stolen. The crazy bitch wrecked it, too."

"A girl wreck car?"

"Yeah. She was crazy jealous, too. Loved me so much

she put an '88 is Great' tattoo where the sun don't shine!"
He winked. "Got hammered one night, took my car out, and
smashed the heck out of it." Ross sighed. "I loved that car."

"Who vas girl?"

"Sorry, can't tell you that. It's complicated . . ."

My mind started working on this revelation—*a woman*
wrecked his car. A "crazy bitch" in his words. Obviously,
he'd lied to the police, claiming he didn't know who stole
his car. Maybe he'd lied to protect this woman. More likely
he'd lied to protect himself from the bad publicity of a sordid scandal.

Whatever the reason, he was clearly guilty of a cover-
up—though innocent of manslaughter. He wasn't innocent
of sexual harassment charges, however. After yet another
swallow of *wodka*, he pinned me to the table.

"Come on, Galina, we're alone," he whispered in my ear.
"No one will know."

"*Nyet*," I countered, slapping his face. Thankfully, he
backed off, and I sat up. "I know men," I told him. "They
boast and brag of their conquests!"

Ross backed off, rubbing his cheek. "Is that all you're
worried about." He smiled. "Believe me, I'm a true man of
discretion." He made a zipping motion across his mouth then
mumbled something with his lips zipped.

"*Vat?*"

"I would never tell!" he repeated. "I'll prove it to you.
The fact is—I'm a guy who knows *all about* jealous hus-
bands. Remember that man who brought you the skates?"

"Comrade Rayburn?"

"*Da*," Ross said, smiling and nodding. "He's a real jealous husband. I work with the guy on promotional events all
the time, *and* I nailed his wife—practically under his fat
nose. You met the missus. That built cougar, Danni?"

I nearly fell off the examination table.

"Nope." Puckett drained his flask. "Evil Eyes didn't
guess squat. And you never read about Danni and me in the
tabloids, either. Do you know why?"

Too shocked to reply, I simply shook my head.

"Because I was a true man of discretion. I kept a secret the whole time we were hooking up last December."

Last December? Oh my God . . .

The timing was irrefutable—the car wreck that killed M's cousin was last December. The car was driven by a "crazy bitch" involved with Ross. And now he admitted the identity of the woman he'd been having a secret affair with last December.

This idiot doesn't know it, but he just admitted to me that Kaitlin Brophy was killed by Danni Rayburn!

Ross belched. Hot, alcohol-laced breath washed over me. He lunged again and our lips locked. During the ensuing struggle, my bun disintegrated.

There was no more to be gained here, and my situation was dire. I had to go. Fortunately, I'd already planned my escape. All it required was a little melodrama on my part.

As Ross moved in for another kiss, I knocked my sunglasses off. Then I covered my eyes and started screaming.

"I *yam* blind! Blind! The light, it *ruin-ink* my eyes."

"Oh man, oh man. Let me find your glasses," Ross said in a tone of drunken panic. Then I heard a sickening crunch. "Damn. Damn," groaned Ross.

Oops. So much for those pricey Kazuo Kawasaki frames.

My screams got louder, until someone pounded on the door.

"Let me in or I break it down!" Boris commanded from the other side.

"I'll be right there," Ross said. He tripped during his headlong lunge for the lock. He staggered to his feet, ripped the door open, and sighed with relief.

"You better get her out of here," he told Boris. "Get her to a doctor, man."

"Boris? Is that you?" I called, eyes closed, arms groping blindly.

"Get away from her, you brute!" Boris shouted, hands

balled into fists. "This is outrage! An international coincidence!"

"I'm gone!" Ross pushed past Boris and staggered down
the hall.

I rolled off the examination table and kicked the ice
pack off my calf. Boris handed me my pumps.

"Thanks, comrade," I whispered as I slipped them on.
"Let's get out of here. Through the back door, this time."

Fifty-nine

꩜꩜꩜꩜꩜꩜꩜꩜꩜꩜꩜꩜꩜꩜꩜꩜

"Cosi, that hit-and-run is a year old," Lori Soles informed me by phone the next morning. "It also took place in Nassau County, on Long Island, so it's out of the NYPD's jurisdiction."

"But—"

"No buts," Lori insisted. "What you have is hearsay, not proof. Ross Puckett has everything to lose and nothing to gain by repeating the story he told you. The man's attorneys would never allow him to go on the record with authorities."

I paced my kitchen, suggesting that Lori at least *review* the files.

"I've got no time for that! Reach out to the shields on Long Island, maybe they can help. Anyway, I can't see how that case is related to the unsolved homicides we *do* have in our jurisdiction."

"It is related, if you consider my theory—"

For half the night, I lay awake going over my memories from both Cookie Swap parties, and I'd come to a firm conclusion: one of two people had to be guilty of killing M. Unfortunately, Lori wasn't listening.

"—by now you *must* know about the evidence your man Quinn dug up," she went on. "Your late employee testified against members of a Dublin car-theft ring, one of whom is still at large. My lieutenant is completely sold on Quinn's revenge murder theory, and he's got half the squad checking alibis on the gangs' known associates in the United States—"

"Listen to me," I said, "Mike Quinn is a brilliant narcotics detective, but his theory about M's murder is totally skewed by the Irish authorities. They have good reason to think what they do, but they weren't at those Cookie Swap parties or at the Bryant Park crime scene. *I was.* And I have my own theory about the connection between my employee's murder and her cousin's death. I admit I can't *prove* it. But I promise you that it does add up."

A long pause was followed by a mumbled conversation to someone on Lori's end of the line. Finally, she came back.

"Look, Cosi, I'll come by the shop tonight, and you can brief me on this theory of yours. But I have to warn you—without proof, theories are about as valuable to me as a kiddie bedtime story."

"Yes, Detective, I realize that."

"Oh, and save me a few of those gingerbread men. Biting their heads off is proving cheaper than therapy." She lowered her voice. "Endicott's snapping his fingers. Got to go . . ."

The line went dead, and I collapsed into my kitchen chair.

I knew in my bones that I was close to solving M's murder. Unfortunately, I couldn't get around Lori's point. For anyone to believe me, I would have to find proof. But how on earth was I going to do that?

An hour later, I descended the stairs to the Village Blend. The scheme I'd come up with was simple enough—and if I executed my plan this afternoon, I'd have the evidence in time for Lori's scheduled beheading of little gingerbread Endicotts tonight.

There was only one drawback. I would have to persuade my most trusted barista to help me. And that barista had every reason to turn me down.

"And here she is! The Great Galina herself!" Tucker Burton grinned as I approached his lanky form behind the coffee bar.

"Tuck, we need to talk. Pull us a couple of doubles and come up to my office."

Sixty

ᘓᘓᘓᘓᘓᘓᘓᘓᘓᘓᘓᘓᘓᘓᘓᘓᘓᘓᘓᘓᘓᘓᘓᘓ

"**S**o?" Tuck began as I shut the door. "Dish! How did it go last night with the horny hockey captain?"

"Well enough to give me a very strong lead on M's murderer."

"Wow. The NYPD should keep me on retainer to costume all their undercovers!"

I settled into my creaky desk chair, took a hit of earthy espresso, and hoped the caffeine would give me the courage to get through this.

"Tuck, I'm so sorry, but I've got some disappointing news for you."

"Uh-oh. I don't like the sound of that."

"The last thing I want to do is shoot down an artist's dream, just as it's taking off. But what I discovered is going to mean an end to your bound-for-Broadway show with the Double Ds."

For a terrible moment, Tuck looked completely stricken—and I felt horrible. Then a whoosh of air rushed out of him and he sat back with an unreadable look.

"Ooooh," he wailed, "thank goodness!"

I blinked. "Thank goodness?"

"Oh, honey, if you can get me 'off the hook' to do this show, I will be forever in your debt!"

"But . . . I don't understand. I thought you were thrilled with the chance to do a show with Danni and Delores?"

"That was before I got to know the real them. Those ladies were heavily packaged by the reality show producers—and it worked for TV. But theater is another animal. On stage, what you see is what you get, and those ladies . . . How do I put this? If talent could be measured on a scale of one to ten, they're in the negative numbers."

"Even with a campy production?"

"Are you kidding? Camp takes courage, CC, and it also takes skill: singing, dancing, comic timing; at the very least, the ability to deliver your lines with a modicum of stage presence! Punch is brilliant at it, and I would *much* rather work with him and any number of actor friends, who are true geniuses, rather than with those true housewives."

"Really?"

"For days, I've been trying to work out how to save the production. Punch suggested a drag show *around* them. They'd make a few key appearances, something simple for them to handle. But Eddie Rayburn wouldn't have it. His Danni and her little buddy Delores had to be the *stars*, so I've been losing sleep, trying to figure a way out. I mean, sure it's every director's dream to be handed a big-budget show, but who needs a bomb so big it explodes your career?"

"Oh, Tuck, I am so relieved that you're relieved!"

"No problem, CC. Maybe I'll get to Broadway someday; maybe I won't. But, honestly, I'd rather my success be based on my own talent and experience—not on a couple of ladies who are simply famous for being famous."

I took another hit of espresso, fortifying myself for the second half of my difficult news.

Tuck studied me. "So? What did you find out last night? Did Ross come out and *say* that one of the Ds killed M?"

"Not M. Her cousin Kaitlin."

"You'll have to explain."

"Last December, Ross told authorities that his BMW was stolen by an unknown thief. But last night, he told me that a jealous girlfriend got herself drunk and took it. He wouldn't tell me her name; only that she was crazy enough to get herself tattooed with *88 is Great*. A few chugs of Smirnoff later, he let slip that he was having an affair, in that same time period, with *Danni Rayburn*."

"No!"

"Yes! Obviously, Danni Rayburn killed Kaitlin when she drove Ross's car into the bakery where the girl worked. The car severed gas lines feeding the ovens. The bakery caught fire, Kaitlin was killed, and Danni escaped manslaughter charges because she and Ross covered it up."

"And how does that connect to M's murder?"

"It seems to me, when M first came to America, she must have lived and worked on Long Island, probably with her cousin Kaitlin, at that same little bakery where the girl was killed. Two years ago, M moved to New York City to pursue her dream of becoming a professional recording artist. That's when she moved in with ex-rocker David Brice."

"The guy you met at the retirement community?"

I nodded. "I'm sure M hoped to hit it big one day, and that was why she changed her name when she came to the city—to prevent anyone from tracing her history to that sordid scandal in Dublin. Then last year, she heard the news of her cousin's death, and it hit her hard, but she kept going, continued working, singing, and dreaming. I'm sure she believed what everyone else did: that Kaitlin's death was a terrible accident and the person responsible was a car thief who got away.

"Then about three months ago, according to Lori Soles, M received a letter. What was in this letter? M never wrote that down in her diary, but she did say it brought 'terrible news.' She obviously thought about the letter a long time and then wrote that 'the letter changes everything.' As of about three weeks before her death, she began to write about the Letter with a capital L, and finally said that it would help her 'build a better future for herself, and for others.'"

"And?"

"I believe this Letter revealed the truth about the accident that killed Kaitlin. It wasn't some unknown thug who caused that fire; it was TV star Danni Rayburn, a rich and famous woman, who never paid for what she'd done. I think M decided to make Danni pay. She used the Letter to blackmail her."

"Oh my goodness, this is actually making sense . . ."

"Danni probably agreed to pay but demanded to see this Letter first. M would have insisted the meeting be in a public place so she could be sure of her safety—but also make sure the tables weren't turned on her."

"What do you mean?"

"Well, what M was doing was a crime. She was extorting money in exchange for silence. M would want to avoid the presence of any witnesses who might help Danni twist things around and charge M with blackmail."

"That's why they met in the Bryant Park carousel?"

"Yes, that broken carousel was in the public eye during the Cookie Swap, yet still private. With carols playing over the speakers and the ice rink the center of attention, no one would notice what was going on inside that dark circle . . ."

"Go on!"

"My bet is, M brought the Letter to the killer, who waited for a chance to bash M to death. Afterward, the killer took the Letter and went back to the party. With the heavy snowstorm predicted that night, M's body wouldn't have been discovered for at least another day—that is, if I hadn't stumbled upon it."

"And you really think Danni Rayburn was the killer?"

"Either Danni or her hotheaded husband, Eddie. He could have done it for her, and he was at the Cookie Swap, too."

"Eddie certainly has a history of violence," Tuck noted. "What about Ross Puckett? Couldn't M have tried to blackmail him with this Letter?"

I shook my head. "I overheard the way Ross spoke to M at the Cookie Swap. There was no bad blood between them.

Ross kidded with her, even made a pass. That kind of behavior doesn't add up to a perjurer talking to his blackmailer."

"What about the blood spatter? Wouldn't there have been blood on Eddie's suit or coat? How could he go back to the party with evidence like that on him?"

"I thought of that, too, but then I remembered what Matt told me about Breanne's leaving her fur at home this season because the hottest fashion item for women this winter is—"

"The Fen reversible coat! Oh my gosh!"

"Yes, *that's* why I think the killer was a woman—Danni and not Eddie. If Danni got any blood on her coat, all she would have to do is wipe away the wetness with a tissue and reverse the thing. Then she could leave the dark carousel, maybe hang around the skating rink for a little while, watching her kids on the ice, and finally walk right back inside to the party, checking her coat before continuing her evening as if nothing had happened."

"Don't the police have anything from the crime scene? Fingerprints? Blood? Hairs?"

"According to Lori Soles, there are no usable forensics on M's murder. The snowstorm in Bryant Park saw to that. They did recover a single bloody fingerprint from Rita Limon's murder at the toy store. But the police are convinced Rita's estranged husband is the killer. They're still looking for him. The thing is . . ." I shook my head. "Given the similarities between M's murder and Rita's, I'd swear they were killed by the same person. But I don't know of any connection between Rita and Danni, so—"

"You're *kidding*! You don't *know*?"

"Know what?"

"Before Rita opened her bakery, she worked as a personal chef for the *Rayburn* family! She cooked for Danni and Eddie!"

I sat back. The revelation was a stunner. But it shouldn't have been. My mind raced, remembering what Rita had revealed at the toy store Cookie Swap. She said, when she first came to this country, she worked at a resort spa in Arizona . . .

"One of the ladies who went there liked my dishes so much that she brought me here to New York, and I became a personal chef to her wealthy family. The pay was good, and . . . I caught a little break with some TV exposure . . ."

The Double Ds reality show was what gave Rita the exposure to find financial backers, quit her job with Danni and Eddie, and open her own bakery. The clues had been there. I just hadn't seen them. On the other hand . . . timing was everything.

I leaned forward in my creaky chair. "Tuck, I never watched *True Housewives of Long Island.* Do you remember if Rita was still working for Danni *last* December?"

His head bobbed. "She was! Rita made brief appearances on both seasons."

This was it, the connection, and it made complete sense with my theory! I threw my arms around Tucker and squeezed. "Thank you!"

"For what?"

"Rita was the one! I'm sure she wrote the Letter. While she was working as the Rayburns' cook, she must have overheard Danni spilling her guts to someone—her husband or her best friend Delores. Then Rita bided her time. She waited until after she left her job with the Rayburns. And when she was out of their house, she felt safe enough to tell M the truth about who killed her cousin. That's why Rita was murdered! Danni found out what she'd done!"

"Oh God," Tucker moaned. "What are we going to do? How are we going to prove *any* of this? Do you want us to question Danni, like you did Ross Puckett?"

"No. If she or her husband is a killer, we'd be putting ourselves in real danger. But I've come up with the perfect solution. We'll go to—"

"Delores, of course!" Tucker blurted.

I nodded. "Delores is Danni's best friend. If anyone knows her secrets, she does. And these people aren't exactly geniuses. Delores won't suspect you and me of ulterior motives. You're her director and I'm just a lowly coffee-house manager. We'll come up with some clever angle to get into her house. I'll bring a digital recorder, keep it hidden, and get Delores a little tipsy on wine—"

"Not wine. Champagne! Delores is a sucker for it. The pricier the better."

"I'll take care of it. If we can get her to corroborate at least part of my theory, I'll play the recording tonight for Lori Soles. Once Lori is convinced, I know she'll help us set up Danni the same way. But when we approach Danni, you and I will be wearing wires, and we'll have police backup."

"Brilliant plan, Shirley Holmes!" Tuck put out his hand and I slapped it.

Quinn would be so proud of me, I thought. *I might be impatient for justice, but I'm not taking any risks this time. Not only am I going in with backup, I'm steering clear of the truly dangerous suspects.*

What could be safer?

Sixty-one

〜〜〜〜〜〜〜〜〜〜〜〜〜〜〜〜〜〜

"THIS is it." Tuck steered Punch's Nissan into a curving driveway.

The Deluca home sat on a quiet road in an upscale section of Long Island, fashionably close to the shore. Surrounded by trees and an expansive snow-covered lawn, the house could be called "modest"—if you compared it to the Palace of Versailles, or Windsor Castle.

"Don't let these imposing digs intimidate," Tuck assured me. "Delores is very approachable."

Recalling the unhappy laser stares that Ms. Deluca had emitted at me—twice, in as many parties—I was doubtful, but it was too late to turn back now.

We strode up to the double-door entrance, where Tuck rang the chimes, and I reached under my coat to activate the digital recorder in my skirt pocket.

I expected Delores to be dressed to the nines, maybe in floor-length silk pajamas. But she greeted us wearing stressed denims and a gray *True Housewives* sweatshirt. Far from dowdy, her top was short enough to display a flash of navel (and a belly button ring). Her blond hair and expensive makeup were perfectly done.

Delores air-kissed Tuck. Then she saw me and her scowl returned, along with a wary tension, as if my presence made her nervous and infuriated at the same time.

I attempted to break the Little D ice by handing over the bubbly bait (appropriated by Matt from Breanne's bar fridge). I'd even nestled the bottle of champagne in ice packs so we could drink it right away.

"Dom Pérignon! If I'd known we were having champagne I would have dressed for the occasion!" Delores fingered her sweatshirt. "As you can see, I've been decorating for the holidays."

"I can't believe you're doing that work by yourself," Tuck said. "Is that skinflint of an *almost* ex-husband nickel-and-diming you again?"

"The kids are with their father, so I cut the maid's hours," she replied.

"Without your children around, it must get lonely in this big house," I said.

Delores shrugged and took Tuck's hand. "Come on. I'll show you around."

But Delores didn't show us around. She ushered Tuck and me through a carpeted hallway, then down a flight of stairs to a basement family room beside the four-car garage.

The large space boasted a big-screen TV with game consoles, a pool table, and shelves packed with expensive toys, and cheaply gilded athletic trophies. In the corner, a Christmas tree glittered like those little statues, in monotone gold. It was big and showy, tall enough to reach the high ceiling.

"I'll be right back and we'll nosh!" Delores exclaimed and took off with the champagne, shutting the door behind her.

I examined a wall of framed mementos. "Check this out. A picture of Ross Puckett, skating with a little boy. Is that a real hockey puck mounted in the frame?"

"It's real. And FYI, that boy is Dino, Dolores's oldest child."

I read the message scrawled in Puckett's sloppy hand: *"Here's a Raider's puck for good luck!"*

"Wow," said Tuck. "Who knew Ross was a poet?"

"Do you know what this means?!" I cried.

"His major influence was Dr. Seuss?"

I grabbed his shirt. "Delores *must* have known about Danni's affair! This photo is proof that both Ds, and their children, spent time with Puckett!"

"Getting Little D to spill might be easier than we thought," Tuck whispered.

"I'm back," Delores called as she pushed through the door.

While Tuck took the heavy tray from her, Delores grabbed a champagne flute already brimming with bubbly.

"I couldn't wait. Bottoms up!" she said, taking a long, happy sip. Then we sat down around the coffee table while Delores poured for Tuck and me.

I took a small sip, determined to remain sober. (*In champagne veritas*, and I wanted all of today's *veritas* to come from *Delores*.)

Tuck didn't get the memo, and nervously downed his bubbly. Delores refilled his glass.

"You're not drinking, Clare."

Her gaze was so intense that I felt it would be rude not to take a second sip. Clearly, she didn't want to drink alone: after I drank more deeply, Delores relaxed.

"This Gruyère's from a cheese monger in East Hampton. Do try!"

I passed on the cheese, while Tuck launched into his prerehearsed spiel.

"I came to talk to you about the production," he began. "I'm composing a first draft, and I realized we need to take this show into unknown territory."

Delores arched a plucked eyebrow. "Unknown territory?"

"I want to get to the heart of your story, and Danni's. That means frankness. Truth. Bold truths, without compromises."

Delores frowned. "I don't follow—"

"Whew," Tuck said. "It's warm in here."

Delores put the flute to her lips and wet them. "You were saying, Tuck?"

"I sense there's a truth behind the reality on the reality show," he replied. "Untold stories. There are clues that Danni's fairy-tale life with Eddie may not be so storybook, after all. Rumors of an affair."

"Do you mean that Eddie is having an affair?"

"No, that Danni is," I replied. "With Ross Puckett."

"The hockey player? Why Danni hardly knows him—"

"Danni knows Ross, and you know him, too," I said, pointing to the picture. "That's your son Ross with Dino— I mean your son *Dino* with *Ross*."

Wow, I thought, Tuck was right. *It is warm in here!*

"Well, Clare," Delores said, "you probably know Ross as well as Danni does."

"What do you mean?"

"You spent quite a long time alone with him after that spectacular tumble on the ice last night."

I stiffened. "Me? Certainly not!"

"So you *didn't* hook up in the first aid room?"

"You must have me confused with someone else. I was working at my coffeehouse last night. Right, Tuck?"

When I received no reply, I turned to find my assistant manager slumped on the couch. I touched him, and Tuck fell forward, bouncing off the coffee table before rolling onto the faux stone floor. I tried to catch him, but my own knees sagged and I sank back onto the couch.

My God, she's drugged us! She must have put the stuff in the champagne bottle. That's why she poured hers first and pressured us to drink up!

Through heavy eyelids I watched Delores gather up the flutes, the champagne bottle, the cheese. When she bent over, her sweatshirt rode up, exposing a tattoo—*88 is Great* spelled out in Raiders' blue letters.

Ross's words about the woman who stole his car flooded

back to me. *"She was crazy jealous . . . Loved me so much she put an '88 is Great' tattoo where the sun don't shine!"*

The evidence was right in front of me. We went for the wrong Double D! Ross hadn't been talking about Danni. The "crazy jealous bitch" was Delores!

"Really, Ms. Coffee Queen, you didn't have to go to so much trouble last night," Delores purred. "Believe me, I learned the hard way. Ross isn't that particular. He takes what he can get, although he does prefer them young, like that orange-haired tramp he carried on with for fifteen minutes or so. I should have killed Piper Penny after I bashed that Irish bitch, but not even the morons in the NYPD would buy *two* attacks in one night."

I wanted to strangle the woman, but I couldn't even get off the couch! The drugs had nearly crippled me.

"You killed an innocent girl," I rasped, losing focus. "An angel—"

"How many angels turn to blackmail, Coffee Queen? That girl tried to shake me down. Are you here to shake me down, too?"

I shook my head.

"My sister crunches crime stats for the NYPD and she knows about you, Clare Cosi. You've helped the cops with lots of cases. You're even involved with a high-profile detective. Are you wearing a wire?"

I thought she was going to frisk me, but Delores wisely kept her distance.

"No. Of course, there's no wire. The NYPD would lure me to the city before they tried to entrap me. Since we're in Nassau County, you're on a fishing expedition. If the police had any real evidence, I'd already be behind bars."

Delores reached into her denims for a medicine bottle, then stuffed several pills into her mouth. She chased them with champagne, draining her untainted flute.

"First my husband dumps me over a *tiny* indiscretion. Then the show gets cancelled. All the real money is supposed to come from syndication, but nobody wants to syndicate our show! Now I'm broke and can't get Ross back on the hook, even after I *forgave* him for cheating on me with my best friend!

"I got even with Danni, though. Good for the goose, right? She doesn't know it, but I slept with her husband. That settled Evil Eyes right down—and me, too. I had to keep things on track, pretend to make nice so we could reboot our careers."

The pill must have kicked in. Delores seemed to be calming down.

"I didn't *want* to kill the little Irish baker, you know? I was going to reason with her. Try to make a deal. The girl wanted fifty thousand to stay quiet. She didn't deserve even one dollar, if you asked me, but I was willing to work something out to keep her from going to the tabloids." Delores shook her head. "Then Ross showed up with that teenage rocker. I'd been drinking, and . . . I lost it. When I tripped over a loose sidewalk stone at the carousel, I thought it must be fate that provided the weapon; that I *had* to kill her."

"Over a Letter?" I rasped, still wondering if that's how M found out.

But Delores was done confessing. She lifted the heavy tray and crossed to the door, where she paused.

"You don't understand, Coffee Queen. The hardest thing about fame and fortune is losing it."

Sixty-two

~~~~~~~~~~~~~~~~~~~~~~~~~~~~~~~~~~~~

As soon as Delores locked the door behind her, I rolled to the floor and tried to rouse Tuck. But he was out cold, and I was slipping fast.

We were both going to die, and I knew what I had to do—I leaned over the edge of the couch and jammed my fingers down my throat. After I emptied my stomach, my head cleared and my strength returned. This time I shook Tuck so hard that he actually groaned.

Thank God! You're not dead!

I couldn't induce vomiting in him. He was still unconscious and could choke to death. I had no cold water to splash in his face, and no smelling salts for his nose, so I slapped him, right in the kisser!

His eyes opened, but they were still unfocused, so I slapped him again.

"Clare?" he cried, cheeks blazing.

I told Tuck what had happened while he was out, and convinced him to lose his lunch, too. Just as he finished, we both heard an engine rumble in the garage beside us.

"Oh no!" Tuck cried. "I know what Delores is doing. I saw that episode of *Criminal Intent*—the one she auditioned for! A police stenographer and her detective lover are *asphyxiated* by the man's jealous wife in their love nest beside a garage! The killer ran a hose from the car exhaust to the room, through the heating vent. When we're dead, Delores is going to weight our bodies and dump us in a lake upstate, just like the TV show!"

I could already smell the exhaust fumes pouring through the vent. Now Delores revved up a second engine. It must have been a truck because the rumble was so powerful it rattled the shelf of cheap gold trophies.

"That crazy bitch really wants us dead!" Tuck cried.

"Calm down. We have to think our way out of this."

"I need air to think," Tuck said with a cough. Soon I was coughing, too.

"Here. I want you to have this," I said, reaching under my skirt and yanking off my tights.

Tuck's eyes widened in shock. "Clare! I know we're about to die, but I'm not that kind of guy!"

"Not that! I want you to have my tights for the 'Whistling Dick' stunt! You taught Punch how to do it, right?" I pointed. "See those high windows, near the basement ceiling. They're sealed, for light only. But you can *break* one of them. Just like Punch broke my French door at the Blend."

Tuck grabbed my tights. "I need a rock . . . Something small but heavy."

I pulled the framed picture off the wall and smashed it on the coffee table. I passed the hockey puck to Tucker.

"This thing must weigh five pounds," he said. "I hope it doesn't rip through."

"Double the thickness. Put one leg inside the other."

Coughing, Tuck did as I asked, then stuffed the hard puck into my tights.

The air was getting heavy as Tuck spun the hosiery. The material stretched, but didn't snap. Tuck aimed for one of the sealed windows near the ceiling and let it fly!

The puck shattered the glass on the first try. Frigid air rushed into the playroom, but not enough to dispel the carbon monoxide. Not enough to save us.

"Break the other window," I said, gagging.

"With what? Your tights are outside!"

"Then we have to get out, too."

The edge of the window was at least twelve feet above my head. Even when Tuck hefted me onto his shoulders, I couldn't grasp the windowsill. So I scrambled off Tuck's back, tipped the enormous Christmas tree, and braced it against the wall.

I climbed up the pine branches, stripping them clean of their gaudy tinsel. Gold ornaments shattered in my wake. I reached the broken window and called down to Tuck.

"Throw me my coat!"

Tuck tossed it up. I bunched the material around my arm and knocked the glass splinters out of the frame. Then I crawled out onto the cold ground.

As I moved through a line of shrubbery, I spied our stocking-wrapped hockey puck, hanging on snow-covered branches like a low-rent Christmas ornament.

I left it there and continued crawling on my knees until I reached the yard. Exhausted and sick, I collapsed, rolling onto my back to catch my breath. Finally feeling relief, I began to sit up when a shadow loomed over me.

"I guess I'll have to kill you the messy way," Delores said as she smacked a hammer into her palm. The woman was taunting me, taking pleasure in what she was about to do.

Good Lord, she's a monster!

I braced myself, ready to fight when the shrubbery behind her moved.

"Hey, De-lor-es!"

Tucker Burton broke out of the bushes, stocking swinging like a lasso.

Hearing her name, Delores turned. With a sickening clunk, my loaded tights connected with her forehead.

Then the unconscious bimbo dropped face-first in the snow.

"Thank you, Whistling Dick!"

Tuck reached for my hand. "Don't thank me. Thank Mister O. Henry."

Sixty-three

⊹⊶⊷⊶⊷⊶⊷⊶⊷⊶⊷⊶⊷⊶⊷⊶⊷⊶⊷⊶⊷⊶⊷⊶⊷

THAT afternoon, I finally heeded Lori Soles's advice and called the Long Island cops. Sirens wailed as men in uniform took Delores Deluca into custody—and Tuck and I took a trip to the local ER.

Our recovery was relatively quick. Oh, there were dozens of questions and recorded statements. But after several hours, and then a few nights' rest, we were back to the calm oasis of our Village Blend . . .

The shop was closed early for our annual holiday party, and it looked downright magical with the overhead lamps dimmed and strings of tiny white lights twinkling around our French doors. Fresh green boughs gave off the scent of pine, a cozy fire crackled in our exposed brick hearth, and Madame's silver menorah flickered on the mantel.

All year long, I looked forward to this night, an evening to relax with my staff while sipping our favorite Fa-la-la-la lattes and munching fresh-baked cookies, provided by Janelle and Boris. As a thank-you to Matt, I'd even baked up my New York Cheesecake Cookies, finishing them with a drizzle of candied strawberry syrup.

Now jazzy holiday tunes played over the speakers, and my baristas mingled with a few friends and loved ones. But I couldn't enjoy it; I was still upset over a missing piece of the puzzle.

Matt and I took a table by the wall of French doors, so I could watch the lightly falling snow while filling him in on Delores Deluca's crazy Cookie Swap crime spree . . .

"So let me get this straight," Matt said when I finished my tale. "You were saved by the Christmas tree?"

"The tree and Tucker Burton. If Tuck hadn't learned how to turn a pair of ladies' tights into an effective slingshot for his production of Whistling Dick's *Christmas Stocking*, you'd be attending my funeral right now, instead of our annual Secret Santa party."

Matt stared. "Whistling *what*?"

I waved my hand. "Forget it."

"Well, what happened after that? Did Delores confess to the Long Island cops?"

"Partly. She admitted drugging me and Tuck, but that was all. Then Lori and Endicott took a crack at her in the interview room. They played her my digital recording, and she admitted she tried to asphyxiate us, too. She also confessed to causing the fire that killed Kaitlin, which her lawyers maintained was no more than manslaughter. And though she confessed to beating M to death, her lawyers argued that Delores was the victim—that she was a desperate woman being blackmailed. A crime of passion, in other words, and not premeditated murder."

"What about *Rita*?" Matt said, fingers tightening on his Candy Cane Latte (fortified with a Matt-size splash of peppermint schnapps). "That poor girl had an awful end, too. Didn't Delores admit to killing her?"

"No. She wouldn't admit to that. Her fingerprint *appeared* to match the bloody print the police picked up at the crime scene, but that print is partially smeared, and it's not definitive enough to be a slam dunk in court. Everything else is circumstantial because they never recovered the link between Rita and M."

"You mean the Letter?"

I nodded, glancing out the window, into the dark, cold night. "Delores must have destroyed it."

"Don't you think M was smart enough to make a copy?"

"Yes, but where she put it is a mystery. The police searched her apartment and came up empty." I sighed. "If only we could find that Letter. I'm sure it would nail Delores for Rita's murder, too, and that homicide was *definitely* premeditated."

"How can you know that for sure?"

"Because my ice skate theory panned out, that's why. The forensics people tested a child-sized ice skate, and it was an exact match for her head wounds."

Matt rubbed his chin. "Why does that make it premeditated?"

"Don't you remember? You told me yourself during the last Cookie Swap. The most famous toy store in the world has thousand-dollar jumbo stuffed animals and a jewel-encrusted Etch A Sketch, but it doesn't sell ice skates."

"Oh, wow, Clare, you're right. That means the killer had to bring it into the store, which means Rita's murder was—"

"It eats at me, knowing that monster is going to escape being tried for Rita's coldly premeditated homicide . . . If only the police could recover the Letter—or a copy of it."

I sighed again, gazing out the window, wishing for a miracle. And a few minutes later, I got one . . .

"Ho, ho, ho!" Jingle bells rang out as our front door opened. "Merry Christmas!"

"It's Santa Claus!" Tuck cried, running up to hug the man in red.

Behind his long white beard, the red-suited figure grinned wide.

"Have you been a good boy?" Punch teased.

Tuck's boyfriend was so lean he needed three pillows to fill the suit. On his back, he carried a red velvet sack filled with my gifts to my baristas and their gifts to one another—the Secret Santa presents that had been piling up all month in the back pantry, beside our little, plastic, motion-detecting Bing Crosby.

As Punch unloaded the presents, I saw Matt saying something to me, but I didn't hear him. I didn't hear *anything*. Staring into space, I was suddenly reliving a moment before that first Cookie Swap . . .

I saw the image of M taking that cell phone call, a call I now knew was from her killer, Delores. The two were finalizing plans for their fateful meeting at the broken carousel. M had walked back to our pantry area so she could speak to Delores in private, and that's when I heard our little Bing Crosby singing his tinny "White Christmas."

"Oh my gosh!" I jumped up.

"What is it?" Matt asked.

I raced over to Punch. "Santa, let me see those gifts!"

"I don't know. Have you been a good little girl?"

"Good enough!" I began frantically unloading the packages onto our counter. Halfway down, I saw it—the mysterious gift that Vicki had mentioned the other day, a gift marked for Moirin, one that none of the baristas had taken back since her death.

I didn't have to ask anyone who put it there. I *knew*. Ripping the paper, I opened the gift and looked inside.

"What is it?" Matt asked, hurrying up to me.

"This is it! The *Letter* . . ."

Obviously, M had learned something from her old boyfriend in Dublin, who'd hidden a handgun under a Christmas tree. Well, this little present was just as explosive.

I pulled out the sheet of Barbie pink paper. The Letter told the whole awful story of how Delores Deluca stole Ross Puckett's car, wrecked it into the bakery, and killed M's cousin. I was thrilled with this discovery, until—

"Oh no . . ."

"What?" Matt asked.

"The Letter is typewritten. And it isn't signed. Without Rita's signature, we're sunk."

"Look," said Matt, peering into the box. "There's something else in here . . ."

And that's when we finally nailed Delores Deluca for Rita Limon's murder—because the box contained a second letter, this one handwritten on a plain piece of notebook paper:

Dear Moirin,
I knew Kaitlin. I went to her bakery often. She told me that she had a cousin who worked in the city for Janelle's Pastries. That's how I found you.
The letter enclosed explains the truth of how Kaitlin died. I overheard it spoken in Danni Rayburn's home. I used her stationery as proof of this.
I didn't sign the letter because I would like to remain anonymous. But I think you should use it to make Delores Deluca pay for what she did.

Peace be with you,
Rita Limon

The "Peace be with you" troubled me—because I couldn't feel any peace.

I'd uncovered the *who*, *what*, *where*, and *how* of M's murder. I even knew *why* the killer did it. What I didn't know was why M had.

Part of me still saw her as the child from "The Little Match Girl," lying in the snow, dreaming her dream as she died. The other part saw her greedy and grasping, resorting to blackmail, and that truly troubled me.

Why had she done it? To enrich herself? Or punish Delores?

Learning what I had about M, neither rang true. I prayed about it, but reached no reconciliation, and cried myself to sleep.

Sixty-Four

@@@@@@@@@@@@@@@@@@@@@@

Two days before Christmas, Detective Lori Soles stopped by to see me. She'd come to fill me in on the repercussions of my final discovery.

When I approached her fireside table, I found her munching serenely on one of Janelle's famous chocolate chip cookies, even though we still had plenty of gingerbread men awaiting execution in the pastry case.

"Off beheadings?"

"*Da*, Comrade Cosi . . ." (Ever since she heard about my little Galina masquerade, she'd taken to spoofing a Russian accent.)

I sat down and pointed to the pile of cookies on her plate, none of which resembled her gingerbread stand-ins for a certain self-satisfied superior.

"Why the stays of execution?"

"First things first. I came by to *thank you* for finding the Letter. Once we got our hands on that, there wasn't a leg Delores Deluca could stand on. If you saw the papers, you know the DA is charging her with the premeditated murder of Rita Limon."

"Actually, I heard the report on New York One. It's all over the media."

"The woman's defense attorneys are scrambling for a plea bargain, and that's always a good sign. They know it's over."

I frowned. "Are you saying Delores is going to plead guilty to a lesser charge?"

Lori shook her head. "That train left the station this morning, when Danni Rayburn's missing nanny walked into my precinct house. She knew all about Delores and the car crash, but she wanted no part of blackmail. When your employee was killed, the nanny got nervous, but swallowed the same delusion Endicott did—she told herself Moirin Fagan was a random victim of the Christmas Stalker."

Lori sunk her teeth into one of Janelle's Eggnog Shortbread Cookies, happily chewed, and chased it with gulps of Americano.

"After Rita was killed at the toy store, the nanny figured Delores was involved in both murders, though she couldn't prove anything. She also figured she was next on Little D's hit list, and took off. She hid at her cousin's apartment in Washington Heights until she read the papers and found out Delores wasn't leaving Rikers anytime soon. That's when she decided to come to us."

Lori grinned. "With the nanny's testimony, Delores Deluca is just like this little goodie—"

She held up a crisp piece of Janelle's Oatmeal Cookie Brittle. With a snap, she broke it in two, then plunged half into her coffee and wolfed it down.

"So why this end to the Reign of Terror?" I said. "Sick of gingerbread?"

"That's the other reason I'm thanking you. Detective Fletcher Endicott is finally off my back!" She grinned wide. "Mr. DNA is taking an administrative leave to write a book about the Cookie Swap Murders. That means I'm being assigned a *sane* partner until Sue Ellen gets off medical leave in February."

"Oh, that *is* reason to celebrate. But you know something? You still haven't explained to me why you call Endicott 'Mr. DNA.'"

"It's the Devo song, right?" Tuck asked, who'd dropped by the table to say hello (and eavesdrop).

"Nothing to do with Devo," Lori replied. "DNA are the initials of Endicott's fictional character: Detective Nat Adams. The *Deoxyribo-Nucleic Acid* Detective—get it?"

"Ouch. That almost hurts."

"If you think that hurts, save yourself some pain and skip searching for his book titles."

I was fine with that advice, but Tuck made a beeline right for the counter, and I knew why. A few minutes later, Lori finished her coffee and popped a Pfeffernüsse—a sugar-coated little spice ball that had a lot in common with the detective herself.

"Got to go," she said, giving me a little hug. "Have a merry one, Cosi."

"You too . . ."

After seeing Lori to the door, I headed back to the coffee bar and noticed Tuck tittering with Punch.

"Okay, what's so funny?"

Tuck pointed to Punch's tablet computer. "The titles in Detective Endicott's DNA book series, that's what. Lori Soles wasn't kidding. These are painful!"

"They can't be that bad."

Tuck pointed at the screen. "His first novel is called *The Secretors.*"

"Which begs the question," Punch said, "what do they *secrete*?"

"That tour de force was followed by *Body Bags,*" Tuck said. "Then *Residues and Don'ts.*"

"Oh, ouch."

"The next book appears to be some kind of ethnic mystery."

"Title?"

"*Seminal, Indian.*"

"Oh no," I said. "Enough!"

"Look!" Punch cried. "He even has a holiday-themed mystery!"

"Don't tell me . . ."

"Have to," Tuck said with a grin.

"Let me guess . . . *Slay Bells*?"

Tuck shook his head. "*Mistletoe Tags*."

THE next day was Christmas Eve. In the lull before our noon rush, our doorbell *jingled* and we had another visitor with a beard, but not a long or white one. This man's trimmed whiskers were tawny and shot with gray, more Kris Kristofferson than Kris Kringle. His shoulder-length hair was pulled into a short, hipster ponytail, and a small loop of gold glinted in one ear.

This guy didn't have a red suit, either.

David Brice sauntered into my shop wearing ex–rock star holiday colors—black jeans, black sweater, and a black leather jacket. What he brought me that morning before Christmas felt just as dark, but there was light at the end of it.

I smiled when Nancy's perky voice sang out: "Hey, Mr. Brice. How are you? I'm surprised you haven't left for your daughter's yet!"

"In a few hours," Dave said, that deep FM voice sending shivers. "She's expecting me before sunset, so we can light the Chanukah candles together."

I greeted the man with a smile, inviting him to sit at the counter as I retrieved his navy sport jacket—the one he'd lent me when we'd been on the run from News Channel Six.

"Thanks for the loan."

"No problem." He made a sweeping gesture across the shop, from our wood plank floor and marble-topped tables to our tin ceiling. "Nancy was right. This really is a great place."

"And you haven't even tried the coffee yet . . ."

I asked Tuck to get us two Holiday Blends and joined

Dave at the counter. "Nancy tells us she's been enjoying her work at Evergreen . . ."

On the night of M's memorial, Nancy had confided with me that she couldn't stop thinking about those "nice old folks." She said her own family was scattered across the country, and she missed the chance to have older people in her life.

"Well, why don't you speak with Mr. Brice?" I'd suggested. "Maybe he'll agree to train you, and you can take on some of M's part-time duties . . ."

She did and the fit was *perfect*.

"The residents love Nancy," Dave told me now. "And everyone's buzzing about the big show tonight. It was good of your people to jump in like that."

"They're doing it for M. She wouldn't have wanted those seniors to be sad and disappointed. Not on Christmas Eve . . ."

Dave nodded his thanks as Tuck brought our coffees. Then he sipped my Holiday Blend, made yummy sounds, and drank more deeply. "I hear Janelle's baking special treats to go with your show?"

I nodded. "When she heard the party was in honor of M, she insisted on providing the cookies."

"Sorry I'll miss that," Dave said. "That woman bakes the best chocolate chips on the planet. The problem is, she doesn't bake enough of them. When I try to order, she's always sold out."

"Well, I promise you, that woman is going to do a lot *more* baking from now on and a lot less bookkeeping . . ."

Earlier in the week, I'd brought her to my coffeehouse and introduced her to another customer who'd come to my attention as needing work—that bank executive who'd thrown his resumes in the air.

I'd kept one of his crumpled CVs and looked it over. His experience was extensive, including financial consulting with small business owners, so I called him up and asked him to come in.

He turned out to be the perfect man to revamp Janelle's

back office, and if he found more clients like her, he wouldn't need a full-time job—ever again.

As for the guy's upsetting outburst, it was a one-time thing. Sometimes a good man could have a bad day. And everyone was entitled to a bad day, though maybe not as bad as Delores Deluca's . . .

Boris arrived with a round of treats (and lucky for Dave, they were his fave). Dave sank his teeth into a warm, fresh cookie with toffeelike notes, the chocolate chips still slightly melted, and told me he felt like he'd just died and gone to heaven.

"Ironic," I said, "because the last time we shared a nosh, you were talking about hell."

"I was talking about *fame*." Dave sighed. "It can be torment, when it comes and when it goes, but it's a hell of our own making."

It was the opening I needed. "Do you think that was what drove M to blackmail?" The question was a harsh one, but I wanted to know. "Was she that impatient for fame?"

"M wanted the chance to sing for *more people*, I can tell you that. She loved making people happy—and that's the difference between her and the monster who killed her. A girl like Moirin doesn't go to hell. No way. In fact, Clare, now that you've brought it up, there's something I want you to see . . ."

Dave reached into his jeans pocket and pulled out a folded piece of paper.

"What's that? It looks like sheet music."

"It is. I found it on my desk the other day. Didn't know what it meant until I got your call . . ."

The day after we found the *Letter*, I called Dave to let him know and asked him to let *me* know if he ever found more evidence of what M had been thinking.

Now he unfolded the wrinkled sheet music, pressed it flat, and turned it over. The other side was filled with doodles and scribbles.

"M made these notes just before Thanksgiving," he said. "Look here, in the corner . . ."

Kaitlin's dad—$25,000
Rita—$5,000 for her new bake biz
EFTF—$7,000
My bills—$3,000 max
Dave—$10,000
Grand Total—$50,000

"Fifty thousand," I whispered. "The exact amount M asked Delores to pay."

Dave shook his head. "Back in the day, that was my bar bill for the year. And for a woman like Delores Deluca? That was probably her seasonal clothing allowance."

I pointed to the paper. "What's this? EFTF?"

"That's the Evergreen Field Trip Fund." He swallowed, clearly emotional. "A few months ago, M wanted to take a group of seniors to a concert, but we had no budget for it. She said we should start raising money for a 'field trip' fund to get the seniors who were strong enough out and about. I said she should keep dreaming—because nobody I knew had money."

"What about this note . . ." I pointed. "The one with your name. Did Moirin ever mention that she'd planned to give you ten thousand dollars?"

"Hell no! Like most struggling artists, for M poverty was a way of life. I never expected money from her."

I tapped the sheet again. "Looks like M only wanted to keep three thousand for herself, to pay off her bills . . ."

It was so hard, this feeling of wanting to turn back time, reach into M's life, and fix it all for her. M had been working day and night to make the rent, finance her dreams. I had a whole shop of baristas just like her, working hard, struggling to make something of themselves and put their passions to good use.

I tried to contain my emotions, like Quinn does, but fury rose in me anyway, because I wanted to slap Delores Deluca, and all women like her. Slap them harder than I'd struck Tuck to wake him from his drugged stupor. I wanted to tell them that they should *wake up*, appreciate, and cherish what they had—not throw everything away to get something they didn't.

Delores could have sold one of her cars. She could have handed M her Birkin and Coach bags, a few designer dresses and shoes. She could have put them on eBay herself and come up with the money to pay the girl off.

But M had been wrong, too, and I wanted to lecture her, as well; tell her she should have gone to the police; advised her that shortcuts seldom worked.

Tucker Burton knew that.

As persuasive as people like Eddie Rayburn and the Double Ds were, Tuck knew to get clear of their kind and rely on his own talent and experience to get ahead. Like Dave told me a few weeks back: *"Fires built on nothing flame out fast."*

Well, it seemed the fires of fame proved fateful this season. Delores had been on her way down that white-hot ladder while M had been on her way up. And when they met inside that dark circle in Bryant Park, they'd destroyed each other.

A tragic tale, but in the end, life was sometimes like that. Hans Christian Andersen knew it. He couldn't save his Little Match Girl, and I couldn't save my Moirin. At least with Dave's visit, I was beginning to feel some peace about the girl's intentions . . . and her fate.

As Dave finished his coffee, I gathered up the sport coat he lent me.

"Oh, I almost forgot." He pulled something silver out of his black jacket. "A holiday gift. This is a CD-R of M's songs. Her lyrics are beautiful, and with all the publicity surrounding her death, two major artists contacted me. They're interested in recording a few of M's songs. She didn't have the resources to record an entire professional album, but she made this rough four-song EP. I wanted you to have a copy . . ."

"Thank you." I wrapped my arms around the man and

he hugged me back. When he was gone, I heard a *jingle-jingle* again. (Nancy in her elf hat.)

"Isn't Dave the coolest?" she gushed.

"Uh-oh," Tuck said. "I sense a new crush in the making."

It will never work out, I thought. *But that never stops a girl from dreaming . . .*

I passed the CD-R to Tucker and asked him to pop it into our player. A minute later, a pure, sweet voice filled the coffeehouse. M sang about pain and longing and a love that could never be.

Hearing her words, and the powerful emotion in her delivery, Boris caught my eye. "*Wery* nice," he said. "The voice is beautiful, lyrics, too, but production *walues* . . ." Boris shook his head. "*Nyet*," he said, giving a thumbs-down. "Takes much money to make professional recording. Ten thousand, just for studio time."

Ten thousand dollars was precisely the amount Moirin had planned to present to Dave, according to her scribbled note. It seemed clear enough: M wanted Dave to produce her songs, even if she had to bribe him to do it.

And from the poignant, heart-tugging lyrics M had written, something else was clear. Ross Puckett and my barista Dante were wasting their time when they hit on M. She wasn't interested, and not because of what happened in Ireland.

It was because M wanted more from David Brice than a production engineer. She wanted the man's love. Making a professional recording was only part of what she dreamed of sharing with him . . .

"Play that last song again," I asked.

As the tune repeated, I gazed through the French doors. The winter sun was strong this morning, and a light snow began to fall. While the flakes swirled in midair, I mentally painted M there, looking in on us before taking her journey.

I didn't see her as an earthly body anymore, or a smoky ghost. Now she seemed more like the snow, crystalline and ethereal; bright and beautiful. My vision was like a little-girl memory—lying in whiteness, working arms and legs until something special was left behind for everyone to marvel at.

It was then I knew what M had become.

An angel.

And when the heavenly host sang their *hallelujahs* at midnight tonight, she'd be right at home.

EPILOGUE

~~~~~~~~~~~~~~~~~~~~~~~~~~~

"I'LL see you tomorrow then, sweetheart, in time for Christmas dinner . . ."

I said good-bye, wishing Quinn a Merry Christmas. Then I put my cell on manner mode and took a deep breath. Mike Quinn had *planned* to be here with me, on Christmas Eve, but something came up at work. Once again, he was stuck in Washington.

I tried not to feel disappointed. Instead, I focused on the positive—and tonight, in Evergreen's Recreation Center, there was enough buzzing energy to power a metropolis.

Even seniors who had a place to go for the holidays told their families to pick them up *tomorrow*. That's how excited they were to see this show.

"Yeah, *The Christmas Stocking* is a great little play," I assured Matt and Madame in seats on either side of me.

Matt pointed to the plateglass windows overlooking the beach. "I don't know, given the rock-in-the-sock slingshot climax, I think Punch's drag version of *White Christmas* is going to be the safer half of the evening."

Madame raised an eyebrow and waved her program. "I

didn't know the *White Christmas* revue was going to be in *drag*."

"You're offended?" I asked, a bit surprised, given her long history with the Village people.

"Offended?" she chirped in outrage. "My dear, how can you even think such a thing! *Torch Song Trilogy* had its first read-through on the Blend's second floor!"

"So sorry," I said, biting my cheek.

She leaned close. "What concerns me is your actor friends. They better watch out for some of these older gentlemen." She switched to mime, pinching her fingers together and pointing to her derriere.

"Mother's right," Matt said. "Some of these geezers still have the drive, but their vision isn't so good."

I waved my hand. "Believe me, Punch can take care of himself."

The *White Christmas* revue began, and we settled down to enjoy a wonderful evening of singing, dancing, and comic repartee. Watching Punch in his blond Vera-Ellen wig, I was amazed. Resplendent in peacock blue, he truly looked like a woman.

That's when I decided Tuck wasn't entirely right about life on the stage. I thought about everything I'd been through this holiday season, all the fake names and false leads, the masquerades and murders. It seemed to me, in the end . . .

Sometimes what you see isn't what you get.

A few hours later, I was sitting on a train in Penn Station, waiting for it to depart.

I couldn't help myself. After Matt dropped me off in Manhattan, my duplex felt far too empty—and I'd had my heart set on making my special *Panettone Pain Perdu* for Quinn's Christmas morning breakfast.

Now I still could.

After a few short hours napping on the rails, I'd be in Washington, in time to surprise Mike when the sun came up Christmas morning. How special would that be?

I smiled, thinking about his arms around me, enjoying breakfast, going to church. I could almost hear the *jingle-jingle-jingle* of the Village Blend–blue snowflake scarf I'd given him. He wore it all the time now, and it warmed my heart.

Jingle-jingle-jingle . . .

I blinked, realizing I actually *was* hearing that jingle bell scarf. I looked out the window, onto an arriving track. Another train was pulling out, and the platform revealed the source—Mike Quinn! Or was it?

Had that crazy guy hatched the same idea I had? Had he taken a late-night train to surprise me Christmas morning?! If it was him, and I didn't do something fast, he was going to spend the holiday alone at my empty apartment while I'd be at his!

I wanted to call to the man, but the window was sealed. I sprang from my seat and moved down the crowded aisle. At the train's open door, I shouted out—

"Mike! Mike Quinn! Is that you?!"

The man turned and peered across the platforms.

"Clare!"

It *was* Mike!

The next thing I knew, the train's air brake whooshed and the cars began to move. I hurried back down the aisle, grabbed my overnight bag, and headed for the exit once more, but the car was so crowded. It took me forever!

When I finally reached the door again, I found Mike jogging down the platform, calling to me. I threw my bag to him, and he caught it.

"Jump!" he cried. "I'll catch you!"

I took a breath for courage and flew into the air. Mike did as promised and I landed in his arms. We laughed and hugged.

"Let's go home," I said.

We climbed the steps, finding the station's large waiting area nearly empty. A small knot of lone travelers sat together on a bench, sipping coffee, a guitar case open at their feet.

A man in the group began strumming "Silent Night." A

young woman joined in. She had dark hair and a lovely smile, and her pure voice made me think of freshly fallen snow.

Suddenly the big board fluttered with news of the updated departures, and I thought of Moirin. Her trip was complete now. She was at peace.

"Look," Mike said, pointing at the station's clock. "It's after midnight."

"So it is."

"Merry Christmas, sweetheart . . ."

I wished him the same, but as he moved to kiss me, I stopped him with an upsetting thought. "Oh, Mike, I just remembered. I had your gift in a tote bag, all ready for the tree. I left it on the train!"

I wanted to cry. I'd picked it out special, wrapped it with care. "I'm so sorry. Your Christmas gift is lost!"

"No it isn't," he whispered, touching my cheek. "It's right here."

He smiled, and I did, too, feeling the magic of the hour as the duet of carolers echoed across the cavernous room. Then he bent his head once more, and together we exchanged the most profound gift of any Christmas.

In a last word to the wise of these days let it be said that of all who give gifts these two were the wisest . . . They are the magi.
—O. HENRY, *THE GIFT OF THE MAGI*

RECIPES & TIPS
FROM THE VILLAGE BLEND

Visit Cleo Coyle's virtual Village Blend at
www.CoffeehouseMystery.com
to download even more recipes, including:

* Janelle's "Best on the Planet"
Chocolate Chip Cookies
* Eggnog Shortbread Cookies
* *Pfeffernüsse*
* New Mexican *Biscochitos*
* Candy Cane Frosted Brownies
* New Orleans Gingerbread (*Gâteau de Sirop*)
* Oatmeal Cookie Brittle
* Clare's Gumdrop Cookies
* Leftover Cranberry Sauce Holiday Pastries
* Clare's *Panettone Pain Perdu* with
Maple Butter Syrup
* Matteo Allegro's 8 Napkin Patty Melt
* and many others . . .

RECIPES

~~~~~~

Janelle's Gingerbread Crackle Cookies

Clare Cosi certainly understood why barista Esther called these cookies "Christmas crack." The spices, brown sugar, and molasses blend together in the oven to produce the quintessential aromas of the Yuletide holiday.

One of the best spice cookies Clare ever tasted, Janelle's recipe produces a balanced, flavorful treat with the perfect contrasting textures of a chewy, spicy center and crisp, sugary surface. Her baker's secret? Just the right amount of butter and molasses to keep the middle soft, while the white sugar inside and the raw sugar outside contribute to that satisfying crunch.

Janelle has a stern warning, though: Follow the recipe exactly. Before baking, roll the cookie dough balls in turbinado or demerara sugar (also known as raw sugar or Sugar in the Raw). If you substitute standard white, granulated sugar for this step, you will not get the same great cookie that Village Blend customers swoon over.

May you bake and eat them with the joy of this special season!

Makes 3 dozen cookies

¾ cup (1½ sticks) unsalted butter, softened
½ cup dark brown sugar, firmly packed
¾ cup white, granulated sugar
1 large egg
2 tablespoons molasses, unsulphured, not blackstrap
1 teaspoon pure vanilla extract
2½ teaspoons ground ginger
1¾ teaspoons ground cinnamon
¼ teaspoon ground allspice
1½ teaspoons baking soda
¼ teaspoon salt
Pinch of ground black pepper
2¼ cups all-purpose flour
½ cup turbinado (raw) sugar for rolling (*see note)

*NOTE: Do not substitute white, granulated sugar for this step. You will not get the same wonderful results. *Turbinado* sugar is the name of a coarse, natural brown sugar. In the United States, you may know it under the brand name *Sugar in the Raw*. In the United Kingdom, a version of this sugar is referred to as *demerara*.

Step 1—Make the dough: Using an electric mixer, cream the softened butter and two sugars until light and fluffy in texture. Add the egg, molasses, vanilla extract, ginger, cinnamon, allspice, baking soda, salt, and pepper, and beat until blended. Stop the mixer, add the flour, and mix only until a smooth dough forms and all flour is incorporated. (Do not overmix at this stage or you'll develop the gluten in the flour and your cookies will be tough instead of tender.)

Step 2—Chill it, baby: The dough will be soft and sticky. To firm it up, you must cover it in plastic and chill it for at least 3 hours (or overnight). This rest period also allows the spices to permeate the dough and the wonderful flavors to develop.

Step 3—Roll in sugar: When ready to bake the cookies, preheat the oven to 375°F. Line baking sheets with parchment paper or silicone sheets. Butter your hands and roll the sticky dough into balls (about 1½ inches in diameter). Gently roll each ball in the raw sugar (*turbinado* or *demerara*), making sure to completely coat. Arrange sugar-coated balls on prepared pans, allowing space for spreading.

Step 4—Bake: In your preheated (375°F) oven, bake 12–15 minutes. The cookie balls will flatten out and crack on the surface. Remove cookies from oven while still soft. If you bake them until they are hard, you have *over*baked them! Remove pan from oven and allow soft, warm cookies to set up a bit before transferring to a wire rack to finish cooling.

Chocolate Candy Cane Cookies

A holiday hit at the Village Blend, these cookies combine the sweet, luscious flavor of a soft chocolate cookie with the festive peppermint crunch of Christmas candy canes. When baked, they taste like a cookie-fied version of a Peppermint Pattie!

While these cookies are fantastic naked, you can also gild the peppermint lily by topping them with Tucker's pink Candy Cane Frosting—a brilliant yet easy recipe that will also transform a plain, boxed brownie mix into a cookie swap treasure.

You can find Tucker's recipe for pink Candy Cane Frosting and many more in Holiday Grind, *another holiday-themed mystery in Cleo Coyle's Coffeehouse series.*

Makes about 3 dozen cookies

> 6 tablespoons unsalted butter, softened
> ½ cup light brown sugar, firmly packed
> ½ cup white, granulated sugar
> ⅓ cup plain whole milk yogurt
> 2 egg whites
> 1 teaspoon pure vanilla extract
> ¾ cup unsweetened cocoa powder
> ½ teaspoon instant espresso powder
> ½ teaspoon salt
> ½ teaspoon baking powder
> ½ teaspoon baking soda
> 1 cup all-purpose flour
> ½ cup finely crushed candy canes
> (To finish) ¼ cup white, granulated sugar

Step 1—Create dough: Using an electric mixer, cream the butter and sugars until fluffy. Add yogurt, egg whites, vanilla, and blend. Add cocoa powder, espresso powder, salt, baking powder, and soda and blend until smooth. Finally add the flour. As the dough comes together, fold in the crushed candy canes. Do not overmix at this stage.

Step 2—Chill, baby: The dough will be sticky, so cover the bowl with plastic wrap and chill for at least two hours (overnight is fine, too). Chilling and resting will make the dough easier to work with and allow the flavors to develop.

Step 3—Roll and bake: Preheat oven to 350°F. Grease hands with butter and form dough into balls. Roll in white, granulated sugar (coat completely) and place on baking sheets lined with parchment paper or silicone sheets, allowing space for spreading. Bake 8–12 minutes. Do not overbake. When edges are firm, cookies are done. Remove from hot pan and cool on a wire rack.

Clare Cosi's New York Cheesecake Cookies
with Candied Strawberry Drizzle

This impressive stuffed cookie was one of Matt's favorites back when he and Clare were married. These days, when he's been very, very good, Clare still bakes up a batch for him. They're easy to make because they use a cake mix starter. The simple addition of finely crushed graham crackers subtly mimics the flavor of a New York Cheesecake, and the sweetened cream cheese filling adds to the flavor illusion. The cookie is not complete until you've drizzled it with Clare's candied strawberry syrup, which makes it an especially festive-looking cookie for the holiday season. Close your eyes, take a bite, and you're practically sitting with Clare and Matt at a Village Blend café table.

Makes 10 big, coffeehouse-size cookies

For the Cheesecake Filling:

4 ounces cream cheese, softened
2 cups powdered sugar
1 teaspoon pure vanilla extract
⅛ teaspoon salt

For the Cookie:

1 box of vanilla cake mix
2 tablespoons finely crushed graham crackers
2 large eggs
½ cup canola oil
1 teaspoon pure vanilla extract
¼ teaspoon lemon extract

Step 1—Make the cheesecake filling: Combine the softened cream cheese, powdered sugar, salt, and vanilla extract in a bowl. Using an electric mixer, beat until smooth. Using a tablespoon or cookie scoop, carve out 10 balls of the filling and set them on a wax paper–covered dinner or pie plate. Place the plate in the freezer and chill for at least 4 hours.

Step 2—Create dough and chill: Finely crush the graham crackers using a food processor. To crush by hand, place crackers in a plastic bag and pound with a rolling pin or other heavy object. Pour the crushed crackers into a large mixing bowl. Add the box of cake mix, eggs, canola oil, and vanilla and lemon extracts. Using an electric mixer, beat until well blended. The dough will be wet, sticky, and difficult to work with, which is why you *must* wrap it in plastic and refrigerate it until firm, about two hours (overnight is fine, too).

Step 3—Assemble: When the dough firms into an almost Play-Doh texture, it's chilled enough. Preheat oven to 350°F. Line a dinner or pie plate with wax or parchment paper and place in the refrigerator or freezer. To assemble the cookie, take a golf ball–sized piece of dough and flatten it in your hand. Place a frozen cheesecake ball in the center of the flattened dough and wrap the dough completely around it. Seal it up so that no cheesecake filling is showing. Gently roll this mass back into a ball and place it on the plate in your refrigerator or freezer. When you've formed all the cookies, line a baking sheet with parchment paper and transfer chilled cookie balls.

Clare's Tip: These cookies spread quite a bit, which is why she advises you to make not more than a few at a time.

Step 4—Bake: In your well-preheated oven, bake these cookies for 12–14 minutes. The cookies will flatten and their surface will begin to crack. Remove from the oven and let the cookies cool on the baking sheet for 5 minutes, then carefully slide the parchment paper, cookies and all, onto a wire rack to finish cooling. If you want to store cookies for more than a day, place them in a plastic container in the refrigerator, taking care to put wax paper between each layer.

Step 5—Finishing drizzle: When the cookies have cooled, they're ready to finish with Clare's Candied Strawberry Drizzle. The sweet tang of this drizzle is the perfect complement to offset the buttery, caramelized richness of the sweet cream cheese–stuffed sugar cookie. If you have no time to make Clare's delicious recipe below, take a shortcut with a premade strawberry ice cream topping and . . . eat with joy!

Clare's Candied Strawberry Drizzle

½–¾ cup granulated sugar (according to your taste)
2–3 teaspoons cornstarch
½ cup water
2 cups chopped strawberries, fresh or frozen (and thawed)

In a large saucepan, mix the sugar and cornstarch with the water. Add 2 cups of chopped strawberries. Cook this mixture about 20 minutes or until it thickens enough to coat the back of spoon. Puree this thickened mixture using an immersion (stick) blender, or a standing blender, or a food processor. Finally, run the pureed mixture through a sieve to strain out any fruit bits. Using a fork, drizzle the finished, room temperature strawberry syrup over the cooled New York Cheesecake Cookies. Store the drizzle in a plastic container or a chef's squeeze bottle in the refrigerator. When chilled, the drizzle will harden up. Before using again, allow it to warm to room temperature. To speed up this process, place the plastic container in a warm water bath, or set it in a microwave for 8 to 10 seconds.

Janelle's Lemon Sugar Cookies

These delightfully crunchy, sweet-tart cookies are among Madame's favorites, although a plate of them prompted a philosophical observation from Sergeant Emmanuel Franco of the NYPD, who declared the treats "a little girly."

"What is it with women and lemons?" Franco asked Clare and Madame. "Lemon cakes. Lemon pies. Lemon bars. I'd mention lemon tarts, but I wouldn't want you ladies to get the wrong idea."

The detective's question was never answered, mainly because it proved to be moot. By the time Clare convinced Madame to go undercover at a Brooklyn retirement home, Franco had wolfed down most of these lemon-kissed beauties himself.

Makes about 48 cookies, depending on size

For the Lemon Sugar:

> 1 tablespoon grated lemon zest (grate skin only,
> no bitter white pith)
> ½ teaspoon powdered sugar
> ½ cup white, granulated sugar

For the Cookies:

> 8 tablespoons (1 stick) butter
> 1 cup white, granulated sugar
> 1 teaspoon pure vanilla extract
> ¼ teaspoon salt
> 4 teaspoons freshly grated lemon zest (grate skin only)
> 1 large egg
> ½ teaspoon baking powder

2½ cups all-purpose flour
¼ cup fresh lemon juice (about 2 large or 4 small lemons)

Janelle's Warning: Be sure to follow the mixing directions exactly in Step 2. Do not add the lemon juice to the dough until the end of the mixing process or your butter may curdle.

Step 1—Make the lemon sugar: Grate the lemon skin (no white pith) and mix it in a bowl with the powdered sugar to dry out any moisture. Then thoroughly mix it with the granulated sugar. Using clean fingers or a fork, work the lemon into the granulated sugar. If using a small food processor, lightly pulse only once or twice (do not overprocess). When well mixed, set aside.

Step 2—Make the cookie dough: In a large bowl, cream the butter and sugar with an electric mixer. Blend in the vanilla, salt, egg, lemon zest, and baking powder. Add the flour and mix *very briefly* until a shaggy dough forms. Finally add your lemon juice and mix until a smooth dough comes together, but *do not* overmix at this stage or your cookies may turn out tough.

Step 3—Chill it, baby: When first made, this dough is wet and sticky. To firm it up for the next step, you'll need to chill it. Cover (or wrap) the dough with plastic and place in the refrigerator 2–3 hours. The well-wrapped dough can also rest overnight in the refrigerator or up to 3 days before baking.

Step 4—Roll and sugar coat: Preheat oven to 350°F. Line baking pans with parchment paper or silicone sheets. Roll pieces of dough into 1-inch balls. Coat balls in lemon sugar (from Step 1). Place on prepared pan and use the buttered bottom of a glass, dipped in the lemon sugar, to gently flatten each cookie.

Janelle's Tip: You'll want to dip the glass bottom into the lemon sugar each time you flatten a new cookie or the dough may stick to the glass.

Step 5—Bake: Depending on your oven, cookies will bake in 12–15 minutes. When cookie edges and bottoms turn a light golden brown, they're done. Move the hot cookies to a cooling rack. If you're in a hurry for them to set, transfer them to a plate in the freezer, where they will harden very quickly into a sweet-tart treat that gives a satisfying snap when bitten into. These cookies also freeze very well; simply store in freezer-safe plastic bags.

Clare's Eggnog Crumb Muffins

The morning after her awful scare, Clare woke Mike Quinn with this sweet holiday offering. Tender and rich, these muffins are superb paired with your morning coffee—as Mike can attest. He happily inhaled them while still in bed, after pulling Clare in first.

Over the years Clare has created two versions of this recipe. Both produce delicious muffins with the seasonal flavors of eggnog and nutmeg. The following recipe is Clare's "from-scratch" version. It makes only six muffins for fresh-baked enjoyment at an intimate breakfast or over coffee. During her years raising Joy in New Jersey, Clare also created a large batch version of this recipe using a cake mix starter. That version bakes up two dozen muffins fast, and is great for parties, school functions, or bake sales.

To download the illustrated recipe for Clare's Large Batch Eggnog Muffins, come to Cleo Coyle's online coffeehouse: www.CoffeehouseMystery.com.

Makes 6 muffins

For the Muffins:

5 tablespoons unsalted butter, softened
⅓ cup white, granulated sugar
2 tablespoons light brown sugar
1 large egg, lightly beaten with fork
⅓ cup eggnog
¼ teaspoon ground nutmeg
¼ teaspoon salt
1 teaspoon baking powder
½ teaspoon baking soda
½ teaspoon pure vanilla extract
1 cup all-purpose flour

For the Crumb Topping:

¼ cup all-purpose flour
¼ cup light brown sugar, firmly packed
¼ teaspoon ground nutmeg
Pinch of baking powder
2½ tablespoons cold unsalted butter,
cut into cubes

Muffins: First preheat your oven to 375°F. Using an electric mixer, cream butter and sugars in a bowl until light and fluffy. Add egg, eggnog, nutmeg, salt, baking powder, baking soda, and vanilla extract. Once blended, add the flour and mix until a smooth batter forms and flour is completely incorporated. Do not overmix at this stage. Line six muffin cups with paper liners, divide batter among them. Make the Crumb Topping (see directions on the next page) and divide evenly over the muffins. Bake for 20 minutes. Muffins are done when a toothpick inserted into a test muffin comes out clean. Remove from oven and cool.

Crumb topping: First a warning from Clare—your butter must be *cold* for this recipe or you won't make crumbs; you'll make a sticky messy dough, so be sure your butter is well chilled.

To prepare with a food processor: Place all ingredients inside and pulse until you see coarse crumbs.

To mix by hand: Place flour, brown sugar, nutmeg, and a pinch of baking powder into a bowl. Whisk together to blend. Add the cubes of *cold* butter and using clean fingers or a pastry blender, work the butter into the dry ingredients until the mixture turns into coarse crumbs. Store in a plastic container, in the refrigerator, for up to 3 days.

Brigadieros (Brazilian Chocolate Truffles)

Given his frequent coffee-buying trips to Brazil, Matt Allegro quickly recognized these caramelly chocolate truffles when he spied them on Rita's Cookie Swap display table. Brigadieros are beloved in Brazil, and no children's birthday party is complete without them. They are especially fun for young children to help make. Once the dough is properly cooked, little hands can help roll it into chocolate balls.

The odd name is a result of the historical period when the sweet was invented. Created during the food shortages of World War II, the Brigadiero was named after a famous Brazilian Air Force brigadier of the time.

Clare often tweaks Rita's recipe, adding a pinch of espresso powder—a baker's secret for deepening the taste of chocolate in any recipe. She also recommends adding salt to balance the very sweet flavor of the condensed milk. Of course, growing up Italian, Clare routinely watched her nonna drench cakes in rum before putting them on sale in her little Italian grocery. Consequently, Clare sometimes adds rum or rum extract to this recipe. It's not traditional, but it is delicious!

Makes about 40 chocolate truffles

> 1 (14-ounce) can of sweetened condensed milk
> 1 tablespoon butter
> 2 tablespoons sweetened cocoa (*See Clare's Note)
> 1 tablespoon unsweetened cocoa powder
> ¼ teaspoon salt
> 1 cup or so of finishers such as chocolate jimmies,
> powdered sugar, finely chopped nuts, sweetened flaked coconut,
> colored sprinkles, etc.

Clare's optional additions:

> Generous pinch of espresso powder
> 1 tablespoon dark rum (or 1½ teaspoons rum extract)

*Clare's Note: For the sweetened cocoa, you can go with a brand like Nesquik or splurge with hot cocoa mixes like Ghirardelli or Jacques Torres. Just make sure the sweetened cocoa does not include powdered milk in its first three ingredients. You're looking for cocoa and sugar in the ingredient list and directions that require you to mix the powder with milk (not water). With the variety on the market, try experimenting with hot cocoa flavors such as: Ghirardelli's mocha, hazelnut, or peppermint; or Torres' "Wicked" with spicy heat. Have fun!

Step 1—Cook the chocolate: The key to getting the chocolates to form balls is to cook it long enough. You must also stir continually to prevent burning. Mix the condensed milk, butter, salt, sweetened and unsweetened cocoas in a saucepan over medium-low heat. (If using espresso powder, add now.) Cook the mixture around 15–20 minutes, until it thickens. A sign to watch for: As you stir, try to see the pan bottom by pulling back the chocolate with your spoon. If the mix holds for a second, allowing you to see the pan bottom, cook another minute and it should be ready. For a final test, place a spoonful of the chocolate mixture onto a cold dish (place dish in freezer). If the mixture solidifies quickly and does not run, you're ready! Remove from heat. (If adding rum or rum extract, stir it in now.)

Step 2—Cool the chocolate: Pour the warm mixture onto a sheet pan that's been covered in parchment paper. Cool the chocolate to room temperature for about an hour, or chill for thirty minutes in the refrigerator.

Step 3—Roll and coat: Grease your hands with butter and roll the mix into balls of 1 to 1½ inches. Toss each truffle in a coating of your choice—chocolate jimmies, powdered sugar, finely crushed toasted nuts, sweetened flaked coconut, colored sprinkles, etc. Creating several varieties with one batch is common.

Step 4—Serve with holiday flair: Clare serves each chocolate truffle in its own little fluted paper cup. Mini muffin pan paper liners work very well for this. Buy them in holiday colors, nestle each little truffle inside, and you'll make any dessert or coffee tray look festive for the season. Or box them up with a bow, and you've got a sweet little holiday gift. May you make them with love and share them with joy!

Clare Cosi's Easy Pumpkin Cake
with Surprise Cream Cheese Swirl

For step-by-step photos of this recipe, come to Cleo Coyle's online coffeehouse at www.CoffeehouseMystery.com.

One cup of canned pumpkin, a little maple syrup, and some classic holiday spices will convert an ordinary cake mix into a stunning pumpkin-maple Bundt. This is a quick-and-easy version of a Village Blend favorite, sold by the slice out of Clare's pastry case. She developed the recipe for her In the Kitchen with Clare column as a great way for busy home bakers to enjoy the taste of a pumpkin roulade without the often heartbreaking hassle of attempting to roll a sheet cake.

The "surprise swirl" of sweetened cream cheese not only brings happiness to your taste buds but impressive-ness to your presentation. Serve as a brunch treat with a light dusting of powdered sugar or dress it up with an easy glaze for a lovely holiday dessert.

This cake also pairs beautifully with Warm Custard Sauce. Clare snagged that amazing "old-school" recipe from her favorite Chinatown baker, Mrs. Li, famous in New York for her egg custard tarts. For the Warm Custard Sauce recipe, turn to page 364 in this book. For a delicious Egg Custard Tart recipe, see Cleo Coyle's Coffeehouse Mystery A Brew to a Kill *and bake with joy!*

Makes 1 Bundt cake yielding about 12 slices

For the Bundt Cake:

4 large eggs
1 package yellow cake mix with pudding in the mix
(Note: This recipe will work with cake mixes in boxes from
15.25 to 18.25 ounces)
1 package (3.4 ounces) instant vanilla pudding mix (boosts structure
and moistness)
⅓ cup pure maple syrup (not pancake syrup)
¼ cup canola oil
1 cup canned pumpkin (pumpkin purée and not pumpkin pie filling)
¼ teaspoon salt
1 tablespoon pumpkin pie spice (*see note)

Note: To make your own pumpkin pie spice, see the brief recipe following this one.

For the Cream Cheese Swirl:

> 1 large egg
> 1 (8-ounce) package of cream cheese, softened
> ¾ cup confectioners' (powdered) sugar
> 1 teaspoon vanilla

Step 1—Make the cake batter: First preheat your oven to 350°F. In a large bowl, break your four eggs. Lightly beat them with a fork and add the rest of the Bundt cake ingredients. Using an electric mixer, blend on low speed for about 30 seconds. Scrape down the sides of the bowl and increase mixer speed to medium, beating for a full two minutes (and no more). You want to whip air into the batter, and you should see it increase in volume, but you don't want to overmix or you'll develop the gluten in the flour and your cake will be tough instead of tender. After two minutes, stop the mixer and set the bowl aside.

Step 2—Make the cream cheese swirl: In a separate bowl, crack one egg and lightly beat it with a fork. Add the softened cream cheese, powdered sugar, and vanilla. Using your electric mixer again, blend the ingredients together. When no more clumps are visible, whip for a full minute until smooth, light, and creamy.

Step 3—Assemble: *Generously* butter the interior of a standard 10 to 10.5-inch (12 cup) Bundt pan or a fluted tube pan of about the same size. Don't forget to butter the center tube. *(Do not use nonstick spray for this cake because it creates a darker, harder, less appealing crust.)* Into the pan, pour about half the cake batter. Add the cream cheese mixture in an even layer. *(Use the back of the spoon to level it off.)* Swirl a knife deep through the layers of cream cheese and cake batter. Make little loops as you move around the entire ring of batter in the pan. Now add the rest of the batter to the pan and level it off with the back of a spoon.

Step 4—Bake: In a well-preheated oven, bake at 350°F for 40–50 minutes. The time will depend on your oven. The cake is done when the visible layer of the Bundt appears to be baked. If you're unsure, insert a toothpick into the cracked areas of the cake. When the toothpick comes out clean, the cake is done. Be careful not to overbake.

Step 5—Cool and glaze: Avoid heartbreak! Cool for a full 30 minutes before removing the cake from the pan. If you try to remove it sooner, it may stick or break on you. To remove cake: Place a serving platter over the top of the cake pan. Flip the pan. With a heavy spoon or knife handle, rap the pan all over to help loosen any areas where the cake may be sticking, and then carefully lift off the pan. Allow the cake to finish cooling before glazing. *(See my Easy Bundt Cake Glaze recipe below.)*

For the Homemade Pumpkin Pie Spice:

To make your own pumpkin pie spice, follow these directions. For 1 teaspoon of pumpkin pie spice, mix these ground spices: ½ teaspoon cinnamon, ¼ teaspoon ginger, ⅛ teaspoon allspice or cloves, and ⅛ teaspoon nutmeg.

For the Easy Bundt Cake Glaze:

> 1½ cups confectioners' (powdered) sugar
> 3 tablespoons half-and-half (or light cream)

Note: Milk and water will also work, but will not taste as rich and may need a bit more sugar to thicken.

Measure out the powdered sugar. Stir in half-and-half (or light cream) until all the sugar is dissolved. With a wire whisk or fork, whisk the mixture until it appears smooth and without a single clump. Test on a plate. The glaze should drizzle easily but should not be thin or watery, and it should set in about ten minutes.

Troubleshooting: If the glaze is too thin and watery, add a little more sugar. If too thick, add a bit more liquid. When you're happy with the consistency, spoon the glaze over the Bundt cake's top and sides, allowing it to drip gently down.

Clare's Tip: You'll notice the glaze pools in the center of the Bundt. When you finish using the glaze in your bowl, take a small spoon and scoop out the pooled glaze at the center of the cake. Continue spooning over the cake. Allow 15 minutes to set and . . . eat with joy!

Clare Cosi's Pepper-Crusted Roast Beef

When Mike Quinn went missing in a freak winter snow-storm, Clare was sick with worry—and eventually hunger. Determined to wait it out, and share this flavorful pepper-crusted roast beef with her man, she ultimately succumbed to the temptations of ex-husband Matt Allegro and his 8-napkin artisan patty melt.

In the end, however, Clare was relieved she had this beautifully cooked beef resting in her fridge, ready and waiting for Quinn's homecoming. Sliced thin when cold, this roast makes an excellent sandwich. Served hot with potatoes and vegetables, it makes a wonderful, hearty winter meal. Just be sure to include some crusty rolls on the table—to sop up the mouthwatering beef juices.

Clare's preferred cut for roasting is eye of round, but all three types of rump roasts (top round, eye of round, or bottom round) will work for this recipe, and don't miss her

Horsey Sauce. The bright, creamy tang of the sauce perfectly complements an unctuous beef sandwich!

1 boneless beef rump roast (eye round), 3 to 5 pounds
1 tablespoon coarse sea salt
1 tablespoon cracked black pepper, coarsely ground
1 teaspoon ground white pepper
1 tablespoon cooking oil (olive, canola, corn, or vegetable)
¼ teaspoon ground cumin

Step 1—Prep: Rinse your raw beef, pat it dry, and place it on the rack of your roasting pan. Allow the beef to rest outside of the refrigerator for at least 40 minutes or up to an hour. If you put cold meat in a hot oven, you risk uneven cooking and tough meat.

Step 2—Encrust: Preheat oven to 350°F. In a dry bowl, combine sea salt, two peppers, and (optional) cumin. Mix thoroughly and pour on a flat dish or cutting board. Coat the beef completely with cooking oil, and roll all sides in the pepper mixture, crusting well.

Step 3—Roast: Place the beef, fat side up, on the pan's rack. Roast the meat at 350°F for 17–19 minutes a pound for rare (or to an internal temperature of 145°); for medium rare to medium, roast the meat for 20–25 minutes a pound (or an internal temperature of 150° to 160°). For well-done meat, roast 27–30 minutes a pound (or an internal temperature of 165°F). Clare roasts her meat to an internal temperature of 150°F, because, she notes, "the meat's temperature continues to rise about 10 degrees after it's taken out of the oven."

Clare's Tip: To take the internal temperature of a roast, use an Instant Read Meat Thermometer. Do not stick the meat too often with the thermometer or you'll lose valuable meat juices. Wait until you're near the end of the cooking time to test the meat and (if possible) do it only once or twice.

Step 4—Rest: An important step. After the beef comes out of the oven, let it sit for at least 30 minutes before slicing or those lovely meat juices will run out and you'll be left with a roast that's far too dry. Place a loose tent of aluminum foil over the beef to keep it warm; then slice it up and eat with joy!

Clare's Horsey Sauce

⅓ cup mayonnaise
¼ cup bottled horseradish (hot or mild)
⅛ teaspoon white pepper
⅛ teaspoon white cider vinegar

Combine ingredients in a bowl and mix well. The mixture will seem watery, but after chilling in the refrigerator for fifteen minutes, the sauce will thicken up. Serve with hot or cold roast beef, or other meat sandwiches.

Clare's Chicken Marsala for Mike

Chicken Marsala is one of the most popular dishes in Italian restaurants worldwide. The chicken melts like butter, the mushrooms provide an earthy richness, but the key ingredient (and the secret to this dish's charm) is dry Marsala, a fortified wine from Sicily similar to sherry or port.

Clare adds an extra step to this one-skillet recipe—an easy marinade. Do not skip this step. The marinade truly heightens the flavor, bringing this dish to a whole new level.

Though Chicken Marsala is traditionally dished over pasta or presented with potatoes, Clare served Mike Quinn her Marsala the way many Italian eateries in New York

City do—on a crispy, fresh Italian roll, the perfect late-night sandwich for Quinn after a day of holiday sightseeing with his children.

Makes 4 servings

> 1 to 1½ pounds boneless, skinless chicken breasts
> 1¾ cups dry Marsala (divided, see recipe directions)
> 4 tablespoons olive oil
> 3 tablespoons butter (divided)
> 6 cloves garlic, smashed
> ¼ teaspoon Kosher salt or ground sea salt (divided)
> ¼ teaspoon freshly ground black pepper (divided)
> ½ cup all-purpose flour
> 1 large onion, diced
> 3 cups sliced mushrooms (baby bellas, cremini, button, or a mix)
> 1 cup chicken stock

Step 1—Prep the chicken and marinate: Wash chicken breasts and slice in half. On a cutting board, use a meat hammer to pound breasts thin. (Or you can buy pre-filleted breasts, but because the goal is tenderness, you still *must pound* the chicken.) In a covered bowl, mix ¾ cup of Marsala with 1 tablespoon olive oil, six cloves of smashed garlic, ⅛ teaspoon salt, and ⅛ teaspoon pepper. Place the chicken in the marinade and refrigerate for thirty minutes, or up to three hours.

Step 2—Dredge marinated chicken and sauté: Remove chicken from marinade, do not rinse. (Discard the liquid.) Dredge in ½ cup all-purpose flour. Heat 3 tablespoons olive oil in a large skillet over low heat. Add 1 teaspoon of butter to the hot oil, then gently sauté the coated chicken until golden brown (three minutes per side should do it, turning once). When the chicken is cooked through, remove from the oil and set aside.

Step 3—Sauté the aromatics: Add the diced onion to the oil, cook over medium heat until the onions are clear and tender (about five minutes). Add 1 tablespoon of butter to the skillet. When melted, throw in your sliced mushrooms and sauté. The mushrooms will quickly absorb the oil, but keep cooking until the edges are brown and they begin to release their juices again.

Step 4—Add wine, reduce: Now pour into the pan your remaining 1 cup of dry Marsala. Increase the heat and bring to a low boil. Simmer until the liquid has been reduced by half (5 to 6 minutes). Add the chicken stock and simmer for another three minutes.

Step 5—Sauce the chicken: Return the chicken breasts to the pan along with any juices that might have accumulated in the holding dish. Lower the heat, and cook until the chicken is heated through and the sauce thickens (about 5 to 7 minutes). Toss in that final 1 tablespoon of butter, ⅛ teaspoon salt, and ⅛ teaspoon black pepper. Serve hot.

Clare's Apple Crumb Pie with Mrs. Li's Warm Custard Sauce

After serving Mike her Chicken Marsala, Clare wanted to share a dessert that conveyed all the sweet, wholesome warmth of a fire-lit home on a cold winter night. This Apple Crumb Pie hit the mark. Mike swooned over the combination of fruity-sweetness, crunchy topping, and warm, creamy custard (adapted from a recipe that Clare snagged from her favorite Chinatown baker, Mrs. Li).

Clare finds cooking the apples before baking helps to caramelize the fruit, and the crumb topping in place of a traditional top crust provides a homey hint of old fashioned cobbler, making it an uplifting dessert for any dark winter night.

Makes one 9-inch pie

> *3 pounds apples (Clare uses 7 Golden Delicious)*
> *2 teaspoons fresh-squeezed lemon juice*
> *¼ cup white, granulated sugar*
> *¼ cup light brown sugar, packed*
> *3 tablespoons unsalted butter*
> *3 tablespoons all-purpose flour*
> *1 teaspoon ground cinnamon*
> *½ teaspoon nutmeg*
> *¼ teaspoon salt*
> *1 uncooked pie crust (premade or homemade)*

Step 1—Prepare the fruit: Peel and core the apples and slice them in ¼-inch-thick pieces. Use clean hands to toss first with the lemon juice and then the two sugars. Place a large saucepan over medium-high heat. Melt 3 tablespoons of butter, add the apples, and cook until tender, stirring often for 8 to 10 minutes. Now stir in the flour, cinnamon, nutmeg, and salt and cook for another minute or until the mixture thickens. Remove from heat and cool to room temperature.

Step 2—Assemble the pie: Fill the pie crust with the cooled apple mixture. Sprinkle the crumb topping evenly over the fruit (recipe follows). Now prep for cooking by sculpting strips of aluminum foil around the crust's thick edges. This foil shield will prevent your crust from burning. If you have a store-bought pie shield, put it to use now. Place a *loose* sheet of foil over the top of the pie to protect the crumb topping from burning. Set the pie in the refrigerator while you prepare the oven.

Step 3—Bake the pie: Preheat oven to 425°F and place a baking sheet on the lowest rack in the oven. Heat the sheet for thirty minutes. Place the chilled pie on the hot baking sheet and lower the temperature to 375°F. Bake for 45 minutes. Remove the aluminum foil from the top and the crust edges and finish baking for another 15 to 20 minutes, until the crust is golden brown. Cool on a rack before slicing and serving with warm custard sauce (recipe follows).

Clare's Crumb Topping

¾ cup all-purpose flour
½ cup light brown sugar, packed
¼ cup white, granulated sugar
1 teaspoon cinnamon
5 tablespoons cold unsalted butter, cut into pieces

First a warning from Clare—your butter must be *cold* for this recipe or you won't make crumbs; you'll make a sticky messy dough, so be sure your butter is well chilled.

To prepare with a food processor: Place all ingredients inside and pulse until you see pea-sized clumps. *To mix by hand:* Place flour, brown sugar, white sugar, and cinnamon into a bowl. Whisk together to blend. Add the cubes of cold butter and using clean fingers or a pastry blender, work the butter into the dry ingredients until the mixture turns into pea-sized clumps. Store in a plastic container, in the refrigerator, for up to 3 days.

Mrs. Li's Warm Custard Sauce

Clare Cosi first met Mrs. Li when she visited the woman's Chinatown kitchen under false pretenses. That rather unusual situation ended in a demonstration of an ancient martial art known only to Chinese grandmothers—but that's another story (namely, A Brew to a Kill*). Despite their rocky beginnings, Clare and this traditional Hong Kong baker were soon in business together, and swapping trade secrets. Clare happily gave up her superb Eggnog Crumb Muffin recipe for the secret behind a warm, rich, traditional custard sauce. The method is old school—no shortcuts with cornstarch or other thickeners—just the purity of egg yolks, milk, sugar, and a dash of vanilla. Add a little heat, and a lot of patient stirring. Though time consuming to prepare, once the custard sauce sets it can be cooled, then whisked and reheated and paired with many fall and winter desserts. Try this warm custard as a lush, silky topping for fruit pies, cobblers, or cakes, especially spice cakes. During the holiday season, Clare often serves this warm custard with Janelle's "New Orleans Gingerbread," aka* Gâteau de Sirop*. You can find that recipe at www.CoffeehouseMystery.com.*

Makes approximately 1 cup

6 egg yolks
3 tablespoons white, granulated sugar
2 cups whole milk (or half-and-half for richer sauce*)
1 teaspoon vanilla extract

Holiday Variation: For the holiday season, when eggnog is available, Clare sometimes replaces half of the milk with eggnog, adds a splash of rum extract, and a sprinkling of nutmeg. Either way, this custard is a delightful add-on to pies, cakes, fruit, or ice cream.

Step 1—Whisk eggs: In a heat-proof bowl, whisk together egg yolks and sugar until the mixture is a lemony yellow color. Set aside.

Step 2—Heat and mix: Place the milk in a saucepan and simmer over medium-high heat. Remove pan from heat and stir in vanilla. Now *very slowly* pour the warm milk and vanilla mixture into the bowl with the egg and sugar mixture while *stirring continually*. You must add the warm milk *gradually* to avoiding cooking or curdling the eggs.

Step 3—Cook for up to 45 minutes: Pour the egg and milk mixture back into the saucepan and return to low heat. Stir constantly until mixture starts to thicken. This is a traditional custard recipe with pure ingredients and no thickeners like cornstarch, which means it will take a long time to thicken up. Once it starts to thicken, check for doneness by tilting the pan. When the mixture begins to coat the side, you're close to finished. Draw the tip of the spoon through the coating. If the cut fills in, continue heating. When the cut remains clear, remove from heat and serve the finished custard sauce warm.

Clare makes it in advance, places it in a small heat-proof pan with a lid and keeps it at low, holding temperature in her oven. Then she stirs it up, making it smooth again before serving it with fall and winter pies and cobblers.

Clare's Frozen Eggnog Latte for Mike

Ever since he moved to Washington, DC, Clare noticed Quinn drinking more alcohol, especially at night. In an effort to keep him sharp on the night after Moirin's murder, she served him this creamy, refreshing holiday treat. It worked, too, although Quinn soon persuaded Clare to give her own worries a rest and turn her thoughts elsewhere.

Okay, technically this is not a latte (because the milk is not steamed), but Quinn loved the rich chilly creaminess of the drink so much that he convinced Clare to add it to the Village Blend's holiday menu.

Makes one 10-ounce beverage

⅓ cup cold milk (whole or 2% for richness)
⅔ cup cold eggnog
6 coffee ice cubes (pour super-strong coffee into trays and freeze)
Whipped cream
Dash of ground nutmeg

Add the milk, eggnog, and coffee ice cubes to a blender and mix for around a minute, until the ice is pulverized. Pour into a serving glass, top with whipped cream and a sprinkle of nutmeg. Serve as cold as the North Pole!

The Village Blend's Gumdrop Spritzers

Clare and her baristas put their espresso bar syrups to good use on the night of the toy store Cookie Swap, creating colorful gumdrop flavored drinks. They were a ginormous hit for the Village Blend, especially with the kids. Clare wasn't all that surprised. Europeans have long had a passion for adding flavored "gourmet espresso bar" syrups to sparkling water to create delicious "Italian sodas."

In North America, syrups are more commonly used to flavor lattes and cappuccinos, but in recent years the companies that make these syrups are providing a dizzying array of possibilities, not just for coffee bars but consumers at home—butter rum, carrot cake, pink grapefruit, kiwi, watermelon, mandarin orange, English toffee, pistachio, piña colada, toasted marshmallow, even tiramisu. The combinations can make your head spin—and your mouth water.

Here are a few simple tips that will help you become a barista in your own home. The next time you plan a party, assemble a number of bottled syrups, place them on a table with ice, club soda, a bowl of gumdrops, and a stack of swizzle sticks, and invite guests to mix their own gumdrop drinks. (And take Clare's advice—buy extra swizzle sticks!)

Makes one 16-ounce beverage

1½–2 ounces* flavored syrup (3–4 tablespoons)
10 ounces club soda
4 ounces ice cubes (approximately 4 cubes)

*Note: 1 ounce = 2 tablespoons

Mixing directions: Fill a 16-ounce glass about one-third full of ice (approximately 4 cubes). Pour the syrup and club soda over the ice and stir well.

Tips for blending flavors: When blending two syrups to create a third taste (say lemon syrup and lime syrup to make lemon-lime), you can either use equal amounts, or you can try for a dominant taste. For example, try 1 ounce of one syrup and ½ ounce of another. Here's a more specific example: Mix 1 ounce of orange and ½ ounce of cranberry, and you've made orange cranberry. If you flip the ratio, you will then make cranberry orange. Use your imagination and your taste buds, mix, match, experiment, and . . . drink with joy!

Where to find syrups: Here are three brand names and their websites to get you started. You can learn more about the flavors they offer and where to purchase them, and you'll even find recipes.

Torani—This is the oldest American brand of gourmet syrup, started in 1925 by Italian immigrants in San Francisco. www.torani.com.

Monin—Monin was founded in France in 1912. Enjoyed for nearly a century by Europeans, it hit the American market in the early 1990s. www.monin.com.

DaVinci Gourmet—This respected brand was launched in Seattle in 1989. www.davincigourmet.com.

Easy Candy Cane Latte with
Homemade Peppermint Syrup

Matt drank a version of this delicious peppermint-flavored latte at the annual Village Blend Secret Santa party. Matt makes all of his own coffee drinks and (being Matt), he slipped a shot of peppermint schnapps into his Candy Cane Latte for an extra holiday kick. Here's Clare's virgin recipe, but feel free to add schnapps, Jägermeister, mint-flavored vodka, or mint liqueur in Step Three to get your own holiday buzz.

Makes two 8-ounce drinks

1 cup milk
½ cup white chocolate, chopped, or white chocolate chips
¼ teaspoon vanilla extract
2 tablespoons Clare's homemade peppermint syrup (see next recipe
or substitute ¼–½ teaspoon peppermint extract)
2 to 4 shots hot espresso or strong coffee (divided)
Whipped cream (optional)

Step 1—Melt the chocolate: Combine milk and white chocolate in a heat-proof bowl and place over a saucepan about one-third full of boiling water. (The water level should be under the bowl but not touching it.) Stir constantly until chocolate is melted. Be careful and make sure not a drop of water gets close to the chocolate.

Step 2—Whisk until frothy: Using a whisk or handheld electric beater, whip in the vanilla and peppermint syrup or extract. Continue to whip about a minute until the warm mixture is loosely frothy.

Step 3—Assemble the drink: Take out 2 large mugs and pour 1 to 2 shots of espresso into each (more shots will give you more coffee flavor and caffeine in the drink). Divide the steamed white chocolate milk between the mugs and stir to blend the flavors. Top with whipped cream, sprinkle with chopped candy canes, and serve with a whole candy cane in the mug as a stirrer. (This drink is absolute heaven. It tastes like a rich, warm coffee-infused peppermint milkshake! Enjoy!)

Clare Cosi's Peppermint Syrup
Homemade from Candy Canes

Got leftover candy canes? Put them to great use with this outstanding peppermint syrup. This sweet, potent syrup is delicious licked right off the spoon, but you may also want to serve it over ice cream, stir it into hot chocolate, or use it the way Clare Cosi and her barista crew do—to make their amazing Candy Cane Lattes and Cappuccinos.

1 cup water
1½ cups granulated sugar
8 large candy canes, broken up

Pour the water and sugar into a large saucepan. Stir until the sugar and water are mixed fairly well, then place over medium heat. Add the candy cane pieces to the mix and continue stirring. When the candy canes begin to melt, the mix will turn a milky pink. Keep cooking until the mix comes to a boil. Boil for 3–4 minutes, then remove from heat. Allow the syrup to cool in the pan before transferring to a storage jar or bottle. If the syrup is too thick to pour, warm in hot water or microwave for ten seconds.

As the surrey swept even with the sidetracked tramp, the bright-eyed girl, seized by some merry, madcap impulse, leaned out toward him with a sweet, dazzling smile, and cried, "Mer-ry Christ-mas!" in a shrill, plaintive treble.

Such a thing had not often happened to Whistling Dick. . . . snatching off his battered derby, he rapidly extended it at arm's length, and drew it back with a continuous motion, and shouted a loud, but ceremonious, "Ah, there!" after the flying surrey . . . "W't d'yer think of dat, now! . . . Mer-ry Chris-mus!"

—O. Henry, "Whistling Dick's Christmas Stocking"*

*Originally published in the December 1899 issue of *McClure's Magazine*, this short story is believed to be the first work that William Sydney Porter published under the pseudonym O. Henry.

Cleo Coyle is a pseudonym for Alice Alfonsi, writing in collaboration with her husband, Marc Cerasini. Like their Coffeehouse Mysteries, their Haunted Bookshop Mysteries, published under the name Alice Kimberly, are national bestselling works of amateur-sleuth fiction for Berkley Prime Crime. Alice and Marc were born and raised in small towns near Pittsburgh, Pennsylvania. They met in New York City, where both began their postcollege careers. After falling in love, Alice and Marc were married in Nevada's Little Church of the West. Now they live and work in New York City, where they write independently and together. When not haunting coffeehouses or hunting ghosts, Alice writes young adult and children's books; Marc writes thrillers and nonfiction—and both are *New York Times* bestselling media tie-in writers who have penned properties for Lucasfilm, NBC, Fox, Disney, Imagine, and MGM.

Cleo enjoys hearing from readers. Visit her virtual Village Blend coffeehouse at www.CoffeehouseMystery.com, where she also posts recipes and coffee picks. Sign up for her newsletter by sending an e-mail that says "Sign me up" to CoffeehouseMystery @gmail.com.